THE
VARICOSE VIGILANTES II

Hedge Money

Also by Jay Lumbert

The Alchemist Conspiracy
The Varicose Vigilantes
The Presidential Pretender
Working HR For Private Business
Retirement Planning Simplified By Jay
Retirement Plans Simplified By Jay

THE
VARICOSE VIGILANTES II

Hedge Money

Jay Lumbert

Shaksper Books
USA

THE VARICOSE VIGILANTES II - Hedge Money

Shaksper books may be ordered through booksellers everywhere, or by contacting:

Shaksper Books
www.shaksperbooks.com   admin@shaksperbooks.com

ISBN -13:978-0-9800501-3-4   (pbk)

ISBN -13:978-0-9827068-0-0   (lg prt pbk)

ISBN -13:978-0-9827068-1-7   (ebk)

ISBN -10:0-9800501-3-8   (pbk)

ISBN -10:0-9827068-0-4   (lg prt pbk)

Printed in the United States of America

For Bill & Marilyn Eaton.

Author's Note

While an author may get the credit for a book, there are usually others that should. A novel like this cannot be written without the sacrifice and help of many.

I have been blessed with the support of my family, without whom, none of this would exist. I thank you all profoundly.

Thanks again to my pre-readers. Your encouragement is great motivation. So, too, is the indomitable spirit of our nation's senior citizens.

I spent over thirty years as a financial advisor. During that time, I started two investment banking (broker-dealer) firms and two investment advisory firms. My companies have advised clients with billions in assets.

I have had the opportunity to work with some of the country's finest investment managers and advisors. I have also seen my share of less-than-honorable men. I have been the personal victim of financial fraud.

The world of investments lends itself to great temptation. It is surprisingly easy to steal a client's money. Sometimes, this is done outright. Other times the "theft" is far more subtle, showing up in exorbitant commissions or fees—often legal, but sadly immoral.

I wanted to write a book where a basically good person (Cantwell) succumbs to temptation and loses his way. He isn't a complete fraud (like Madoff). Instead, he travels the far more slippery slope, one his clients don't notice. He systematically shifts billions from his clients' pockets to his own. The crime is one thing; the cover-up is the killer. So is the man protecting Cantwell.

Enter Mabel Witherspoon, our sight-challenged, incontinent senior who cares more about honor than her life.

Mabel's fight for justice, against men with enormous power and influence, becomes a unique and powerful story. It should resonate with anyone who has invested money, or been the victim of a financial crime.

No book about high-society finance in Palm Beach could ignore Donald Trump. Although he appears in this book, this is a purely respectful and fictionalized portrayal. I'm not sure how he would react to being pinched in the butt by a seventy-five-year-old woman with failing eyesight and a weak bladder.

"If we do not maintain justice, justice will not maintain us."

"The place of justice is a hallowed place."

"Truth is a good dog; but always beware of barking too close to the heels of an error, lest you get your brains kicked out."

Sir Francis Bacon

"Lawless are they that make their wills their law."

William Shakespeare

"Beyond a doubt truth bears the same relation to falsehood as light to darkness."

Leonardo da Vinci

Chapter One
V

BEN JOHNSON

I never thought retirement could get so dangerous.

After soldiering for the CIA, the NRO and the NSA for forty years, being shuffled between them like playing cards…snooping into other people's business…mostly foreign governments and terrorists, stuff like that…I always envisioned sitting down on a wooden dock in Key West, watching the sun set as I sipped on a Corona with a cute little girlfriend about thirty years younger than me, with smooth skin, perky breasts and size five jeans.

I took my retirement. Bought a place in Key West. Got a boat and did lots of fishing. I have a freezer full of enough fish to stock a restaurant for a year. Haven't caught the girl. Probably never will. But that doesn't keep me from looking.

I never found contentment, though, having nothing to do but play. I had my gadgets. Still did some hacking, mostly into the systems of foreign dictatorships, maybe planting a worm, or some program to move a little money to some charity somewhere. But something was missing. It was like a hole in my heart.

Last year I got a call from an old friend, Tony Trance. He'd started this group called SOSCADA, the Society of Senior Citizens Against Drug Abuse. They were working to take down this big drug dealer in Miami and they needed my help. So, I complied. And then, damn-it, I realized how bored I really was.

So, there I was in South Beach, putting up my shingle for a detective agency. Why I'd want to deal with Miami riff-raff is beyond me. But that was the calling. Gotta go where the fates send you.

My new place is actually quite nice. I've got this little two story building on Seaway Drive. The view is a killer and I get to watch a lot of twenty-somethings walk by with these tiny little bathing suits that make me want to go pop a Viagra. None of them seem to have any interest in a retired guy with silver hair and a replaced hip.

That's not why I am writing this journal, though. No, I'm writing this because of Mabel Witherspoon.

I thought this gig was going to help keep me from being bored, just enough to get the blood flowing, and maybe even help some people in need.

I never thought this job would lead to kidnappings, bombings, billions of dollars in stolen cash and politicians on the take. I never expected to be smack in the middle of an event that could shake the world like this one. But I'm getting ahead of myself here. I want to tell the story as it happened, from the beginning, as if I didn't have 20/20 hindsight. Because, if I had 20/20 hindsight, I might never have taken on this case.

Chapter Two

V

As the private elevator door began to slide open, Mabel Witherspoon squeezed tightly upon the handle of her black metal cane. The veins on the back of her hand popped up like purple ropes, seeming to slither up her arm before disappearing beneath the cuff of her white cardigan sweater. Mabel gazed through her thick black eyeglasses into the deep folds of the office that stretched out before her. She felt small, dwarfed by the looming walls of dark wood. She felt pinched by the chandelier that stretched down like an old oak, dripping crystal orbs off the high ceiling like winter icicles on her New Hampshire barn.

Mabel set her jaw and stepped forward. She walked slowly, using the cane to support a leg that hadn't fully recovered from a mild stroke. She held her chin high, refusing to be intimidated by what she could see was the intent of the room—the long walk across an Oriental rug so large it must have needed a container ship to transport it across the ocean, the raised mahogany desk at the end that made her think of the Titanic, the vivacious receptionist that sat behind that desk with her smooth blond hair, her clear blue eyes and those perfect white teeth. Then, there was all that art along the walls.

"Welcome to Cantwell Investments. May I help you?" said little miss perfect.

"Name's Mabel. I'm here to see Cantwell."

The receptionist frowned, then peered into a computer screen that was built into the bulwark of her desk. "Do you have an appointment, Miss…Mabel?"

"He wouldn't give me one. Kept trying to pawn me off on some assistant."

"Excuse me?"

"Cantwell. I've been trying to get an appointment with him for weeks, but he keeps dodging me. So I came in unannounced. I'm here to give him a piece of my mind."

The receptionist seemed confused, or was it concerned? She stood and peered around her desk, as if searching Mabel for a weapon. "Excuse me, but how did you get past security?"

Mabel smiled. "Just flashed a little skin, honey. You're not the only one who can turn a head."

The receptionist's mouth opened. Her lower jaw hung down, quivering in space, before closing shut like a snapped trap before any of her thoughts could escape. She turned and began walking to her left, down a long, low-lit hallway adorned with more expensive paintings and a city of marble sculptures resting on a row of pedestals.

"I'll be right back," she mumbled.

"Good. Be quick. Tell him it's Mabel Witherspoon."

A few minutes later, little miss perfect returned. The smile came back to her face, plastic and rigid, as if glued in place. "Mr. Cantwell will see you shortly." The receptionist pointed toward a grouping of chairs that were lurking against the wall to Mabel's left. "Please have a seat. May I get you something to drink?"

"Got any scotch?"

"Of course. Mr. Cantwell likes his clients to be as comfortable as possible."

"Then why does he duck them?"

"I beg your pardon?"

"Why does he avoid his clients?"

"Mr. Cantwell doesn't avoid his clients, Ms. Witherspoon. He is a very busy man, and his schedule is full for months in advance—"

"I've got five million bucks invested with him and I want some. I've called here every day for the past month and he won't see me, or send me a check. I find that rather rude and ungrateful."

"Well, he will see you now. You said scotch?"

"Chivas, if you've got it. On the rocks."

"On the rocks it is, then."

The receptionist walked back down the hall, moving like a sleek panther in her black suit with her tight little twenty-something ass. Mabel watched as miss perfect reached a door on the left and walked inside. She returned less than a minute later, holding a squat rocks glass filled to the brim with ice and its shimmering, soothing amber liquid.

Mabel slipped the handbag off her shoulder, then took the drink from the receptionist's outstretched hand. She sniffed it, before taking a healthy swig. She settled back into a chair, cradling the drink like she might a newborn baby. "That's better, dear. Now, you go get your boss."

A few minutes later, Rial Cantwell strode down the endless, softly-lit corridor. He was wearing a blue pin-stripe suit. Sapphire cufflinks the size of acorns were poking through the French cuffs of his white, silk shirt. His shoes were Barker Blacks, rich with a sleek ostrich cap. To Mabel they looked like sawed off cowboy boots, but what did she know? She figured they were expensive; everything about Cantwell was expensive.

Cantwell's hair was a long mane of silver, combed straight back over his head. It flopped down around his ears in an elegant, but haphazard manner, one that could only come from a haircut that cost more than Mabel's wardrobe. Mabel didn't like him at once. He was too refined, too slick, too controlled. He was stealing her money.

"Mabel Witherspoon," said Cantwell in a deep, basso voice. "What a pleasure it is to meet you." Cantwell placed his hands upon Mabel's shoulders and pecked her once on each cheek.

"Careful, or I'll bite," said Mabel.

Cantwell smiled. He motioned down the hallway and nudged Mabel gently in the direction of his hand. Fifty feet down the hall they came to a large conference room with a frosted glass wall. Cantwell opened the door and ushered Mabel inside. There was conference table in the center of the room, crafted from a ponderous chunk of shiny burled walnut. The table made Mabel think of the deck of a ship; it looked strong enough to walk on and solid enough to withstand any storm. There were twenty-four chairs arranged around the oblong block, in six groupings of four. Cantwell pointed toward the head of the table.

"Please, sit," he ordered. "I am told that you have an urgent matter to discuss with me?"

"Yeah, and I've been trying to see you for a month."

"I'm sorry. I have been overseas until three days ago, scouring the global capital markets to help you make more money."

"I've got all the money I need and I want it. At least three million of it."

Cantwell pursed his lips, then made a soft sucking sound with his teeth, and said, "Well, that is a problem."

"What, you don't have it? You some sort of Madoff? You scamming me?"

Cantwell laughed. "I am not a fraud like Madoff. And I have all your money. But, unfortunately for you, your husband chose our most aggressive investment account."

"Well, turn it to cash and write me a check."

"That is simply not possible."

"Why not?"

"You are in a hedge fund, Mrs. Witherspoon. Do you know what that is?"

"A license to steal?"

Cantwell chuckled. "It's a license to make *you* money. To do so, we take strategic positions, often with substantial leverage, that can take years to pay off. If investors demand their money at the wrong time, the entire strategy can turn belly up, as you might say. That's why we have, what we call, 'lockup' restrictions, on your access to funds."

"I never agreed to restrictions. And what's this…this locking up thing? You running a prison?"

Cantwell ignored Mabel's taunt and said, "Your husband understood the restrictions."

"Well, Archie's been dead for three years, God bless his soul. So, we need a new agreement."

"It doesn't work that way."

"This can't be legal."

Cantwell laughed again. He walked to a large flat screen that was built into the wall and touched it. The surface flashed instantly to life. Upon the screen, Mabel could see several rows of numbers. The upper left hand corner showed a "deposit" of $675,000. Her husband's name was splashed across the top, to label the account.

"This is your account, Mrs. Witherspoon, with your year-by-year returns."

There was a column labeled *S&P 500*. A second was labeled *Barclays/Lehman Agg Bond*. A third was labeled *DOW*. A fourth was labeled *Account*. Over the eighteen year investment period, Witherspoon's account had grown to more than $5.4 million. The Bond column showed a terminal value of $945,000, while the S&P column grew to $2.2 million. The DOW was slightly higher than the S&P, at $2.4 million. The figures were graphed into several brightly colored charts.

"As you can see, Mrs. Witherspoon, in the time that we have been managing your money, your account has grown from $675,000 to well over $5 million. Through yesterday, your average annual after-tax compounded return has been 12.2%. Your returns have far outpaced those of any major index."

Mabel stared at the board and nodded. She understood. "Do you know Kenny Rogers?" she said.

"Excuse me?"

"Kenny Rogers. He sang a song called *The Gambler*."

"Yes, I know the song. Don't know the man personally."

"You got to know when to fold them and walk away. I'm walking away. I want my money."

"You don't understand…Mrs. Witherspoon. Our agreement allows you to withdraw as much as ten percent of your funds in any given year, with six months advance notice. After five years, you can withdraw the balance."

"That's absurd."

"That's how we stay effective. A lot of my competitors have gone out of business. Many have lost their clients' money. I've done neither." Cantwell shrugged. "I wish I could deviate for you, I really do. But unless you die and your family has estate tax issues, I am afraid there is nothing I can do."

"That sucks."

"Excuse me for asking," Cantwell said softly. "But, why do you need the money?"

"It's for my grandson. He wants to buy an entertainment center…here in Miami."

"An entertainment center?"

"Yeah, for kids. It's called Jiggles."

Cantwell hid a smile. Jiggles was a well-known gentleman's club on NW 183rd Street. The club was not far from Cantwell's office and quite close to LandShark Stadium, home of the Miami Dolphins, and site of the upcoming Super Bowl. "Sounds risky to me, Mrs. Witherspoon."

"This isn't just for my grandson. It's for all the kids, the kids he'll entertain."

Cantwell's lips twitched. "I'm sure it is. But there's nothing I can do. If I break your contract, it isn't fair to my other investors. Integrity is crucial in my business."

Cantwell looked discreetly at his Patek Philippe watch.

"Going somewhere?" said Mabel.

"I was in a meeting when you came, Mrs. Witherspoon. Still am, with the SEC. They are waiting for me. I must get going. I wish there were more I could do."

Mabel stood up and crooked her arm around Cantwell's elbow. "I'll walk you back to your meeting."

"But—"

"I insist."

When they reached the door to Cantwell's office, Mabel increased her grip on his arm. Cantwell tried to shake her off, but she held tight, flopping with his arm like a rag doll.

"You've got to…let go!" said Cantwell, as he tried to pry Mabel's fingers away from his whitening flesh. He wasn't sure, but he thought that she might have actually drawn blood.

"Not 'til I have my money."

"You can't have it. I'm going to call security."

"I'll cry rape."

Cantwell's face spread into a wide grin. Then he laughed loudly. "They are sure to believe that, Mrs. Witherspoon." Cantwell's demeanor softened. "Okay," he said. "Why don't we discuss this with the Securities Exchange Commission? Two of their representatives are on the other side of this door."

Mabel huffed, "Fine."

Cantwell opened his office door and motioned for Mabel to enter the room. Two men were seated comfortably in easy chairs. They were looking out a large picture window over a lake of shimmering blue water, to the Dolphins' stadium, less than half a mile away. One of the men was willowy thin, with a carrot top of curly red hair and a face smothered with brown freckles. The other was much shorter, with a nearly-bald head. He had a large round belly that teetered precariously over a worn leather belt.

"You get rid of her, Rial?" said the red-haired man, without looking back.

"No, he did not," said Mabel. "The old broad brought him back here so she could get her money."

The SEC examiners jumped to their feet. The speaker pulled his hand to his mouth and muttered, "Sorry," as a splash of crimson spilled across his face.

Cantwell cleared his throat and said, "Gentlemen, this is Mabel Witherspoon, one of my early and most important investors." Cantwell pointed toward the tall man with the red hair and the even redder face. "This is Timothy Galway." Cantwell pointed toward the heavy-set man. He had a flabby, pinched face that made him look like a constipated toad. "This is Millard Cramp."

Mabel flashed a coquettish smile toward both men. She made a sort of awkward curtsey, nearly tipping over, before catching herself with her cane and the edge of a chair. "Hello, Tim. Hello, Millard. Which one of you is in charge?"

Galway stepped forward. "That would be me, Ms. Witherspoon."

Mabel regarded Galway from his head to his feet. She gave him a wary sneer, as if she weren't completely impressed. Then she smiled. "I am so glad you are here, Mr. Galway. I came to withdraw a portion of the money I have invested with Mr. Cantwell. He won't give it to me. I have some very important, community investments to make and I need the cash."

"Her grandson wants to buy Jiggles," said Cantwell.

Galway began to smile, but turned away before Mabel could react. When he looked back, Galway's face had sobered. He said, "He'll give you your ten percent, won't he?"

"I need three million. That's fifty-five percent."

"He can't do that," said Galway, after sneaking a quick glance at Cantwell. "Not if you're in the standard portfolio."

"Well, why not?"

"Because that is your agreement."

"What if I were dying?"

"Then you'd get your money."

Mabel fell to the floor, her head flopping against the side of one of the chairs. Then she lay there, eyes closed, saying nothing. She didn't even breathe.

"Ms. Witherspoon?" said Galway. "Ms. Witherspoon, are you all right?"

Mabel opened her eyes and narrowed them, peering first at Galway and then at Cantwell. "I think I'm dying."

Galway's eyes darted from Cantwell to Cramp and back. He motioned for Cantwell to walk with him to the office door. They exited the office, closed the door behind them and stood alone in the hallway. Galway leaned forward and whispered, "Why don't you just give her the money, Rial?"

"I can't, you know that."

"It's just three million, and she seems like trouble."

"My agreement with investors states that, if I make an exception for one investor, I must offer it to everyone. I've got the Saudis wanting to withdraw ten billion from the same fund that Witherspoon is in. If I give her three million I have to give them ten *billion*. That would sink my ship. I've got loans. I've taken positions. You know that…You *know* that."

"I do."

"And you know that I run an honest and ethical organization. Every three months, I open my books for you and your colleagues. You've got unfettered access to every account I manage, every trade I make. You *know* that everything I do is clean. So squeaky clean it makes your ears hurt. I'm not one of those charlatans that promises twenty and thirty and forty percent to their clients. I'm happy to get them twelve to fourteen over time…Sure, I've got to take risks, make some big bets, but I don't lose my clients' money. Never.

"I'm going to need your help on this one, Tim. Witherspoon's invest-ment contract states that she can withdraw ten percent per year for the first five years. After five, she can take the balance. I need you to tell her that. Make her understand that she needs to abide by her contract. It's legal. It's moral. It's honest. It's ethical. It is the agreement we have. She needs to understand."

"I'll tell her," said Galway.

Cantwell patted Galway's shoulder. "Thanks." He paused. "Tell you what. I'm going to make a donation to your favorite charity. Fifty thou-sand. In cash. Tonight, before you leave my office. You can decide which organization to give it to. Fair enough?"

Galway nodded slowly and smiled. "Sure. She's got to abide by her agreement. Otherwise, investors could get hurt."

Cantwell pulled a folder from inside the pocket of his suit coat and placed it into Galway's palm. "This is a copy of Mabel's agreement. When she started calling, I had my secretary scan the agreement and print it for me. Page six outlines the withdrawal provisions. Clear as day.

"You tell Witherspoon that we just went to retrieve this. Tell her you reviewed it. Repeat what you told her earlier, that there is nothing underhanded going on, that it's just 'business as agreed'."

When Cantwell and Galway returned to Cantwell's office, Cramp was lying face down upon the floor, naked to the waist. Mabel was standing upon his back in bare feet, walking heel-to-toe along his flabby frame.

"Oh, my God," mumbled Cramp. "You've got the feet of a magician."

"Yeah, and I've got other things that work even better—"

"Excuse me?" said Cantwell. "What are you doing?"

Mabel spun on her feet, still keeping them upon Cramp's back. She looked at Galway, and then Cantwell. "He needed an emotional enema, to get rid of the baggage that's been building inside him…see all that flab…nasty stuff…just *nasty*."

Cramp let out a long, loud fart.

"That's it, baby," said Mabel. "Let it all out."

Cramp farted again and then groaned.

Mabel jumped down to the floor and crouched beside Cramp. She adjusted her glasses and angled her head so that she could get a better look at his face. The she said, "Now you go home tonight and make passionate love to your wife. Afterwards, you both write out a plan on how you are going to lose five pounds a month with diet, exercise and sex. Lots of sex. You got that?"

"Eat right. Get lots of exercise and sex."

"There you go. You've now got the keys to a happy, healthy life."

Mabel looked up to Cantwell. "You have my money?"

Galway stepped forward and flashed the contract that Mabel's husband, Archie, had signed almost twenty years before. He opened the document to page six and held it in front of Mabel's face. "Mr. Cantwell and I just printed a copy of the agreement executed by your husband, Ms. Witherspoon. Page six outlines the withdrawal parameters—"

"Wait a second, honey," said Mabel. She reached into a pocket of her skirt and removed a magnifying glass. The glass was about two inches in diameter and rested on the end of a white plastic handle that also had a push-button light. Its 4x magnification turned the contract's small type into letters the size of a small dinosaur.

Mabel put the magnifier close to the paper and peered down at the contract. After several minutes, she mumbled, "Damn. I thought Cantwell was lying to me about my agreement. As I understand this, I can withdraw ten percent of the prior calendar year-end balance, each January, for the first five years. Then I can take out the remainder?"

Galway nodded. "Correct."

"So, getting three million for my grandson's amusement center will take all of five years?"

"Correct again."

"He won't get the place."

"I'm sorry."

"He'll be crushed. You should have seen his face, talking about helping all those kids."

Cantwell rolled his eyes. "I'll bet."

Mabel offered her hand to Cantwell. Cantwell took it and brushed his lips across her spidery nest of veins.

"I'm sorry I was so tough on you," Mabel said.

"That's okay, Mrs. Witherspoon. Even in the hedge fund business, this is a highly restrictive wind down. I only did it only to protect the assets of *all* clients, you included. You understand this now?"

"I do. And I want to make it up to you. How about dinner?"

Cantwell's eyes flicked toward the two SEC examiners, before settling back upon Mabel. "Dinner would be wonderful, Mrs. Witherspoon. I will have someone call and make the arrangements."

"What about tonight?"

Cantwell motioned toward the two SEC agents. "We're working late."

Mabel pulled a Blackberry from a holster hidden somewhere underneath her skirt. "Draw your gun," she said.

"My gun?"

"Your Crackberry. Draw it out and shoot me your contact info. Send me a vCard via email or bounce your contact info by infrared. I'm not going to play the gatekeeper phone tag game with you again. I want your cell number and private email, now."

Cantwell chuckled and pulled out a Blackberry. "What's your email address, Mrs. Witherspoon?"

"Mabes@Superhotbikerchick.com."

"Super hot biker chick dot com?"

"You got it. That's me. Now, give it here."

A moment later, Mabel's Blackberry vibrated. For a brief moment, Cantwell wondered if she kept her gun (as she called it) strapped to her thigh, like an old gunslinger. Mabel's lips raised with satisfaction and she nodded. She shook hands with Cramp and Galway, then looked at Cantwell. "This has been fun. I've got to take a leak, then get home and sit down with Oprah. Where's your bathroom?"

Cantwell gave Mabel directions to the bathrooms. Mabel let herself out the office and walked toward her destiny.

Chapter Three
V

Ben

It was a nasty day in early January. The sky was gray, looking like an old silver platter that needed a good polishing. There were these little black streaks that ran through the gray, kind of like Zorro slashes made with some great cosmic sword. A heavy mist was hanging in the air, a bank of moisture thick enough to slice. It was rolling off the water in waves. A steady wind was coming out of the northeast, making it feel more like San Francisco in July than southern Florida at any time of year.

I heard the rumble of a motorcycle outside my office entrance and decided to see who it was. I was coming downstairs, just as Mabel walked into my office, without an appointment. She was wearing a plaid wool skirt, something a girl might wear at a Catholic school, or a hardy competitor in the Scottish games, take your choice. The skirt was green with black stripes, down to the knees and kind of cute. I might have gone for her then, if she were thirty years younger.

Mabel took off her coat, to reveal a white cardigan sweater. It had a design of orange and yellow butterflies. Monarch's, I guessed. The butterflies were stitched along the right sleeve, looking like a basketball player's tattoos. The sweater was tight and I liked that. Come to think of it, Mabel didn't really look too bad. I might have exchanged those thick, cat-like glasses for some Lasik. Maybe put a little make-up on her face. Her eyes are green and really quite beautiful. I couldn't see that then, not through the thick lenses, just a hint. But she had this way about her, like she knew she was a hot mama deep inside. I did like her motorcycle, a Harley Softail.

"I hear you're good," she said.

"If I were good, I'd have clients," I said. I really didn't want to work, not yet. I was enjoying my new surroundings and that was enough. Just having an office to come to had put my boredom on hold. I would milk that as long as it lasted. Why rock the boat by taking on a client? When that black cloud of depression began to hover again, I would act. But not now. Certainly not now, not while I was content.

Mabel pulled out a Blackberry and peered at it with a magnifying glass. After a moment, she turned it toward me and stuck it in my face. I could see my ugly mug, smiling for the camera on my spanking new, very extensive website.

"This is your website, isn't it?" Mabel said.

"Maybe."

"These credentials that you list. That all true?"

"Perhaps."

"What the hell are you doing here, Ben Johnson? You should be working as a consultant to foreign governments or something, making millions."

"Money was never my thing."

Mabel looked around my small little building. It was a weird hybrid between a colonial and a ranch house, with a little Cape Cod thrown in, like its builder wanted to combine the best of New England tradition, then bring it to southern Florida. Instead, all he got was a camel. A camel is a thoroughbred racehorse designed by committee. It can run, it has endurance, it can go for days without water…it just can't win any races. My office building was a committee's nightmare, and it would never grace the cover of Architectural Digest.

"You own this place?" Mabel asked.

"Yeah, what about it?" I said indignantly.

Mabel gazed around the room with a smug little smile upon her face. "Looks like it was built by a contractor on LSD."

I laughed. She was right. "I got it cheap. Structurally, it is very sound. Are you here for something, other than to criticize me and my building?"

"I want to hire you."

"I'm still setting up."

Mabel stared around the office. There was a cluster of unopened cardboard boxes in one corner and a dozen un-hung pictures sitting in frames against another.

"I'll help you then," Mabel said. She tossed her cane to the floor and limped toward my jumble of boxes. "You got a box cutter?"

"I'm not a terrorist."

"Could have fooled me. Get me something to open these boxes with, or I'm going to use my teeth and bleed on your floor."

That's how it started with Mabel. By the end of that day, we had unpacked all of my boxes, which had been lying there for weeks. We hung all the paintings and arranged the furniture. To tell you the truth, the office looked pretty damned good, for a place designed on LSD.

Chapter Four
V

Mabel closed Cantwell's door behind her, leaving him alone with the two lackeys from the SEC. Lot of good they had been, she thought. Still, Mabel felt better. She had $5.4 million dollars and she could get to ten percent a year, if she needed it. Cantwell's withdrawal previsions were downright draconian. But they were not illegal. Mabel had done her research. She knew that most hedge funds had provisions limiting the amount and the timing of withdrawals. Newer funds had far more liberal policies, brought about by the gyrating markets, the mortgage debacle and pressure from the SEC. The failures of such bell-weather funds as Long Term Capital, Tiger and Madoff, had forced the hedge funds to give clients easier access to cash. Cantwell had modified his own restrictions for new investors, but he had held fast to agreements made in the past. That was fair. It sucked, but it was legal.

Yes, Mabel felt better. It was time to empty her bladder, maybe even take a good dump, now that the stress was gone. Her grandson would have to find a different way to entertain himself.

Mabel peered down the dim hallway in the direction Cantwell had said the bathrooms would be. She began to shuffle, using her cane as little as possible, willing her leg to work on its own. Mabel came to a water cooler, with a door just beyond it. The door had one of those stick figures they used these days to differentiate between men and women. She wondered why they didn't just put a penis on one of them. That would make it a hell of a lot easier for the sight challenged, like her.

Mabel sighed. She could still see things in the distance. But up close, her world was a dizzy haze. She'd been fine until those stupid little pieces of plaque had clogged up the arteries behind her retinas and then burst, right where the light focused. "Your eyes can't focus through the blood," her ophthalmologist had said. "But, the rest of your vision is holding up quite well, for someone your age."

Mabel had the beginnings of macular degeneration, but that was no big deal, at least not yet. She could still ride her Harley. Yeah, the world was growing a little pale. Yeah, the black was fading to gray and the contrast was slowly blending. But she could still ride. Let them *try* to peel her off of her hog.

Mabel peered at the black shadow before the bathroom, trying to discern if it was male or female. She reached into her pocket for her magnifying glass, but it was gone. *Damn.* She'd left it in Cantwell's office. No matter. She had a dozen more at home.

"God, I wish they would just give you guys a penis," she muttered. All the men looked like Barbie's Ken, neutered and useless. At least they could build them a "package" like they had John Kerry, for that magazine cover, back when he was running for president. Just a little bulge would help.

Mabel opened the door slightly. "Hello," she said softly. No answer. "Hello!" Again, no answer.

"What the hell." Mabel stepped inside the bathroom. The light was unusually bright and she had to shield her eyes, after the contrasting dimness of the hallway. There was a row of what looked like marble sinks, with those automatic faucets that turn on when you put your hands under them. Mabel tried one and the water flushed out in a warm jet. Mabel hit her cane against one of the sinks to see if the stone was real. She was rewarded with a solid, tinny *clink.* The sink was real stone. Mabel looked to the bank of mirrors that stretched along the wall for a good twenty feet. She stepped back so she could see herself with more clarity. She straightened her hair. Then she adjusted her top row of teeth.

As Mabel turned to step into a stall, she saw a row of urinals. "Damn," she had done it again. "Why the hell won't they give Ken a penis?" If they would just give Ken a penis, she wouldn't do this anymore. A big penis; big enough so people like her couldn't miss it. Mabel debated whether to walk out and find the ladies' room. She was going to have to walk out this door anyway. Then she would have to find the other bathroom. She decided to stay; it was easier. If someone came in while she was in a stall, she would just lift her legs. She already knew what she would do if someone came in while she was standing like this; she'd pretend to be a man, a man in drag. She would grab her crotch, fart and spit into the sink. Then she'd say, "How are ya? I'm on my way to a costume party. How do I look?" in the deepest voice she had. Then she'd get out fast.

The stall was spacious, and it was clean. Like Cantwell. Even so, Mabel reached into her handbag and removed a small bottle of Lysol, which she used to spray the seat. She wiped the seat dry with toilet paper, then sat down, wondering if she was going to poop today. She was still waiting when she heard voices outside the bathroom door. Male voices. She rapidly pulled up her skirt and stood on the seat.

Mabel heard Cantwell say, "I've got Galway and Cramp in my office for another hour or so, Lou. Then I'm taking them to dinner, maybe out to the clubs. So, let's make this quick."

"Just a sec."

A long period of silence followed. Mabel could hear the shuffling of shoes, moving slowly in her direction. She could hear a soft scratch of leather, then silence. Someone was checking the stalls. Soon, Mabel could see the shadow of legs outside her stall door. The edge of a face appeared. She couldn't see the eyes, but she could feel them. He was checking the floor beneath her toilet perch. The feet moved on. After another minute she heard, "Okay."

"How much we have this time?"

"Two hundred fifty two million."

Cantwell whistled. "That's one sweet month, Lou." Cantwell's deep, powerful voice echoed through the bathroom like a bassoon. "Bring it to the boat tomorrow. Tell our friend in the Caymans to expect us."

"The usual place?"

"Yeah." Cantwell paused. "I've got something for you to do before then. I want you to research one of our clients, Mabel Witherspoon."

"She going to be trouble?"

"I hope not, but we need to prepare. She came in today, demanding three million from an account of five."

Lou sighed. "You couldn't just give it to her?"

"I might have, but she confronted Galway."

"And the SEC knows, that if you make an exception for one, you must offer it to all?"

"Correct. He tried to bait me, but I wouldn't bite."

"You think Witherspoon's trouble?"

"Don't know yet. She is a bitchy little thing. I'm going to take her to dinner, later this week. I'll know more then."

Bitchy thing, my ass, thought Mabel. He hadn't seen bitchy, at least not yet.

"Why don't you just pay her off?"

"I won't do that."

Lou paused. Then he said softly, "Why don't we just shut this down, Rial? We've got over thirty billion. We could shut it all down and no one would know."

"I want fifty."

"You're too goddamned greedy."

"And you're a sociopath who likes to kill people. That's why we make a good team."

"Killing is dangerous," said Lou. "I prefer *not* to kill."

"I just said to find information on Witherspoon, not kill her."

"Information leads to death. Always does with you. That's your code."

Cantwell remained silent for a long time. Mabel could hear his breathing, and she wondered if he were hearing hers. Killing? They going to kill her? She peed in her diaper.

"We kill only when we need to," continued Cantwell. "Besides, you enjoy it. I know you do."

Mabel felt herself begin to shake. She wasn't sure if it was fear or rage that made her feel like a leaf in a tornado, probably a little bit of both. These men were thieves and killers. She was a deer in their headlights. She prayed that they wouldn't hear her now, because she knew, she *knew*, that if they did, she wouldn't leave this bathroom alive. Five minutes later, the men were gone.

It took half an hour for Mabel to stop trembling. During that time she began to formulate a plan. She needed a plan. It was a long time since she had left Cantwell's office. She was going to have to walk past little miss perfect in the reception area. Little miss tight ass might note the time and pass it along to Cantwell. How could she explain forty minutes in the bathroom? She might even run into Cantwell in the hall. What would she say then?

When she was sure the bathroom was empty, Mabel stepped out of the stall. She walked to the door and peered outside, looking both ways before jumping into the hallway. She continued down the corridor, away from the exit, until she found another stick figure outside a door, one with a dress. She stepped inside the bathroom and went straight for a stall. She pulled off her skirt and removed her Depends, which was now soaked into a heavy load. She squeezed the diaper to wring a stream of urine around the outside of the toilet, especially in front. *That should do it*, she thought.

Mabel rolled up the Depends and stuffed it deep into the used paper towel bin. She washed her hands, exited the bathroom and began to shuffle back toward the entrance to the offices. Little miss blondie was seated at her desk, looking as regal and smug as a music diva.

"Excuse me," said Mabel. "I had a little bit of an accident back there…in the ladies' room. I'm not as good a shot as I used to be. You know how it is, you can't sit on the seats anymore because you might catch AIDS or some other nasty venereal disease. So, you've got to stand up and shoot for the water. God didn't see fit to give me very good aim at this late stage of my life so I kind of pissed all over the floor. I got the poop cleaned up, but you might want to send someone in to clean the floor. I'm sorry about this, but, if you live long enough, you might learn what it's like.

"Please thank Mr. Cantwell for his time. Tell him that I understand his process now and feel much more comfortable about my money."

Chapter Five
V

Ben

After we set up my office, I pulled a couple of Coronas out of the fridge and walked toward the stairs that led to my second floor. "C'mon," I said. "Let's talk on the balcony."

Mabel followed me up to the faux widow's walk that the drug-induced architect had slapped onto the front of my building. Imagine a ranch/colonial hybrid. The main part is just one floor, stretching far back with a walk-down mud room. The front of the structure has a colonial façade just one room deep, with a second-floor balcony that curves out over the front of the home like a southern mansion. The balcony has a white wooden railing and a floor made with greenish recycled plastic, which looks like it belongs on a school playground. French doors open out to the balcony. Beside them is a pole, painted white, with a brass ship's bell attached to it. Sometimes I ring the bell at the girls walking by. They usually wave and that makes me feel like part of the scene.

We sat in chairs that looked out toward the ocean. I handed Mabel a beer, then said, "So, what is so important that you need my help?"

"Rial Cantwell is trying to kill me."

"The hedge fund guy?"

"The *scum bag* hedge fund guy."

"He's a pillar of our community, Mabel. Does a lot of charity work."

"He's stolen thirty billion dollars."

"So, tell the police. If money's been stolen, they'll find whatever's left."

"I already went to the authorities. They think I'm nuts."

"Well, maybe you are."

Chapter Six
V

As Mabel walked out into the lobby of the Cantwell building, she was sure there were eyes upon her. Was Lou, the sociopath, tailing her every step, looking for the chance to put a shiv in her side? She looked around, seeing nothing but the two security guards. One of the guards was seated at a desk, picking his nose. The other watched a wide-screen television that was tuned to a football game. It had been showing market updates when Mabel had walked in. The markets must be closed now, leaving the inmates to rule the asylum.

Mabel waved gaily to the guards. "Goodbye!"

The nose-picker waved back, with a booger on the end of his finger, while the other guard remained fixed to his game.

Mabel felt her shoulders slump as she walked outside. She had made it, at least this far. She looked around the street. Cars were passing; that was good. There was a line of modest two-story office buildings and re-tail stores stretching in both directions. Mabel thought how odd it was for a prominent hedge fund manager to office in such a blue-collar neigh-borhood. Pickup trucks and jalopies with dents and mismatched paint seemed to be the predominant vehicles here, not the BMWs and Mer-cedes that one would expect to prowl the streets outside a company that claimed to manage over a hundred billion dollars. Mabel made a mental note to ask Cantwell why he had his office here, rather than some ritzy high-rise. Provided her let he live, of course.

Mabel began to shake again. All she'd wanted was to withdraw some of her money, so her grandson could buy Jiggles. Now, she knew some-thing she shouldn't know. Something bad. Rial Cantwell had stolen thirty billion dollars from his investors. He was planning to move another quar-ter billion offshore in the morning. He had a henchman named Lou who liked to kill people. And, through bad luck, they had targeted her.

Mabel sat down on the curb and threw up into her mouth, absorbing the bitter taste of fear like a determined cage fighter after a kick to the groin. She knew what she should do. She should sell her Miami condo and go back to New Hampshire. A farm in Durham was a far safer place than a street curb in Miami Gardens. She should just forget about what she'd heard, take her ten percent for the next five years and cash out, provided the money was there. She didn't need the money anyway. UNH leased a portion of her farmland for a hundred fifty grand a year. That was enough. She should forget about Rial Cantwell. She should forget about Lou, the killer sociopath. She should forget about the money that was going to the Caymans tomorrow. She should walk away.

"Damn it," she said.

Mabel pulled her Blackberry out of its holster and fingered it awake. She opened the Internet browser and searched for an address. Soon she stood up. She knew what she *should* do. She also knew what she *must* do.

Mabel walked down the street and stopped beside a hulking Harley Davidson Softail. She ran her finger across the smooth red and black fuel tank that rested above the twin cam 96A Evo engine, with its 1594 CCs of pulsating power. What a wondrous thing to strap between the legs, she thought. Even better than riding a horse.

Mabel slid the helmet off the handlebars and strapped it on. She attached her cane to the back saddlebags with a bungee cord, wrapped her good leg over the frame of the bike, jammed a key into the ignition and cranked the sucker awake.

The air thundered with the rumble of the Harley. Mabel juiced the engine several times, before pulling out into the street with a long, loud squeal.

Mabel pulled into a parking lot across from 16320 NW 2nd Avenue. She stared at the modest white structure, which was surrounded by leafy trees. Did she really want to do this? She should sell her condo and move back north. Why put a bull's-eye on her forehead? Why alert Cantwell that she was onto his scheme? Why rock the boat that had, at least on paper, turned a modest land sale into $5.4 million? Why not take the money and run? Because, she had to do the right thing. *Stupid.* She'd always been stupid, doing the right thing. Why did she always have to do it this way?

Mabel removed her helmet and slung the strap around the left handlebar. She fluffed her plaid skirt, smoothed out her sweater and walked to meet with the FBI.

"I want to see the agent in charge," Mabel said.

A woman peered at Mabel through a thick plate of bulletproof glass.

"Do you have an appointment?"

"No. But, I've got a tip about fraud and murder."

"Fraud and murder?'

"Billions stolen. And a sociopath who kills to keep it quiet."

"Could I see some form of identification, please?"

Mabel slipped her driver's license through a narrow slot in the window, her eyes darting to the door. "Make it quick. They may be after me."

The woman called for someone. A man soon appeared, took the driver's license and disappeared inside. A few minutes later, the man returned and said, "Let her in."

Mabel was buzzed inside. She passed through a metal detector and was allowed into the inner sanctum of the FBI's Miami field office.

The man guided Mabel to a second story office with no window. It had a small metal desk and two chairs. There was nothing else on the walls or the floor. The room smelled of moldy dust and ripe sweat.

"My name is Agent Cross," the man said. Cross was young, mid-forties, maybe. He had thinning brown hair and an angular face that made Mabel think of a hawk with hair. His nose was large, like a beak, with a sharp point on its end that might have been good for cracking nuts.

"You're not the agent in charge," said Mabel.

The man laughed. "No, Ms. Witherspoon. I'm just the man you want to see if you have information on fraud."

"What about murder?'

"I don't do murder. That's another department. You see a murder?"

"No."

"Did you see fraud?"

Mabel paused. What was she going to tell Agent Cross? That she was in the men's bathroom and overheard Cantwell talking to Lou, the killer? He'd think she was insane.

"I don't see very well," said Mabel.

"Pardon me?"

"Never mind." Mabel paused. This was going to be harder than she thought. How could she alert the FBI without sounding like a ditz? "I have $5.4 million invested with Rial Cantwell's hedge fund, and I think that he may be committing fraud."

Cross's eyes narrowed. His lips tightened and then twisted to the side, as if he were trying to bite his cheek. "Do you have any evidence of this?"

"Yes, but I can't tell you what it is."

Cross stared at Mabel for a long time. "Have you committed fraud, Ms. Witherspoon?"

"Me? Of course not!"

"Then why won't you share evidence that will support your claim? You must understand that an accusation of fraud against one of our communities' most visible residents will need to be substantiated."

"I overheard them talking."

"Who?"

"Cantwell and Lou."

"Lou?"

"His hired killer."

"And what did the two men say?"

"They've stolen thirty billion dollars and they are moving two hundred fifty million more offshore in the morning."

Cross stared again. His lips twisted to the other side. His pointed nose crinkled, as if Mabel had just opened a can of oily sardines. He was serious for a long moment. Then he laughed. "Thirty billion, you say? And I'm the tooth fairy… You do know that Mr. Cantwell is one of the most celebrated residents of Miami?"

"Well, duh."

"Successful people are often the target of false allegations. Are you looking for money, Ms. Witherspoon?"

"Money? I have money. He won't give it to me, but I have it."

"What do you mean, he won't give it to you?"

Mabel closed her eyes. This wasn't going well. What was she going to do, tell Agent Cross that Cantwell had refused to deviate from the *contract* he had with her? Was she going to say that the SEC examiners had attested to the validity of the agreement? Was she going to tell him that

Cantwell would only give her $540,000 this year? He'd laugh at her.

"I was in the bathroom."

"Ah, Ms. Witherspoon, we don't need to discuss that here."

"No, I was in the men's room."

"You were in the men's room? Why were you in the men's room?"

Mabel closed her eyes. "Never mind."

Cross smiled. "Let me assure you, Ms. Witherspoon. The FBI has a thick file on Mr. Cantwell. You are not the first person to issue a complaint against him. He has a very strict policy about paying his investors. We know that. We have reviewed his customer contracts…and his files. We have consulted with the SEC. He is clean, so far as we know."

"What about murder?"

"Don't know anything about murder. That's another department. But I wouldn't go around accusing Cantwell of murder, Ms. Witherspoon, unless you have evidence. That's the kind of thing that ends up in court, or worse. Know what I mean?"

"What do you mean?"

Cross shrugged. He looked solemnly at Mabel and said, "I'm just trying to protect your reputation ma'am."

"You think I'm crazy."

Cross laughed. "No...I think you're angry. You're not the first person to be upset with Cantwell. Nor will you be the last. I'm sorry I can't help you. I really am. But that dog won't hunt.

"If you've got evidence of other crimes, I can tell you who to see. Did you want to file a report?"

Mabel sighed deeply and shook her head. Agent Cross thought she was bananas. She'd told him about the men's room. How could she have told him that? Fortunately, she hadn't mentioned the Depends. "Thank you for your time, Agent Cross. I am sorry to have wasted it."

"No, Ms. Witherspoon. Thank you for your concern. Most of our tips come from people like you. Unfortunately, Cantwell is old news. He's probably clean. If he's not, he's too smart for us, and the SEC."

Chapter Seven
V
____

Ben

I settled more comfortably into my chair and took another sip of my beer. The beer tasted good, better than good. It was cold and crisp, putting a pleasant tingle on my tongue. It reminded me of college, what little I remembered of it now.

Two young ladies walked by on the other side of the street. They *looked* like college kids, young and still innocent to the true perils of this world. I took a sideways glance at Mabel. She was slumped down in her chair, but she was nowhere near as relaxed as I was. There were hard, taut lines crowding around her eyes. The edges of her lips were pinched into round white dots. She was wearing a scowl, making me think of Sigourney Weaver in one of those horror flicks, where the unsuspecting alien was about to meet its gory demise. She was a soldier preparing for battle, while I was an old gunslinger who had hung up his pistols, content to ride out his final days on the porch.

I didn't want to take on this case. What I wanted was to help some distraught woman who suspected that her husband was cheating on her. I could set up a little surveillance thing, get to use some of my toys and catch the bad guy in the act. I would help my lady client get a little justice, a good chunk of alimony, then take her to dinner and let her buy me a fine bottle of cabernet. Instead, I had Mabel Witherspoon, a Harley riding farmer's wife from New England, who wanted to take on a highly respected billionaire and his killer henchman. Shit.

"Who did you bring this to?" I said.

"The FBI."

I felt my eyebrows rise. Mabel's allegations were certainly salacious enough to draw the attention of the fibbies. If they didn't bite, then why should I?

"What did you tell them?" I said.

"The truth."

The truth, I thought. Nobody knows the truth, the real truth. We only see what we perceive to be correct. Show the same crime to twenty people and you'll get twenty versions of the facts. As they say, 'it is what it is,' but it is never what we think it is.

"You better tell me what happened, Mabel. From the beginning. Leave nothing out."

Mabel told me.

When I finished laughing…something Mabel did not find amusing at all…I said, "Mabel, you are some piece of work."

"So, you'll take the case?"

I looked through her glasses into those intelligent, determined green eyes and said something stupid. I opened the door. It was just a tiny sliver, but enough for Mabel to come barging through it like a Pamplona bull. "If there was some dirt on Cantwell, the FBI and the SEC would certainly be all over him."

"He's paying them off."

"You're dreaming. Doesn't work that way anymore."

"Then he's conning them, too."

"I doubt it. After Madoff, the Feds and the SEC have grown hyper-vigilant. They won't be embarrassed again. If Cantwell was scamming clients, they'd find it."

"Not only is he scamming clients, he's killing them. Clients like me."

I stared at Mabel. I wanted to believe her. She didn't seem crazy, just passionate. If Cantwell was conning investors out of billions, shouldn't he be stopped? If he was killing people, which was too much of a stretch for me to believe, shouldn't he pay for his crimes? If Mabel wanted her money, shouldn't she get it?

"Okay," I mumbled. "I'll help you."

"So, what's the plan?"

The plan? That all depended on what Mabel wanted. If she wanted three million dollars I could get that before she left the office. If she wanted justice…well, that was something different. Something danger-ous. I didn't want to open that Pandora's box. No frigging way.

I walked over to my computer and flicked it awake. "Have you got your account number with Cantwell?"

Mabel pulled a folded envelope out of her pocketbook and handed it to me. I stared at the summary page for a moment. She really did have $5.4 million. "What's your Social Security number?" She told me. "Maiden name? Address? Your other addresses? Place where you were born?" She told me again.

"Why are you asking me all this?" she said.

"I'm going to get you your three million. Shouldn't take me more than, say…twenty minutes. Since Cantwell uses the Caymans, we'll set up an account for you there. We'll transfer money from your investment account to your new Cayman account. We'll bounce it to a few more places before moving it to, say… the Bahamas. Yes, perfect place. We'll take a boat ride tomorrow from West Palm, get your money, in cash, and be back by nightfall. That work for you?"

"I don't want my money."

"What do you mean, you don't want your money? You went to Cantwell for three million dollars. He wouldn't give it to you. I can. Problem solved."

"I don't want you hacking into Cantwell's computers and setting up offshore accounts. That's illegal."

"You're accusing Cantwell of doing illegal things. The authorities won't help you. I will. Hacking is how I do it, Mabel."

"Not for me. I don't want my money. No. I'm hiring you to *expose* Cantwell."

I groaned. No frigging way. I tried to think of a tactful way to say it. The best I could come up with was, "No frigging way."

"What are you, scared?'

"I'm not scared. I'm just not stupid."

"Yeah, you are. You're scared as shit. You don't want to mess with this because you are a scaredy-cat, dickless pantywaist."

"A dickless pantywaist? I'm not a dickless pantywaist. I've done things that would make your skin curl. I've left my calling card on the doorstep of dictators all around this world. You don't call me a dickless pantywaist and get away with it. You take that back."

"I'm not taking it back. You're a little weenie who's afraid to save lives. You're afraid to risk your little chicken neck to help others."

"Well, let me tell you miss, potty pants…I stuck my neck out for this country for forty years. I was *the man*. I've helped save thousands, maybe millions of lives. I've hacked the inner sanctum of every terrorist organization from Cuba to Iran. I've tracked down rogue extremists with nuclear weapons, helped foil dozens of terrorist plots on *our* shores…so don't go calling me a dickless pantywaist."

I heaved a heavy sigh. In a way, she was right. "I've retired from all that, you see. I'll get your money if you want me to. But I'm not going to be sticking my neck out, not anymore. Nooo. I'm too old for that."

"Then you're a liar."

"What do you mean, I'm a liar?"

"Go look at your website. It says you help people find justice."

Oh, shit, I thought. Now this was a case of honor. I pulled up my website and read through the fluff I'd written for it. She was right. I'd stretched the truth, made everyone think that I was some crimestopper, hell-bent on justice, rather than a tired old man who wanted to hang out on his office balcony, drink beer and watch the eye candy.

"Oh, Mabel…"

Chapter Eight
V
____

Rial Cantwell pulled up to the entrance of the Miami Beach Marina garage at precisely 8 A.M. He swiped his access card and drove to his assigned parking spot. He hefted a crocodile suitcase out of the trunk of his BMW 650i convertible and set it upon the garage floor. A minute later, a dock attendant came running over to grab the bag.

"Good to see you again, Mr. Cantwell," the attendant said, as Cantwell palmed him a $100 tip.

Cantwell walked into the marina, where he checked into the U.S. Customs area. He palmed another tip to the clearing agent, who checked his bag with just a cursory glance.

"Where're we heading this time, Mr. Cantwell?" said the agent.

"Going through the Windward Passage to Montego Bay, Mr. Nelson," said Cantwell. "Got some investors with a place down there."

"Must be nice."

"Oh, it's not as nice as you might think. Sometimes I wish I were standing in your shoes."

Nelson laughed. "Anytime, Mr. Cantwell."

Cantwell grinned and headed back outside. He turned right and took a leisurely stroll toward the last of a dozen docking runways that ran like giant hair pick tines out over the water. When he reached the end, he continued into the Meloy Channel, with the morning sun glowing between the high-rises behind him. The dock attendant followed closely with his suitcase. They reached the far end of the straight dock and angled left toward Cantwell's deep water mooring spot. His luxury, 220' Rodriguez yacht rode high in the water, rolling up and down with a slow, measured beat in the early morning breeze.

Cantwell jumped on board and headed for the control room, where he found his captain, checking the yacht's electronics.

"Hello, Mr. Cantwell," said his captain. "A fine day for a sail."

"It is, Acacio. How soon will you be ready?"

"Just a few minutes, sir. Will you be wanting the hard top today?"

Like a luxury convertible, Cantwell's yacht had a hard top that could be removed for open-air cruising.

"Open her up. Let's enjoy the day."

Acacio spoke into an intercom to alert the crew. Then he engaged the hard top's power mechanism, which acted much like that of an automobile, except with a far larger roof. Cantwell could hear the motor engage, while a low hum filled the air.

"I'll be in my cabin," said Cantwell. "Let me know when we're set to depart."

Ten minutes later, Cantwell's yacht, *HEDGEMONEY*, motored away from its slip.

As Cantwell's yacht pulled into the Meloy Channel, Ben Johnson started the engine to his own 48' Sea Ray Sundancer.

"Nice ride," said Mabel. "What'd this cost you, Ben? Must have been a quarter million, at least."

"Add a million to that, Mabel. Give or take." Ben motioned toward Cantwell's mansion-sized yacht. "About three percent of what it cost for Cantwell's toy."

"You make that kind of money doing government work?"

Ben laughed. "Nah. I've done some consulting now and then. Enough to get what I need."

"Who needs a boat like this?"

Ben shrugged. "I like to fish for big game. Can't do that in a seventeen footer. This thing's got a standard four hundred gallon tank, with a two hundred gallon spare. We can cruise forever, at least 300 miles, without pushing it."

Mabel looked out over the water at Cantwell's sleek motor craft. "That's some kind of ride. Probably used my money to buy it."

Ben hung well behind Cantwell's yacht for hours. Using the ultra-sensitive radar he'd installed for his fishing, Ben followed Cantwell at a distance of a mile, well enough behind to avoid suspicion. They were twenty miles south of Key West when Ben saw the blip of another boat begin to drift suspiciously toward Cantwell.

"Well, hello," Ben said. He flipped on a radio, with a scanner that read all open channels. After a moment he heard, "Permission to approach, sir."

"That's him," whispered Mabel. "That's Lou, the killer."

"You don't need to whisper, Mabel. Our mic is not engaged."

Lou's boat approached from the south, making a wide circular turn, as if searching out pursuers.

"You have the package?" said Cantwell.

"I do."

"Welcome aboard, then."

Ben recognized Lou's boat as a custom Halvorsen of about forty-five feet. It was a magnificent looking craft, with clean white lines and dark blue trim.

"Now that is a boat," Ben said.

"Tiny little thing," said Mabel, as the Halvorsen pulled beside Cantwell's much larger craft.

"Size isn't everything, Mabel."

"Men think so."

Ben chuckled. "You know how to rig a skipjack?"

"What?"

"You know how to rig a skipjack tuna, for marlin fishing?"

"Do you know how to birth a cow? Or a horse?"

"I take that as a 'no.'"

"I'm a simple farm girl."

Ben's boat was outfitted with two curved-butt Shimano Tallus IFGA 130# fishing rods, with Tiagra 130A big game reels They were slipped into holsters on the side of two fishing chairs that were bolted onto the back of the boat. Ben reached into a cooler and removed a live skipjack tuna. The fish would have made a good meal on its own. He rigged the tuna and gently lowered the squirming fish into the water. He snapped the rod into its pole clips and motioned for Mabel to sit in the chair beside it.

"Sit in this chair. Yell if something happens. We're over Woods Wall, so it's possible, even at this time of year."

There was an Anglr fighting harness draped over the chair. Ben checked to make sure that the harness was attached, just in case.

Ben edged his Sea Ray slowly forward and stopped as close to Cantwell as he dared. He lifted a pair of Fujinon Stabiscope 40x Superpower Gyro Stabilized Binoculars to his eyes. He had a camera rigged to the binoculars, for taking pictures. Ben adjusted the focus and snapped off a couple shots. He looked to the digital viewer and nodded. Good enough for what they needed. Ben watched while Lou edged his Halvorsen beside Cantwell's Rodriguez. The forty-five footer was dwarfed by the leviathan bulk of Cantwell's superyacht. Two of Cantwell's crew tossed ropes overboard, while two men on the Halvorsen grabbed the lines to secure the boats together, which Lou used to board the *HEDGEMONEY*. Ben took photos as Lou climbed. He snapped off another series as Cantwell met him with a handshake.

A loading boom swung over the side of the *HEDGEMONEY*. There was a cable hanging from the boom, which the Halvorsen's crew attached to a square steel crate that sat upon its deck. The crate was secured by a cable at each corner, with the four meeting in the middle to allow for one attachment point. The crate lifted slowly, until it swayed above Cantwell's yacht like a giant pendulum. Ben's camera clicked off shots until the crate had been lowered safely upon the *HEDGEMONEY*'s deck.

"That's the cash," said Ben.

Then something unexpected happened. Lou took Cantwell's place on the big yacht, while Cantwell lowered himself down into the Halvorsen.

At that moment, there was a loud, piercing scream. The Shimano rod bent almost in half, looking like an inverted letter J. Line poured out from its Tiagra reel like it had been shot from a cannon.

"Holy shit," said Mabel. "We've hooked a whale."

Ben groaned. This wasn't supposed to happen; this was *not* supposed to happen.

"Put on the harness, Mabel," yelled Ben. "You're going to catch yourself a marlin."

"The hell I will."

"The hell you *will*. I've got to man the boat, so you'll need to bring it in."

At that moment a huge blue marlin launched itself fully into the air, shaking its head as it tried to spit out the circle hook.

"Oh, my God," shouted Ben. "That thing is huge. Could run a thousand pounds. You *do* have yourself a whale, Mabel. I said, strap in!"

Mabel quickly put on the harness, which was attached to a BlueWater Large Marlin fishing chair. Mabel tried to place her feet against the chair's footrest, but her legs were too short. They dangled out over the end like those of young child at Thanksgiving dinner. Ben secured his boat's wheel and ran back to adjust the footrest up to Mabel's feet. Mabel would need her legs, and more, to fight that fish.

"You are in for the time of your life, Mabel. Even better than sex."

"Sex? What's sex?"

"It's something you do to make kids."

"Oh, yeah. I remember that. Haven't had sex in eight years…My husband's been dead for three."

Ben smiled. "Don't grab the rod until I tire this gal out a bit."

"How do you know it's a *she*?"

"Because of her size."

"But what about Cantwell?"

"We've got what we needed."

"Aren't we going to follow him?"

"Where to? Back to Miami? We know where he lives."

Ben did his best to keep a gentle tension on the fishing rod, without letting the line play out and snap. After fifteen minutes, the fish seemed to tire enough for Mabel to take charge. Ben put the boat into neutral and set up a rod holder between Mabel's legs.

"I'm going to place the rod into this holder, which you will use for leverage. It's got gears and an adjustable tension. I'm going to set it to something you can handle. Whenever you feel some slack, you reel in as fast as you can. You got that?"

"I've fished trout and bass, you know."

"This fish is going to run on you like you've never—"

At that moment, there was another loud *whine*, as the marlin ripped off a hundred more yards of line. Ben looked down and saw that the reel was nearly played out. The fish had run close to a thousand yards away. Another few feet and the line was going to break. Ben finished setting up the rod for Mabel and ran back to the helm of his boat.

"Don't want to do this, but I'm going to back us up a bit. You're going to have to reel in like hell. Don't let the line go slack."

"Got it."

Ben gently nudged the boat backwards, while Mabel reeled as fast as she could to keep the line taut. After they'd pulled the fish three hundred yards closer, Ben put the boat into neutral and walked back to

Mabel.

Ben said, "Lucky we didn't lose her. How strong are you?"

"You ever milk cows? Muck a stall?"

"No."

"Builds wrists like iron. If we arm wrestled, I'd kick your ass."

Ben smiled. "Well, all right, Ms. Popeye. I'm going to set your drag at forty pounds."

"You think I'm kidding."

Ben laughed. "If you can handle forty pounds, I'll eat a skipjack, raw."

"You're on." There was a quick glint in Mabel's eye and a look of determination that sent a shudder across Ben's heart. Something told him that he didn't want to be on the wrong end of her fishing rod.

Mabel could actually handle a constant forty pound drag. With the harness holding her in, plus Ben's pole support, she was able to fight the fish's fury for another hour. Mabel began to tire, so Ben reduced her drag to a more manageable thirty pounds.

After the marlin jumped full out of the air again, nearly pulling the rod out of Mabel's hands, she yelled, "I've got to pee!"

"The chair's got slats," yelled Ben from the cockpit. "Let it go, Mabel. Just let it go."

"I'm wearing Depends," yelled Mabel.

Oh, yeah, Ben thought. It was so easy to forget. Ben put the boat into neutral. He ran back to Mabel, took hold of the rod and sat himself down in the second chair. "Go use the head," he said. "I won't tell. Our little secret."

"You don't reel that thing in; not a bit."

"Agreed."

Big game fishing is like golf; it is a sport of honor. You take a fish down, you do it on your own, all the way, if you can. That way, when you point up to that fish on the wall, or to the picture in your palm or on your computer screen, you can honestly say, "I caught that fish." Not some tour guide. Not some guy who hands you the rod at the very last minute. You. You fight that fish until you think you can't fight anymore. Then you go on. You pee in your chair. You fight through the cramps. You ignore the sunburn and the blisters. It is you against the fish, mano a mano. Until one of you surrenders.

After less than a minute, Mabel returned.

"I took the diaper off," she said. "I don't cheat. Next time, it's on the chair."

Ben gave the pole back to Mabel. He shook his head. "You are some chick."

It took nearly five hours for Ben and Mabel to pull the massive marlin alongside the Sundancer. Ben wrapped something that looked like a rubber theraband around the fish's sword. He attached this to a steel cable that ran to a winch that he'd swung out over the boat. He slipped a noose over the marlin's tail and secured it to a clamp on the boat's aft corner. The fish had finally worn out, and it flopped anemically against the side of the boat. It wouldn't stay that way for long. All it needed was a breather; then it would be ready for more. Ben was careful to keep the fish's gills underwater, until Mabel gave the word.

"What do you want to do with her?" Ben said.

"Let her go."

"She's worth a fortune at the fish market."

"Let her go."

"Don't you want a picture?"

"Not if I kill her."

Ben quickly pulled his camera off the Stabiscope and set it on a flexible mounting that could hang out over the boat. He pulled up on the marlin's sword with a winch, just enough to bring the fish to the top edge of the water. Then he used a remote trigger to snap off a dozen photos of the big blue beauty.

Ben measured the fish's girth in a number of places. He ran a tape from the fish's lower jaw to its tail.

"All right," he said. "We're going to take one last photo."

Ben adjusted the camera. He pressed a button and the winch whirred. The fish came out of the ocean like it had taken a full jump. Ben snapped a photo, then let the fish splash back into the water. The entire process took less than five seconds. Ben looked carefully at the fish. She was beginning to stir again, looking as restless as a wild horse at a rodeo. Ben removed the tail loop. Then he unwrapped the rubber strap that held the marlin's sword. The fished drifted for a moment, then began to calmly swim away.

"Be free, you beautiful thing," he said.

"You've done this before," said Mabel.

"Not with a thousand pounder, I haven't."

"Are you disappointed? That I let her go?"

"Hell no. Are you?"

"Only that I won't have a photo with me standing beside that little monster."

Ben motioned toward the rear of the boat. "Go stand over there."

The sun was now low in the sky. It cast an ethereal glow upon Mabel's face. She looked beautiful, despite the glasses that were reflecting hot blinding sunbursts into Ben's eyes.

"Off with the glasses," he said.

"I've got raccoon circles."

"I want even light across your face. Your glasses are reflecting rays like a laser. Take off your glasses. I'll tan your eyes in the lab."

"I wear glasses and I'll keep them on, thank you."

"You afraid you'll be too pretty?"

"Yeah, and it'll ruin your day. 'Cause you ain't getting any."

"Getting any what? I just want a good picture. Besides, *you're* not getting any, so take off the glasses. I'll put them back on with the computer, if you want."

Mabel removed her glasses. Ben shot her with a dozen different poses and from multiple angles. When he was done, he scrolled through them on the back of his Nikon. Satisfied, he waited for Mabel to follow him into the boat's cabin.

"Down here," he said.

Mabel didn't move. "I'm not going in there alone with you."

Ben laughed. "You think I want to jump you?"

"Don't you?"

"I like women decades younger than you, ones with big tits and tight asses."

"I've got big tits and a tight ass."

"You've got a tight ass?"

Mabel shrugged. "Well, it might be a *little bit* loose. It's sure as hell tight enough for you."

"But are you thirty-five?"

Mabel's lower lip curled, then she smiled slyly. "I'm a little more seasoned."

Ben motioned with his head. "C'mon, girl. I've got a computer with

Photoshop inside. Let's see if we can put you up beside your fish."

The inside of the Sea Ray was surprisingly spacious. There was a broad galley with a teak table. In the foredeck, there was a shower and a bedroom with a full sized, island style bed. Ben sat down at the table, turned on a notebook computer and cabled his camera into the side.

After twenty minutes, Ben's printer spit out a magnificent color photo with Mabel standing *beside* her large fish, as if it were dead on the docks.

"How'd you do that?" she said.

"You'd be amazed at what I can do—"

"You coming on to me again?"

"—with a computer."

Ben opened another computer program. This one was a custom job, into which he fed the fish's girths and lengths. Then he stood back and grinned. "Congratulations, Mabel. You've bagged a grander."

"Is that good?"

"It's a very exclusive club."

Mabel's grin was even wider than Ben's. "You're going to join an exclusive club, too."

"I am?" said Ben.

"You owe me a raw skipjack."

"Awww, Mabel."

"A deal's a deal. I handle a forty-pound drag, you eat skipjack sushi."

Ben sighed. He motioned with his head for Mabel to follow him up onto the ship's deck. "Tell you what. We're a hundred and fifty miles from Miami, but only twenty from my place on Key West."

"Don't think you're going to get fresh with me, just because you helped me bag a grander."

Ben laughed. "I've got a guest bedroom. We'll bunk at my place, fill up with gas, and have a nice leisurely cruise back to Miami tomorrow."

"You have a good knife?"

"What?"

"You're going to need a good knife, to eat your raw fish."

Chapter Nine
V
___

It was after dark the next day when Mabel pulled her Harley beside the Michael Graves building at 1500 Ocean Drive. She looked up at the well known structure, which housed her twelfth floor condo. She gazed out to the water. Lights bounced off the waves, sparkling like dancing fairies. She liked this place, with its curving façade, its little forest of palm trees and the cute cabana boy that catered to her like a princess. It was a far cry from her rambling, eighteenth century farmhouse in New Hampshire. It was warm, with sand and sun and island drinks. She didn't want to leave it.

Craig, the concierge, happened to be in the lobby when Mabel walked through the doors.

"Hey, cutie," she said.

"Hello there, superhot biker chick."

"I bagged a marlin yesterday."

"Didn't think marlin were much in season."

"They were yesterday."

"Mabel, that's awesome."

"Let me show you."

Mabel pulled the 8x10 photo out of her purse and put it into Craig's hands. Craig stared at the photo for a long while, without saying a word. He peered more closely at the picture, as if not wanting to believe what he saw.

"This some kind of trick?" he said. "That a fish or a house?"

"No trick," said Mabel. "I bagged her with a hundred thirty pound test, a forty pound drag, a thousand yards of line and five hours of sweat. Off a Sea Ray Sundancer."

"How'd you last that long?"

"I peed in the seat."

Craig looked embarrassed. "I mean, how did your arms last that long?"

"Spent my life running cows and horses, sweetheart. Five hours and I'd just be getting ready for breakfast."

"How much you get for her?" Craig said.

"At the market?"

"Yeah."

"I let her go."

"Good for you."

"Buy a round for everyone at the bar, will you? I'd join you, but I can barely move."

At that moment, Craig noticed that Mabel was walking without her cane. He hadn't seen her without it in over half a year, since the stroke. Before that, she'd always be out on the tennis court or running the beach, wearing down any guy who would take her on. Since then, it had been mostly swimming, doing laps in the pool for hours on end.

"If you're so tired, Mabel, where's your cane?"

Mabel looked around, as if the cane would be standing beside her on its own.

"Guess I forgot it." Mabel laughed. In the excitement of Cantwell's theft and the giant marlin, she had forgotten all about her bum leg. Turns out, it wasn't so bum after all.

When Mabel reached her twelfth floor suite, the door was ajar. Mabel nudged it open with a finger and peered inside. She could see no one. Even so, she spun back toward the elevator, walking as fast as she could. They'd come for her.

Mabel found Craig in the bar, hoisting a beer, while toasting her.

"And, here's to—"

"Excuse me, Craig…"

"Well, here she is!"

"Someone broke into my condo, Craig. Could you please call security? I'm afraid to go in alone."

Dale Archer, the house security guard, was an imposing figure. He stood six-foot-two, with a bald head and a nose shaped like a squashed eggplant. He was a former Miami-Dade beat cop, with a beer keg belly that had seen its share of both donuts and sit-ups in its day. When he reached Mabel's door, Archer withdrew his gun. He held it barrel up with both hands.

"Security," he barked. "Come out if you're in there."

Archer waited a full minute, before swinging the door open with the toe of his shoe.

The suite was empty. But the intruder had made sure that Mabel would know he'd been there. The kitchen drawers had been pulled and left open. In Mabel's study, the drawers to her desk had been removed and placed upon the floor.

"Anything missing?" Archer asked.

Mabel shook her head. "Not that I can see."

"Any idea what they were looking for?"

"Perhaps."

"You'll need to file a police report."

"I will. But, I'm tired, Dale. Went to war with a marlin yesterday."

"You win?'

Mabel showed him the picture.

"Holy moly, Mabel. That thing's a monster."

"One thousand twenty-four pounds. Didn't pull her much out of the water, though. Set her free."

"How's it standing with you on the back of the boat then?"

"Photoshop. My friend didn't manipulate the fish, just put her next to me. He measured my darling in a bunch of places, then fed the data into a computer. Definitely a grander. And alive to fight again."

"Very cool, Mabel. Very cool."

Chapter Ten
V
———————————————

Mabel parked her motorcycle across from a modern looking building made of brick, concrete and glass. The building was solid and rectangular, with its corner resting at the intersection of Miami's NW 2nd Avenue and NW 4th Street. The top floor was all windows, angled outward and capped by a row of white concrete. The place was surrounded by a ring of deciduous trees. From her vantage point, Mabel could just make out the big blue letters, saying POLICE DEPARTMENT.

For the second time in two days, Mabel talked her way past protective glass and reinforced steel. She was directed to an area where a woman sat behind another thick window. She took a number and waited. When her number was called, Mabel walked to the window. "I need to file a police report," she said.

"What kind of report?"

"A B&E."

The woman handed her a form, then pointed. "Take it to Criminal Investigations, after you've filled this out. You'll see Officer Carmen Jimenez."

An hour later, Mabel was sitting beside a woman wearing police blues, with short, closely-cropped hair, dark brown eyes and a gun strapped to her hip. The woman took Mabel's form, leaned back in her chair and read through it quickly.

"Your home was broken into, but nothing was taken? Is that correct?"

"That is correct, Officer Jimenez."

"Anything else you would like to report?"

"I have a name."

Jimenez sat up and leaned forward. "A name? You know who broke in?"

"Louis Masco. He's works with Rial Cantwell."

The officer whistled softly.

"That a problem?" said Mabel.

"Well, yeah."

"Why?"

Jimenez put her hands behind her head and leaned back in her chair. "Let me count the ways…" She stared up at the ceiling and watched the blades of a fan, as they circled slowly. "Rial Cantwell plays golf with the governor and the mayor…He's donated tens of millions to local charities…He even gave a million to the Two Hundred Club, which aids the families of downed officers and firefighters. That enough?"

"I thought justice was blind?"

"Oh, it is, Ms. Witherspoon. It is. Once you've got evidence. You have any evidence?"

"I've got five million invested with Cantwell and he won't give it to me."

"Call the SEC."

"I met with the SEC."

"And?"

"He's within his rights."

"Then why would he have someone break into your home?"

Mabel closed her eyes. She couldn't go through the bathroom thing, not again. And she couldn't tell Jimenez that she'd overheard them talking. Too many people knowing that little fact could be trouble. If the FBI wouldn't bite, the Miami PD sure as hell wouldn't.

"Forget what I said."

"Good choice." Jimenez scanned through the report again, then added a note to the bottom. "Tell you what," she said. "You're the second person who's accused Masco of breaking and entering in the past six months. So, I'm going to pay Cantwell a little visit. Just a courtesy call, to let him know we're watching his people. That okay with you?"

"Don't tell them it was me. Okay? I don't want to die."

Jimenez laughed. "Rial Cantwell is a good man, Ms. Witherspoon. Lou Masco? Well, that's a different story. He's got a history."

"What kind of history?"

"Private."

"Oh. Of course. You can't tell me that."

"Correct."

Jimenez stood up from her chair, signaling that the meeting was over. "I'll call you if I find out anything." She pulled a card from her shirt pocket and handed to Mabel. "You call me if you think of anything else."

Chapter Eleven
V

Ben

"They broke into my house, Ben."

Mabel burst into my office like she'd just robbed a convenience store and was looking for somewhere to hide. She began pacing around the room like a caged tiger, head down and actually *huffing* as she walked from one edge of the room to the other. Her eyes were wide and frightened.

"Sit down, Mabel. Relax."

"I can't relax. It's like being *raped*. I feel violated."

I nodded. You get your house broken into and you *do* feel violated. You see eyes behind you, everywhere you step. You feel the presence of the intruder. And you feel fear, fear that the next time they intrude, you will be there. And…

"I understand, Mabel. I really do."

"Do you?"

I wasn't sure how to answer. Should I tell Mabel that part of my job with the CIA and the NSA had been to snoop into other people's lives? Should I tell her that I'd broken into dozens of homes, on government orders. Sometimes legal, sometimes not. All of it had been for the right reasons, to stop crime, to prevent terrorism. But there was always a price. There were always innocents around criminals, fine people believing in the good of others, no matter how wrong they might be. I could see the faces of those innocent people. I could hear their cries. They haunted me at night. Always had.

"I do, Mabel. You feel powerless against that feeling, I know. But there is something you can do, something *we* can do."

"We fight back?"

"Correct."

"Good. I feel better already."

At that moment, I realized that Mabel wasn't using her cane. "Where's the cane?"

"Don't need it anymore. That marlin scared my leg back into shape."

No, I thought. Mabel's body was preparing for the challenges ahead, strengthening itself for what we both knew was going to happen. Yes, it would be a battle, maybe to the death.

"Let's go up to the balcony," I said.

I poured us a couple of coffees and led the way upstairs, with Mabel on my heels. I wondered how she did it. After fighting that Marlin, her legs must have felt like sacks of concrete, yet she seemed to have gotten stronger, not weaker.

When we were seated, we stared out over the ocean. The sun was just beginning to rise. It began as a tiny crescent on the horizon, just a tiny yellow slice shimmering on the water. It rose quickly, as if standing up after a long night's sleep. Soon, its rays bounced playfully upon the water. For some odd reason, it made me think of children.

"Let's think this through," I said. "From the beginning."

As Mabel took a sip of her coffee, I could see that she was trembling. She was a tough old broad. She'd bagged a thousand pound marlin without a word of complaint. But she was starting to crack, her mind like the shell of an egg under the pressure of a squeezing hand. One more incident with Cantwell, and I was afraid that she would break.

"Okay," I said. "We know that Cantwell is stealing money from clients. He's got Lou Masco, who fixes things. Masco intimidates people into silence. He kills them if he has to; and he enjoys it. The SEC doesn't have a clue. If they do, they look the other way. Maybe they're on the take. The FBI is suspicious. They've had other complaints, but no hard evidence. The police have had one complaint besides yours about Masco, at least one that they'll admit to. They feel intimidated, because Cantwell is connected to everyone that matters. Cantwell plays golf with the governor and the mayor. He gives to all the major charities. He maintains the image of a saint, and everyone around him has a vested interest in keeping it that way."

"He's like an impregnable castle," mumbled Mabel.

I said, "He made one big mistake. He messed with you. And you hired me."

"Can you expose him?"

"Is that what you want? Or, do you want something more?"

Mabel thought hard. Her eyebrows furrowed into a deep V. I could almost hear the gears working in her head, clicking like safe tumblers, as they checked through the options. Was it enough to expose and ruin Cantwell? Or, did she need to recover the stolen money, and see that it got into the right hands? Did she want to try to find a body count, of any people he'd ruined, or even killed? And how much was she going to put her own life at risk?

Finally, Mabel said, "I want to learn everything."

"That will be dangerous," I said.

Mabel shrugged. "I'm seventy-five years old, Ben. What have I got to lose? I spent most of my life working a farm, insulated from the worries and chaos of the outside world. Sure, we had to worry about the elements and commodities prices. But we never had to deal much with people. People are far more complicated. This will be a welcome challenge."

I looked into her eyes and found myself wondering how she got here, so I asked.

"How did you come to invest with Cantwell?" I said.

"Cantwell was the nephew of one of my husband's childhood friends. He started at Fidelity, as a junior analyst, I think. Worked his way up to managing one of their smaller funds. Something global, I think. He got burnt out by the hundred hour weeks, so he went out on his own.

"A bunch of the locals got talked into investing with him, including Archie. He'd just sold a piece of our land to UNH, the University of New Hampshire, and he didn't know what to do with it. We didn't need the money, and Cantwell seemed like a nice kid…smart. He said he'd protect our money like it was his own. He did, at least on paper. While the stock market has staggered, our investment has steadily grown, assuming the money is there.

"To tell you the truth, I don't really care about the money. But my grandson? That's a different story. He's had it kind of hard.

"Our son enlisted in the Army after med school. Served ten proud years, then got out unharmed. He married a fine young lady and bought into a medical practice in Portland, Maine. They had one child. Then his wife…she came down with breast cancer. Didn't make it."

Mabel paused. Her lips twisted, and her face seemed to scrunch together like a sponge. I looked away, but heard her sniff back tears. I pondered my coffee cup, then looked out at the water. There were two spectacular sailboats passing about a quarter mile offshore. They were like tall ships with triple masts, probably more than a hundred years old, sailing with crews of eight or more. There was also a power boat pulling two kids on a big yellow tube. After a minute or so, Mabel continued.

"A few years later, Archie, we called him Junior, was called up from the reserves. They sent him to Iraq.

"Archie, the third…we call him Buddy, was young then. We took him in while his father was deployed. We then raised him, after our son rode home in a flag-draped coffin. So, Buddy is more like a son to me than a grandson.

"When he came to me about Jiggles…" Mabel paused. A small smile creased across her lips. "I know it's a gentlemen's club, Ben. But it's a good one. The girls there are artists, not strippers."

Mabel paused and smiled again, in a shy kind of way. "I was a line dancer in Vegas when I was in my early twenties. Didn't strip and I didn't fool around. I just loved to dance, and that was where you found good steady work, back then.

"Archie came to town for a dairy convention. It wasn't like the conventions of today, just a few fellas gathering from around the country to share the latest in dairy technology. A lot of his friends had farms in California, so Vegas was a natural meeting ground.

"I was up on stage at El Rancho, before it burned down…I saw him staring at me. Something clicked between us, and I couldn't keep my eyes off of him either."

Mabel laughed. "It was love at first sight, if you can believe it. Me, a Vegas dancer with pink fingernails. Him, a grizzled farmer with dirt under his."

Mabel held up her right hand, her fingers stretching toward the sky. She turned her hand so I could see her knuckles. She wore a brilliant emerald ring with an elegant platinum setting, sparkling in the light, as if it were alive. The stone must have been at least two carats, maybe three. It was the kind of ring that would make a Vegas dancer go weak in the knees.

"After the second night, Archie came backstage and he gave me this." Mabel looked to the ring and tears misted into her eyes. I looked away for a few moments, allowing her to regain her center. After a while she continued, "I've never taken this off." She sniffed, then laughed. "Within three days we were married. It was a good marriage, a great marriage. I moved back with Archie to the farm. Traded dancing for breeding cows and growing corn. Traded calluses on my feet for ones on my hands. I loved that man with all my heart. But there was always part of me that…well, you know.

"When we bought our first place in Miami, I dragged Archie to all the dance clubs, trying to see if we could find one that was any good. Of all places, we found Jiggles. The girls there are good, as good as any New York or Vegas showplace. After a while, I think Archie began to enjoy the dancing as much as I did. It was like being young again."

Mabel swiped a tear off her cheek and sniffed again. I looked out over the water, then found something very interesting about my fingernails. Finally, Mabel continued, "I think Archie told Buddy about Jiggles. Probably told him how much we both enjoyed it…I don't go there anymore, not since Archie died. I think Buddy wants to recover something his granddad loved. And I think he wants to see me happy again."

"You're not happy?" I said.

"Why should I be?"

Mabel had a point. Sometimes you reach a stage in life when you begin marking time rather than making it. I guessed that Mabel had lost her way. Maybe Buddy was trying to help her find it again.

Mabel fell silent. I didn't know what to say. I knew nothing about marriage; I'd been a bachelor all my life. I'd had a long string of girlfriends. Came close to tying the knot on a couple of occasions. But work always pulled me away. I was addicted to the chase, to the kill. Settling down and raising a family was too pedestrian for me. I needed action. Now, all I had was boredom. At least until Mabel.

"Tell you what we're going to do," I said. "We are going to learn everything we can about Cantwell's operation. We're also going to let him know that you can't be intimidated. Threats against you will be met with equal force."

"How are we going to do that?'

"Come with me," I said.

I walked back into my office. I continued downstairs to my main laboratory in the rear of the building. It was a spacious room with a ten-foot ceiling. I had four computers lined up against one wall. I had three workbenches stuffed chock full with plastic and electronic gear. I had several still and video cameras, and a latex molding machine that could turn out a face mask as real as the original. Adjacent to this room, there was another one. It was filled with more electronic gear and two lathes, one for wood and one for metal. I also had a plastic injection molding machine that could be engineered to make things of almost any shape.

"What's all this?" said Mabel.

"This is where I ply my trade," I said. "We're going to put together a little something, something that will give us a window into Cantwell's operations."

I walked over to one of the walls and rummaged through a couple of cabinets, until I found what I was looking for. I pulled a thin, 8 by 10 inch sheet of plastic out of a box and placed it beside one of my computers.

Then I sifted through a container of sealed, wafer-thin microchips, until I found six that were the right size and shape. I carried these over to one of my workbenches.

I returned to the computer and opened up Photoshop.

"You sure like Photoshop, don't you?" said Mabel.

"For most of the basic stuff, I get away with Photoshop or InDesign," I said. "I've got more sophisticated graphics software, but what we're doing here is pretty simple."

I set the program onto "browse," found the two custom templates I was looking for and opened the files. I imported a logo into each file. One was for *Intel*. The other was *Microsoft*. I placed my plastic sheet into a printer and printed six small images, three saying *Windows* and three saying *Intel*. I examined the sheet carefully. I took several measurements and checked my figures against another file I had inside my little brain trust.

"What are you doing?" asked Mabel.

"I'm creating something to attach to Cantwell's computer, something to record his keystrokes and send them to us without his knowledge."

"Can you do that?"

I shrugged. "Nearly every PC comes with advertising logos slapped onto the box or keyboard pad. I doubt he's using a Mac. The investment world, at least on the individual and retail level, runs on Microsoft or

Linux. We're going to visit Cantwell in his office, remove a logo off his laptop, and put one of these babies in its place."

I took the newly printed logos and attached them to microchip wafers using a thin layer of glue. I placed each of the chips onto another thin sheet, which had a perforated layer of specialized adhesive on the top and a peel-off layer on the bottom. I used an exacto knife to cut away the excess. Soon, I had six logos that I could place on any computer, looking exactly like the one I'd remove, provided it was there.

Now, all I needed was to figure out some way to get a minute in Cantwell's office alone.

Chapter Twelve
V

The moment Officer Jimenez walked into the Cantwell offices, she began to have second thoughts. She'd received permission from Chief Esposito to speak with Cantwell. But that permission had come with a warning: *Don't make accusations unless you can make them stick.*

The outside of the Cantwell building hadn't been very intimidating. It was a simple, three-story structure in modest Miami Gardens, not the typical flash of a big-time money manager. The building's facade was chrome and glass. The inside had marble floors and two guards packing 45s.

The building hadn't put her hair on end, not like the walk toward the receptionist's mountain-sized desk at the end of that sea of Oriental rug. Jimenez stared up at the chandelier looming overhead. It seemed to glare at her. This was not a place where she was welcome. She was out of her element and she knew it. She looked to the walls, at all the original art, each painting costing more than a year's, maybe a lifetime's salary. What was she thinking? Even if he was guilty, she couldn't go up against this man, not with the money and the machine at his disposal. Still, duty called. And for her, duty was everything.

Jimenez reached the elevated desk at the end of the hall and looked up to the receptionist. The young woman had a perfect face, immaculate blond hair, extraordinary blue eyes and the straightest white teeth she'd seen outside of a toothpaste commercial. It was as if the receptionist were a china doll, painted by a master artist, with not a flaw in place.

"Hello, Officer Jimenez. Mr. Cantwell is expecting you. But he will be a few more minutes. May I get you something to eat or drink?"

"No, I'm good," said Jimenez. She wished that she'd groomed herself before coming inside. She felt like a donkey standing next to a gazelle. She reached up to her curly black hair and tried to shape it into place with a cup of her hands. Never happen. The receptionist smiled, then went back to typing on her perch high above, looking down like a Supreme Court judge.

Jimenez took a seat and waited for Rial Cantwell. After just a few minutes, she could see him begin the long walk down the softly-lighted hall, moving deliberately, almost like a monarch approaching a commoner. He was wearing a blue silk suit and a bright red tie, with a matching handkerchief in his suit coat pocket. Cantwell looked at his watch. Jimenez looked at hers. He was right on time.

As Cantwell stopped beside her and stretched out his manicured fingers, Jimenez felt the urge to kiss his ring.

"Officer Jimenez…Rial Cantwell. So pleased to meet you."

Jimenez gripped Cantwell's hand and shook it firmly. His palm was smooth and cool. His fingers lingered, just a bit longer than she would have expected, as if he were measuring her by feel.

"Come this way," he said. Cantwell began the endless walk down the hallway. Jimenez followed at his shoulder, half a step behind. There was even more artwork along the walls and a bunch of Roman sculptures. She recognized one of the paintings as a Monet, a scene with ducks and lilies on a bluish purple pond.

When they reached Cantwell's office he closed the door behind them. Straight ahead, across a good thirty feet of space, stood Cantwell's desk. It was antique and made of polished teak. Probably off some old ship, she thought. There was a large plate window behind the desk, revealing a broad view of his blue collar (and no collar) neighborhood. To her right, Jimenez could see another wall of windows, looking out to a blue body of water and then to LandShark Stadium about half a mile away.

"I know what you're thinking," said Cantwell.

"Sir?"

"You're wondering why I office here, when I could be housed on Fisher Island, or in some fancy high rise looking out at the ocean."

Jimenez looked to her shoes. Was she that apparent?

"I get asked that all the time. Truth is, I started here, back when I had no money, just a few investors and a crazy dream. I bought a modest two-bedroom house nearby and got used to the neighborhood. I like it here. It keeps me grounded, seeing normal humanity every day. It's too easy to forget who we are, Ms. Jimenez, and where we came from. Working here keeps me in touch.

"But we're not here to talk about that, are we? You said you had something important to discuss, about one of my employees?"

Jimenez could feel her tongue swell, until it felt almost like a tennis ball, too dry and too large, big enough to clog her throat. She looked out at the stadium, then back to Cantwell. He smiled and waited for her to respond. After a moment, a look of concern spread along his face.

"Are you okay, officer?"

Jimenez steadied herself. This was just a simple meeting. Why did it feel like she was walking into a field of land mines?

"Yes, thank you. I'm fine." She took a deep breath and motioned toward the table and chairs that looked out toward the stadium. "May we sit down?'

Cantwell shrugged. "Sure." He looked at his watch.

Jimenez said, "We won't be long."

After they were seated, Jimenez said, "Could you please tell me about Louis Masco?"

"Has he done something wrong?"

"Not that we know of."

"Has he been accused of anything?"

"No, not really. But, over the past couple years, several people have come in saying that they feel…uneasy about him." *Oh shit*, she thought. She'd wussed out.

"Is that a crime?"

"No, but—"

"Mr. Masco is my partner, but also my bodyguard and troubleshooter, Officer Jimenez. He's supposed to make people feel uneasy."

"Some…people have said that they think he might be breaking into their homes."

"They *think* that he *might* be breaking into their homes?"

Jimenez looked back to her feet. "I know. It sounds sort of silly. I'm sure it's nothing. But I thought you might want to know, just in case you've heard anything from your side."

Cantwell reached into the inside pocket of his silk suit coat. He removed an aluminum tube, screwed off the end and withdrew a fat Siglo VI cigar. He put the cigar into his mouth but didn't light it. Jimenez was sure that he would have, were she not there. Had she made him feel the nervous need to suck on something? The hairs on the back of her neck rose again. There was something amiss here, something she could sense, deep in the back of her mind.

"A man in my position, Officer Jimenez, is always a target. I've got disgruntled investors who want to get at money I can't give them. I've got protestors of every sort saying that I'm a capitalist pig. They say I'm supporting a shadow government, I'm promoting global warming, or I'm burning down the rain forests. I never know when somebody is going to come at me with a stick or a gun or a pint of blood in a jar.

"I need Louis Masco to make people uncomfortable. He, and the other people paid to keep me safe, are *supposed* to intimidate. So, if you have people accusing *him* of making *them* feel uncomfortable, I see this as a sign that he is doing his job.

"Now, if you want to supply me with the names of those who've complained, I will be happy to speak with them personally, to assure them that we don't go around hurting people. We may defend ourselves, but we *don't* hurt innocent people."

"I can't give you names."

"Can you give me evidence of wrongdoing?"

"No."

"Then what are you doing here?"

Cantwell looked at his watch again. Jimenez took this as a sign that the meeting was over. She stood and offered Cantwell her hand.

"I am sorry to have wasted your time, Mr. Cantwell. I'm just making sure that people are safe. Sometimes that means following up on erroneous information."

"My time was not wasted, Ms. Jimenez. I had the chance to meet a concerned officer of the law with the public's safety in mind. I also confirmed that my partner is doing his job. I feel safer now. Thank you for coming by."

Cantwell placed a gentle hand on Jimenez's shoulder and nudged her toward his office door.

"I can find my own way out," she said.

"You sure?"

"Of course."

"Please close the door behind you."

The moment that Jimenez walked out of the office, Cantwell punched his intercom.

"Lou. Are you there?"

"Yeah, Rial."

"Come here."

Once Lou Masco was inside his office, Cantwell motioned for him to shut the door. When it closed, he said, "Did you break into Witherspoon's home?"

Masco didn't answer at once. He looked into Cantwell's eyes. In some ways, his partner was a dunce. Sure, he was extraordinary at managing money. But with people, the man was a Neanderthal. He had no clue about how the real world worked, or how people thought. Cantwell had no frigging idea how many times Lou Masco had stepped in to save his ass.

"Yeah," Masco said. "Someone needed to deliver the message."

"She went to the police."

"You sure?"

"Officer Carmen Jimenez was just here, from Miami PD."

"Shit. She give Witherspoon's name?"

Cantwell shook his head. "No. But I assume it was her."

"What do you want me to do?"

Cantwell interlaced his fingers and pressed them against his chin. He stared out at the Dolphins' stadium and thought about football. It wouldn't be long before his city would be hosting the Pro Bowl, and then the Super Bowl. Miami was going to be overrun with even more tourists than normal, hundreds of thousands of them.

"Maybe it *is* time," he said softly.

"Time for what?"

"Never mind…For now, leave Witherspoon alone. I think she's had her say with the police. She's no real threat to us now."

"I'll watch her."

Chapter Thirteen
V

Mabel settled deeper into the seat of the darkened car. She looked along the deserted street, which curved around the end of Biscayne Point. Light was sparkling off the blue-black water from the city beyond. Two miles across the bay, half a million people were awake, going about their boring day-to-day lives. Here, an eerie stillness had filled the air. Nothing moved; there was no sound. Mabel's gray turtleneck clung tightly to her skin, as if she'd thrown it on after jumping out of a pool. She could feel sweat congeal beneath her armpits, sogging the already wet fabric of her shirt. And why not? She'd never broken into somebody's home before, particularly not the lair of a killer.

There were a dozen or so homes that curved out into the bay along this secluded drive. The street lights were minimal, casting eerie shadows against the palm trees that lined the curbs. Ben could hear the soft rustle of their leaves, sounding like ghosts in the stillness of the night.

They were on the south side of the point, just far enough to shield them from the home of tonight's quarry. Ben peered through the side window of the Chevy he had rented, using an assumed name. Neither he nor Mabel said a word. Finally, a couple hundred yards ahead, just around the bend, Lou Masco pulled out of his driveway.

"You sure he won't come back?" said Mabel.

"Yes, dear. Every night it's the same. He leaves at 7:45. He goes to the gym, works out, gets a massage, then eats a late dinner. He won't return until after 10:30."

"Will we have enough time?"

Ben laughed. "We're just breaking in, Mabel. We're not throwing a party."

Ben didn't say anything more. He looked at his watch, then followed the tail lights of Masco's Mercedes as it traveled east down Cleveland

Rd. They sat in silence for the next fifteen minutes. Finally, Ben looked to his watch again and said, "You getting cold feet?"

"My feet are always cold. It's a circulation thing."

"You want to go home?"

"I guess not."

"Well, do you or don't you? You either want to do this or you don't. There is no 'guess' about it. It is a 'yes' or a 'no'."

"You don't need to be so testy."

"I'm not being testy."

"Yes, you are."

"No, I'm not."

Mabel grinned. "We sound like we're married."

"I always get on edge before I break into someone's home."

"Yeah, me too."

Ben laughed. "Since you're such a pro, why don't I stay here and let you do the work?"

"I never break and enter alone."

"Why don't you follow me, then? You know how to handle a Glock?"

"A what?"

"A Glock. A pistol."

"Oh, a pistol. Sure. Do it all the time."

Ben pulled a Glock 19 semi-automatic out of his glove compartment and held it in front of Mabel's face. "This, is a Glock."

Mabel took the gun out of Ben's hand. She released the clip magazine and counted the fifteen bullets inside it. Then she snapped it back inside, slid the barrel to chamber a round, fingered the safety and said, "Of course I can handle a Glock. Can't everyone?"

Ben shook his head. "You never cease to amaze me, Mabel."

"Keep your mind out of the gutter, Ben."

"I was just giving you a compliment."

"Just shut up and break into the house, will you? Before I have to pee again."

"You always have to pee."

"So do you."

"I've got an enlarged prostate. What's your excuse?"

"I'm old."

"The last thing in the world you are is old."

"Well, my body thinks so."

Ben opened the car door. He reached behind him, grabbed a black backpack off the rear seat and stepped outside. He took a long look around, before closing the door. This part of Biscayne Point Circle was out of sight from any residents. They were between homes on the right, while the large house to the left was protected by a tall stucco wall. Mabel remained inside the car for a few moments more, before joining Ben on the bay-side sidewalk.

Both were dressed in dark gray running sweats. Ben knew that gray was nearly as invisible as black, but less suspicious if they ran into anyone along the way. As they made their way north around the point, they passed a man walking a Golden Retriever on the other side of the street. He was speaking into a Bluetooth headset and didn't even glance their way.

When they came to Lou Masco's impressive place, Ben stopped. He looked cautiously around, then slipped through the side gate of a three-foot, white picket fence.

"Wait here," he said to Mabel.

Ben placed his backpack upon the ground and rummaged inside. He removed a pair of infrared goggles and placed them over his head. He picked up the backpack and motioned for Mabel to follow behind him, as he walked slowly to the back of the home. The rear of the house had a large patio that looked out over the water. Mabel gazed into the bay, soaking up the view of the city beyond. Ben slipped the goggles up on his forehead and walked to the back door. He examined the locks. Then he looked closely at the windows, all without touching a thing. He put on the goggles and peered inside.

"Well, isn't this convenient," he said.

"No alarm?" whispered Mabel.

"Oh, yeah," said Ben. "He's got a high-end security system and it's turned on."

"How's that convenient?"

Ben pointed toward an ADT sticker.

Mabel said, "ADT. That's a big outfit. Maybe the biggest. They know what they're doing."

"They do," said Ben. "But I've been at this a long time, Mabel. So have they. We both go back to a time when we used the names of our dogs as file and system passwords, not multiple layers of twenty-five-character strings of numbers, letters and symbols. I built a back door to the ADT system years ago." Ben paused. "The other problem with big security is that they're always open. And open means *open*. I can get to them now."

Ben pulled a notebook computer out of his backpack and flipped it on. Using a broadband wireless connection, he hacked into the ADT security database. Less than three minutes later, he'd written out Masco's security code.

Ben closed his notebook and put it back into his backpack. He set the pack upon a chair and pulled out a black leather case. He unrolled the case onto a square metal table and removed two small, wire-like tools from inside it. He took these to the door and used them to unlock the two Schlage deadbolts and the standard Yale door lock. He opened the door and walked calmly to the security keypad. He entered in Masco's code and waited. Nothing happened. That was good.

Ben put the goggles back on his head and checked for a secondary system of motion detectors. He saw nothing.

"Okay," he said. "C'mon in."

As Mabel walked inside, the hair rippled along the back of her neck. Her hands began to tingle and she needed to pee.

"It's like walking into the house of the devil," she whispered.

Ben chuckled. "Masco's just a two-bit thug, Mabel. Nothing to be scared of."

Ben pulled a flashlight out of his backpack and turned it on. The light's face was covered with a red lens. There was a tiny opening in the center, the size of a pinprick, which allowed a narrow shaft of white light to shine out. The pale red light, combined with the tiny beam of bright was enough to allow Ben to see.

Ben made a quick tour of the home, before stopping in a room with a large, pale oak desk. Upon it was a standard four-line AT&T phone, plus a Polycom speakerphone. The desk's left corner sported an in/out tray. It had a stack of papers in the top tray, and nothing in the bottom. The right side of the desk had a brass table lamp. Behind it sat a tall, blue leather chair.

Ben looked around for a Wi-Fi router, which many homes use to access the Internet without a cable connection. If Masco used Wi-Fi, even if it

was security-enabled, Ben could breach the router in a few short seconds. Masco didn't use Wi-Fi; he hooked to the Net directly with an Eth-
ernet cable. Cautious man. Ben looked for a decal on Masco's desktop.
It was a high-powered Dell, with no decals. Strike two.

"Hmm," said Ben.

"What?" said Mabel.

"We're on to plan C." Ben shined his light down from above the brass
table lamp and looked in. He smiled. "That's better." Ben unscrewed the
bulb. "Seventy-five watts," he said. "Phillips energy-saver."

Ben reached into his backpack and removed an elongated, box-shaped
case. He flipped open the top, pulled out a matching Phillips bulb and
screwed it into the light fixture.

"You're changing his light bulbs?" said Mabel.

"Can't ride his computer, not without something more sophisticated
than what we've got here tonight. So, I'm planting a bug."

"You've got bugs in light bulbs?"

"Phillips *and* Sylvania. Can you think of a better place?"

"I thought you'd tap the phone or something?"

Ben shook his head. "Too obvious…too easy to detect."

"Where'd you learn all this?"

Ben drew a long breath. He sat down into Lou Masco's chair and laced
his fingers behind his head. "Got my start as a math geek at The University of Chicago. They taught me to crack safes."

"They had courses in safe-cracking?"

"Well, sort of…There was this little group of us…We were taught how
to open all of the most sophisticated vaults in the world—the ones used
by embassies and banks…brokerage houses. If a vault wouldn't open
somewhere, whether it be in New York or Hong Kong, one of us could
be sent in to fix it."

"You were taught to rob banks?"

"I was taught to *help* banks. They sent my fingerprints to the Fed, just
in case I ever wanted to go freelance…Like they thought I'd be too stupid to wear gloves."

"Ever go freelance?"

Ben smiled. "I got recruited into the CIA, where I received a whole
new set of training."

"Like what?"

Ben Johnson grew silent. He was telling too much and he had to stop. "That's about all you want to know, Mabel."

Ben picked the locks on Masco's desk and rifled through the contents. He found nothing of value there. Same thing with Masco's filing cabinet.

"Damn. They must keep everything at the office," Ben said. "Smart."

"We'll have to bug Cantwell's office then," Mabel said.

"I've decided I'm too old for that," Ben joked. "Masco's home will have to do."

"You weren't before. You chicken out?"

"Chicken out?"

"Yeah. That's what I said. Are you a chicken?"

"Are you calling me a chicken?"

"What are you, deaf? Chicken.....*Bluck...bluck...bluck.* You're a chicken."

Ben sighed. "Oh, Mabel. Years ago I would have done it, no problem, with the government's help and blessing. Of course, we'd usually have a team of guys...and the most sophisticated gear." Ben sighed again. "But not now. Now that I'm retired..."

"Chicken."

"At lease I don't wear a diaper."

"Live long enough and you will, bucko. Something for you to look forward to."

Once they were done inside, Ben went out onto the back porch. He reached into his backpack and removed a silver metal box. It was the size of a cigarette pack and had solar panels along one side. Ben looked around the rear of the house and found what he needed. There was a pair of decorative lights, shaped like large diamonds, attached to the back of the home overlooking the porch. They were the kind usually seen on the front of a house like this, large and elaborate, enough to impress the neighbors, or anyone who passed by on the street. There was a similar light about ten yards into the yard, out toward the water. This was attached to a metal pole.

"Perfect," said Ben.

Ben walked into the house, found the utility room and switched off the breaker that controlled power to the back patio. When he came back out, he slung his backpack over his shoulder, grabbed one of the patio chairs and carried it to the light pole. He stood on the chair and removed the top to the ornate fixture. He put the fixture top on the ground, then found a pair of electrical pliers. Ben got back up on the chair and used the pliers to cut the wires leading into light's bulb. He spliced another set of wires into these and attached them to the silver box. He set the box onto the floor of the light fixture, then closed the top back up. When he stood back to look, he could see no trace of the transmitter.

"What're you doing?" whispered Mabel.

"This will pick up the signals from the light bulb bugs we've placed inside the house. It will store conversations onto a micro hard drive, until we come to pick them up. We'll swing by on the boat and download the data. It's got a range of a couple thousand yards, maybe more, depending upon the power charge."

Mabel looked closely at Ben. "You've done this a lot, haven't you?"

Ben smiled. "Usually, it's just foreign terrorists that get such fine attention."

"But, you've done it here, too? In the United States?"

Ben shrugged. "The CIA would never operate on U.S. soil, Mabel. It's against the law."

"I'm glad you're on my side."

"Me, too."

Chapter Fourteen
V

The day was predicted to be clear, with a high of sixty-eight degrees. The morning's usual layer of low, slate-colored clouds had yet to dissipate, so the temperature still hung in the fifties. Patches of sun were beginning to peek through the clouds with increasing frequency, so it wouldn't be long before they yielded to bright sunshine.

Mabel Witherspoon parked her Harley outside the offices of Cantwell Investments and unzipped her black leather jacket, while Ben Johnson slid off the back of the bike.

"Remind me never to ride with you again," Ben said.

"Don't like my driving?'

"You call that driving? It's attempted suicide."

"I can't see. What can I say?"

"Act your age."

Mabel laughed. "Get your own bike and stay off the back of mine."

Mabel preceded Ben through the revolving doors into the Cantwell building. They signed in at the security desk, where they were asked to place their belongings onto trays, before passing through a metal detector.

"This is worse than an airport," said Ben. "You want me to take off my shoes?"

The guards said nothing. One of them began to look closely at the fountain pen Ben had removed from his shirt pocket, far too closely. Ben did his best to look bored.

"What's this?" said the guard.

"It's an antique Montblanc Meisterstuck 149 pen. Never seen one? It's a piece of art."

"Why's it so fat?"

"It's a fountain pen, not a ball point. Uses a lot of ink. Be careful. It squirts like a son-of-a-bitch."

Ben held his breath. The last thing he wanted was to try to explain what he was hiding inside this pen.

The guard peered at the pen. He began to unscrew the body, but then looked at Ben. "This gonna get ink all over me?"

"Probably. And the stain's impossible to get out. Want me to show you? Stand back, this thing could spray everywhere."

The guard shrugged and handed the pen back to Ben. "No. You're okay." He motioned for the two of them to pass onward to the elevator. "Third floor."

Rial Cantwell walked down the cavernous hallway as he always did. Head held high, his long mane of hair flowing like Fabio's in a wind tunnel. Today, he was wearing a maroon and white, two button seersucker suit. No tie.

"I see we're casual today," said Mabel, as Cantwell laid a gentle hand upon her shoulder.

"I'm doing research. This is my only meeting." Cantwell looked at Mabel's leather pants and matching jacket. "Thought you'd be casual, but I see you wore a suit."

"Rode over on my Harley. Won't mess up our lunch plans, will it?"

"No." Cantwell looked keenly at Ben, as if assessing the value of his navy blue suit. It was a deliberately cheap one and Cantwell could tell. "And who is this important looking gentleman that came without an appointment?"

"This is Mr. Benjamin Johnson, my financial planner."

Cantwell smirked. "Financial planner, huh?" He extended a manicured hand. "Rial Cantwell. Pleasure."

Before Ben could speak, Cantwell turned on his heels and began walking down the hallway. "This way," he said.

Cantwell stopped outside the same conference room where he'd first taken Mabel. Mabel looked at Ben, who furtively shook his head.

"Your office, Cantwell," said Mabel. "I want to show Ben your view of the stadium."

Cantwell hesitated, but moved along. He pulled a Blackberry off his hip, spoke into it and said, "My office, Lou."

Oh, shit, thought Ben. This wasn't going to be as easy as he'd hoped.

Lou Masco was waiting at the entrance to Cantwell's office. Cantwell smiled and introduced him.

"Lou Masco, head of operations." Cantwell motioned toward his guests. "Mabel Witherspoon and Benjamin Johnson, her…financial planner." Cantwell, looked at Ben. He lowered his voice and said, "Lou will be your contact, if you have questions beyond today."

Masco extended a hand and wrapped his fingers around Ben's, squeezing down with a grip that would have crushed an apple.

Ben's eyes widened. "Whoa, big fella. No need to break fingers."

Masco's lips smiled, but his eyes remained cold. "Don't know my own strength sometimes," his threat covered with just the smallest hint of veneer. Message delivered and received.

"Yeah," muttered Ben. "Me neither. But odor isn't everything."

As Cantwell ushered them into his office, Mabel pointed out toward LandShark Stadium. "Isn't that beautiful!" she said, with an exaggerated wave of the hand.

"Magnificent!" said Ben. He turned to Cantwell. "You going to the Super Bowl?"

"Of course. You?"

Ben shook his head. "Nah. Like to, though."

"Perhaps you and Mrs. Witherspoon would like to be my guests?"

Mabel gushed, "That sounds like the bee's knees." She looked expectantly at Ben. "You want to go?"

Ben looked slyly at Cantwell. "You gonna have free food?"

Cantwell frowned. "Of course." He paused, as if pondering whether or not to change his mind. Finally, he said, "I'll see that you get invitations. Do you have a card, Mr. Johnson?"

Ben pulled a gold plated case from his pocket and removed an embossed card with an exaggerated flourish. The card said, Benjamin Johnson, MBA, CFP™, CLU, ChFC, CLTC, CFS.

Cantwell perused it. "Don't usually trust a man who puts so many initials after his name."

Ben smiled playfully. "Requirement of my job, Rial. Gotta be honest, particularly when the credentials are real." Ben paused, leaned toward Cantwell, then said, "Do you know what the costs would be to settle your estate?"

"What?"

"You've got a family, right? Probably married more than once…You want to pass this business along to your kids, right? Before that happens, your heirs are going to have to pay a boatload of estate taxes. You have any idea what those might be?"

"Are you soliciting me, Mr. Johnson?"

"Aw, heck no. I just want to help you avoid big tax problems. Who owns your life insurance?"

It was obvious that Cantwell wasn't going to allow Ben to be alone in his office, no matter what antics Mabel might try. So, Ben was on to Plan B. He had to remove himself as a threat to Cantwell, at least the perception of one. That would give him more opportunity later, provided there was a later.

"You invest in mutual funds?" Ben asked.

"I manage money, Mr. Johnson. Mutual funds are for people like you."

"Yeah, but you need to diversify—"

Cantwell held up a hand. "While I'm sure that you have my best interests at heart, Mr. Johnson, I must politely decline your offer of help. I've got a team of tax attorneys on payroll. Nixon Peabody, from Washington, handles my estate issues. I've got a hundred million of life insurance owned by a defective grantor trust, and more held in offshore accounts. I manage over a hundred billion dollars and I *don't* like mutual funds. Understand?"

"Sorry. How about your health insurance? Who handles your company health insurance? You have a Section 125 Cafeteria Plan? A 401(k) for your employees? Who gives them financial advice?"

Cantwell looked over to Mabel, his eyes pleading for help. It was obvious that he didn't want to be rude, but his patience had worn as thin and cold as winter frost.

"He's all set, Ben," said Mabel.

Ben's shoulders slumped. "Oh."

Cantwell said, "I'll keep you in mind, though."

"Yeah, and…" Ben's eyes suddenly brightened. "Hey, perhaps you can be of help to one of my clients?"

"I doubt it."

"They're a little bit out of my league, you see."

"Mr. Johnson—"

"It's a non-profit, with an endowment of five hundred million dollars and—"

"*Now*, you've got my attention, Mr. Johnson."

Ben thought, *I'll bet I do.* "I do?"

"You do. Non-profit charity organizations deserve the best professional help."

"It's called SOSCADA."

"The Society of Senior Citizens Against Drug Abuse?"

"You know it, then?"

"Of course, I do."

"The head dog is a client of mine."

"Wendell Holmbs or Tony Trance?'

"Know 'em both. You want me to arrange a meeting?"

Cantwell immediately shifted into selling mode. "I'm not taking on new clients at this time, Mr. Johnson."

Ben recognized the reverse selling tactic, the same one that had been used so effectively by Bernie Madoff. Two could play this game. "Oh, c'mon. They're a really good cause…"

"Good cause or not, I owe it to my current clients to stay focused on investing, and not on obtaining new clientele."

"It's okay with me, Rial," said Mabel. "Don't let me stand in the way of your business."

"Oh, I couldn't—"

Mabel said, "Really. It's okay. The more the merrier."

"I could bring Tony here to meet you," said Ben. "You won't even have to leave your office."

"Oh, I don't think so, Mr. Johnson—"

"But it's a really good cause! Not only does SOSCADA reduce drug usage in America, it gives seniors a reason to live, something to keep them going."

Cantwell seemed to waver. His eyes narrowed, as if he were in deep thought. Then he finally said, "Well, maybe. Because they do good work."

Ben beamed. "Great. Tony will be *so* pleased." Ben snuck a glance at Lou Masco. Masco was scowling, as if he had a painful case of hemorrhoids. Ben wondered if he'd been that apparent, or if Masco was just sour by nature. He'd learn that soon enough, once he began listening to his conversations. Masco glanced at his watch.

"Going to join us for lunch, Lou?" Ben said cheerfully.

Masco shook his head. "I have work to do."

"Too bad," said Mabel. "You seem like such a nice fella."

A nice fella, he wasn't.

"Where're we going, Rial?" said Ben, while giving Cantwell a friendly slap on the back.

Cantwell seemed to hesitate, as if he were rethinking his choice of restaurants. *Perhaps*, he thought, *McDonald's would be a better choice.*

"We're going to The Setai," said Cantwell. The Setai, on South Beach, was a 5 Star hotel and resort, known for its elegance and quiet serenity, where a suite could cost thirty thousand dollars a day or more, and lunch might cost a normal house payment.

Ben said, "That a good place? They got fried clams there? I *love* fried clams..."

Chapter Fifteen
V
____

Ben pulled his white, 1964 Jaguar XKE convertible up alongside a twelve-foot, pink stucco wall, then shut off the engine. He sat for a moment, as if deciding what to do.

"What are we doing?" said Mabel. "You got a flat or something?"

Ben held up a hand for silence. He pulled his PDA out of its holster and spoke into its face. "Dial Tony."

A few moments later, Ben said, "Hey, I'm looking for Antonio Sollozi." He smiled at Mabel, then laughed. "Uh-huh. I'm outside the gate…Sure."

Ben fired up the engine on the Jaguar. It gave a loud, throaty growl, before settling into a contented purr. He put the car into gear, then drove forward slowly, until he came to an opening in the wall. Before them stood a gate made of thick, black iron bars slung between two stone pillars. Beside the large gate, built into the imposing pink wall, was a black metal box. Upon the box were two glass bubbles covered with wire mesh. One was colored red and brightly lit. The other was green and dull. Beside the lights was a small keypad that looked much like a pocket calculator. It was covered by a hard plastic housing. Ben got out of the car and inserted a magnetized key card into the box. The plastic covering slid back and he punched a series of numbers into the keypad. The light switched from red to green. Satisfied, Ben entered in another set of numbers and the gate swung open. Ben hopped back into the car and began to drive slowly, along a winding path of barely tamed jungle.

Ben said, "This is one of the few estates that hasn't been fully cut up over the years. The fence is electrified and surrounds the entire grounds. As you see, the top is covered with spikes and wire. Very private. Twelve acres, six hundred feet of water frontage, an indoor pool, an outdoor pool, two Jacuzzis and tennis courts. The house is small by today's standards in some parts of Florida, but a good size for this area. And the view is spectacular."

"You sound like a tour guide," said Mabel.

"You should understand how this came about, Mabel." Ben closed his eyes for a brief moment, then continued. "This place used to be owned by a crime boss named Sanchez. He was murdered by his lieutenant, a guy by the name of Cesar. Cesar took over and became one of the biggest drug dealers on the East Coast.

"A couple of years back, he kidnapped Jaime Crandall—"

"The big pop and country singer?"

Ben nodded. "Uh-huh. She wasn't famous back then, just the grand-daughter of two of the residents of The Final Rest. You know the place?"

"That big retirement community, where people live until they die? Archie and I looked there, but we weren't real keen on senior living."

Ben checked his rearview mirror to make sure the gate was closed. "When Jaime was kidnapped, the residents banded together and formed The Varicose Vigilantes, a group of senior citizens dedicated to finding Jaime, and then eradicating illegal drug use in America.

"They saved Jaime, and formed SOSCADA."

Mabel nodded. "The drug fighters that you talked to Cantwell about."

Ben smiled. "They've got thousands of members now, with over half a billion dollars in endowment."

"You know the owner?"

"There is no owner, Mabel. It's a non-profit, focused on fighting drug crimes. But there is a leader."

"And you want to bring him to see Cantwell?"

"Cantwell won't know what hit him."

The old Sanchez mansion was twelve thousand square feet of exotic Italian marbles and rare woods. There was a plush green lawn spreading out from the main home. The grass was as smooth as a golf course, with manicured gardens spreading everywhere about the grounds.

Mabel's first glimpse of the home was through a thick grove of bam-boo trees, with Biscayne Bay fanning out behind it. "Seriously nice place," she muttered.

Then Mabel saw the side yard. Stretching out to the side and behind the home stood at least two hundred people. They were dressed in white robes, and they were all moving in unison. "What it this, a monastery?"

Mabel looked more closely. The people in the robes were running through an elaborate set of martial arts moves.

"Is that karate?" she said.

Ben nodded. "That is Tiger Form Three. The Vigilantes study many katas, while they learn to control the mind and body."

As they drew closer, Mabel could see that the robe wearers were the same age as she. "They're old!" Mabel yelled. "Is this some kind of cult?"

"What does it look like?"

"I don't know. What's the point?"

"They're training."

"For what? Death?"

Ben used a second plastic card and a different combination to gain access into the opulent Spanish style home.

"Why don't you just knock?" said Mabel.

"They're at the range."

"That explains it."

They passed through the electronically controlled front doors, which were a good eight inches thick.

"This house is a vault," Mabel said. Her attention was drawn to a floor of opaque marble, then upward to a thirty-foot entryway ceiling that was dominated by a ten-foot-wide chandelier made of multi-colored crystal. "More like a mausoleum," she continued.

As they walked inside, their rubber soled shoes began to scrunch noisily upon the smooth stone surface. Ben led them through the home, until they came to what was once the grand ballroom. This ceiling was also thirty feet high, with elaborately carved, gold trimmed wooden beams that criss-crossed from one side to the other. But, instead of furniture and a polished floor, the room was encased by wood and concrete, the floor covered with pine planking.

"It's a shooting range," said Mabel. "You bring your Glock?"

Before them stood seven shooting stations, with narrow corridors that ended with large, black and red circle targets. Behind the round bull's-eyes were backstops of lead and sand. The targets were attached to smooth gray wires, which ran through small motors, so they could be retrieved. There were seven elderly people taking aim, each holding a High Standard .22 caliber pistol, with a silencer on the barrel.

Mabel could hear a constant *pft, pft, pft,* as shot after shot was fired.

A man turned away from the shooters and approached them. He wasn't tall, perhaps five-foot-nine. He looked much larger, at least more solid. Mabel wasn't sure how old he was—he could have been seventy, or he could have been fifty. His skin was smooth, tanned and pliable, but his face looked like it had seen many years, with wisdom lines stretching out from his ever-so-slightly Japanese eyes.

The man opened his arms and wrapped them around Ben with a robust, brotherly hug. Mabel could see strong, sinewy muscles bulging from the man's frame, as if he were a young weightlifter, not a man in retirement.

"Hello, Tony," said Ben.

"Good to see you, old friend. How's the agency working out?"

Ben stood back and motioned toward Mabel. "My first client."

Tony grinned at Mabel. "You sure you want to trust your life to this old hack?" He stuck out his hand. "I'm Tony Trance."

When Mabel grasped Tony's hand, it was like holding the end of a sledge hammer. His skin was hard and cool, his fingers calloused with something akin to steer horn. Mabel turned Tony's palm over and said, "Let me guess, karate?"

Tony smiled. "I've had some training."

At that moment, an elegant blond woman of about forty came around the corner. She looked like she had stepped out of a Cosmo magazine, except that she was holding a baby against her shoulder, patting it softly as it drooled into a white burping rag. The woman took the baby off her shoulder, and with both hands thrust it into Tony's face. "Take your son," she said. "I need to use the bathroom."

"So do I," said Mabel.

The woman looked at Mabel and smiled. She extended her hand and said, "I'm Pat Trance." Then her eyes narrowed and she smiled. "Oh, you're Mabel Witherspoon! How have you been?"

"I'm good." It took Mabel a moment to recognize Pat's face, but after a moment she said, "I remember you. You used to be Pat Crawford, real estate agent to the stars."

Pat smiled. "Now I'm a sleep-deprived mother, changing diapers and wiping drool off my shoulders."

"You helped us buy our condo."

"Remember it well. How is Archie?"

"He passed away."

Pat's eyes softened, their empathy strong and sincere. "I'm sorry for your loss. Archie was a fine man." Pat hesitated. "May I ask why you're here?"

Mabel shrugged and pointed toward Ben. "Ask him."

Pat gave Ben Johnson a hug and a peck on each cheek. "How've you been, stranger?" she said. "Long time, no see."

"Been setting up shop."

Pat laughed. "That's not what I hear. I hear you've been procrastinating for months."

"True," said Ben, shuffling his feet. "But I finally got off the schneid. Mabel's my first client."

Pat looked to Mabel and touched her shoulder. "You're in good hands, Mabel. C'mon, I'll show you the bathroom. It's obvious that Ben needs help with your case, whatever that might be. Let's let the boys talk."

Pat led Mabel out of the shooting area, back into something more like a typical Miami mansion.

Pat said, "Care to share your problem?"

"Rial Cantwell is trying to kill me."

Pat showed little surprise, as if she dealt with this sort of thing all the time. "Really?"

"Well, maybe…"

"Rial doesn't seem like the killing type."

"You know him?"

"We dated once, for a short while. Between wives…number three and number four, I think. He was an okay guy. A gentleman, to me."

When Pat and Mabel returned to the shooting range, Tony motioned for them to follow him outside. He led them to an expansive patio that looked out toward the water. There were three picnic tables, painted green, along with a dozen or so white plastic chairs. Beyond the patio, the Vigilantes still ran through their karate forms. Three instructors walked among them making corrections with their hands.

"Sit," said Tony.

Once they were settled, Tony's face grew somber. He leaned across a picnic table and said, "What brings you here, Ben?"

Ben told Tony about Cantwell. He told him about the transfer of money and the overheard conversation. He told him about Mabel's money and her bull-headed insistence on justice.

"What can we do?" said Tony.

Ben said, "I told Cantwell that I would bring the head of SOSCADA to see him. I sorta said that you were looking for a new money manager."

Tony looked out over the water. He curled his lower lip, looking somewhere inside. He didn't say a word. Instead, he pulled a Sectéra Edge PDA off his hip. He punched a number and waited. A moment later he said, "Murray, what's your twenty?" Tony looked at Ben and nodded. He spoke back into the phone, "Come to the back patio when you get here, will you? Task someone on Rial Cantwell. ASAP."

Tony's eyebrows lifted, and he said, "Really? Can't wait to hear about it."

Tony hung up his phone. "Cantwell's got a history."

Mabel stood and began to walk among the picnic tables. After a while, she said, "Okay. I've been patient enough. What is this place?"

Tony looked at Ben. "You haven't told her?"

Ben shook his head. "Not for me to tell, really. I told her about SOSCADA and Jaime. No specifics, though."

Tony spent the next ten minutes telling Mabel about the Varicose Vigilantes. He told her about Jaime's kidnapping and the white slavery ring. He told her about the drugs and the hundreds of millions of dollars. He told her about Talid and Cesar and about Jack Trance.

"The billionaire Trance?" Mabel said.

"My nephew."

Mabel looked at Ben, with a playful look in her eyes. "You really weren't lying on your website."

Ben shrugged. "I do have resources, Mabel."

At that moment, they saw a white, stretch Cadillac limousine pull into the driveway. It was a convertible, with a stern-faced Oriental driver who moved with a resolute, perfunctory demeanor.

Inside the car, Mabel could see a man with flowing white hair, dressed in a bright white suit. He appeared to be eating something, perhaps an apple. Beside him sat two women who looked like prostitutes. Except that they were…old. There was one other man inside the limo. He looked unusually somber, with salt-and-pepper hair and thick black glasses, much like hers.

The man in white jumped out of the limo when it stopped. He opened the door with an exaggerated flourish, allowing the women to step out like movie stars. Maybe porn stars. They were both wearing pink hot pants, spike heels and black fishnet stockings. The serious man followed out of the car with deliberate slowness. He was wearing a gray pinstripe suit that looked like it was at least two sizes too large and forty years out of style.

The man in white began walking toward them, with an odd kind of shuffle that made Mabel think of a pimp walk. He greeted Ben with a loud, hearty voice. "Well, if it isn't the Benster! What's up, dude?"

Ben and the white-suited man went through an elaborate handshake that must have lasted ten full seconds. When they were done, the man looked at Mabel and said, "Take off your glasses."

Mabel's normal reaction would have been to tell the man to buzz off. But the white-suited man had such a carefree and innocent air about him that she pulled off her glasses and smiled, turning her face from side to side for him to see.

The man walked slowly around Mabel, regarding her studiously from head to toe. He said, "Uh-huh...Mmm...Not bad. We could use you, out on the streets." The man suddenly thrust out his hand. "Hi. I'm Doctor Love. Who are you?"

Mabel looked briefly at Ben, whose face had broken into an amused grin. "Doctor Love? What kind of name is Doctor Love?"

"I'm a pimp. It's my handle."

Mabel looked at Ben, at Tony, and then back at Doctor Love.

Ben said, "His real name is Mortimer Winkelman. We call him Gumbo. He's not a pimp. He just pretends to be one, to get information from drug dealers."

Mabel's jaw quivered. She didn't know what to say. She looked to Gumbo's open shirt and noticed his colorful, American Eagle tattoo. "Nice tat," she said.

Gumbo opened the final two buttons on his shirt and spread it apart, so Mabel could see the full wing span of the bird. "You dig it?"

"Sweet. I'd show you my butterfly, but...we'll you know."

Gumbo winked. "Believe me, sister. I know."

The man in the oversized pinstripe suit cleared his throat. Mabel looked to him and he held out his hand. "My name is Murray Stein," he said. Stein's New York accent was as thick as the state of New Jersey.

Mabel took Murray's hand, then curtseyed, as he gallantly kissed the back of it. "Mabel Witherspoon."

"Murray is our lead analyst," said Tony. "If there is any chink in Cantwell's armor, he'll find it."

"Cantwell's a drug dealer," Murray said. "At least he used to be. Once had a decent size operation, based in Miami Gardens. Then he fell off the grid."

"You do any work for him?" Tony said. Tony looked at Mabel. "Murray was a CPA. He had some clients who used to bend the law."

"One law-bending client," Murray said. "A big one. Not a drug dealer, but he was into everything else."

Mabel sat down into a chair and sighed. This was all coming too fast. She was in this gaudy mansion with a shooting range inside. There were a couple hundred geriatrics doing karate in the back yard. There was this guy, Doctor Love, who looked and acted like a pimp. Then there was this Jewish guy who used to be a crime boss CPA. Two of the women looked like hookers, but they were at least her age. One of them had a chest the size of Montana, with a waist like Dolly Parton. The other was thin and so fit that she looked like she could run a marathon.

Gumbo motioned toward the slim woman. "This is Millie, my wife." He pointed toward the woman with the balcony chest. "This here is Sophie."

"Are you prostitutes?" Mabel said.

"Nah," said Sophie. "Just pretend to be…Best way to learn about the drug trade. We just started working Atlanta. Got back in today." She paused. "Lot of drugs in Atlanta." She smiled playfully. "But not for long."

Gumbo said, "Millie and Sophie are my two best operatives."

Mabel's jaw hung open, and remained that way, unmoving. For once in her life, she couldn't speak.

Ben looked at Murray. "Tell us about Cantwell and his drug trade."

Murray scratched the back of his neck and looked out at the bay. He pulled a bottle of Poland Spring water out of an ice-filled cooler and took a long sip. "We're going back almost twenty years, Ben. As I recall, he came down here as a wet-behind-the-ears money manager. Ran into some trouble in the markets and got bailed out by one of the local drug dealers. Gomez, I think. Gomez is long-since dead. I'm pretty sure Cantwell's interest in the drug trade didn't die with him, though."

"Why haven't we targeted him?" asked Tony.

"Because he's too smart and too well insulated, that's why. He's got connections like a Clinton. He's got a Farbrecher named Masco who isn't afraid to intimidate.

"We focus on less organized prey, Tony. This man's a master."

Tony and Ben locked eyes. They'd been through this sort of thing, too many times before, to feel any sort of intimidation. For them, this was fun.

"Murray," said Tony. "Please task a dozen people on Cantwell. I want to know everything he does, everywhere he goes. I want to know where he shops, where he banks, who he sleeps with… Everything."

"Sure thing, boss."

Tony looked at Ben. "I suspect you have a plan?"

Ben smiled. "Of course."

Chapter Sixteen

V

The day dawned hot and bright. Despite being low in the sky, the sun beat down with summer-like ferocity. The temperature was already in the seventies, and it was barely nine o'clock.

Ben pulled the Sundancer out of its slip at the Miami Beach Marina and began to head into Biscayne Bay. He removed a pair of easy chairs from a storage hatch and set them on the back deck. Mabel settled herself down to read a book, while Ben navigated north toward Biscayne Point.

Ben dropped anchor when they were across from Lou Masco's waterfront home, but still a half mile offshore. He turned on his notebook computer and opened a program to download the data from Masco's conversations. It took less than five minutes for Ben to empty the disk. Once it was done, he fired up the Sundancer's engine and began to meander southward.

Ben dropped anchor when they were off the southern tip of Key Biscayne. He and Mabel went down below and sat at the galley table. Ben scrolled through twenty-two Masco conversations and put them into a digital playlist. He imported the files into a program, which converted the conversations into Word documents. Ben printed out over two hundred pages of text. He took half the stack and handed it to Mabel, keeping the rest for himself.

"Let's see what we find," he said.

Most of the conversations were useless. One did provide entertainment. It was a call to a 900 number, which ended with Masco breathing heavily into the phone, crying, "Baby…baby…baby."

"At least he practices safe sex," said Mabel.

Then Ben read a conversation between Masco and Cantwell, one he wasn't sure he wanted Mabel to see. He located the conversation on his computer, put on a pair of headphones, and gave it a listen.

"I'll tell you, Rial," said Masco. "Witherspoon is trouble. She comes in here and demands money. Then she comes back with her financial planner, who's a poster child for incompetency and boorishness."

Cantwell laughed. "The bozo ordered fried clams at the Setai. Fried clams, can you believe it?" Cantwell paused for a long moment. Ben wondered what it was he was doing. Lighting a cigar? Scratching his butt? Taking a drink? Finally, he said, "You check him out?"

"Yeah. He's legit. I went into his website. He's listed with the CFP Board. Beats me how he passed the exam."

Ben smiled, pleased that he'd removed his detective site from the Web, and that that the new one he'd created, and listed on his business card, had held firm. He was glad that he'd taken the time to hack into various professional websites to insert his name and bio. Masco had viewed the CFP Board of Standards site, where Ben had listed his name among the Certificants. Who knew where else he'd been?

Cantwell said, "He's good enough to deliver Tony Trance."

"That scares me. It smells."

"You're too paranoid, Lou. I think he's just a member of the lucky sperm club. He's got that feel."

"My job, Rial, is to keep you out of trouble."

"Are you suggesting something?"

"I want to send her a message."

"Didn't you do that already?"

"Obviously, it didn't work."

"She's a ditzy old broad, Lou. That's all. She's not a problem. Leave her alone."

"No. She *is* a problem. You remember Taylor? What did we have to do with her? Huh?"

Cantwell remained silent.

"And Jameson?"

More silence.

"And Vermeer? He got really close."

Cantwell sighed deeply. "All right, Lou. I get your point. You know best about these things. Send another message. But I don't want a mess, or a body. Not yet."

"We don't need to do this, if you want to cash out. We can just walk away. Right now. What do you say?"

"Not yet, Lou. Fifty billion. We're too close. Five more years. Maybe less."

"We're playing with fire."

"That's my call, isn't it? Goodnight."

Ben pulled off his headphones and debated what to do. Finally, he handed the paper with the conversation to Mabel. "Take a look at this."

As Mabel read the transcript, her face grew progressively pale, as if she were applying layer after layer of thin, light makeup. Small rivers of sweat began to break out across her forehead. Her fingers began to tremble and she curled them into fists to keep them still. "He wants me dead."

"You want out?"

"Hell, no. Just makes me mad."

Ben remained silent. After a while, the color began to return to Mabel's cheeks. Once he was sure she wouldn't faint, Ben said, "We've got two ways to play this, Mabel. We can go dark, keep everything under the radar, out of sight. Or, we can confront them, stick it right in their faces."

Mabel stood up without saying a word. She walked out onto the deck of the boat. The sun had risen as high as it would go today, maybe higher than it should have. The temperature had climbed into the high-seventies. It was a glorious winter day, with not a cloud in the sky. A slight breeze tugged on the water, not enough to raise the chop, but enough to keep them from baking. Ben came up behind Mabel and put an arm around her shoulder. She flinched, but then relaxed.

"So, what do you think?" he said.

"I think this is exciting as hell. Let's kick them in the balls."

Chapter Seventeen
V
____

Ben Johnson pulled his Glock from the shoulder holster he wore under his sport coat. He gripped it in both of his hands, barrel upward, and nudged Mabel's partially open door with the toe of his shoe.

"It's déjà vu all over again," muttered Mabel. "Asshole."

Ben had insisted on coming back to Mabel's condo with her, suspecting that Masco would be striking again. He'd been right.

"I even had the locks changed," said Mabel.

Ben moved slowly through the entryway, his head swiveling in every direction. "A sealed vault won't keep out a pro, Mabel. If he wants in, he's in. What we need to do is install a camera that he won't see. Catch him in the act next time. That way, we'll get leverage. Once we can tie him to you, it gets risky…too risky to…" Ben hesitated. "…to do anything nasty."

"You mean kill me?'

"I didn't say that."

"You think he killed the others? The ones he mentioned in his conversation with Cantwell?"

Ben shrugged. "We'll put Murray on that and find out soon enough, won't we? Right now, let's see what message our friend left for you today."

They found it in the kitchen. There, in the sink, was the dead head of a fish. A snapper.

"The least he could have done was leave the body. Then, we could have eaten the darn thing," said Mabel.

Ben continued to look around the condo. He found a listening device in the bedroom and one in the living room. Sophisticated, but not state-of-the-art. Masco had done this on his own.

Ben unscrewed the phone and found a bug in there. Before removing anything, he motioned for Mabel to join him out in the hallway.

"We've got another choice here, Mabel. We can remove the listening devices. Then they'll know that we are on to their game. Or, we can leave them in place and feed them disinformation."

"Let's feed them some crap. First thing I'm going to do is call a 900 phone sex line, give Lou a taste of his own medicine. Wait 'til he hears *my* heavy breathing."

"He's liable to place you on YouTube," said Ben.

"Then we'll put *him* on the Internet."

"Oh, Mabel. Thou art so devious. Remind me never to cross you."

Chapter Eighteen
V

Gumbo's white stretch limousine nudged to the curb outside the Cantwell building, followed closely by Ben's white Jaguar. A 1965, cherry red Mustang pulled in behind that, with Tony Trance and his wife, Pat, stepping out onto the sidewalk.

Gumbo and Murray Stein emerged from the limo. Gumbo was wearing his trademark white suit, while Murray had swapped his baggy gray suit for an equally baggy one of navy blue. They were followed by Millie and Sophie, who were wearing outfits that would make a Jiggles dancer blush.

Tony Trance was dressed in a light brown turtleneck, a cream-colored wool suit and brown loafers. Pat was wearing a light blue dress, custom-made by one of the local fashion designers. She wore minimal jewelry, a two carat engagement diamond with a solitary diamond pendant necklace to match.

Mabel wore another Scottish kilt, with black leggings under the blue plaid wool. She had on a pale yellow sweater, with bright blue and yellow butterflies sewn into the sleeves. The butterflies continued down along the left side of the front.

Ben wore a pair of tan Dockers, beneath a tweed blazer with leather patches on the elbows. Ben had added a touch of "silver spoon," by sewing a patch sporting the emblem of Exeter's Philips Academy onto the coat's left breast.

It took a full ten minutes for the group to clear security. Tony had brought a suitcase filled with papers, which the guards insisted on reviewing, page by page. Ben's fat pen had lost its novelty and wasn't examined at all. Now, it was just another pen.

Cantwell met them with his usual aplomb, walking down the long corridor with his hair flowing behind him. Mabel thought he looked like a pampered, long-haired Afghan at the Westminster dog show.

Cantwell held out his hand for Pat Trance. She placed it into his palm and he kissed it fondly.

"Patricia. So good to see you again."

"It's been a while," said Pat.

"Since you married, you've dropped from sight."

Pat had once been a fixture in Miami society. She had been escorted, but not bedded, by many of Miami's most powerful and influential figures.

"I'm a content mom now, Rial."

Cantwell's eyes widened, then softened. He looked at Pat's shapely frame, thinking how she hadn't aged a day in the past decade. She still looked like she could be a runway model, with the long lines and angular cheeks that had made her so fashionable among the men.

"Congratulations to you both."

Cantwell extended his hand to Tony. "We've never had the pleasure."

Tony met Cantwell's hand with his iron fist. Cantwell frowned, but didn't comment.

Cantwell said, "Mr. Johnson tells me that you may be looking to change money managers."

Tony glanced over at Ben and said, "I'm afraid that Mr. Johnson exaggerates—"

"The hell, I do. Why, just the other day you were saying—" said Ben.

Tony held up his hand and Ben shut up, as scripted.

"Sorry," Ben said.

"I'm really not taking on clients at this time, Mr. Trance," said Cantwell. "But, as a favor to Mrs. Witherspoon…and my old friend, Patricia…I agreed to review your portfolio."

"Thank you, Mr. Cantwell." Tony turned to the others. "These people are all trustees of the SOSCADA foundation. Any change of endowment management would need to be approved by the board."

Cantwell looked at Gumbo, in his bright white suit, his shirt open to the navel, with three heavy gold chains hanging from his neck. One of the chains hefted a gold medallion that must have weighed a full pound. There was a tattoo emblazoned across the man's chest. It looked like a bird, maybe an eagle.

Gumbo shuffled forward and grasped Cantwell's hand, with his 'cool dude' shake. "The name's Love. *Doctor* Love."

"Oh…well…it's a pleasure to meet you…Doctor."

Millie and Sophie sidled up to Cantwell. As they drew beside him, Cantwell couldn't help but think of Jiggles. These women looked like they would have fit right in, forty years ago. Even so, Cantwell felt his eyes being drawn to Sophie's chest like a moth to light.

"Mind out of the gutter, Cantwell," said Sophie. She stuck out a hand. "I'm Sophie. Don't worry about the chest thing. I get that all the time." She hefted her bosom and gave it a little pat. "Just shows you're a man. These puppies come in handy, in my line of work."

"And what might that be?" said Cantwell.

"You can't tell?"

"I'd hate to guess."

Tony said, "Sophie, Millie, Murray and Gumbo…Doctor Love…They work the streets."

Cantwell raised his eyebrows, as if in surprise. Tony noticed a slight flush to his cheeks. *Good*, he thought. *Off-balance is good.*

Cantwell said, "Well, they certainly look the part."

Cantwell began walking down the hallway. As he passed his trophy receptionist, he said, "Please bring refreshments to the main conference room. And call Mr. Masco. Have him meet us there."

"Of course, sir."

Cantwell ushered them all into his conference room. As they passed beyond the frosted glass into the imposing space, Tony took in the heavy walnut table and the twenty-four chairs. He looked to the set of six high definition screens that made up one wall. One of the screens was on, and tuned to the Fox Business Channel. This room was meant to impress, and it did.

As they were settling into seats, Lou Masco slipped into the room. Cantwell motioned toward him and made introductions. Masco took a seat at the head of the conference table, while Cantwell remained standing, as if ready to present.

"I need to use the little girl's room," said Mabel.

Masco spoke quickly. "I'll bring you."

"No need," said Ben. "I've got to drain my little wiener myself. You all start talking turkey. We can find our way around."

Cantwell and Masco looked at each other. Cantwell subtly nodded and Masco seemed to relax.

"I brought statements showing our current portfolio," said Tony. He hefted his briefcase onto the table. Masco leaned forward, while Cantwell hovered above the briefcase like a hunting hawk.

As Tony was pulling out the first stack of papers, Ben and Mabel stepped out of the conference room and began walking quickly down the hall.

"If we're lucky..." Ben whispered. "...We'll only need a minute."

Ben slipped into Cantwell's office. Mabel stood watch outside the door, peering into her purse as if she'd lost something. Ben walked to Cantwell's desk and opened up his HP EliteBook notebook. In the lower right hand corner, there was a Windows sticker. Ben smiled. He pulled out his Mt. Blanc pen and unscrewed the cap. There was no pool of messy ink inside. Instead, there was a small metal tube, with a thin razor on its end. The razor was barely the width of a small fingernail. But it was sharp and efficient.

Ben quickly scraped off the Windows sticker. He reached into the pen and pulled out a piece of cotton, which was soaked in an odorless solvent, something like Goo Gone. He used this to remove any remaining glue. He wiped the residue with the edge of his pinky finger, then the tail of his shirt. He blew on it for a moment, just to make sure. Then he pulled a replacement sticker out of his pen and placed it on the machine.

Forty seconds after entering Cantwell's office, Ben slipped back into the hallway. He and Mabel began walking, continuing toward the men's and ladies' rooms.

"You've got to tell me which is which," said Mabel "The guy on the sign doesn't have a penis."

Just as they turned the hallway corner, Lou Masco stepped out of the conference room and began walking toward the bathrooms.

Ben Johnson was standing at a urinal, vigorously wiggling his penis, when Masco came inside. "Damned prostate," Ben muttered. "You gotta good prostate, Masco? Or do you dribble like me?"

Masco took the urinal beside Ben, then peed with a hard heavy flow. Ben peered over and said, "I'm friggin' jealous, Lou. Takes me a full two minutes to drain my Johnson." He laughed. "Get it. My name's Johnson and I've got a Johnson—"

"You don't fool me, Ben," said Masco.

"Excuse me?"

"Nobody as stupid as you act can be as successful as you appear to be."

Ben Johnson laughed. Without zipping up his fly, he pointed at the

Phillips emblem on his sport coat. "I may be stupid. But I'm a charter member of the lucky sperm club, Lou. Went to prep school just down the road from where Cantwell grew up. He can check me out…I'd rather be lucky than smart any day. How 'bout you?" Ben looked down to his open pants and blushed. He began to zip up his fly. "Oh…sorry. Guess Little J needed some air."

Ben washed up and walked outside to wait for Mabel. Masco followed and stood guard beside him. Several moments later, Mabel emerged from the ladies' room, smoothing the Depends beneath her skirt. Ben escorted Mabel back toward the conference room, while Masco stayed behind and slipped into Cantwell's office.

"Think he'll know?" said Mabel.

"I didn't see any cameras or sensing equipment in there."

"I want to leave here alive."

"Let's hope we do."

"There you are!" said Cantwell, as Ben and Mabel slipped back into the conference room. "I thought you'd gotten lost."

"At my age, things don't flow like they used to, Rial," said Ben. "Got to do a lot of shaking to get my old bird to spit."

"Amen, brother," said Gumbo.

"Well?" Ben said to Tony. "What do ya think?"

Cantwell said, "We've only just glanced at the SOSCADA portfolio, Mr. Johnson. But it appears to be a simple system of laddered bonds. Conservative, with little potential for growth."

Ben said, "Laddered bonds? What do you mean laddered? What kind of bond buys ladders?"

Cantwell gave Ben a patronizing glance. He looked at Tony, who motioned for him to explain.

"The SOSCADA endowment is invested in bonds of different maturities. Each year, about ten percent of the bonds mature. This allows the portfolio return to be higher, more like longer term bonds, with a shorter-term average maturity, about five years."

Ben said, "If you say so. You think you could get him to buy some mutual funds from me?"

"Sorry, Mr. Johnson. No mutual funds for this account." He paused. "But under SEC regulations, I *am* allowed to legally pay *you* as much as thirty percent of our fees. As a finder."

Ben's eyes widened. "Get out of town...Now we're talking! That could be a lot of money, right?" Ben looked at Tony. "Well, what do you think? I think you should move your account. This guy's a magician."

"We haven't had the chance to discuss what Cantwell Investments can do for us yet, Ben. If you'd stop talking, we might even get to that."

"May I ask how you two know each other?" Cantwell asked.

"Family friend," said Tony. "Ben is related to my brother's side of the family, the Hopewells. You know, Hopewell Industries? Too close and too powerful to ignore."

Cantwell shook his head slowly and looked at Ben. "Lucky you."

Ben grinned. "Yeah. Too bad all my money's in trust."

Rial Cantwell spent the next two hours discussing his investment strategies. He brought in half a dozen programmers, who explained his algorithms and his program trading operations. He brought in three of his analysts who talked investment theory. And he spent a good deal of time showing charts and graphs of his historical performance. He was good. Really good. His Alpha was high. His Beta was low. His equity R Squared was still near one hundred, so his Beta was valid. This was an enviable combination in the money business.

As the meeting drew to a close, Tony said, "What are your lock-up provisions?"

"Five years," said Mabel.

"One year for *new* money," said Cantwell. He looked at Mabel and shrugged. "Our policy since the meltdown."

"Why can't I get my money then?" said Mabel.

Cantwell's eyes flashed briefly. Mabel was sure that she actually saw flame. His eyes quickly cooled to a soft glow, and he said, "All investors are treated the *same*, according to their agreements, Mrs. Witherspoon. We've discussed this."

"Oh, I know. Just thought I'd try one last time."

Cantwell smiled. It was a slick smile, just at the corners of the mouth, not with the eyes. But it seemed to put Mabel at ease.

Tony stood from the conference table. "You are very persuasive, Mr. Cantwell. We'll be having a meeting of our full board shortly. Perhaps we could have another meeting then?"

"But, of course."

"Good." Tony extended his hand. "I'll look forward to it."

Chapter Nineteen
V
___

After meeting with Tony and the others, Cantwell had to rush from his offices to attend an investors conference, where he delivered the keynote address. It wasn't until after he had spoken to a sycophantic audience, and then endured a "rubber chicken" convention dinner, that he and Masco were able to discuss their meeting with Tony.

It was late. Cantwell was at his computer, scrolling through the day's market data, when Lou Masco sauntered into his office.

"I don't like it," Masco said.

"What?"

"Something's fishy. They did something."

"They couldn't have been gone for a minute before you bolted out of the conference room, chasing after them like a horny hound after a bitch in heat."

"I'm not a fucking dog, Rial. I'm as important as you are."

"You know what I mean. You just made it obvious."

"What?"

"That you don't trust them."

"I don't."

"But that makes *us* look untrustworthy. I'm looking to take on a new client and you're acting like *we're* untrustworthy."

"Oh, bullshit."

"Why are you so edgy about this?"

Masco began to walk around Cantwell's office, pacing more like a hyena waiting to scavenge a lion's kill than a horny dog.

"We've got that deal going down. Our biggest yet. By far."

Cantwell sighed. "Why do you still insist on dealing drugs? Haven't we moved beyond that now?"

"Because you want a frigging fifty billion, that's why."

"I want fifty billion because I love the game, Lou. It's not about the money. Not anymore."

"That's why I deal the drugs, Rial. Because of the *game*."

Cantwell walked over to his large picture window and stared out at the Dolphins' stadium. "Maybe we *should* pack it in. I don't like this new deal you've cut. You've gone out on the edge, way too far."

"It's the goddamn Super Bowl, *plus* the Pro Bowl, Rial. How often do we get a chance like that? We can use this to establish ourselves across the *country*."

"But three *billion*? Wholesale? Then taking on the downstream? What were you thinking? No football game is going to generate that kind of demand. It'll take us a year to unload that kind of inventory, no matter what contacts you make." Cantwell sighed and sank into one the chairs looking out toward Miami. "You know why I've been able to siphon our clients' money? It's because I'm *good*, Lou. Maybe the best. I've never stolen. Every dime that I say they have is there. I just haven't given them all they've earned."

"Some people might call that theft, Rial."

"Who's been harmed? I just changed the profit sharing parameters. That's all. I *earned* that. Mabel Witherspoon has made a goddamned *twelve percent* on her portfolio, while the rest of the investment world has gone bankrupt. So what if she's actually earned a few million more? She's done *well*. Nobody's been hurt."

Cantwell closed his eyes and whispered, "But this drug thing…I don't like it. People do get hurt with drugs."

"Didn't seem to bother you seventeen years ago, Rial. Back when you were sucking wind and about to go belly up. Who saved you then? Who saved your ass then? I'll tell you who. *I* did."

Cantwell let out another deep sigh. "I know."

"You've earned *five* billion and siphoned off twenty. The other five is from *me*. I've earned us another five *billion* dollars. Shouldn't I get some respect for that? You and I, we've actually *earned* the same amount of money."

"It's not the same," said Cantwell.

"Fuck you, it's not the same. Money is money."

"Is it? I'm not sure it is. I'll give you this, though. You've earned five billion. I've earned five billion in fees and profit splits, above expenses. That was *before* taxes, just three billion after taxes. I've siphoned ten.

The other thirteen we've earned *together*, by investing. We're partners. You know that."

Masco snorted. "Don't go getting all soft on me, Cantwell. Not when it's been *you* that's wanted fifty billion. I said I'd be happy with thirty. But nooo...*You* said we needed more."

"I've changed my mind. I say we shut it down. We shut down the drug deals. We shut down the siphoning. From now on, we play it straight."

"After nearly two decades, you want to play it straight?"

"Yeah. Stop the drug buy."

Masco laughed out loud. He began to pace the room even harder.

This time, Masco made Cantwell think of a gorilla pacing in captivity, it's caged instincts driving it to obsession. Lou seemed agitated, like a junkie sweating for a fix. Then a horrible thought came into Cantwell's head.

"Are you using, Lou? Is that it? Are you taking the drugs you sell?"

Masco guffawed. "You have no fucking clue, do you? You sit up here in your fucking Ivory Tower, peering at your fucking charts, schmoozing you're your fucking clients, traveling the fucking world, while I do all the hard work.

"I'm the one that cleans up your mess. I'm the one who has to test the product—"

"We don't need drugs!" yelled Cantwell.

"That's easy for you to say."

Cantwell groaned. He had a good thing here; they both did. They were billionaires. They were each listed on the Forbes 400. Sure, Forbes had no clue about the stolen money, how much they really owned. But that didn't matter. They had *respect*. They could go anywhere, do anything. They could dine with the president, or with the Queen of England. They could do the weekend morning shows, they could go on Leno. They had it all. Now Lou was about to screw it up.

Lou had gone into business with the most brutal cartels. He had promised them three billion dollars for product, blatant enough to attract the attention of the Feds with a big red flag. Even Cantwell's influence couldn't keep the Feds away on that, not if they got a bug up their ass about taking them down.

"Shut it down, Lou."

"I can't shut it down now, you know that. They'll kill us."

"They might do that anyway."

Cantwell looked closely into Masco's eyes. Yes, he was using. He could see it now. How had he missed the escalation? He'd been too preoccupied with Mabel Witherspoon.

"How long you been using, Lou? And why?"

Masco's shoulders slumped. He dropped into one of the chairs and let out a long, weary groan. "Until now, we've just been a lender. We put out the money for a buy, we get double back within six months. But you wanted fifty billion, so I changed the game. By taking the lead, we can earn *three hundred* percent, far more than you ever dreamed of.

"I'm dealing with the frigging cartels, Rial. Santiago…he makes you test the product every damn time, like he knows it's going to make you weak." He paused. "It just sort of happened…*You* try snorting pure blow and see what it does to you, you holier-than-thou fucking money manager…and Khan…I don't even want to talk about Khan."

"You need treatment."

"Treatment? The only treatment that will cure this is a car bomb."

"Let's pay them off. We'll pay them off. We'll give the cartels whatever they want. I don't care about the money. Offer them five, five billion. They keep their product. We'll have it wired, tomorrow. We'll get you into rehab…"

Masco shook his head. "Doesn't work that way, my friend. I made a choice. Now, I'll have to live with it, at least until after the Super Bowl. After that? Yeah, maybe after that we can shut it down. Sure. After that."

"Go home, Lou. We'll talk more on this tomorrow. I'm tired and so are you."

Chapter Twenty
V

Ben

It was nearly 10 P.M. I was seated at my computer, finally getting the first of Cantwell's keystrokes onto my laptop. Wouldn't be long before I had all his user names and passwords. Then I could surf his cyber world and find out everything. I'd probably be able to return all the money stolen from investors right here from the office.

I looked at Mabel. She was preparing to sleep on my couch. "You sure you don't want me to bring you home?" I said.

Mabel shook her head. "I'm scared, Ben."

"Yeah. I'd be scared, too."

At that moment, we began to hear the first audio from Cantwell's office. I switched on the digital recorder in my laptop and settled back in my chair. Mabel and I listened without speaking. Cantwell laid out how much he'd stolen, and what Masco had earned from dealing drugs. This was more than we expected, more than we'd hoped for. I could feel my spirits soar. We now had enough on Cantwell to take him down, at least privately. This wouldn't hold up in court. In fact, the recording might be enough to send *us* to jail. But a conversation like this, put in the right place? It would make Cantwell's career implode like the World Trade Center. My guess was that he would jump at the chance to return money to investors and then quietly slink into oblivion.

Then they started talking about the major drug deals, and Masco using. I could feel my spirits begin to fall, like Icarus, plunging into the earth in a pile of melted wax and feathers. The Columbians? The Afghans? Bad news. Really bad news. One didn't get in their way, not without enough firepower to level a Middle-Eastern nation, maybe not even then. The United States government couldn't stop these people, so how could we ever hope to? We couldn't; that was the truth. All we could do was shake sticks at them and hope we didn't piss them off enough to retaliate.

Sure, SOSCADA had been able to slow the growth of the drug trade in America. Internal estimates showed an effective rate of ten to twenty percent. That was *huge*. SOSCADA had been able to educate youths against drug use. They had even been able to take out some of the biggest U.S. distributors.

But these cartels were beyond brutal and ruthless. If Masco was involved with them, I wasn't sure I was up to the task. Even the old Ben might have walked away. It made me think we should just return the money to investors, not start a war as big as Desert Storm.

Mabel said, "I didn't know you had audio with that little thingy you put on Rial's computer?"

"I'm riding Cantwell's whole system, Mabel. Soon, I'll be able to make it do anything I want."

"But will you want to?" said Mabel. "Now that you know what's involved? This is far more complicated than we thought. Far more dangerous."

"What's life without a little risk?" I joked.

"Longer."

I smiled. It wasn't a happy smile. No, it was a wry, forlorn smile, because Mabel was right. We were walking into a gunfight with popguns.

Chapter Twenty-One
V

Lou Masco left the Cantwell building and aimed his Mercedes into the street. He maneuvered over to NW 32nd Avenue and set his cruise control to exactly one mile under the speed limit. When he reached Brentwood Park he pulled into the main parking lot. There were thirty or so cars already there, using up half of the spaces. More cars were pouring in, so there must be some sort of event about to begin. *Good*, thought Masco. *The more the merrier.*

Masco waited inside his car. He was parked on the north side of the lot, facing east. He looked out at the expanse of well-trodden grass. To his left, there was a path that wound around most of the park. There was a scattering of people upon it, walking dogs, swatting a flies, staring at the sky. A couple of joggers got out of their cars beside Masco and began to stretch. Lou estimated the path to be about half a mile around, nothing daunting, for even the out of shape recreational runner.

Although the temperature had yet to make it out of the fifties, Masco could feel himself beginning to sweat. How did he let this happen? He already had more money than he could spend in a lifetime. He had a spectacular home on the water. He owned a 45 foot Halverson. He had a place in Costa Rica, up on a hill with a view that even Cantwell would die for. He even had a mistress who gave him great sex. Granted, it was over the phone and he'd never seen her face or touched her skin. But it was better that way, cleaner, safer. He wasn't one of those freaks who had to bang everything with open legs. He didn't have to sit at the blackjack tables, betting twenty-five grand a hand to get a thrill. No, he was a simple man. Let him sit out on his boat with a beer in his hand. Let him wrap his fingers around the throat of some innocent woman every few years. Let him fill a crate with a quarter billion dollars of cash every once in a while. That was all he needed. Why had he felt the need to do *this?*

Masco closed his eyes. It wasn't often that he got this way, pondering life like fucking Nietzsche. But he had nothing else to do right now, except to wait.

Shit. His career had started out with such innocence, working as a fixer for a small-time drug dealer by the name of Gomez. He made five hundred bucks a week in cash. No Social Security taxes, no income taxes, just green in the jeans and hit the bars on Friday nights. Life had been good. Then Cantwell showed up.

Cantwell had offered him five grand, just to set up a *meeting* with Gomez. He should have walked away. Maybe then, his life wouldn't have spiraled out of control into this—sitting in a parking lot waiting to dance with the devil.

Five thousand had become ten thousand. Then twenty-five. Overnight, Gomez had become a major player in the drug trade, fueled by Cantwell's money.

When Gomez's old lady shot him over the second half of a turkey sandwich, Masco had taken over the operation as his own. A partnership was born. Cantwell became the money man. Masco's drugs supplied the cash flow Cantwell needed to show stellar returns, and attract his first significant investors. Billions followed. It had been a partnership made in heaven.

So, why was he lurking at the gates of hell, sitting in his car, strung out on coke, waiting for a meeting with men who could just as easily shake his hand, spit on him or slit his throat? There was no way out, not anymore.

Masco saw a red handkerchief wave across the park. Time for the meet. Masco slowly got out of his car. He thought to sneak another snort; he needed one. But he'd be forced to take a line by the cartel, probably more.

Masco jogged along the path until he approached the far corner of the park. It couldn't have been more than three hundred yards, but his heart began racing like he'd sprinted five miles. When he neared the corner, he bent over and sucked up huge gasps of air. He could feel his heart thumping like a car piston with a stuck valve, not quite working as it should. He'd have to cut back on the drugs; they were killing him.

"Hello, Mr. Masco," came a voice from behind him.

Masco turned his face. A man with pockmarked skin and the black beady eyes of a rat was staring down at him. He wore a thin smile, the kind a serial killer might wear as he stalked his next prey. There was something feral there, something not quite right.

"Hello, Angel," said Masco.

"Our friend is waiting."

Raul Santiago. The boss.

Masco stood up and arched his back. His head began to spin. He felt like he was on a carnival ride, maybe the Disney teacups. The world went around and around and around. He remained rooted in place, waiting for his brain to settle.

"Let's go," said Angel.

Masco shook his head. "Just a moment."

After a minute more, Masco nodded. Angel frisked him quickly, then began to walk along the path. They turned the corner and moved another thirty yards south, until they were across from NW 195th Street. This sleepy street ended in a cul-de-sac against the park. There was a clear view across the expanse of grass, enough for Santiago and his people to make sure Masco wasn't followed. A silver Rolls Royce limousine was parked at the end of the road beside the park. It looked odd in this neighborhood of small ranch homes with their peeling stucco facades, their old boats, junked cars and run-down campers in the driveways. Two men stood at the side of the limo, their feet planted in the mangy, burnt-out grass, with binoculars in their hands. They spread behind Masco as he passed them.

When Masco reached the limo, the rear door opened. A solitary man sat inside. He was wearing a suit of black tropical wool. Beneath the jacket was a white silk shirt with a slightly ruffled collar. It was oddly feminine, particularly for a man famous for such brutality. A pair of black penny loafers, without socks, covered Santiago's feet.

"Come in, my friend," said Santiago.

Once Masco was seated, Angel and the two bodyguards slipped quickly inside. The car began to speed off, even before the door was closed.

The limo drove around the city for a full five minutes, before anyone said another word. Santiago simply stared at Masco. Masco didn't know what to say, so he remained silent, staring back. What he wanted to say was that he was having second thoughts. He wanted to tell Santiago to take a flying hike, that he had no more use for his product, didn't even want the money. He wanted to tell him he was *done*. It was over. It had been a good run, a great run. But his days of riding the razor were over. It was time to cash out and settle down.

Masco could feel sweat beginning to pool beneath his armpits. A thin layer of moisture began to seep along his scalp, followed closely by oily bubbles along his forehead. Soon, he began to tremble.

Santiago frowned. "You don't look very good, Lou."

"I'm fine," he said.

Santiago nodded toward one of his bodyguards. The man pulled a small table out from beneath a seat and locked its legs into the floor. He reached into a maple cabinet that was built into the back of the limo, removed a black leather pouch and unrolled it onto the table. The case held several vials filled with white and brown powder. There was an assortment of spoons, some small, some larger, a butane lighter and a few virgin syringes encased in plastic.

Santiago said, "You will sample our latest wares."

Masco shook his head. He was done. He was going to shake this monkey, beginning now.

"I trust your product quality, Mr. Santiago. No need to waste it on me."

Santiago laughed. "Oh, but I insist."

One of Santiago's guards pulled an HK out of a shoulder holster. He dropped the magazine and began to count the bullets. He glanced over at Masco and smiled. He had a gold front tooth, which glinted blood red in the dim light of the limousine. Masco closed his eyes. He held them that way for a long moment. Then he took a spoon and dipped it into one of the vials. He brought the spoon to his nose and snorted. The cocaine rushed through his head like a hurricane. He felt his eyes bug wide. His heart began to race again, harder and faster than when he'd been running. He felt the world begin to pull away, as if he were riding upwards in a balloon, watching as the land began to telescope into tiny black specs.

"What's in this?" Masco whispered. This wasn't just cocaine. It was pure and it was powerful, but there was something else, something in it that mulched the reality of Masco's mind into tattered little shreds.

"You like?"

Masco felt his world began to whirl. "Too much. I don't like…I don't think I want to do this anymore. I…I…"

"Try the other," said Santiago.

"No, I—"

Santiago's guard chambered a round with a loud *snap*. Masco looked to the guard. The guard smiled at him again. This time the gold in his tooth appeared to melt. It seemed to go soft and began dripping out of his mouth, like blood. The guard made a gun with his free thumb and forefinger and fired off a symbolic round. "Pow," he said.

Masco looked at Santiago. He smiled weakly and said, "Sure. I'll try it."

Masco dipped the spoon into the second vial. This one didn't give the same crazy kick. It was just cocaine. But it was as powerful as a thoroughbred racehorse. It took him flying across the countryside, driving the world past him like he was in the Kentucky Derby.

"Which do you like best?" Santiago said.

Masco felt his eyes roll, around and around, then into the back of his head. He didn't like either of them, not anymore. But he was trapped. Trapped in the limousine, trapped in the drugs, trapped in the life. He struggled to focus and said, "Both will have their fans."

Santiago grinned. "I thought so."

"Listen...Mr. Santiago…I've been giving this a great deal of thought…I've decided that I'm going to retire…I thought I would want to do this forever…But I'm getting too old…I need out."

"We are as old as we feel, Mr. Masco."

"It's just that…I don't want to have to worry…to have to watch over my shoulder…I just want to be…done."

Santiago smiled again. He nodded toward the guard with the gun. The guard leaned over and calmly forced the barrel of his Heckler & Koch into Masco's mouth.

Santiago said, "You want this to be over? Is that what I'm hearing?"

Masco felt like he was about to puke. He leaned over, the gun still pressed in his mouth. He felt his shoulders heave and he gagged, once, twice. Santiago motioned for the driver to stop the limousine. They were on NW 186th Terrace. It was a lazy residential street with little traffic and modest ranch style homes. Masco opened the door, jumped out and threw up onto the sidewalk. Nobody saw it happen, except for a young boy, who happened to be riding by on a small bike. The boy stopped and stared at Masco, wide-eyed and silent. Masco stared at the boy. He looked to be about ten years old. He was wearing a red and white shirt. The shirt was covered with grass stains and it had a large rip on the collar. His bicycle was blue, with rusted handlebars. Masco and the boy locked eyes for several long seconds before Masco said, "Boo!"

The boy's mouth opened with a silent scream. He pushed off on the bike and began pedaling as fast as he could. Once he was fifty yards away, the boy turned back and stuck out his middle finger, before continuing down the street. Masco cleared his throat and waited for a moment, before stepping back into the car.

"There," said Santiago. "You feel better now?" He paused. "I think we had a little misunderstanding there, ese. My man seems to think you said you wanted to die. You don't want to die now, do you?"

"No," choked Masco.

"No. I didn't think so."

As Lou Masco left the limousine on 195th, and began his walk back across Brentwood park, Ben Johnson lowered his binoculars. "Meeting's over," he said.

Mabel continued to gaze through her Zeiss spotting scope. "He doesn't look very good, does he?" she said, without pulling away from the single eyepiece.

"Must not have gone too well."

Masco's body looked like it had wilted while he was inside the limo. He looked two inches shorter and twenty pounds lighter. His swagger was gone, and he appeared to have aged ten years. Mabel wasn't sure, but it looked like he was dragging a leg, as if he'd had a mini-stroke or something.

"He's stoned," said Ben.

"He's beat," said Mabel. "If he weren't such a killer, I'd be tempted to feel sorry for him.

"That'd be like thinking that a cobra looks cute, and then trying to pet it," said Ben. "You *never* feel sorry for a man like that. You do, you die."

"I'll remember that."

"You better."

Ben wondered if she would.

Chapter Twenty-Two
V

As Ben's Jaguar approached the old Sanchez mansion, the gates seemed to magically swing open. They passed onto the grounds and Ben could see why. Tony had two new guards manning the gatehouse.

"Just like old times," muttered Ben.

Mabel said, "What's that?"

Ben waved at the armed men, then began the winding drive through the estate's mini forest. Ben said, "When Tony first moved into this place, he used to have men stationed at the old guardhouse. He stopped the practice when Cesar died. Cesar was the drug dealer that led to all this. Now that Tony's working with us on the Cantwell thing, he obviously sees the need for precautions. Hence, the guards."

"Do you blame him?" said Mabel.

Ben shrugged. "We'll see."

Ben parked his car in the circular drive of crushed white shells, then led Mabel to the rear of the home.

Tony Trance had assembled his team on the back patio. They were standing in the shade of an old oak tree. It was a crisp winter day, with the temperature in the low sixties. Gumbo was there, wearing his customary white suit. Murray looked like a nightclub comedian, dressed in a pair of brown corduroy slacks slipping off his hips, and a blue blazer large enough for a hippo. He had on a bright red tie with a design of little gray pelicans. Most of the others were wearing jeans, with matching fleece jackets that had the letters VV stitched across the back.

Ben pulled a bottled water out of an open cooler, sat down at one of the picnic tables and gazed out at the bay. Oh, what he would give to be out there right now, dropping a mullet or a pinfish over the side of the boat, to see if he could snag himself a tarpon. Instead, he was reeling in a shark, a hedge fund manager that was chumming with some of the biggest carnivores on the planet.

Tony Trance motioned for everyone to gather around Ben at the table, while Murray hefted a black briefcase onto its surface. Gumbo walked up beside Murray, pulled an apple out of his suit coat pocket and began to polish it on his sleeve. He took a bite, then waved over toward the house. Millie and Sophie emerged from the back door. They were dressed in normal pant suits. Must not be "working" today, thought Ben.

A man Mabel hadn't met followed the ladies out of the house. He looked to be about seventy, with the confident air of a man in control of his life. Beside him came a woman of similar age. She crooked her arm inside his elbow and they walked toward the group.

"Ah," said Tony, as the couple approached. He motioned toward Mabel, then toward the newcomers. "Mabel Witherspoon, meet Wendell and Gertrude Holmbs."

Mabel's eyes widened when she looked at Wendell. "I know you. You're the SOSCADA guy, the head dude. I've seen you on TV."

"I'm just the figurehead, Mabel. The front man. Tony runs the show; have no doubt about that."

Wendell smiled and offered his hand. Mabel shook it; then they all sat down.

"C'mon everybody," said Tony, impatiently. "Let's get started."

"You in some kind of hurry, Tony?" said Gumbo.

Tony smiled and shrugged. "Pat informed me that she and I are taking baby Jack to the beach this afternoon."

Gumbo laughed. "Teach you to have a child at your age. You going to take a nap first? Maybe soak your feet or your teeth before you go?"

"Yeah, yeah. Unlike you, Gumbo—"

"Doctor."

Tony smiled. "—I still *have* my original teeth."

"That's why they're not as white as mine. If you had new ones, particularly the super deluxe model, they'd be whiter than your old things."

Gumbo looked at Mabel and smiled. She almost had to turn away, Gumbo's teeth were so bright.

She said, "Wow, Gumbo. Your teeth are like lasers. What'd you do to get them so white?"

"Like I said, they're the super deluxe model."

"I don't follow."

"You get what you pay for, Mabel. I ordered the top of the line—"

"He used to *have* no teeth," interrupted Millie. "That's why we call him Gumbo, 'cause all he had was a set of pink gums."

"Yeah," said Gumbo. "Then Tony needed me to go undercover, to take down Cesar. I had to get a set of teeth, to fit in with my image."

"You look like a pimp, Gumbo."

"Please…Doctor."

"But you're not a pimp? Are you?" They'd been through this before. But he seemed so...so *real*. Mabel just had to be sure.

"Course not. Everybody thinks I am, at least out on the streets."

Mabel looked over at Ben. She'd always been a little unique. But this bunch…Gumbo, he took the cake. "You work the *streets*?"

"I thought you knew? I work the streets with my girls." Gumbo motioned toward Millie and Sophie. "I've got others. A few dozen of the hottest babes in Miami. Guys from SOSCADA, mostly from The Final Rest, come by and pretend to be their Johns. This gives us street creds, credibility. That way we can find out things, like who is dealing what, who's new and moving up the ranks of the drug trade."

"Isn't that dangerous?"

Gumbo smiled. The sun reflected off his piano-key teeth and Mabel had to shield her eyes.

Gumbo said, "Sure. That's why we study karate, in case we get rolled." Gumbo motioned toward the back lawn, where over a hundred Vigilantes were going through karate katas. "We have classes all day. Trains the body *and* the mind."

"But you're…old."

"We are?"

Mabel rolled her eyes. "You actually fight?"

"Only when we have to, Mabel. That's not often, not anymore. Now that we've got our reputation as a bunch of freaks. Only rookies have to be put in place now."

Tony Trance walked up beside Gumbo and put a hand on his shoulder. "That's enough, Doctor. She gets the point."

Tony moved to the head of the table and nodded toward Murray. "Murray's tasked a team to look into Cantwell's involvement in the drug trade." He pointed in the direction of Gumbo and his ladies. "Gumbo's had the others asking around, to find out who's got product, and who's looking to expand. They've prepared reports."

Tony sat down and said, "You first, Murray."

Murray Stein reached into his bag and removed a thick stack of brown manila folders. He lifted the top folder off the stack, then pulled out a pile of papers. He broke the papers into two parts and handed them to either side of the table. "Take one and pass it along."

The paper was a graphic hierarchy chart. It started with three names on the top. Beside the names there were printed small thumbnail photos. Below the top three names, there were two more, Cantwell and Masco. Below these, a dozen others were listed. A few of them were well known in Miami social circles. All were dangerous.

When each person had taken a chart, Murray said, "This is what we are looking at, guys."

Mabel squinted at her chart, but she couldn't see much more than fuzzy photos and squiggly lines of text. She thought to pull out her 4x, but vanity ruled and she didn't. She had ears. That was enough.

Murray continued. "The U.S. drug trade is as large as any single American industry—health care, electronics, or food production. And it is the most profitable. We are talking hundreds of billions in annual revenues and tens of billions, if not hundreds of billions, in profits. Left unchecked, drugs could poison our nation irreparably. Already, they cost over $500 billion in lost productivity, every year. We spend tens of billions annually, in this country alone, just to fight them.

"Since SOSCADA began, cocaine use among America's workers has declined by 38%. Cocaine and marijuana use among teens is also down significantly.

"While the fight is hard, we *are* making a difference. The problem is that we can never rest. Sources tell us that there is a major initiative going on to dramatically increase drug supplies in the southeast, particularly here in Florida. This push is being led by three men."

Murray looked at Mabel. "As you may or may not know, the great majority of this country's cocaine comes from Columbia. Much of this enters into Florida by sea.

"In recent years, the Columbians have partnered with a couple Mexican cartels, who haul the product over our southern borders by land, often using human mules." Murray pointed at one of the top photos.

"This is Raul Santiago. Santiago controls the majority of the cocaine production in Columbia. Probably the most powerful drug dealer on earth." Murray pointed to the picture next to Santiago. "This is Fausto Diaz. He heads the largest Mexican cartel. Two years ago, Diaz began buying product from Santiago and moving it over the U.S. border.

"These two men, alone, are responsible for more than half of the cocaine that poisons this country."

Murray paused and took a sip of water from his plastic bottle. He wet his lips with his tongue. Then he pulled off his glasses and cleaned them with the tail of his shirt. He put his glasses back on, took another sip of water and continued.

"This third guy…" he said, pointing to the last photo on top. "…is the worst of the bunch. This is Abbas Mohammad Daud Khan, from Afghanistan.

"The Afghans have been producing close to ninety percent of the world's heroin. Supported by the Taliban, and ignored by his nation's government, Khan has become Afghanistan's leading producer and distributor. If America ever hopes to stem the growing tide of U.S. heroin use, Khan is the man to stop."

"What about Cantwell?" said Mabel. "Looks like he's smack dab in the middle of these creeps."

Murray looked over at Tony. Tony gave him a slight dip of the head, as if to say it was all right to continue.

"I was just getting to that," Murray said. "Until you came to us, Mabel, we were not fully aware of the extent that Cantwell and Masco had penetrated the trade. We knew about Masco, dating back to when he used to work for Gomez. We knew that Cantwell had banked other dealers in the past. But we let both men fall under our radar."

Murray's cheeks began to splotch into a patchwork of red and pink and white. A pained look came over his face. He looked almost ready to cry.

"That was my screw-up," Murray said. "In recent years, Masco has been careful to keep a low profile. He has been using go-betweens, all meetings at night in the anonymity of Miami Gardens. While we suspected that he and Cantwell provided liquidity to the markets, we always thought it was in the way of loans, not as a direct investment. Now we see that Masco's become one of the biggest wholesalers in the southeast.

"Over the past few months, we've heard rumors of a huge influx of cash and drugs coming into town. We thought it was just because of the

Super Bowl. Now we know that it's something more. It's an escalation. We're talking billions here.

"Wholesale prices have risen during the past year, significantly. Masco's big purchase should lower them a little, but not much…We've seen $50,000 per kilo for cocaine in America, far more in Europe. This means big profits for those with the financial resources to cover the carrying costs…Men like Santiago or Khan don't floor plan their product. There's no financing; it's cash on the barrelhead.

"For the past few weeks, we've had people tracking Cantwell and Masco. Cantwell seems oblivious, but Masco has been meeting with all sorts of unsavory characters."

Murray held up a sheet of paper with the chart. "As you know, Masco met with Santiago this week. We have reason to believe that he will be meeting with Khan shortly, perhaps Diaz, too."

"What about the guys down below?" said Mabel "The guys on the bottom part of the chart?"

"Those are major distributors, Mabel. The typical wholesaler makes a major buy. He takes possession of the raw product, like heroin paste. He might break it up and sell it, as is, to the biggest dealers. Or, he could refine it and cut it, then sell it at a greater markup. The more of the downstream a dealer controls, the more he makes and the more he risks. Until recently, we thought that Cantwell and Masco simply banked major purchases. Now, we see they do more.

"We have been monitoring Masco's telephone conversations, thanks to the bugs you and Ben placed in his home. He has spoken with each of the players profiled below. Nothing meaningful is said on the phone, other than to arrange a meeting. Our friend is careful. He has also been a very busy man. He has over a dozen meetings scheduled in the next two weeks."

Mabel frowned. This wasn't what she intended when she'd hired Ben. She had hired Ben to protect her, and to see that she got her money, maybe a little justice. Now she had put herself into the middle of a major drug ring, maybe a war. It wouldn't be long before the Feds came knocking on *her* door, asking how she was involved. Heck, they might think that she was involved with Masco. After all, she was an investor. Then, of course, there was the breaking and entering, the illegal wiretaps and computer surveillance. Somewhere along the line, she had become a criminal. Now, *she* was doing things that were against the law. Where was that line? she wondered. When was it right to break the law? Was it ever right at all?

"I've got to go pee," Mabel said.

"Me, too," said Gumbo. He motioned toward the house. "You go first. Second door on your left. I'm right behind you."

Chapter Twenty-Three
V

Ben and Mabel were sitting contentedly on Ben's balcony. It was an intensely sunny day, so Ben had unfurled a canvas overhang to give them shade. It was still cool, but comfortable.

Ben unfolded Wednesday's copy of the "Shiny Sheet," The Palm Beach Daily News. He glanced at the cover briefly, then did a double-take. Shannon Donnelly was profiling the gala events of the New Year, and one of them drew Ben's attention like a spotlight.

Rial Cantwell and Louis Masco were hosting a fundraiser at the private Mar-a-Lago Club. The cause was breast cancer. Worthy, but nothing unusual, and not enough to draw a cover article in the Daily News. Ben had heard Cantwell and Masco speak about the benefit on several occasions. Cantwell was a member at Mar-a-Lago, and he was often traveling to the nearby Trump International for a round of golf. Sometimes he'd play with Trump, but more often with investors or their representatives.

When the two men had discussed the fundraiser, it hadn't seemed like anything more than a little get-together with friends, something to make them look good, a chance to rub some shoulders and have a cocktail party with shrimp and mini dogs, maybe host a silent auction and have too much to drink. But, at $50,000 a plate, this was a *major* event, even by Palm Beach standards.

Both of Florida's U.S. senators were scheduled to attend. There was a rumor that the president would join them, on his way to a South American business summit in Rio. Business leaders and royalty from around the world would be descending upon Trump's sprawling jewel on this exclusive island.

"This looks like something worth attending," Ben said to Mabel. He tried to hand her the paper, but Mabel kept her eyes fixed on a group of sailboats that were staging a regatta offshore. Ben placed the paper on the small table between them, next to his Corona beer, and followed her gaze.

"Just a minute," Mabel said. She watched until the final sailboat rounded a race buoy, less than half a mile away. The boat's crew ran a sail up the main mast. An orange and white spinnaker caught the wind and puffed out majestically like a giant robin's breast. The sail pulled hard on the boat, making it leap forward, as if sprinting to catch up with the ones ahead.

"I love it when they turn downwind," said Mabel. "They look so powerful and graceful and beautiful."

Ben watched the sailboats with mild distain. He was a power guy, a fishing guy. Sailboats just got in the way. Still, they did have a simplistic beauty, and an almost cleansing purity. He could almost feel them refresh his spirit, like fire and rain.

"They are beautiful," Ben said. *Like you*, he thought, but didn't say.

Mabel said, "Sometimes I think of just sailing away, of going to a place where life is simple. I think about having days where I don't have to look around all the time, or hold my breath before I open the door to my house. I think about walking down the street and not feeling eyes upon my back."

Oh, Mabel, thought Ben. *Life isn't simple; it never really was. And it certainly never will be again.* "We're going to deal with Masco and Cantwell, Mabel. Just wait and see."

Mabel's lips stretched into a thin tight smile. "Sure." She motioned for the paper. "Give me the Shiny Sheet, Ben."

Mabel read the article about Cantwell's fundraiser. It was one of the "can't miss" events of the year. Everyone that mattered in Palm Beach was expected to attend, as were the anointed from across the country and overseas. The entertainment alone would cost Cantwell millions—Carrie Underwood, Michael Bublé and Elton John. Cantwell was donating the entertainment, which could be enjoyed for a mere fifty grand a head.

"Looks like we're going to a party," Mabel said.

"A bit expensive, even for you, isn't it?"

Mabel shrugged. "I've got a over ten thousand acres of land up north, Ben. Lots of it is waterfront. You know what that's worth today? More than I care to admit. I lease some of it to the university, at a fraction of the market value. I rent more to local growers, for just enough to pay the taxes. If I needed a hundred grand for you and me to support breast cancer research and shake some feathers, all I need do is make a couple calls. But I don't need to. I've got the cash."

Mabel took a sip of her beer. "That reminds me…we've never discussed your fee."

Ben grabbed hold of his Corona. He stared out over the water with a wry, crooked smile pinching the edges of his lips. "I was wondering if we'd ever get around to that."

"How much you want?"

"What am I worth to you?"

"Don't know yet. Haven't taken you out for a test drive." Mabel's voice was low and deliberately sexy.

"Way too much body rot on this old clunker for a test drive, Mabel."

Mabel laughed. She took a gulp of beer and stared out at the boats.

"How does it happen, Ben? One day you're in the prime of your life, and the next…Where does the time go?"

"It's like sand running through your fingers."

"More like water." Mabel rose from her chair. Her left knee popped loudly and she groaned. "That was my good knee, Ben."

"One you were actually born with?"

"Got all my original parts. You?"

"Almost. Just one titanium hip."

"It's my plumbing I'd like to replace."

"Your plumbing's just fine, Mabel."

"Except for the leaky faucet."

Ben shrugged. "Wouldn't let it bother you, dear. Every guy's got a leaky faucet. You take a wiz in a toilet, and no matter what you do, you're going to drip into your drawers. You can dap it, shake it, even whack it and it's still going to leak."

"Really?"

"Archie never told you?"

"Hell, no. Just thought he was careless. That wasn't the kind of thing that Archie would have talked about. He was an old Yankee, Ben, all the way. I was lucky he ever saw me dance. He'd been dragged out by a bunch of his buddies. Not that our show was anything close to risqué."

Mabel took another sip of beer. She burped politely, then sighed. "After we retired, he came to the dance shows as a favor to me. It was all about seeing me happy." Mabel paused. She looked out at the water, then swiped at tears that were rolling down her cheeks. When she spoke again, there was a little *croak* in her voice.

"When Buddy told me how Archie had raved about Jiggles, I knew what he was doing. Archie was reaching out, you see, even after he was gone. He wanted me to have something fun, something to keep me going. He knew I would never do it on my own. But, for Buddy? I'd do anything for Buddy.

"Archie knew that our grandson would play the game, and that I would play right along. One day I would 'discover' that Jiggles was a gentleman's club. I would show the appropriate outrage. Then I would swoop in like a mother hen for those girls. It would be like having a whole new family."

"Why don't you just sell some of the land? Use that to buy the club?"

Mabel dipped her head. Ben could see more tears begin to well in her eyes. He looked away, back out to the water, to give Mabel her privacy. After a long while, she spoke again. "I could never sell anything that Archie owned."

"Loved him that much?"

"Not a day goes by that I don't ache."

"Excuse me for saying this, but you once implied that you and Archie didn't have sex during the last five years of your marriage."

Mabel grinned. "That was the diabetes, not Archie. Archie would have…well…you know…"

"Ahhh."

Ben and Mabel fell silent. They finished their beers, and then one more each. They watched as the water turned from emerald green to dark blue to black, while the sun behind them faded into night.

Finally, Ben said, "Pizza or Chinese?"

"Italian, I think. You have an Olive Garden nearby? I think it's an all-you-can-eat salad kind of night…Or, maybe a Denny's Grand Slam. You choose."

Chapter Twenty-Four
V
____

Mar-a-Lago was the creation of Marjorie Merriweather Post. She was Mrs. E.F. Hutton at the time, wife to one of the nation's richest investment advisors. The property's 114 rooms stretched from the Atlantic Ocean to Lake Worth, hence the name, Ocean to Lake.

The mansion was built with an extravagance that would be impractical to recreate today, a living testament to the last gasps of the roaring twenties. Mar-a-Lago's twenty thousand square foot ballroom was monstrous, even by Palm Beach standards, with a Louis XIV gold and crystal finish that seemed almost too opulent, even for men like Trump and Cantwell.

Tonight's five hundred guests had raised a generous sum for the Susan G. Komen Foundation. Nancy Brinker, founder of the organization, was stepping off a raised stage, gazing out at the substantial gathering of influence and wealth, after having thanked them for their support and generosity.

Rial Cantwell greeted Brinker with a hug and an air kiss, then bounded up onto the stage. He was wearing a white tuxedo with a pink bow tie and cummerbund. "Good evening," he boomed, with his James Earl Jones voice. "I know that you all have many charities to choose from…" Cantwell paused and looked out to the grouping of familiar faces, many of them clients. "…I know that a number of you have your own foundations, which absorb your time and resources. I would like to thank you all for sharing your evening with us, and for opening your wallets for this event.

"We have over five hundred guests here tonight. I am happy to report that this has raised more than twenty-five million dollars for the important mission of breast cancer awareness and treatment."

Cantwell pulled a checkbook out of the breast pocket of his tux. "Lou and I are making a donation of our own, in the amount of twenty-five million dollars." He looked up and grinned. "I hope the rest of you brought your wallets, because I am going to challenge each and every one of you to give what you can to this great cause." Cantwell ripped out a check, held it aloft, and said, "Ambassador Brinker, this is for you and your fine organization. Your sister would be so proud. Please come back up here and accept my profound thanks for the work you do."

Cantwell's guests broke into spontaneous applause. Some of them reached for their own checkbooks, most feeling generous, others not wanting to be outdone by this newcomer, Cantwell. They began holding checks aloft, as if waiting for them to be plucked out of the sky by a passing bird. The PR cameras clicked away. Cantwell put an arm around Brinker and flashed a toothy smile.

Cantwell said, "Nancy, I see that we have some other admirers in our midst."

Nancy Brinker began walking among the guests, accepting the checks. "Thank you…Thank you…Thank you," she said. "My sister would be so humbled, as am I."

"All right," boomed Cantwell. "It is now time for dinner. After which, we will have our silent auction.

"I am pleased to announce that one of our unique items is an invitation for two, to my private box for the upcoming Super Bowl. Through negotiations with NFL Charities, this package includes a meet and greet with your choice of Super Bowl quarterbacks. You'll meet during the Pro Bowl, the week before the game. You will also have a five minute visit with the *winning* quarterback, just moments after the Super Bowl."

After dinner, Cantwell and Masco moved to a quiet corner of the ballroom. A receiving line of guests gathered before them, investors looking for tips, others simply wishing to rub shoulders with greatness.

Ben and Mabel slipped into the line and waited for their chance to meet face-to-face with the two killer crooks. After twenty minutes, Mabel and Ben reached the on deck circle, just one guest away from gaining Cantwell's undivided attention.

As she and Ben stood there, Mabel began to study their reflection in a large mirror across the room. Mabel was wearing a blue evening dress, created for her by a designer friend of Pat Trance. It featured her own trademark butterflies, blue and yellow ones, which had been dyed into the custom fabric. Ben stood at her shoulder, wearing a white tuxedo that was eerily similar to the one worn by Cantwell. No cummerbund, a vest instead. He, too, wore a pink bow tie.

Cantwell caught Mabel and Ben in the corner of his eye and froze. He glanced over at Masco, who nodded that he had seen the pair.

"Well, isn't this a surprise," Cantwell said, when Mabel drew to the head of the line.

"Wouldn't want to miss the first major social event of the year, would we?" said Mabel sweetly.

"Didn't know this was your thing."

"You don't think that the $5.4 million you're keeping from me is all I've got now, do you?"

Cantwell's face grew wary. He glanced around the room, his eyes absorbing everything in a few short seconds. Ben was the next person in line, but he didn't matter. He was also the last in line, and that *did* matter. No one had overheard Mabel's taunt.

Cantwell lowered his deep voice and said, "I don't *keep* client money, Mrs. Witherspoon. I *invest* it."

"What about killing, then?"

Cantwell's face paled white, as if Mabel had sprayed him with decorative Christmas snow paint. All he needed was a couple of pine cones and his head could pass as a Christmas ornament.

"Killing?" Cantwell whispered.

"Sure," said Ben, stepping in front of Mabel. "Just give a listen."

Ben Johnson pulled a pair of white ear plugs out of his tuxedo pocket and placed them into Cantwell's palm. "Really. Give a listen."

Cantwell placed the plugs into his ears, while Ben pulled an iPhone out of his tux. Ben plugged the earphone jack into his iPhone and fingered it to play.

Cantwell heard, "But this drug thing…I don't like it. People do get hurt with drugs."

"Didn't seem to bother you seventeen years ago, Rial. Back when you were sucking wind and about to go belly up. Who saved you then? Who saved your ass then? I'll tell you who. *I* did."

Cantwell let out a deep sigh. "I know."

"You've earned *five* billion and siphoned off twenty. The other five is from *me*. I've earned us another five *billion* dollars. Shouldn't I get some respect for that? You and I, we've actually *earned* the same amount of money."

"It's not the same," said Cantwell.

"Fuck you, it's not the same. Money is money."

"Is it? I'm not sure it is. I'll give you this, though. You've earned five billion. I've earned five billion in fees and profit splits, above expenses. That was *before* taxes, just three billion after taxes. I've siphoned ten. The other thirteen we've earned *together*, by investing. We're partners. You know that."

Masco snorted. "Don't go getting all soft on me, Cantwell. Not when it's been *you* that's wanted fifty billion. I said I'd be happy with thirty. But nooo...*You* said we needed more."

"I've changed my mind. I say we shut it down. We shut down the drug deals. We shut down the siphoning. From now on, we play it straight."

"After nearly two decades, you want to play it straight?"

"Yeah. Stop the drug buy."

Masco laughed out loud.

There was a long pause, before Cantwell said, "Are you using, Lou? Is that it? Are you taking the drugs you sell?"

Masco guffawed. "You have no fucking clue, do you? You sit up here in your fucking Ivory Tower, peering at your fucking charts, schmoozing you're your fucking clients, traveling the fucking world, while I do all the hard work.

"I'm the one that cleans up your mess. I'm the one who has to test the product—"

"We don't need drugs!" yelled Cantwell.

"That's easy for you to say."

Cantwell ripped the plugs out of his ears and whispered, "How dare you?"

"Excuse me?" said Mabel. "How dare *I*?"

"You're going down for this."

Mabel shook her head. "No, Cantwell. *You're* going down for this."

Cantwell began to laugh. "Mabel…Mabel…Mabel…you are one naïve little bitch."

"What's going on, Rial?" said Masco.

Cantwell handed the ear phones to Masco. He looked at Ben and said, "Play it."

As Masco listened to the recording his face grew progressively red. Soon, it began to look like a huge cranberry, not perfectly shaped or evenly colored, just a mass of round mottled red with a pulpy nose. He looked at Mabel. "I didn't know you had a death wish."

"You mean like Taylor? Or Jameson? Or Vermeer? You planning the same fate for me, Lou?"

"You have no idea what I can do...What I will do."

Ben looked quickly around, to see that no one was listening. He leaned between Cantwell and Masco. "Here's the deal, guys. We're going to pretend that these recordings never existed. You're going to return the money you stole from investors, along with all their investment gains. You can keep the drug money, but no more dealing. Then you close up shop and ride into the sunset."

"We can't do that," said Masco.

"That's the deal. Otherwise, we go after you for everything."

Cantwell said, "We can, Lou—"

Masco said, "We can't Rial! We can't stop. You know that. We're in too fucking deep. We've made commitments."

Ben said, "Take it to the Feds. They'll clear things up."

Masco laughed. "If I take this to the Feds, it's *you two* who go to jail."

Mabel said, "I think not."

Masco scowled. "What do you mean, 'you think not'? Who the fuck do you think you are?" He laughed again. This time it ended with a high pitched raspy whine, almost like the howl of a wolf. "You've got no power over the Feds, Witherspoon. *We* do. And don't forget…We didn't illegally tap other people's offices. *You* did that. You broke the law. No, I think it will be *you* spending time in jail, not me, not Rial." Masco paused. A smile spread slowly across his face. "Yeah. Why don't you go and take these recordings to the Feds and see what they say—"

Cantwell pleaded, "Lou—"

"Shut up, Rial!"

Several heads turned in their direction. Masco saw them and immediately began an exaggerated laugh, slapping Cantwell on the shoulder. "Shut…up. That's just too funny!"

The guests drifted back to their conversations.

"I was thinking more like YouTube," said Mabel.

Masco's face blanched, his cheeks draining color until he looked as pale as a hard-boiled egg. "Do that and you're dead."

Ben cheerfully said, "Looks like we've got a Mexican standoff, boys and girls."

Masco muttered, "Provided you get out of here alive." Masco's chest heaved slowly. His hands clenched and unclenched, his knuckles turning white, then red with the pulsating movement of his fingers. He stared at Ben, then at Mabel. His eyes were wide and wild. They reminded Mabel of the eyes of a horse, just before it was put to sleep. There was an awareness there, an awareness that something bad was lurking just around the corner, maybe that death was calling out his name from that bright white place in the great beyond. This was a fight, a cage match. This was a battle to the death; they all sensed it.

Ben smiled. He took Mabel by the elbow and began to lead her away. "The night is still young, fellas. I think it's time for us to go socialize, maybe check out the silent auction. We'll hang around to see if you want to change your minds."

Ben looked at Cantwell. His eyes were hard and focused. After a few moments, his lids narrowed to accusing slits. "If we die, this goes everywhere. We will not be intimidated by your threats."

"Yeah," said Mabel. "Besides. We paid a hundred grand to be here, so we're sure as hell going to get our money's worth. Maybe I should go pinch Bublé's ass."

Chapter Twenty-Five
V

A valet stepped out of Ben's Jaguar, while another opened the side door for Mabel to get inside.

"Nice ride," the driver valet said.

"Thanks," said Ben, as he placed a twenty dollar bill into the man's discretely outstretched hand. "You know your cars."

A valet at Mar-a-Lago must drive every rare and expensive car known to mankind. While Ben's half-century-old XKE might retail for a fraction of a Bentley, Ferrari, or a Rolls, there was a rare elegance and purity in its design, one that had been lost in most cars over the years.

"One of the finest rides ever made," the valet replied.

Ben smiled and handed the valet another twenty dollars.

"You're a sucker for praise," mumbled Mabel, as she sat inside.

Ben nodded; she was right. As he drove away from the old estate, Ben took one last gaze at the opulent structure. The place had been built at a time when wealth wasn't just owned, it was displayed like a military medal. Marjorie Post never could have foreseen the economic carnage that was lurking just around the decade's corner. Life was simple for the rich. It was the Roaring Twenties. Wealth was forever. It just had to be spread like fertilizer, at parties in places like this. Here, it would sprout new opportunities, growing from quiet conversations made amidst billows of cigar smoke.

The Great Depression had put an end to all that. Life had changed. The world had changed.

Tonight, the conversations had not taken place in smoke filled rooms. Men had not huddled on one side of the parlor, while women clung to the other, prancing around in bright, low-cut dresses like peacocks trying to please the men. This time, an aging woman with a weak leg and bladder had attacked one of the nation's richest men like a fearless Doberman. Mabel Witherspoon had pressed her face so close against Cantwell's that she could smell the shrimp on his breath. She had delivered her message, not like a peacock, but with all the ferocity and temerity of a wolverine.

The problem was, Cantwell and Masco weren't petty criminals being run down after robbing the local bank. Cantwell was one of the biggest names in world finance. He could buy Mar-a-Lago with his pocket change. That wasn't what made him dangerous, though. Cantwell and Masco killed without conscience. They had endless resources. They could summon an army against them. They were men who wouldn't blink an eye if Ben and Mabel vanished forever.

As they pulled onto South Ocean Blvd, Ben said, "What the hell were you thinking?"

Mabel said, "What do you mean, what was I thinking?"

"You know what I mean."

"No, I don't."

"Yes, you do."

"Don't"

"Do."

"Don't."

"Aw, c'mon, Mabel. You knew the plan."

"The plan was to confront Cantwell and we did."

"The plan was for *me* to confront Cantwell. Not you. Now you've put a big red bull's-eye on your forehead. You're paying *me* to be the target. You're paying *me* to take the heat and get your money."

"I haven't paid you a dime."

"You know what I mean."

"It's not about the money, Ben. It's about what's *right*."

Ben drove along Southern Blvd., out across the water toward the mainland. They had to stop because the bridge was open. Probably some billionaire heading out for a midnight sail, thought Ben. He glanced in his rearview mirror, hoping Cantwell hadn't sent someone after them, perhaps to kill them. How had he allowed himself to be caught up in this? This was insane.

"Nothing in this world is ever completely right, Mabel. Everything is a compromise. There is bad in everything good, avarice in all profit. There is self-congratulations in all charity."

"I hired a detective, not a philosopher."

"Yeah, well you hired *me*."

Mabel smiled. She looked out across the water. Lights were sparkling like fireflies on the shimmering Lake Worth. The air was cool and clean, with a hint of barbecue floating in the breeze. "I think this is going quite well, Ben."

"Going well? You think this is going well? You just challenged two ruthless killers to a pissing match. And you think this is going well?"

"I did no such thing. You know I can't pee, at least not far."

"Then you'd better learn."

"I didn't play the recording, Ben. You did that."

Ben sighed. "I was supposed to do that when you weren't standing next to me. The plan was to protect you from all this. *I* was going to tell them that *you* had no idea what was going on. I was trying to draw them away from you. But you had to stick your little nose right into the middle of everything."

Mabel grinned. "Kinda fun, isn't it?"

"Fun? It's suicide!"

"What's life without a little risk?"

"Longer."

Mabel looked out over the water. It made her think back to a time when Archie was still alive.

Mabel and Archie were at North Jetty Park, on the southern end of Casey Key Road in Nokomis, Florida. It was a blistering summer day. The sun was just beginning to sink down into the ocean. A thin layer of clouds was hovering out over the water, turning a spectacular purple and gold as the sun dropped slowly into the sea. They were sitting on folding chairs, having come to the west coast of Florida to do this very thing.

"I'm not going to live much longer, babe," Archie said.

"Nonsense," said Mabel. "You're going to outlive me by a decade."

Archie's hair had turned completely white. His original six-foot height had shrunken by inches, as if a vacuum cleaner had sucked his skin and bones back inside him. His once-muscular frame had now dwindled to skeletal remains, covered by a wrinkled patina of skin. His face was just a hollow carving, the remnants of what had once been the picture of rugged vibrancy, the face of a man who had spent his life in the elements, soaking in the sun and the rain like a growing tree. Now, only the outer bark remained, a crumbling shell of something that had once been as solid as young oak.

"My ticker is slowing down, Mabes. Like an old clock with no one to wind it. I've got renal failure that no amount of dialysis will fix. It is time for me to say goodbye.

"I feel blessed to have been married to you. Old farmers like me don't usually get the chance to marry a woman that can turn heads like you did, like you still do. Why you agreed to leave the glamour of Las Vegas for a life growing corn and setting teat cups is far beyond me."

Mabel felt tears rise into her eyes. How could she tell her husband that it had been no sacrifice? Leaving Las Vegas had been an easy choice. She had never liked it there, except for the dancing. That, she had loved. Leaving the dancing? Well, that had been something different, hadn't it? That had been like cutting off a piece of her body, cremating it and spreading the ashes out over the dirt, never to have it back again. But that had been her choice. *Her* choice. She had made it freely and she had never looked back. Not really.

"I love you, Archie. Always have. Always will."

"You sacrificed it all for me."

"I sacrificed nothing."

Archie smiled. He looked at Mabel with eyes that made her feel warm. She slumped deep into her chair and stared out at the ocean. The sun was barely a crescent now, dipping into the calm sea. A cooling breeze began to drift in off the water.

Archie said, "You should start dancing again. There was this light in your eyes when you danced…something I haven't seen in a long, long time."

"I can't dance anymore. My knees creak."

"You're never too old to dance, sweetheart."

"Oh, Archie." Mabel reached over and stroked her husband's white hair. It was so thin that it felt like air.

"Why don't you buy that club?" he said.

"What club?"

"If you can't dance, you can help the ladies who do."

"What are you talking about, Archie?"

Archie didn't answer. Mabel looked toward him. His head had slumped forward. His right hand had fallen down beside his chair, as if it had dripped off of him.

"Archie?"

Archie didn't move.

"Archie!" Mabel reached for her husband's hand. It was as limp and lifeless as cooked spaghetti. "Oh, Archie…" Mabel began to moan. She had spent half a century with this man, her husband. They had raised a child, then a grandchild, together. They had loved and laughed. They had fought like tomcats on occasion, but they had always made up. They were friends and lovers and soul mates. Now he was gone.

A sleek, two-masted sailboat passed slowly through the causeway. Then, finally, the bridge began to move. Mabel remained silent; she didn't feel like talking. She could almost see Archie hovering above her, as if he were guiding her, maybe even protecting her.

Ben continued on Southern Blvd. until they reached Interstate 95. They passed beneath the freeway, then turned left onto the long highway feeder ramp.

"Penny for your thoughts," Ben said.

Mabel smiled but said nothing, not for a long while. Ben remained silent. She must be in a hidden place, someplace dark, a room he could never enter unless she opened the door.

"I was thinking of Archie," said Mabel. "He was a good man. I loved him, you know."

Ben nodded. "I know."

Mabel raised herself up in her seat and allowed the wind to blow her hair into a wild frizzle. "Ahhh," she said, smiling pensively. "I loved my life with him. It was…pedestrian. Know what I mean?"

"Safe?"

Mabel thought for a moment. "Comforting. That's about as good as it gets. Life with Archie was like wearing an old pair of shoes. I miss him terribly."

"I love old shoes." Ben drove into the night, heading back toward Miami, saying nothing more.

Chapter Twenty-Six
V

Ben

I am at a loss today. I really don't know what to do. I've got enough conversations between Cantwell and Masco to send them away for a very long time, provided I can get the authorities to listen. I've got them discussing murder and fraud as casually as the weather. I've got them admitting to dealing drugs. I've also got tapes of politicians, lawmen and bankers helping them, although, I suspect that none of them know the full scope of their crimes. I've even got a recording of Florida's new governor discussing a bribe.

From the Windows logo chip I placed on Cantwell's computer, I now have access into his entire network. I've gone peeking in there at night. He's got enough firewalls inside to withstand a cyber army, with passwords everywhere. But I've got all that, now, thanks to Cantwell's keystrokes, as well as a few of my own.

I nearly freaked when Cantwell logged into his accounts in the Caymans. He's really got thirty-three billion dollars down there. He manages it like some Rain Man idiot savant. He played the tech boom to a T. He got out of the market near the top in 2008. Then he went short on margin. His account is up nearly 800% in the last nine years. I did the math and came up with a compound growth rate of 24% per year, compared to about zero for the overall market. I can see how he could siphon funds off investor accounts and still keep them happy. He's been on the run of a lifetime.

Now, if Cantwell would just fix things. All we asked was that he return the money he'd stolen. Heck, a couple billion of that would have been his anyway, from normal profit splits with investors. The thing is, he didn't *need* to steal the money.

I've always wondered what it is that makes successful people feel the need to bend the rules. I mean, how much is enough? Maybe it's some kind of hoarding instinct that some people have. Personally, I think it's an addiction to the thrill. Plain and simple. Like a retired athlete who has to gamble. Or an executive with an adulterous sex addiction. Or, like Tiger Woods on his rampage, a man who always needed to be on the edge.

Then there is Lou Masco and this drug thing. Sounds like he does have his head in a noose. He's been lending to wholesalers for nearly two decades. Now, he's decided to escalate, to become one of the biggest operators in the country. He's committed three billion dollars to men who will slit your throat as easily as pat you on the back. The problem is, they've taken his promise of more funds and used that to order enough cocaine and heroin to choke New York City. The cartels' growers have burned down new stretches of mountain and rain forest. They've imported fresh laborers to plant more crops and work the fields, all with the expectation of getting paid. If Masco doesn't deliver, he dies. This poses a unique problem for Mabel and me.

With Mabel breathing down their necks to stop dealing, to make good with investors and shut things down…With me standing behind her with evidence…With the drug dealers ready to kill Masco and Cantwell if they ever stop dealing…It appears that the only logical conclusion is for one side to give—for Masco and Cantwell to kill *us*. That isn't real high on my goal list.

So, in order to stay alive, we are going to have to fix things. And that…will be a challenge.

Chapter Twenty-Seven
V

Lou Masco pulled off I-95 onto the Dolphin Expressway. From the Dolphin, he took Biscayne south, until he reached Port Blvd. Here, he turned out into the industrial Port of Miami.

As he drove, Masco stared at the thousands of cars that passed by, every one of them filled with people, people who laughed and played and loved. They were also people who hated and cheated, and people who sucked his product as greedily as a hungry baby on a mother's breast.

He had always seen cars as "demand." The cars held the people that held the cash that bought the drugs that gave him the rush—that great *whoosh* of adrenaline that made everything else seem meaningless.

Masco didn't feel the rush today. Instead, he fought off a sickening dread. The pit of his stomach felt like it was filled with sour milk, drying and congealing into a slimy puddle of goo. He could almost smell the putrid stink, rising up into his nostrils on bony fingers that poked and prodded at him with malevolent glee.

He didn't want to make this trip. Not today; not ever again. Yet, here he was, crossing into the Port. He could see a line of cruise ships off to his left, stretching ahead like a string of small islands. Tens of thousands of people were resting inside, or were out sightseeing or preparing to board for exotic lands. They had no idea how much cocaine and heroin…how much death...lurked within a leisurely stroll of their bucolic floating towns.

Masco turned onto Australia Way and followed it along the southern edge of the port. He passed a string of warehouse buildings, stacked against each other like city row houses. They were all unremarkable, just piles of brick and stone and wood and glass. Ask anyone what they looked like and all you'd get would be a shrug. They might remember the noise, the bellow of horns, the *beep, beep, beep* of trucks, or the clanking of chains. But that was all. This was the anonymous, unre-markable world where the demons lay. The buildings looked like every-thing else on the outside—boring and benign. Yet, on the inside, they protected men like Abbas Mohammad Daud Khan and Fausto Diaz. Masco's meeting today was with Khan.

Masco carefully maneuvered his thirty-two foot, silver eighteen wheeler along the wide Port road. It was a Sunday and the traffic was light. Masco glanced into his rearview mirror to check for a tail. All he could see were two black H2s. He smiled. That was good. The Hum-mers held his bodyguards, and there was no one else behind them.

Masco reached his destination. It was a windowless, flat-roofed ware-house made with chipped brown bricks. He backed his semi-trailer down a small alley, then up against the skids of a loading platform, moving slowly until he hit the spring-loaded ramp and the truck shuddered to a stop. He closed his eyes. He was piloting a billion dollars of cash. A *bil-lion* dollars. Ten million bills. Twenty-two thousand pounds of paper to turn to poison gold. How many men would kill him for this? He shud-dered at the answer. Far too many.

Masco watched his posse stop beside him, twelve men armed with enough weaponry to assault a medieval castle. He remained in his semi, making sure there was no one else in sight. Masco's men sat in their Hummers, waiting for a signal.

Masco dialed his phone. It was answered quickly.

A voice said, "This is Henry."

"This is Lou. We clear?"

"All set, boss."

Masco waved his hand. His men jumped out of the cars at once. Half of them remained outside, crouching with their weapons at the ready. The others marched single-file into the warehouse.

"Clear!" someone yelled. This was followed by a chorus of other, "Clears!"

Satisfied, Masco walked inside. The inner warehouse was one large cavern. It smelled of stale diesel fuel and fresh mold. The floor was lit-tered with shreds of old newspaper, grease and sawdust. Thousands of white Styrofoam peanuts gave the surface a look of light snowfall. The walls were covered with grayed plasterboard. Pipes ran horizontally along one of the walls. Another was lined with peg boards. Most of the boards were empty, but a few held an assortment of tools. The ceiling was high. It was filled with a criss-cross of wires and metal beams. Some of the beams could be used to transport freight from the loading platform. Others provided simple support for the roof.

Masco's men fanned out around the inside, to their pre-determined places. Two of them climbed up into the rafters and took position as snipers.

A row of offices ran along the right side of the warehouse. Inside the first office, there was a grouping of video monitors. Henry sat before the screens, watching every inch of the building, both inside and out.

Henry had a face that looked like it had never seen the sun. His eyebrows were a bushy white, growing like unkempt weeds. His head was shaved, and glowed like a pale moon under the harsh florescent lighting. His skin was smooth and fleshy pink, like polished Italian marble, making Henry look almost cherubic.

As Masco peered into the office, Henry looked up from his screens and waved. "Hey, boss."

"How we look?"

Henry shrugged. "Nothing yet."

"We've still got half an hour. Tell me when they're here."

Masco walked farther into the warehouse. He stopped at the far corner office, unlocked the door and stepped inside. The room was furnished like any executive suite on Wall Street. There was a round conference table in one corner, with six Henry Miller chairs. There was a corner lounge area, with a couch and two upholstered chairs.

A flat-panel computer TV hung along one wall. The opposite wall held a series of three large salt-water fish tanks. Inside the tanks swam tropical fish of all sizes and colors—Powder Blue Tang, with wide blue bodies and bright yellow dorsal fins, False Percula Clowns, with vertical stripes of orange, white and black. There were various types of Annularis Angel fish, with brilliant striping showing all colors of the rainbow.

A cherry executive desk jutted out from the far wall, with a green banker's lamp on one side and one made with tall crystal on the other. Behind the desk was a red leather chair.

Masco let himself down into the chair and sighed. He felt deflated. He should have felt energized. He always did at this stage, trading cash for drugs. But today? Today, he felt his life slipping through his fingers, like fine, Sarasota sand. He closed his eyes and began to think. How could he end this?

"They're here," Henry said.

Masco opened his eyes. How long had he been sitting there, staring into the empty black holes of his mind? He looked at his watch. Half an hour. It had passed like a moment.

"Be right there," Masco said. "In three minutes, you let them inside."

Masco checked the Beretta nine millimeter that was nestled in his belt. He chambered a round and engaged the safety. He reached down to the Smith & Wesson twenty-five caliber backup that was snapped into an ankle holster. He made sure it was primed with the safety on.

Masco adjusted his sport coat so that the Beretta was out of sight. Not that it mattered; it was no secret that they would both be packing. Still, it was bad manners to display the heat.

Masco left his office and walked to the center of the warehouse. He stood there, hands at his side, waiting. After another minute, he heard the *click* of Henry releasing the lock to the warehouse door. One of his men swung it open and stood to the side, allowing Khan and his soldiers to step inside.

Khan was wearing a white kaftan robe which stretched nearly to the floor. The elaborate garment was intricately embroidered along the front and sleeves, befitting Khan's status as a leader among leaders. Beneath it, Khan wore sandals on bare feet.

Khan walked slowly toward Masco, looking up and around, while assessing the forces against him. Behind him came six men, the same number Masco had been allowed to bring inside. Khan's guards were carrying AK-47s, held out before them, ready to strike like vipers. Spare ammo magazines were strapped across their hips, clanking softly as they moved.

Khan stopped when he reached Masco. The two men stood there alone, face to face, like men preparing to duel. Khan wore a scowl, making no attempt at civility. He didn't offer to shake hands, nor did Masco.

"You have the money?" Khan said.

Masco replied, "You have the product?"

Both men nodded.

"You want to count it?" Masco said. *Good luck*, he thought, counting ten million bills.

"No…You want to test the heroin?"

Masco smiled. "No." How was he going to test two semi-trailers filled with horse?

"Good."

"Come," said Masco. He turned, then motioned with an arm for Khan to follow him to his office. "Leave your guards."

When they reached the office, Masco removed his pistols and laid them on the desk. Khan did the same with his weapons, a pistol and a dagger inside a jewel-covered scabbard. Masco took a seat in one of the upholstered chairs and motioned for Khan to do the same. Khan hesitated. Masco was pulling him out of his element. He preferred to stand, the position of confrontation, the position of control.

"Please sit," said Masco, with a friendly voice. "We are business partners."

Khan sat warily. He topped the FBI's Most Wanted List, so he rarely left the safety of the Afghan mountains. Only a billion dollars and the opportunity to destroy Americans had drawn him to Miami. He needed to look Masco in the eye before letting him take so much killer paste.

"Let's have a little chat," said Masco.

Khan said, "Chatting is for women. I have nothing to say." Khan stared at Masco. His eyes were narrowly set and as dark as black marbles. His left eye angled inward slightly, something Khan tried to hide by looking at Masco from the side. Khan had a three day growth of dark brown beard, and he smelled like he hadn't showered in days.

"You bring me two trailer loads of heroin. You take possession of a billion dollars in cash. And we have nothing to talk about?"

"What do you want me to say?"

"Oh, I don't know…Maybe, 'how've you been'?"

Khan laughed. His eyes drew into puffy slits. They reminded Masco of a lizard sitting in the sun, looking half asleep, but ready to strike in the blink of an eye. "I despise men like you," Khan said.

Masco curled his lower lip, but said nothing. He despised men like Khan. But that didn't keep him from being civil.

Khan continued, "You Americans…you think that you can bully your way around the world, spreading your filth and decay like confetti. You steal our oil. You pollute the air and the water. You poison the minds of our leaders. You corrupt our people with Brittany Spears and Madonna videos..."

"That's the price of freedom, Khan."

Khan spit onto Masco's shoes. "That's what I think of your freedom."

Masco slowly stood. He walked over to his desk, being sure to keep the weapons out of reach. He snapped a tissue out of a box on the corner and used it to wipe off his shoe.

"But you like my money," he said.

Khan scoffed. "You think this is about money?"

Of course it was about money, Masco thought. Why else would Khan risk being caught inside the American borders? Why else would he deal drugs in such large quantities?

"If it's not about money, Khan, what's the point?"

Khan stared at Masco.

Masco could feel the hatred in Khan's eyes. It was raw and red and unchecked. Then Masco knew; Khan wasn't lying. It wasn't about the money; it was about hate.

"This is war," whispered Khan. "And you help us wage it, against your own people."

Masco pondered Khan's words for a moment and shrugged. "I suppose you're right."

Masco sat down beside Khan. Neither man spoke for a long while. Finally, Masco said, "Why don't we call this off? You keep your drugs, I keep my cash."

"No."

"Really," said Masco. "You're right. I am waging war against my own people and I should stop—"

"I said, 'No!'"

With a movement too fast to see, Khan pulled a second dagger from beneath his robe. He climbed upon Masco and pressed the end of the blade against Masco's lower eyelid. Masco leaned back, but Khan moved along with him. He pressed the blade deeper into Masco's soft tissue, until a trickle of blood began to appear.

"You're crazy," whispered Masco.

Khan withdrew the knife for a moment. Then he thrust it forward again, this time placing the blade flat against Masco's tongue. He pressed down and slid it back, until the tip of the blade pushed up against Masco's uvula. Masco fought not to swallow. He tried to pull away, but Khan grabbed him by the shirt collar and held him fast.

"Let…me…go…" said Masco.

Khan loosened his grip on Masco's shirt and let him fall back into his chair. Masco felt his throat and began to massage it.

Khan said, "Like you said, we are partners." Khan reached over and patted Masco on the knee. "I think we will continue working well together, you and me. Don't you think?"

Chapter Twenty-Eight
V
____

Cantwell's powerful yacht cut through the water like a carving knife, slicing through the four foot waves like they were mere shaving cream foam. Cantwell and Masco sat upon the upper aft deck in lounge chairs, remaining silent as they rounded Bill Baggs Park, off the end of Key Biscayne. The sun rose behind them as they entered the bay, glowing unusually warm for late January. The air smelled faintly of flowers and salt, along with a hint of cigar smoke, from some other boat off in the distance.

Cantwell was sipping a Diet Coke through a straw, his drink in a tall clear glass, with a bright green wedge of lime. Masco was drinking the same, except that his had two shots of rum, despite the morning hour.

Cantwell ordered his crew to drop anchor in the middle of the bay. The surf was lighter there, and the boat barely rocked in the small swell. The yacht twisted slowly in the soft easterly breeze, until its bow pointed into the sun and the wind.

Cantwell shed his windbreaker and his sweat pants, down to a pair of Hawaiian swim shorts and a white T-shirt. He opened his arms and threw back his face to soak in the sun. Masco remained tightly wrapped in black khaki pants and a navy fleece jacket. He kept his arms crossed, and he seemed to be trembling.

"Why all the drama?" said Cantwell.

"What do you mean, drama?"

"Well, let me see…You tell me that we need to talk, but only on the boat, and miles away from Miami. I call that drama."

"Screw you."

Cantwell sat up. His face grew somber and he said, "I know you're under pressure."

Masco laughed. "Pressure? Is that what you call it? On one hand, we've got Mabel Fucking Witherspoon and her so-called financial planner with tapes of our conversations, threatening to expose us if we don't shut it down. On the other hand, we've got drug dealers who will *kill* us if we walk away."

Cantwell pulled on a pair of Oakley sunglasses and relaxed back into his chair. He said, softly, "They'll kill *you* if we pull out."

Masco sneered. "You think they don't know that we're joined at the hip? They may not have put a knife in your eye or down your throat. But when they did it to me, they did it to you, as sure as I'm sitting here."

Cantwell raised his chin to expose his neck to the sun. It was important to have an even tan; essential, in his line of work. He ran his fingers through his hair, making sure that every strand that had been disturbed by the wind had been put back into place. He closed his eyes and smiled. "You can deal with it, Lou. You always do."

"Not this time."

"Oh, c'mon," said Cantwell. "We've been in tougher spots. Remember that time with the pictures? What about that? And the time with the...the video recording?"

"Those were normal people, Rial, not ruthless killers."

"Are you calling Witherspoon a ruthless killer?"

"No, but Santiago and Khan? They kill for fun."

"Santiago and Khan aren't so bad. We'll find their price."

"You have no clue."

"Let's deal with Witherspoon and Johnson first. Maybe it *is* time to kill them."

"We can't kill them now, Rial. They've got evidence, evidence they say will be *released* if they are harmed."

"We'll shut it down, then."

"We can't shut it down."

Cantwell shifted his head to the side, so the sun would tan behind one of his ears. "Ah, Lou…Lou…Must you be so myopic?"

"How 'bout I put a blade down your throat and see how myopic you get? Huh? Let's see how far your eyes can see with death in your face."

Masco pulled a knife from inside his jacket pocket. Before Cantwell could scream for his bodyguards, Masco pressed the blade against his tongue. Masco kept the knife there for just a couple of seconds, before pulling it out and throwing the knife into the surf.

"Sorry," Masco said. "Just thought you should know how it feels."

Cantwell looked to his bathing suit. It now had a dark urine stain leaking across the fabric. He closed his eyes and fought the urge to faint. Sweat popped out across his upper lip and he began to shake, like an addict coming down. He breathed in deeply, then out through his nose. In…out…in…out. After a minute he said, "Do that again, I'll boil you in acid."

Masco laughed, "If I do that again, I won't stop."

The men sat in silence for several long moments.

Cantwell grabbed a towel and threw it over his lap. He didn't pay much attention to the sun anymore. His tan didn't seem quite as important now. An elderly woman and her tech-savvy financial planner were in the front of his mind. Something had to be done about them. Something that would keep their information from becoming public, something that would make this all go away.

Masco had a smug smile upon his face. He'd always been the one to do the dirty work, while his partner remained aloof, oblivious to what it really took to keep him in his exalted, holier-than-thou place. Now Cantwell knew. He knew what it was like to stare death in the face, what it was like to feel his bladder go to jelly, what it felt like to be *scared*.

"It's not fun, is it, Rial? Makes you feel unclean. Maybe now you know what I do for you, what I've been doing for all these years."

"Thank you," said Cantwell. His voice was soft, barely a whisper. "I never knew."

"Well, now you know."

"I do. We're going to figure out a way to fix this. We have to."

Chapter Twenty-Nine
V

___

Ben

It wasn't hard for us to follow Cantwell out of the marina. He and Masco took great care when leaving their homes or the office, making sure they weren't followed. But they didn't look twice when taking their boats out for a spin. It was as if they thought of the water as sacred ground, where pursuers wouldn't tread. My forty-eight footer was like a little gnat tailing behind the gargantuan bulk of Cantwell's craft. We edged out of my slip unseen, just after Cantwell ordered his crew to leave the yard.

We followed Cantwell into the Atlantic, around Fisher Island and south past Virginia Key. There was a good chop today, the remnants of a storm that was now off the Georgia coast and threatening New England with snow. The sun was beginning to rise nicely, and it looked like it was going to be a fine winter day.

Mabel sat beside me. She was wearing jeans today. She had them tucked into a pair of black Cowboy boots with chrome rings along the outside ankles. Her top was a powder blue sweater with pink and yellow butterflies fluttering across the chest. Her hair was pulled into a ponytail, and held tight beneath a black cowboy Stetson, which she had cinched beneath her chin to keep it from flying away in the wind.

Cantwell's ship turned into Biscayne Bay and the surf mellowed to a gentle roll. A mile inside the bay, the *HEDGEMONEY* dropped anchor and pointed into the wind.

"Whatcha want to do?" said Mabel.

I said, "When the water's warmer, there's some pretty good snook and tarpon fishing along here. I brought along a few pinfish to use as bait, just in case we wanted to search for a straggler. I've also got some killer plugs, if you're up for a little more work."

"Ahhh," Mabel said, smiling. "I see why you wanted to trail Cantwell today. I've been keeping you from your fishing. You had to have a fix."

In a way, she was right. I was used to fishing twenty times a month. But with this Cantwell thing, I hadn't held a rod in weeks. I could feel my hands itching to feel the pull. My nerves craved the rush, that first pump of adrenaline as a fish jumps the bait. My ears wanted to hear the tick and the whine of a reel as a fish played it out. Bonefish would probably be the best bet today. The water was edging up toward 72 degrees in spots, still cool and early in the season for tarpon fishing, far too cold for snook. Most of the fish were in warmer waters. But there were always a few hardy ones that braved the winter or came back early. That made it more fun. I could use some fun. This Cantwell thing was bumming me out.

"Shouldn't let a good fishing day go to waste," I said.

"Don't you want to get closer to Cantwell, maybe take some video? See if we can read their lips? They might be talking about things they won't say in their offices or at home."

"Do you read lips?" I said.

Mabel frowned. "I thought you did."

"Why would you think that?" I did read lips. But I didn't feel like getting any closer, because we could give ourselves away. I might be able to use a scope to zoom in, maybe well enough to see what they said. But the angle wasn't good. Cantwell and Masco were about three stories in the air, while we weren't much above water level. Besides, it was a great day to fish. My fish finder radar had shown some promise in the bay, and I needed my fix.

Mabel said, "I just thought you'd be able to read lips. Seeing that you'd been a spook and all."

I decided to fess up. There was something about Mabel that made me want to be straight. Maybe it was because she was always that way. I was used to being quiet, keeping everything to myself, like a good card player. "I do read lips," I admitted. "But we can't get close enough, can't get the angle."

"So, we fish?"

"Unless you'd prefer wild sex?"

Mabel laughed. "The only bone you're getting today is a bone*fish*, sonny."

I laughed back. "Then bonefish, it is. I brought some shrimp along. There's a dredged channel nearby, one that's been known to produce a few keepers, even this time of year."

We fished for a while with no luck. Didn't surprise me. All the while, Cantwell and Masco sat on the back of the *HEDGEMONEY*. I wasn't sure what they were talking about, but I did see Masco leap up, as if to choke Cantwell. I wasn't sure, but I thought I saw the glint of something, maybe a knife, flutter into the bay. We weren't the only ones feeling tense.

After half an hour of nothing, Mabel said, "I won one of the silent auctions, you know."

"Which one?"

"The one that mattered."

I didn't know what Mabel was talking about. We'd each bid upon a couple of items. I'd been notified by email that I'd won dinner with Vanessa Fabergé, a hot local model who had offered her companionship for the cause of breast cancer research. She'd be disappointed in me. What she wanted was to hook up with some rich guy who would buy her lots of expensive toys. Instead, she was going to have a photo op with a guy long past his prime, who still had hopes of kissing a woman half his age, despite twenty years of futility.

"Which prize mattered to you?" I asked.

"The one with the quarterback. I was hoping for Tom Brady, but they lost the wildcard game. I thought Favre would make it. I'd sure like to squeeze his butt cheeks. But, he just lost the NFC championship."

I said, "I don't think that grabbing ass is part of the deal, Mabel."

"Brett would have never seen it coming."

"Someday, you're going to get sued for sexual harassment."

"If that ever happens, I'll insist on demonstrating my technique in court."

Chapter Thirty
V

Gumbo Winkelman motioned for his limo driver to turn north off 14th Street onto Collins Ave. A few minutes later, he motioned again, this time for his driver to slip the white Cadillac into the first available parking space. Within seconds, people began to converge upon the car. They came from all directions. Most were women, dressed in extremely short skirts or hot pants, tube tops and black fishnet stockings. A few were male, mostly young, wearing pants hanging half way off their butts. There were some older men, SOSCADA members, scattered in the crowd, their faces looking like dried prunes when compared to the youthful kids.

As Gumbo emerged from his limo's moon roof, a roar erupted from the crowd. Then people began screaming.

"Yo, doctor!"

"What's up, doc?"

"You the *man*!"

Gumbo thrust a fistful of hundred dollar bills into the air. He began passing them into the outstretched fingers waving frantically around him. "One for you…and one for you…and one for you…" said Gumbo, as he performed his locally-famous ritual.

Gumbo pulled fresh stacks of bills from his suit pockets, several times. As he did, nobody tried to rip the money out of his hands. There were some tough people in this part of town, but Gumbo was an icon. He would be protected by this crowd as if he were the pope.

When the money was gone, Gumbo held up his hands and yelled, "That's all I got, folks. But drinks are on me, at Club Deuce, for the next hour!"

As the crowd swarmed away, Gumbo got out of the limo and walked the short distance south to the Essex House Hotel. Inside the lounge, he found Sophie and Millie. They were modestly dressed tonight, wearing skirts that came all the way down to mid-thigh, lace tops (showing only modest cleavage), black leggings and red spike heels. They were sitting at a table with two men. The men looked to be in their middle thirties, although they were so weather-beaten by life that they could have been far younger.

One of the men was drugged-out thin. He was wearing a pair of ripped blue jeans, a black Phish T-shirt and Nike Air running shoes. A brown leather jacket was draped across the back of his chair. The other man wore a silk charcoal suit, with a turtleneck that was just a shade darker. He had a pair of dark-red Berluti Rapiécés Reprisés on his feet. The delicate shoes, with their trademark patches, looked out of place on a man well over six feet tall, weighing at least two hundred and fifty pounds. *Thin* man and *big* man, thought Gumbo.

"Nice threads," said Gumbo, as he studied the big man with the suit. "Are those Berlutis?"

"Yeah."

"Sweet."

Gumbo stepped back for a moment and posed like a male model. He adjusted the gold and diamond cufflinks on his sleeves, and then ruffled his shirt, opening his collar enough for the strangers to see his tattoo. "I respect a man who knows how to dress. Get those duds at the Upper Cut?"

"Yeah."

"That's where I shop. Best place for the discerning gentleman."

Gumbo looked over at the man in the T-shirt. "I was a Grateful Dead head, 'til Jerry died."

"Before my time," said the thin man. "Phish is all I know."

"I'm down with that."

Gumbo sat down, without shaking hands with the men. Instead, he pulled two envelopes from his suit coat and laid them upon the table. Each man took an envelope and stuffed it into a pocket.

"Ten grand each, as agreed," said Gumbo. "We cool?"

"Yeah," said Big.

Gumbo leaned forward and whispered, "So, what's the word on the street?"

Neither of the men wanted to speak first. They looked at one another, as if playing a game of verbal chicken. Finally, Thin said, "It's like nothing I've ever seen, man. Everybody's geared up big-time, like they're on steroids or somethin', for a competition. Mombo Smith made a fifty million dollar buy yesterday. I hear Blackjack Jeter's done the same. The whole game has been kicked up, like someone's stokin' the fires. With cash. Word is the wholesalers are extending *credit*, if you can believe that monkey."

Thin scratched at his arm. Gumbo could see that he was beginning to twitch.

"You gotta fix yourself, man?" Gumbo said.

Thin smiled grimly and shook his head. "No, man. I'm good."

Gumbo said, "So, who's behind all this?"

Thin looked at Big. The big man nodded.

Thin said, "Don't know. Word is, it's one guy. They call him the *Money Man*. That's all I know."

Gumbo looked at Big and said, "You have anything to add to this?"

"Yeah."

"I'm waiting."

The big man pointed toward the thin man. "He got it right. The Money Man is calling the shots. Whoever that is."

I'll need to bring this to Tony, thought Gumbo. Probably to the authorities, so they can decide how to play it. The Money Man had to be Cantwell.

Chapter Thirty-One
V

Two limousines turned right off 5th Street onto 2nd Avenue. One car was black. The other was white. They glided to the curb outside a building made with brown bricks, white concrete and darkened glass. The Miami Police Department headquarters.

Gumbo, Sophie, Millie, Murray and Wendell stepped out of the white limo. Tony, Pat, Mabel and Ben stepped out of the other. Together, they entered the building.

The former Chief of Police, Michael McBride, met them at the entrance and escorted them through security. He led them upstairs to a conference room that overlooked the street. In the center of the room was a large oval table surrounded by brown chairs. At one end of the conference room was a media center, with flat panel monitors and two laptop computers. The other end had a wooden table with two large coffee thermoses, as well as several boxes of donuts and bagels.

A group of people were gathered around the coffee, munching on the food, talking softly. They all turned in unison, as McBride led Mabel and the others into the room.

McBride said, "Okay, folks. Let's get started."

McBride had spent thirty years with the Miami PD, with a decade as chief. Under his guidance, the department had grown into an efficient, $100 million crime stopping organization with a reputation for excellence. Unfortunately for McBride, he had also fallen prey to the temptations of crime.

It had begun with an informant, the lawyer to one of Miami's largest crime syndicates. Cesar. When the syndicate's boss had been murdered, and Cesar had assumed control, he and McBride had formed a partnership. Together, they took down many of the city's largest criminal organizations. Along the way, McBride started taking bribes. Small tributes at first—jewelry, a lawn tractor, a set of gold pens, golf clubs. The gifts soon became cars and boats and then cash, until McBride was in so deep that he couldn't stop. He took money to look the other way, while Cesar grew to become Miami's biggest drug dealer.

Eventually, McBride had worked with SOSCADA to take down Cesar. With a presidential pardon, he had begun a new career. He was now a special liaison between the various drug fighting organizations in Florida.

McBride had assembled the important players for this meeting. They were as follows: Miami Chief of Police, Álvaro Esposito; Deputy Chief, Miguel Cabrerra; Major Ronald Magnetti, the head of the Special Investigations Section; Diane Magneson, head of the South Florida Money Laundering Strike Force; Reginald White, head of the High Intensity Drug Trafficking Area (HIDTA); Charles Griffin, head of the FBI's Joint Terrorism Task Force (JTTF); Mark Trout, Special Agent in Charge of the Miami Field Division of the Drug Enforcement Agency (DEA).

"Wow," mumbled Gumbo, as they entered the conference room. "I can actually *feel* the testosterone in this place." He looked at Magneson. "Except for you, honey. You are a beautiful flower."

Magneson blushed to a purple-hued pink, as Gumbo gallantly kissed the back of her hand.

McBride cleared his throat. "Gentlemen…ladies…Let's get down to business."

Within moments, everyone was seated at the main table.

"I have asked you here because we need to address a major new drug push that is underway in our city, and in our state."

McBride motioned toward Tony, Wendell and Murray.

"You all know Misters Trance, Holmbs and Stein. They head up The Society of Senior Citizens Against Drug Abuse, which has become an important tool in our region's fight against drugs."

McBride pointed toward Gumbo and his ladies. "These are a few of their senior undercover operatives."

McBride motioned toward Ben. "This is Mr. Johnson. Ben worked at the NSA, NRO and the CIA. He now practices as a private investigator in Miami."

Finally, McBride turned toward Mabel. "This is Mabel Witherspoon, and she has a story to tell."

Mabel stood up from her seat and walked to the head of the table. She told them about her first time in the Cantwell offices. She told them how she first learned that Cantwell and Masco were siphoning investor cash, leaving out the part about how she'd peed in her Depends. Mabel then told them how she had hired Ben, and how they had discovered that Masco was dealing drugs and killing people.

"Do you have any evidence?" said Esposito.

"Not that we can give you," said Ben.

"But you have it?"

"Let's say, we are sure about which we speak."

Trout, the DEA representative, said, "We've heard rumors about Masco. But we've never been able to nail him."

Magneson, head of the money laundering strike force said, "Same here. Cantwell's been on our watch list for years."

"Well, don't you tail them?" said Mabel. "How about wiretaps? Surely you can gather the evidence. We did."

Ben Johnson cringed. You did *not* just tell the FBI that you had wiretapped someone's home and offices without warrants, he thought.

"What evidence?" said Trout.

"Never mind," said Mabel. "You get your own evidence."

Griffin, head of the FBI's JTTF, said, "It's all about economics, Ms. Witherspoon."

Mabel looked at Ben. Then she looked at Tony. Finally she looked at McBride, who shrugged.

Mabel said, "Well, somebody needs to explain this to me. Or, I'm going to raise holy hell and go to the media."

McBride said, "We all get a budget, Mabel. And the budget is never enough. Our job is to take the money we're given and get the best results we can. You follow, so far?"

"You need to get the most bang for your buck."

"Correct." McBride paused. "Men like Cantwell and Masco have endless resources. What they earn in a month is ten times the amount we are given here locally to fight them. Truth is, we could catch them red-handed, get all the evidence, produce videos of them making a buy, even supply witnesses…and all we'd get would be trouble.

"Even with a rock-solid case, their lawyers would tie us up in court for years. The public would have to fund tens of millions in court costs. Politicians would work behind the scenes to take our jobs. And in the end, they would probably skate."

McBride set his jaw. He looked around the room, to the clear, intelligent eyes of his people, and said, "Even with these obstacles, we might still go after them. But Cantwell and Masco are far too careful to let us get direct evidence. We could get circumstantial crap out the yin-yang, but what good would it be? Try to bring them to court with that, we'd get screwed. Royally.

"So, we focus on smaller fish, ones that don't have the resources and lawyers and connections to fight us and bring us to our knees. The ones we can put away."

"So, what you're saying is, you're eunuchs," said Mabel. "You've got your balls cut off."

McBride laughed, shaking his head with a forlorn smile. "That's one way to put it."

"Shit," said Mabel.

"That's where we come in," said Tony.

"Ahhh," said Mabel, suddenly understanding. She looked at McBride. "We're the farmers and you're the Redcoats."

"Come again?"

"You play by the rules. You march down the middle of the road in a line wearing red targets on your chests, while the farmers shoot at you from behind trees."

"Are you talking about the American Revolution?"

"Isn't that what this is? A street fight for freedom? Our laws and your meager budgets prevent you from stopping these criminals. So, it is up to the citizenry to help you get justice."

McBride's mouth opened, but he said nothing. He looked at Tony, who shrugged. He looked to all the others, who stared at him with steely determination.

"You cannot do this, Ms. Witherspoon. These are ruthless people. They will kill you with no conscience, as if you were a fruit fly on a kitchen counter. You cannot take the law into your own hands. You will not get in our way."

"Seems like you *have* no way, unless it's backwards," Mabel said. She looked around the room. "Anyone here going to take on Cantwell?" She paused. "What if I were to give you audio? Video? Would you do it then? Huh? Huh?" Mabel waited, but no one answered. Finally, Mabel muttered, "Pussies."

Trout said, "Not true, Ms. Witherspoon. Our people put their lives on the line every day to attack crime. It takes enormous courage just to be in this fight, balls the size of watermelons.

"True. The people we ultimately target is a function of cost and benefit. If we go after Cantwell and Masco, we tie up valuable resources, resources we could better allocate to get far more done."

Mabel nodded. "I take back my remark. I was wrong. Pussies, you're not. You are *victims*. Of the imperfect system. I applaud your work and your sacrifice. And I wish it were different, that you could do your jobs without the draconian limitations and restrictions that society places upon you, so as not to violate anybody's rights, even the guilty."

"Amen," said Trout. This was followed by a chorus of "amen" from around the room.

"So, why are we here?" said Mabel.

McBride said, "When Tony came to me, and told me what you were doing, I thought you should know the score."

"That we're on our own."

"Far from it," said McBride. "We are behind you all the way. Just don't break the law. If you do, don't get caught."

Chapter Thirty-Two
V

Ben

As I pulled off of NW 183rd St. into the parking lot of Jiggles, I found myself guiltily looking around, to make sure I wasn't being seen by any-one I knew. I wasn't used to such places, even if it *was* a place where women kept on their clothing—provided you call a thong and tops the size of teabags clothes. I suppose it's no less than what the women wear on South Beach. I just wasn't used to the thought of sitting in a chair watching a woman gyrate on stage. I'm more of the sit on my balcony and secretly use my imagination type.

There was a light in Mabel's eyes that I hadn't seen before. She looked like my niece, many years before, walking down the stairs to show off her first prom dress, with the innocent abandon of youth shining out like the sun. Mabel slammed the door to my Jaguar so hard that it jarred my teeth.

"Easy, girl," I said.

Mabel grinned. "Can't you just feel the energy?"

If I felt anything, it was *shame*. The thought of women choosing to display their artistic talents for money, and the vision of guys shelling it out for the chance to press their palms against a sweaty thigh, gave me the willies. *My* shame came from the secret knowledge that I *wanted* to be there. I wanted to see what was inside. I wanted to stare at those young nubile bodies and let them trade a piece of their youth for my pocket change.

I'd never set foot in a gentleman's club before, so I didn't really know what to expect. I imagined it to be something like what you see on TV—a loud, smoky room with guys sitting next to a stage with their tongues hanging out. Dudes with wife-beater T-shirts and nerds with thick glasses and sweat all over their brows. Guys with boners tenting their pants, licking their lips as they slip dollar after dollar into a dancer's honey bank.

What I didn't expect was a ten dollar cover charge. I didn't expect the patrons to be dressed in suits. I didn't expect the waitresses to be wearing tasteful black dresses. Granted, they all had boobs the size of cantaloupes. Truth be told, they weren't much different than the trophy wives at Mar-a-Lago. Maybe more friendly. Finally, I didn't expect the women to be wearing so many clothes, or dancing on a stage that was big enough for Broadway.

"What do you think?" shouted Mabel, over the pulsing din. The noise was the only thing I'd been right about.

"Extraordinary," I said. And I meant it. The place had class, a ton of it.

I gazed across the room and saw a number of people I recognized. Mostly financial types, probably treating clients to the high-brow entertainment.

Just before looking back at Mabel, I saw two faces that sent a shiver down my spine. Rial Cantwell and Lou Masco. I glanced at Mabel and pointed. "Look who's here."

Mabel squinted, and then laughed. She said, "See those two guys with them?"

There were two men seated with Cantwell and Masco. One of them was thin, with red hair and a face full of freckles. The other had a nearly bald head and a round pot belly that must have taken years to perfect.

"Yeah?" I said.

"They're from the SEC. One of them is Galway. The other is Cramp."

"Did you say Cramp?"

"Uh-huh."

"And I thought the name Johnson lent itself to teasing."

Mabel began walking toward the four men. I followed. When we were half way across the club I could see Cantwell stiffen. He'd seen us. I smiled.

"Well, if it isn't my investment manager and his SEC buddies," Mabel said, once we reached them.

Cantwell said, "Good afternoon, Ms. Witherspoon. Have you come to watch the dancing, or are you now the owner of this fine establishment?"

Mabel remained evasive. "Just visiting." She smiled at Galway and Cramp. "Hello, gentlemen." Mabel ignored Masco.

Galway and Cramp looked like I would have, were I in their position.

They looked like they'd been caught with their pants down.

"You remember Mrs. Witherspoon?" Cantwell said to his guests.

The men nodded.

"How's the program?" Mabel said to Cramp.

"Six pounds, so far. Having problems with the sex, though."

"Can't get it up?"

Cramp smiled. "No. That's working fine. It's my wife."

"You may have to give her time to adjust. She on board with this?"

"Yeah. But not three times a day."

Mabel laughed. "You may want to tone back the sex a bit, Millard."

"Oh, good. I was getting pretty worn out."

We stood there, saying nothing more. Finally, Mabel said, "Well, we've got a meeting. Good to see you all."

With that, Mabel turned on her heels and began walking toward a hallway that ran behind the stage.

We were greeted there by a mountain of a man. He must have stood six and a half feet tall and weighed close to three bills. There wasn't a shred of fat on him. I'm no doctor, but he looked like the poster child for steroid abuse. He stood with his arms crossed, his muscles so defined I could count their striated ridges. There were blood vessels running above them, spidery, worm-like veins that looked like trail maps. His head was shaved, and he had big gold loop earrings that waggled menacingly as he breathed.

"Can I help you?" the man said. His voice rumbled deeply, like a freight train.

"We're here to see Elmer," Mabel said.

"Is Mr. Bagwell expecting you?"

"Tell him it's Mabel Witherspoon."

The man spoke into a band on his wrist. He pressed a finger to what must have been an inner earpiece, then nodded. He stepped to the side and unhooked a red felt rope that was draped across the narrow hallway. We entered the inner sanctum, expectantly, as if it were a hallowed Buddhist temple and we were seeing its Prophet.

"Third door on your right."

Elmer Bagwell was seated at a desk inside a large corner office. Before him were eight flat monitors, each showing a different part of the club. Bagwell was dressed in tan corduroy pants, a white shirt with a bowtie, and a funky plaid sport coat with patched leather elbows. He wore a pair of Docksiders with white socks. Made me think of Pee Wee Herman.

When he saw us, Bagwell jumped from his chair. "Mabel!" he cried. "I haven't seen you in years. What've you been up to, stranger?"

"Hello, Ellie."

Mabel and Bagwell exchanged a hug that went on forever. I grew slightly jealous.

"I suppose you're here to talk about the club?" Bagwell said.

"I hear it's for sale."

Bagwell held out his hand, palm down, and waggled his fingers. "Maybe yes, maybe no." He motioned toward the video screens and said, "Who would want to leave all this?"

"My grandson says you want three million."

Elmer squirmed uneasily. "Look…I had no intention of selling. I still don't. But when your grandson came to me and asked me to name a price, I did.

"I take three hundred grand a year out of this place and I like my job. But, I am starting to slow down. A little vacation home on some island sounds kind of nice. So, I gave him a figure, and it's firm. Won't take a penny less. And I won't sell to someone who will ruin the integrity of the show."

Mabel said, "My grandson will give you four million. Half a million a year for the next five years, the balance in a lump sum."

Bagwell shook his head. "It is all or none, Mabel. Good waterfront is expensive, and I don't want a mortgage. Plus…if I finance your grandson, there's no guarantee I'll get paid. He could run the thing into the ground."

"I'll secure it with my investment portfolio, $5.4 million, invested with Rial Cantwell. I can withdraw ten percent a year for five years if I cash out. Then I can get the balance…Tell you what, you can have it all."

Bagwell shook his head again. "I don't trust Cantwell."

"You know something I don't?"

Bagwell stared at Mabel, debating how much he should tell her. While Jiggles, itself, adhered to the fine art of dancing, Bagwell could not control what his dancers did in their off hours. A few of them had dated Masco and Cantwell over the years. They'd heard things, things said under the influence of alcohol or drugs, things he wouldn't dare repeat.

"Sorry, Mabel."

"How 'bout if I secure it with real estate? I'll pledge thirty million, if you want."

"You got that kind of land?"

"I do. And more."

"Maybe I should up my price?"

Mabel slumped down into a chair. Suddenly, she looked older. The arch seemed to have fallen off the rim of her eyes, crumbling, like there'd been an earthquake inside her. Her jaw slackened, the folds of her cheeks drawing into long vertical lines. Her skin began to look like a patchwork of dry riverbeds.

After a long while, Mabel said, "Shoot." When she raised her head there were tears in her eyes. "I promised Archie that I wouldn't sell the land."

"Take out a mortgage."

"I couldn't sleep at night."

"Maybe you could get someone to buy your Cantwell portfolio at a discount? Someone should be glad to pay you three or four million for it, I'm sure."

"That's just not right."

"Correct," said Bagwell. "It's not. But that's not my fault." Bagwell walked over to Mabel and put an arm around her shoulders. "Don't worry, dear," he said. "I won't be selling this place anytime soon. And, if someone does make me an offer, I'll let you know, so you can match it."

Mabel nodded sadly. When she stood back up, she looked stooped, as if she'd aged a decade in the last ten minutes. Funny, I thought, how attitude could so affect one's age.

I placed a hand upon Mabel's shoulder. She pressed against me, as if hugging for warmth. It felt good. She sniffed, so I pulled a tissue out of my coat pocket. I handed it to her and she gave it a good blow.

When Mabel tried to hand the goopy paper back to me, I said, "I don't want that."

Mabel laughed. "You take all my other crap."

I patted Mabel's back, then pulled her tightly against me. "I wouldn't take any crap from you."

Mabel sniffed one last time, then tossed the tissue into a waste basket.

"You're a good man, Ben Johnson."

"And you're a fine lady, Mabel Witherspoon."

We walked back into the dark club, with its loud music and its brilliant flashes of skin. Mabel looked to the stage, where a dancer with extraordinary talent was doing Broadway in a man's tuxedo. Mabel gazed out at the crowd. I could read her mind. She was wondering if the club's patrons could truly appreciate the skill with which the dancer moved.

Mabel's eyes stopped when they reached Cantwell. He was staring at her with a scowl upon his face. When she caught his eyes, Cantwell hesitated briefly, then smiled and raised his glass, as if toasting her. Mabel flipped him the bird and we walked out.

***

When Mabel and Ben stepped outside, the sun was laser hot and bright, accosting their eyes with a torturing vengeance. *Punishing us for our pleasures*, thought Ben.

Mabel didn't seem to notice. She was still fighting tears, her eyes half closed. She slipped on a pair of sunglasses, and began walking toward Ben's car.

"Man, that hurts," said Ben, as he stepped into the light. He shielded his eyes, but still had to struggle to keep them open.

Mabel smiled. "You'll learn how to deal with it." She tapped on the edge of her Oakleys. "Bring shades next time. Helps with the transition."

"Who says I'm coming back?" said Ben.

"You will."

"Will not."

"Will so."

As Mabel neared the passenger side of Ben's Jaguar, Ben said, "Wait."

Ben remained in place, motioning for Mabel to come back toward him. When she reached his side, Ben triggered the remote starter to his car. The engine fired and purred.

"Getting a little paranoid, aren't we?" said Mabel.

"Humor me."

They waited for sixty seconds before Ben stepped toward the car. As he did, he glanced around the parking lot, looking for anyone who might wish to harm or follow them.

"You're scaring me," Mabel said.

"Better safe than sorry."

Ben pulled onto 183rd Street and began heading toward the Florida Turnpike. He drove slowly, five miles under the speed limit, looking at the cars passing by, and staring repeatedly into his rearview mirror.

"What's up?" said Mabel.

"Don't you feel it?"

"My head hurts from crying. I'm stuffy. I've got a cramp in my left foot and I need to pee. Does that count?"

"Tighten your seat belt."

Mabel did. However, the shoulder strap on Ben's Jag wasn't part of the car's original equipment. It was made for someone taller and didn't adjust, so as Mabel tightened it, the belt rode up across her neck. "Don't decapitate me, Ben."

"Roll your arm over it."

Mabel lifted her right arm and placed it over the belt. This pulled the strap away from her neck, but it pressed awkwardly against her breasts. "Now, you'll cut off a boob."

"Be quiet. You've got enough to spare."

Ben's eyes narrowed as he glanced into his rearview mirror. Behind him, a black BMW began to crowd against his bumper. Then a second BMW slipped in ahead of the Jaguar. Through a darkly tinted window, Ben could see someone staring at them from the back seat of the lead car.

"Mabel," said Ben. He reached into his car's glove box and removed an untraceable burner phone. He handed it to Mabel and said, "Dial 911 and tell them there's a robbery underway at the Dixon Nursery. Tell them shots have been fired and someone may be hurt. Make it sound as serious as you can."

Ben slowed farther below the speed limit. The car ahead of them slowed even more, until Ben's front bumper rode just inches away. "Make the call. Now, Mabel."

Mabel dialed 911. When the operator answered, she said, "There's been a robbery at Dixon's Nursery on 183rd! Someone's been shot and there's blood everywhere. Guys are wearing black ski masks and they're driving these big black BMWs with dark tinted windows. I think it's a drug deal gone bad or something…these guys are…Oh…Ahhh…"

Mabel hung up the phone and said, "How was that?"

"Good. Now, hold on." As they came to the intersection at 17ᵗʰ Avenue, Ben suddenly swerved to the left. He crossed the median and began driving into the one-way traffic on the other side of the street.

"You're crazy!" yelled Mabel, as Ben swerved around an oncoming car.

Ben replied calmly, "Reminds me a little of your driving, Mabel."

Horns began blaring. Lights started flashing. Ben weaved his small sports car around the oncoming cars like he was playing Super Mario on the computer. But now, only one of the BMWs was on his tail. The one in front had not been able to make the turn. Ben cranked his steering wheel, narrowly missing a truck who had refused to give way. They heard a *crash* behind them, as the BMW met the truck head on.

Ben swerved his car into the Dixon Nursery. His tires spun as he drove into the driveway, then over the grass and around several small trees into the parking lot next door. He drove through this parking lot until he came back to 17ᵗʰ Ave. He turned right and began driving at five miles over the speed limit. He took a quick left onto 183ʳᵈ Drive, another left on 17ᵗʰ Court and came back onto 183ʳᵈ Street, heading west.

"They won't catch us now," said Ben, looking in is rearview mirror at the accident behind them. He looked over at Mabel. "You okay?"

"I peed in my Depends."

Ben laughed. "I would've peed, too."

"Let's go back to Jiggles and shoot Cantwell."

Ben pursed his lips, as if considering Mabel's request. But he drove on past Jiggles, not even glancing at the place.

"You better have a plan," said Mabel.

"I say we take the gloves off."

"Shoes, too."

Chapter Thirty-Three
V
____

"You really screwed up on this Ben Johnson guy," said Cantwell.

Masco said, "I *told* you he was trouble."

Both men looked out at the water. It was a raw, gray day. There was an oily breeze coming out of the east, and Biscayne Bay frothed with a heavy chop. The *HEDGEMONEY* moved slowly up and down, as if it were a giant, sleeping on its back, breathing steadily with a long, slow cadence.

Masco said, "Norman was not pleased, having three of his men arrested for crashing into one-way traffic. They also had to explain their way out of a 911 call that said they'd robbed Dixon's Nursery, at gunpoint."

"They're cops. They'll sort it out," Cantwell said.

"They're *Daytona* cops. Not the same thing."

"Nothing cash won't fix."

Masco stood up from his chair and began to pace around the boat's rolling deck. He scratched at his arms, at an itch that wouldn't go away. He needed a line; he needed it soon. But first things first.

Masco said, "You think everything can be fixed with cash, Rial. Well, some things take more than cash, like Witherspoon and that creep she hangs with. And hiring those cops, without telling me—"

"I just had them tailing her. And when she came into the club…I just figured we could scare them, make them see that we were serious. How the hell was I supposed to know he could drive his old antique like an Indy car?"

"I *told* you he was trouble."

Cantwell nodded. "You did. I tried it my way. It didn't work. I'm sorry."

"Not as sorry as you're going to be when they cart your ass away in chains."

Cantwell scoffed. "Better make sure that doesn't happen, Lou."

Masco looked out to the gray-green water that was churning and sloshing all around them. With the heavy winds and the chop, there were few boats in the bay today. There was a cluster of sailboats off in the distance, probably in some kind of race. Two people were on jet skis, wearing aqua dive suits to keep them warm. A pair of hundred footers motored south about a quarter mile away. They were identical. Masco wondered if they were *he* and *she* boats, owned like matching Rolexes or Mercedes in the driveway. About half a mile away, he could see what looked to be a Sea Ray Sundancer. It appeared to be trolling in one of the channels. Not the best kind of weather for fishing, he thought. But vacationers didn't have the luxury of choosing their days.

"What about tonight?" said Masco.

"You mean the meeting with Witherspoon?"

"What the fuck else would I mean?"

Cantwell drew up the collar on his windbreaker and adjusted the blanket he'd thrown over his legs. He was pissed. It was a damp, bitter day. He'd wanted to hold this meeting in his office. They'd swept the damned room a dozen times and found nothing. The only place they'd found listening devices was in Masco's home. Light bulbs, can you believe it? They hid the bugs in fucking light bulbs. Still, Masco wouldn't take any chances, not anymore. So, they had to meet out here in the middle of frigging winter.

Cantwell said, "Can't wait to see what Ben and Mabel have to say now."

Masco smiled to himself. He wondered what Cantwell would say if he knew how that meeting was probably going to end.

Chapter Thirty-Four
V

Mabel and Ben were deliberately kept waiting in the reception area of Cantwell Investments. During the long hour, Mabel patiently sipped a scotch on the rocks. Ben spent the time examining the paintings that hung along the walls. Ben would clasp his hands behind his back and press his face up against a painting. Then he would stand back and admire the work from a distance. After each examination, he would look at Mabel, then at the receptionist, who wouldn't take her eyes off of him.

Ben was admiring his eighth painting when Rial Cantwell began his long walk down the hallway.

"Hey, Mabel. Here he comes!" cried Ben, with a half shout.

Cantwell was dressed in a white, tropical wool suit with an open collar. There were faint blue lines that ran along the fabric, barely visible to the eye. Cantwell's shirt was pale blue silk. It had a tight, expensive weave and glowed softly in the low lights. He wore a pair of gold and lapis lazuli cufflinks. They were nearly the size of match books, providing the necessary color to his otherwise drab outfit.

Cantwell boomed, with his basso voice, "Hello, again, Mrs. Witherspoon. I'm so glad to see you…and your friend."

"Great to see you, too," said Ben, ignoring the slight.

Cantwell looked at Ben. The tips of his mouth rose in a forced smile, just a quick twitch of muscle. He extended his hand and Ben shook it vigorously.

"A pleasure," said Ben. "A real pleasure."

"Yes," said Cantwell softly. "This way."

Cantwell began walking quickly down the hall. He slowed beside the conference room, as if debating whether to stop there, but continued on toward his office. When they were inside, he pushed an intercom on his desk and said, "They're here, Lou."

A few moments later, Masco sauntered into the room. His lips meandered into a lopsided smile. It wasn't a real smile; it was more like the psychopathic twitch of a sadist after blowing up a frog with a firecracker.

Masco extended his hand. When Ben took it, Lou whispered, "I hear you're quite the driver."

Ben grinned. "Heard about that, did you?"

"We take an interest in our clients."

"I'm not a client."

"Ms. Witherspoon is. We were worried for her safety."

Ben shrugged. "Ah, it was just a couple of teenagers out in daddy's car, trying to have fun. That's all."

Masco nodded, but said nothing more. He had a bad feeling about Johnson. Johnson was different than what he portrayed, someone much more dangerous than a bumbling financial planner, like a pretty snake with a deadly venom. Masco had tasked some of his people to look more deeply into Johnson's identity, but it had held. He was a pro. What was he? FBI? DEA? Was this a sting?

Mabel cleared her throat. Everyone turned in her direction. She was standing at the window, gazing out at the football stadium in the distance. She pulled away from the window and said, "We know it was you that sent those cars after us, Rial."

Cantwell's eyes widened with mock surprise. Masco's rounded into worried ovals.

"That's a serious accusation," said Masco.

"More serious than theft or murder?"

"Such claims are outrageous."

Mabel continued. "We know you've been stealing money and moving it offshore. We know that you have silenced others who have challenged your false purity and professionalism. We know that you are dealing drugs."

"So, go to the police," said Masco.

Cantwell's face had grown sickly pale. It looked like a giant slug, pulpy and wrinkled with random lines and folds. He dropped into his office chair with a soft *grunt*.

"We went to the police. They said to buzz off," said Mabel.

This time, Masco's smile grew almost friendly. His lips parted, to reveal his yellow, canine teeth. But, soon, the mirth faded. What remained was the sinister look of an incurable reprobate.

"You should take their cue," Masco said.

"Can't do that," said Mabel. "Too many people have been hurt."

"I've never hurt an investor," shouted Cantwell.

Mabel said, "You nearly did yesterday."

"That wasn't me," Cantwell lied. He'd only wanted to scare them, not put them in any danger.

Mabel smiled, turning her gaze toward Masco. "Perhaps it was Lou, then?"

Lou looked sharply at Cantwell, warning him not to say what he knew was coming. Cantwell ignored him. "Even if it was, Lou wouldn't want to hurt you. Maybe just warn you." His voice softened. "Why would we ever want to hurt you?"

"Because I'm taking you down if you don't return all the money you stole."

Cantwell's eyes knitted into a single brow. Mabel could see the color rise in his face. It reminded her of hot water, flowing up through the pipes of her New Hampshire radiators, starting cold, then burning to a temperature too hot to touch. The tip of Cantwell's sweaty nose began to glow, turning red, until it shone like a stoplight.

"Settle down, Rial," said Mabel. "Don't pop a cork."

"I've never stolen a dime of client money."

"I've looked through my contract, Rial. Where does it state that you get a sixty percent split after I've made eighteen percent in any one year?"

Cantwell's chest heaved. He fought the urge to strangle Mabel where she stood. How could she know that number? Nobody knew his personal target, that magic return that triggered his extra "bonus." Even Masco didn't know that number. Had they hacked his computer?

"You're a good money manager, Rial. A great one. You don't need to steal."

"I don't steal. No client has ever lost a dime. A *dime*. How many advisors can make that claim?"

"Very few, I'm sure. Still doesn't give you the right to embezzle."

Masco quietly slipped out of the room.

Mabel looked over toward the newly renamed Sun Life Stadium. It was lit up like a Christmas tree, as preparations for the Pro Bowl were now fully underway. Mabel could see large trucks driving along the road, looking like black beetles in the distance, as they carried the provisions for nearly seventy-five thousand fans.

Mabel said, "I won the auction, you know. The meet and greet."

Cantwell laughed. "Yeah, I saw that. Congratulations."

"I've always wanted to pinch Brett Favre in the ass."

"Sorry he didn't make it."

"There are other fish in the sea."

Cantwell walked over and stood beside Mabel, looking out at the stadium. Ben remained off to the side, smart enough to remain silent.

After a long while, Cantwell said, "It just sort of happened, you know."

Mabel sighed. "I understand. Care to explain?"

Cantwell nodded slowly. "We made a little killing one time, through a brokerage house in the Philippines. This investment banker there…he offered to pay some in cash, rather than by wire…for a small finder's fee. He explained how he could tweak the numbers so nobody would know…It was so easy."

Cantwell shrugged. "Many of our investors have offshore trusts, money that is being hidden from U.S. authorities. These clients are far more concerned with secrecy than with returns. Give them a steady, tax-free gain and they're content. A few extra percent doesn't really matter to them. It's all about the confidentiality."

Mabel said, "What about us, the legal ones? Why take from us?"

Cantwell pressed his hands against his face and massaged his eye sockets. Then he ran his fingers in wide circles against his temples. He seemed to be thinking, deciding just how to answer. Finally, his shoulders slumped and he said, "I think I got addicted to the game, Mabel. There's a rush that you get when you make a killer trade, like a snort of coke that can last for hours, even days. I found there was an even bigger rush when I could keep the money…steal it…Guess it was the danger." Cantwell paused, then sighed. "You know, there were years when my investors lost money, but never knew. That means you. In those years, I would take some of the siphoned funds and put them back into investor accounts. You might have lost ten percent in a given year, but when you got your statement, you broke even. Never a down year, for you. I'm not all bad, you see…It was like taking out insurance payments and paying claims when the market went down.

"I never filched a dime. Not really. It was insurance."

"Say what you want. It's theft, Rial. It's not right."

Cantwell turned toward Mabel and said, "I'll give back the money. I'll declare a monster year for everyone…But we can't stop the drug deals, at least not yet. These people are heartless…brutal. If we don't follow through, they'll kill us."

"That's not my problem."

"It *is* your problem, if you force our hand."

"It's a matter of law, Rial. It's about what's right."

"What if I give you your money? Right now. I'll include the extra gains. That's over seven million. I'll write a check. I'll wire it. I'll even get you cash. I'll pay it anywhere you want. Anytime."

Mabel shook her head. "Sorry, Rial. You had your chance."

Cantwell stared at Mabel. His eyes pleaded. They had the look of a sad dog being left at home, the sudden drop from expectation to reality, as the family closed the door. "Please don't do this, Mabel."

Ben stepped forward and said, "We'll think about it, Cantwell. Won't we, Mabel?"

Mabel seemed to hesitate. After a moment, the fight seemed to leave her body. She wobbled, like a boxer who'd taken a quick, paralyzing punch. She stepped backward and looked questioningly at Ben. There was a hard look in his eyes, a demand that she back down.

"Okay," she said. "We won't do anything, for now. But I want the money returned to your investors, all of it. I want it paid out. And I want your promise that you'll stop the dealing."

"After the Super Bowl," said Cantwell. "We can meet with the cartels then, maybe work out a deal."

"You can do it, Rial. I know you can."

Mabel nodded, as if satisfied. She stuck out her hand to shake. Cantwell grasped it and held it. When he looked into her eyes, she saw something there. Was it fear? Sadness? It certainly wasn't anger or malice. The bravado had drained out of Cantwell like a leaky balloon. He seemed beaten, deflated, resigned.

"Goodbye, Mrs. Witherspoon."

Chapter Thirty-Five
V

Ben

As we exited the Cantwell Building, Mabel said, "I think that went pretty well. Don't you?"

I wasn't sure how to answer. Cantwell's words had seemed more like a stall technique to me, not a genuine promise to make things right. But Mabel seemed to be in high spirits, and I didn't want to squash them. I stood there looking at her, debating whether I should give my professional opinion, or the one she wanted to hear.

"We're definitely making progress," I said. Let her believe the best. Maybe it was true.

"It's a step in the right direction, anyway."

Mabel began to walk toward my Jaguar, which was parked along the curb. I took hold of her shoulder and squeezed it firmly. "Let's talk here for a minute," I said. "Before we leave."

"Okay."

"First, I want to know something. Why didn't you take your money?"

"Because it wouldn't be right."

"You could have had Jiggles."

Mabel shrugged. "Honor is more important than any possession, Ben."

"Second," I said. "Do you really believe that Cantwell can walk away?"

"Sure."

I wanted to tell her that men like Cantwell could never quit. He was like a star athlete. He would play the game as long as he could, probably longer, until he was forced out.

"Third. You do understand that Santiago, Khan and Diaz will never let Masco walk away?"

"Cantwell said he could fix it."

I shrugged. With enough money, maybe he could. Probably not with what money we'd leave him, though.

"Maybe we should let him use some of the stolen investor money to pay off the cartels," I said.

Mabel shook her head violently. "And give *them* that much more cash? They'd use it to grow crops and kill more kids. Hell, no. Not on your life."

"You have Cantwell and Masco between a rock and a hard place, Mabel. You're giving them no room to wiggle."

"They made their own bed. Now, they've got to sleep in it."

"There's another option for them, Mabel." I didn't want to say this, but she had to hear it. The best option was to see us dead.

"I know," she said softly.

Brave girl. I motioned with my car clicker. "I'll start the car from here."

I pressed the ignition remote and the Jaguar began to roar. A moment later, the sky filled with fire. A loud, teeth-jarring *boom* split the air. It compressed my ear drums, like I'd been boxed with two strong hands. I felt sick and dizzy, but I had enough sense to pull Mabel to the ground and lay over her. A piece of the Jaguar's hood came crashing down upon the back of my legs. I was able to throw it off, but not before it set my pants on fire. A shower of sparks came down after it, looking like fireworks in the dark night air. I fluffed at my clothes and was able to snuff the sparks before they did too much damage. Small chunks of molten metal came down upon my head, sizzling my scalp like little brands. I could smell the char of burning hair and skin. I heard Mabel shriek beneath me. I jumped up and saw that her sweater had caught on fire. It wasn't really in flame, just a melting of the wool. I thought to roll her, as I'd been taught. Instead, I decided to pull the sweater off of her, before it caused more damage. Even so, Mabel began to moan.

"Those assholes," she said. "That was my favorite sweater."

Cantwell's guards finally came crashing out the office building's doors. They stood in place, staring at the burning car, paying no attention to the wounded on the street. What did I expect? They were rent-a-cops anyway. I could hear a fire siren off in the distance. At least someone had called it in.

Finally, one of the guards said, "You guys okay? Can we do anything to help?"

"Help *her*," I said, pointing at Mabel. Then I said, "Mabel, are you okay?"

"Yeah. Just burnt like a French fry."

Mabel looked to my bleeding legs and said, "Oh, my God, Ben. You should sit."

I looked down. The bottoms of my pants had been burned and cut to tatters. There were big red welts on my calves. My left leg had pieces of metal sticking out of it like the butts of steak knives. There was also a deep gash that was spilling blood onto the sidewalk.

"I'm okay," I said, but I began to feel a little woozy.

I turned toward the entrance to the building, waiting for Cantwell or Masco to emerge. They never did.

A few moments later, an ambulance arrived. They put us both inside. Unlike the movies, we were allowed to remain seated, buckled up against the side of the vehicle, while EMTs worked on our wounds.

"Can you tell me what happened?" one of them said to me.

I said, "My car exploded. It was an old clunker. I think it was a gas leak."

Mabel looked over to me and I shook my head. Better to remain quiet about this, at least right now.

Mabel had minor burns that didn't need bandaging. Mine were mostly second degree, painful, but nothing dangerous.

The wounds in my leg were something else. The car shrapnel in my calf seemed okay, although it looked like a blanket of porcupine quills. The gash from the piece of car hood was deep and bleeding like a river. The EMTs fixed me with a tourniquet, which slowed the bleeding to that of a springtime stream.

When the trauma team doctor released the tourniquet in the hospital, the blood whooshed out like a dam had burst.

"Let's get this gentleman to the OR. STAT," said the doctor, calmly. I fainted.

They wheeled me into an operating room and went to work. Four pints of blood and sixty stitches later, I was moved to a semi-private room. There was one other man inside my suite. He'd been shot in a gang fight, I overheard. From what little I could see through and around the white curtain, he looked to be about sixteen. He was groaning and weeping and calling for his mother. Not so tough when they're alone.

They released us that night, after all of the insurance arrangements had been made, of course. Tony and Pat Trance picked us up and took us to the SOSCADA mansion, where there were a lot of extra beds. I think we were all in a mild state of shock, because nobody said a word while we were riding in the limo. At the mansion, they wheeled me into the kitchen, where Pat heated up some chicken soup.

The soup did wonders. When the color began to come back to our faces, Tony said, "Was this Cantwell?"

I nodded. "Car bomb outside his place."

"You threaten him?"

"I wouldn't call it threatening," said Mabel. "We just made a little request—"

"Yeah," I said. "We did."

Tony said, "What do you want to do about it?"

"We might tell the police," I said.

"They'd probably like to know," said Tony, smiling. "You want me to call McBride?

"Got a better idea?"

Tony shook his head. "Nobody's going to want to hear this, Ben. But McBride's our best bet."

Chapter Thirty-Six
V

Former police chief, Michael McBride, was staring out the conference room window as the last people sauntered inside. It was an effulgent sunny day, with the high forecast in the low sixties. There was a grouping of wispy cirrus clouds floating in the upper atmosphere. McBride could see the shape of a dragon, lumbering across the sky in a slow, disintegrating march. By the end of this meeting, perhaps even before it began, the dragon would be gone, as if it never existed. Like a case against a major drug dealer.

McBride wondered if their case against Cantwell would vanish in the same, inexorable way, slipping through their fingers like a cloud.

McBride had reassembled the important players for this meeting: Chief Esposito; Deputy Chief, Cabrerra; Magnetti, from Special Investigations; Magneson, from the Laundering Strike Force; White, from HIDTA; Griffin, from the JTTF; and Trout, from the DEA. None of them were pleased to be here. They'd already played this song, and it was a scratched record. Cantwell wasn't worth the effort; he was too big to take down.

When the players had arrived, McBride said, "Sorry to pull you in here again, but I thought we might want to reassess Cantwell and his danger to the region."

"We've been through all this, Mike," said Chief Esposito. "No one is debating his danger to the region. But we've got to deal with reality here. If we go after Cantwell, we'll set ourselves back five years, at least.

"We'll take white heat, from the governor on down. We'll tie up valuable resources, ones we can use to actually get convictions."

McBride nodded. He understood the game. It wasn't always the worst criminals that got arrested and charged, it was the ones that could be convicted.

"You might think differently, once you've had the chance to hear what

Ben Johnson has to say."

McBride turned toward Ben. Ben was dressed in a pair of blue khaki shorts and a white golf shirt. He was seated at the conference table, so there wasn't much evidence of the car bombing, at least in plain view. His hair was shorter on one side from the burning. There were round nubs on the end of some hairs, where they had rolled up and melted. His cheeks had a red, freshly scrubbed look, where the burns had singed his skin. There were several dark red scabs on his scalp, but they were mostly hidden by the remaining hair.

Ben's leg was something else. As he climbed onto his crutches, several people gasped. The criss-crossed rows of black stitches along his calf looked like railroad tracks in a train yard. The wound was still oozing and it was now covered with a layer of dried, yellowish crud.

Ben hobbled to the front of the room. When he reached the end of the table, he looked back toward Mabel and smiled. She smiled back to give him strength. He looked at Tony Trance, who also nodded encouragingly.

"I wasn't going to tell you this," Ben said. He looked around the room. The eyes he saw were alert and intent. "When we last met, Tony Trance and Chief McBride didn't explain my role at the CIA. I was trained to look into things. My job was to find things out, in whatever way I could. I spend forty years as a snoop. A serious snoop. A weaponized snoop. There isn't a man, or even a government, that can keep me from finding out their deepest, darkest secrets.

"So, when Ms. Witherspoon came to me and asked for help, I kinda reverted to my training. Now, you might want to say that I did things that were outside the law. You might want to raise holy hell and accuse me of doing stuff that I shouldn't have. But, you see, I wasn't trying to get information to put Cantwell away. I was just trying to get what I needed, to see that my client got her money, her hard-earned, legal money…"

Ben hesitated. He looked out the window, brought his hand to his mouth and stroked his chin.

"Relax, Ben," said McBride. "We're not going to prosecute you for anything." McBride looked to the people in the room and said, "Are we?"

After satisfying himself that Ben was safe, McBride said, "Tell us all you have."

Ben nodded. He took a deep, centering breath and said, "Okay. Here we go. I was hired by Mabel Witherspoon to do two things. She wanted to recover money that was stolen from her. She also wanted protection against potential threats upon her life.

"The perpetrator on both accounts was Rial Cantwell. Mabel was convinced that Cantwell was stealing money from investors. She believed that Cantwell knew that she knew, and that he would do anything to keep her quiet.

"When I took the case, I did what I do best. I put something on Cantwell's computer to capture his keystrokes. This gave me access to his files. It also allowed me to listen in on what he said while in his office. I also put listening devices in the home of his partner, Louis Masco. This allowed us to hear what *he* said.

"We learned that Masco and Cantwell have been financing drug deals, for nearly twenty years. They have also been skimming money from investors. These two endeavors have helped them accumulate thirty-three billion dollars. Most of it is held offshore, in secret accounts."

Trout said, "Did you say thirty-three *billion* dollars?"

"I did."

There was a chorus of whistles around the room. They all began to talk, their voices making a rumble in the conference room.

After a moment, Ben continued. "In recent months, Masco has escalated his drug operations. Now, rather than simply finance major wholesalers, he wants to control all levels of distribution, from grower to street dealer.

"We suspect that this escalation evolved from some sort of competition between the two men. Cantwell maintains the high profile. He's the one getting written up in the journals, getting his face on the cover of *TIME* and *FORBES*. He is the one that goes on Oprah and Fox Business. He's the one speaking at conventions and conferences, and receiving honorary degrees from colleges around the globe.

"From what we've learned, Masco wanted to shut things down. But Cantwell was addicted to the game. Masco wanted to quit. Cantwell wanted fifty billion.

"This led Masco to up the ante. Rapidly and forcefully. Then, *he* became addicted. Except, his addiction is to drugs, not the adrenaline of the deal. Now, he can't quit.

"Masco has gone into business with some of the biggest bad-asses on the planet: Khan, Diaz and Santiago. Together, these men manage powerful oligopolies in the cocaine and heroin trades. These are the kind of men who, once they sink their teeth into you, will never let go. Masco is trapped and he's getting desperate."

Ben took a sip of coffee. He scratched lightly on his leg, just enough to quell an itch, at least for the moment. He began again. "Masco has been protecting Cantwell for years, eliminating anyone who tried to stand in his way."

"Hold it," said the FBI's Griffin. "Are you saying that Masco has been killing people? For Cantwell?"

"I am. He tried to kill us last week, with a car bomb."

"And Cantwell is now in business with Khan, Diaz *and* Santiago?"

"Kinda like the Four Horsemen, hey?" said Ben.

Griffin's cheeks puffed, as he blew out a deep breath. "Shit. If word gets out about this, and that we did nothing to stop it…"

"Am I safe from prosecution?" said Ben.

"Yeah, of course," said Griffin.

Ben looked over at Esposito. Esposito frowned, but said, "You're safe, Mr. Johnson."

Ben said, "And Mabel?"

"Yeah, yeah," said Griffin. "You're all safe. The question is, how do we nail these suckers so they can't slip away?"

"I can give you access to all their data," said Ben.

Griffin shook his head. "Can't use it, Ben. We'll have to get our own. Even so, that's not enough, not enough for a trial. We need something visual, something a jury can *see* and *understand*."

"How about a confession?"

Griffin smiled. "A confession is good. Very good. How do we work that?"

Ben thought for a moment. He wondered if Mabel was strong enough for this. It was one thing to have your house broken into, or to be chased in a car. It was a far different thing to survive a deadly explosion that was meant to kill you.

"What do you think, Mabel?" Ben said.

"Go for it, Ben."

"You sure?"

"As sure as you're sitting there."

"I'm standing, Mabel."

"You know I can't see, Ben. You know what I mean."

"All right," said Ben. "Here's the plan: Mabel won a silent auction at a Cantwell fundraiser. She gets to meet the Super Bowl quarterback of her choice, at the Cantwell suite at Sun Life Stadium."

"Nice," said Griffin. "What'd you pay for that?"

Mabel smiled. "Fifty grand. Didn't want to pass up the chance to lip-smack Brett Favre."

Griffin chuckled. "Too bad he lost—"

"Uh-hem," said Ben.

Griffin said, "We'll set you up with a wire." He looked at Mabel. "You sure you can get Cantwell to confess?"

"Of course, I can."

"No wire," said Ben. "I'll fix something less obvious. And we won't want you around, any of you. Masco will smell you a mile away." Ben paused, then said, "I've still got the highest levels of security clearance, guys. I'm sure we can work things out?"

McBride looked over to the representative from the FBI. Griffin eventually nodded. Exposing a massive securities fraud and taking down one of the nation's biggest drug dealers, all at one time? Arrangements could be made.

McBride walked over and stood beside Ben. He placed an arm over his shoulder and said, "You sure you can do this?"

Ben shrugged. "It's what I do, Mike."

McBride looked toward Mabel.

"Sure you want to take this risk?"

Mabel snorted. "Can't be any more dangerous that riding in Ben's car."

She wouldn't have laughed, wouldn't even have smiled, if she'd known what was about to happen.

Chapter Thirty-Seven
V

"This is a madhouse," said Mabel, as she passed through a private side entrance into the newly-named Sun Life Stadium. "I'm not used to such crowds. With my vision issues, I'm afraid I'm going to knee some guy in the balls."

Ben took hold of Mabel's elbow, helping her negotiate the 72,000 people that were assembled for today's Pro Bowl. "I'm sure Cantwell's place will be far more subdued."

Ben and Mabel followed a stadium valet to Cantwell's executive suite, which overlooked the fifty yard line. Inside, there were at least a hundred guests standing in conversation, with drinks in hand. Most of the women were wearing knee-length dresses, with black the clear color of the day. The men tended toward sport coats with dress shirts and open collars.

Mabel felt briefly awkward, in her skin-tight, black leather pants, her white butterfly sweater and snakeskin cowboy boots. Then she thought of the quarterback and smiled. She'd worn this outfit for him, not everyone else. Her one big worry was that she was flying solo — no Depends. How can you grab the backside of an NFL quarterback when you're wearing Depends? You can't. Mabel's rule.

"Do you see Cantwell?" Mabel said. She looked out over the crowd. Who were all these people? she wondered. Friends of Cantwell's? Clients? Probably both.

"Over there," said Ben. He pointed toward a wall of windows, where Cantwell was standing in quiet conversation with Donald Trump. "He's with The Donald."

Mabel said, "Let's go see them."

Ben guided Mabel across the room.

"Well, if it isn't Mabel Witherspoon," said Trump.

"Hello, Donald."

Cantwell said, "You know each other?"

"Mabel pinched my butt at a fundraiser once. Couple years back," said Trump. He smiled at Mabel. "Where was that?"

"Your golf tournament."

"Ah, yes."

Ben whispered into Mabel's ear. "Are you a serial tail grabber?"

Mabel laughed, "Donald was my first." She looked at Trump and batted her eyes. "And only. So far, at least."

Cantwell looked at Trump. "Mabel was the high bidder for the quarterback meet and greet."

"Ahhh," said Trump. "I would have bid on that, except I'll get to hang with them anyway."

Mabel said, "I was hoping for Brett Favre."

"Thought you'd go for someone younger, Mabel." Trump laughed, then placed a hand on her shoulder. "You want to meet him anyway? He might be here, injuries and all."

"You can do that?"

"If he's here, I can. We'll see." Trump scribbled his phone number onto a napkin and handed it to Mabel. "Call me. I like you, Mabel. And I want to see Brett's reaction when you squeeze his backside."

Mabel looked out toward the stadium field. Some of the players were warming up, wearing an assortment of odd, mismatched clothing. Hundreds of people were milling about the grounds like ants—media members gathering interviews, film and lighting techs making last minute adjustments, and a lot of ex-players catching up on old times.

Mabel said, "Never knew this was such a production."

Trump said, "This one's more than most Pro Bowls, Mabel. With the Super Bowl here next week, today's game is a chance for the technicians to work out the kinks, even though the broadcast's on a different network. This is also the start of the big schmooze."

"The big schmooze?"

"You know how many deals get done at the Super Bowl?" Trump smiled. "I just hit Cantwell up for five hundred million. A little deal I've got going over in China."

Mabel shot a glance at Cantwell. Her eyes narrowed and she said, "I hope Rial didn't use my money for that, Donald."

Trump looked quizzically at Cantwell, who shrugged dismissively.

Cantwell said, "Well, Mr. Trump, I'm sure you have other parties to attend."

"I do. I'm off to see Ross right now." Trump shook hands with Cantwell. Then he planted a kiss on Mabel's cheek. "Good to see you again, dear. You look great in those pants."

After Trump left, Cantwell said, "I thought you were joking about Favre."

"I was. Sort of."

"But, Trump—"

"I couldn't resist Donald, Rial. Who could?" She sighed. "He *was* my first. And probably my last."

Cantwell shook his head and chuckled. "Mabel, Mabel, Mabel…What am I going to do with you?"

"It's pretty simple, Rial. Give back the money you stole and stop killing people with drugs."

"And the evidence you have? What happens to that?"

Mabel hoped that the button microphone she wore on her sweater was working as well as Ben said it would. She angled herself slightly, so that Cantwell's voice had a clear shot.

"How much did you actually steal, Rial?"

Cantwell looked out over the field below. More players were beginning to show. A few of them were his clients. He had taken money from these gladiators, men with a short earning window, men who would spend the rest of their lives popping pain killers and trying to remember the names of their kids.

"Ten billion, give or take. I never thought of it as stealing, though."

"You took money that wasn't yours. What else would that be?"

Cantwell's shoulders slumped. He let out a long sigh and brought a hand to his face. It was trembling. "The first time it happened, I needed money. I was leveraged to the teeth. I hadn't paid my employees in weeks, my mortgage in months. So, when this small-time trader says I could skim a little off the top and take it in cash…I had to do it. Otherwise, I would have lost everything. Others would have suffered.

"Then I went on a run, a good run, a great run. I thought I better skim a little more, create a bankroll that would get me through the next low spot. Nobody noticed, and the low spot never really came. Like I said before, sometimes I even put money *into* accounts." Cantwell paused. His eyes were pleading, like a cheating husband caught in the act. "I never took anything unless we did well, unless we were really kicking ass."

"It was your investors kicking ass, not you."

"I know," said Cantwell. "I know…But once you've started…it becomes a habit. You know?"

Mabel looked around. "Speaking of habits, where's Masco?"

Cantwell shook his head. "I don't know. Haven't seen him in days. He should be here, though. He wouldn't miss this."

"Where does he stand on the drug thing? Will he stop dealing?"

"I'll need to get him into rehab first. He's pretty messed up."

At that moment a hush fell across the room, as if it had been covered by an invisible blanket. All talking stopped for a few brief seconds, before beginning again with the volume raised.

"That must be Winde," said Cantwell. "Here to meet you."

Suddenly, Mabel had to pee. "Shoot," she muttered. She turned to Ben. "I've got to pee."

"Can't you hold it?" said Ben. Winde was scheduled for five minutes only. If Mabel went to the rest room, she might lose her chance.

Cantwell began walking across the suite. A large crowd had already surrounded Winde. He was talking with them jovially, although he did sneak a couple quick glances at his watch. He was on a tight timeline, with two dozen charity meetings planned throughout the game.

"Ahhh, Mr. Winde," said Cantwell. "So nice of you to join us." Cantwell took Mabel by the shoulder and tried to thrust her toward the quarterback. "Let me introduce you to Mrs. Mabel Witherspoon." Cantwell's gathering had morphed from mildly exuberant elegance into a boorish free-for-all. The guests were clambering around Winde like he was a rock star after a concert.

"Hello…hello…" said Mabel, as she tried to approach Winde.

"Let the woman pass!" shouted Cantwell.

The mob parted, Winde's fans drifting away with their heads hung down. The quiet endured for a few short seconds, before the guests resumed wolfing shrimp and drinking their drinks and talking far too loud.

Winde extended a hand. "Hello, Mrs. Witherspoon. It is a pleasure to meet you."

Mabel curtseyed, then squeezed her legs together tightly to keep from peeing in her pants.

"Are you all right?" said Winde.

"Sort of...I just need to pee."

Winde laughed. "I get that way before every game. I get dressed. Get all psyched to go out and play. Then I suddenly have to pee. Every time."

"Kinda sucks."

"May I escort you to the bathroom?"

Mabel looked over to the suite's private restroom. There was a line three ladies deep.

"You're such a charmer," she said.

Winde saw Mabel glance at the line and said, "There are bathrooms outside, just down the hall. Why don't I bring you there?"

Mabel smiled shyly and shook her head. "I can't believe you would do this."

"Like I said, I've been there. Every game."

Winde spoke to his bodyguards, telling them to remain at the reception. Mabel crooked her arm into Winde's elbow. The sea of guests parted and they began to walk toward the hallway.

As Mabel and Winde began to leave, Cantwell tapped Ben on the shoulder and said, "Can we talk?"

Ben glanced toward Mabel as she left with Winde. He decided she'd be safe. "Sure."

Cantwell pulled Ben over toward the window. "I've been doing an accounting, of what I...what my investors would have earned, had I not...borrowed."

Ben thought to tell Cantwell that he knew all this. He was tempted to tell him that he knew about the Swiss account Cantwell had just established through a Panama trust, and about the three billion dollars he had directed into this account. Once a crook, always a crook, thought Ben. However, if Cantwell learned that Ben could watch his every move, he might take precautions, precautions that would close the door to him, and the FBI. So, he kept silent.

"How much should Mabel's account be worth?"

"As of yesterday...seven million five hundred and seventy-eight thousand four hundred seven dollars and eighty-eight cents."

Ben whistled. "Must hurt like hell to return all that money, Rial."

Cantwell shrugged. "Not really." He smiled. "I've got some left."

"What about Masco?"

Cantwell spread his hands apart, his shoulders rising submissively. "That's why I wanted to talk. I don't know where he is."

Ben peered into Cantwell's eyes, trying to gauge the true meaning of this statement. Cantwell looked scared, almost bewildered. Was he? Or, was it just a good act?

"How long he been gone?"

"Close to a week."

"You think they have him?"

"Who?"

"I don't know," said Ben. "The cartels? Didn't he tell them he wanted out?"

"He did, but we paid up and took delivery."

"How much?" said Ben, but he already knew.

"All told?"

"Yeah."

"Three billion."

Three billion dollars, wholesale, thought Ben. What a frigging nightmare. How many people would die because of this?

Ben said, "Where do you think Lou is?"

"Don't know. That's what scares me."

"You think he skipped?"

Cantwell shrugged. "Not without his money. I've got his money."

"He'll show up."

"It's not like him, Ben. I'm worried."

"That scares *me*."

Chapter Thirty-Eight
V
____

"This will probably be the highlight of your Super Bowl week," said Mabel, as she and Winde exited Cantwell's suite into the hallway.

Winde smiled, while touching Mabel lightly on the shoulder. "I'm sure I'll never forget it."

"I appreciate this, I really do. I didn't wear my Depends 'cause I wanted to look good in my leather pants."

Winde laughed. It was a friendly chuckle, like he was laughing with Mabel, not at her. He said, "I needed the quiet anyway. You do look great."

"You think so?"

"Absolutely."

Mabel nodded. "Nothing like a geriatric in tight leathers."

Winde guided Mabel along the corridor. It was empty, except for two men standing beside a large cleaning cart over near the bathrooms. The men were wearing gray hoodie sweatshirts, like Bill Belichick often wears, with the hoods pulled over their heads.

"They're running you around like a rat in a maze, aren't they?" said Mabel.

"Yeah, but it's fun. How often do you get to play in the Super Bowl?"

"Never done so, myself," said Mabel.

"Me neither."

By the time they reached the bathrooms, the men by the linen cart hadn't moved. They appeared to be talking to one another, their backs toward Mabel and Winde, their cart blocking the entrance to the ladies' room.

"Excuse us, please," said Winde.

Both men turned. Mabel could see that one of them was Lou Masco. He had a crooked smile on his face and a pistol in his hand. His partner had a pistol, too. Before Mabel could cry out, both men pulled their triggers. There was a soft *pfft, pfft,* as the guns released their darts.

Mabel felt herself swoon. The world seemed to darken around her, like a candle snuffer being dropped around her brain. Her knees buckled and she tipped to one side, but not before Masco caught her by the armpits. He picked her up and tossed her into the cart like a load of laundry.

It took a couple extra moments for Winde to go down. He lunged forward and tried to wrap his fingers around the neck of his shooter. He fell into the man's arms. The man turned him around, bent him over and slung him onto his shoulder like a fireman. The shooter was careful to dump Winde into the cart without hurting Mabel. Even so, as he lowered the quarterback over Mabel's inert body, she let out a soft *squeak.* Mabel didn't appear to be hurt, just covered with two hundred and fifty pounds of limp quarterback.

The man said, "Think she'll be able to breathe with him on her?"

"Stop worrying, Jimmy. She's tougher than both of us combined." Masco pulled several folded towels from beneath the cart and threw them over Mabel and Winde. When their bodies were concealed, Masco said, "That was easy."

"Did you see who that guy was?" said Jimmy.

"Wrong place, wrong time."

"Jesus. I've got money on this game…on *him.*"

"You might want to bet the other side." Masco looked at his watch and grinned. "Like in the next ten minutes."

"What the hell did we do? Do you know what we just did?"

Masco shrugged. "We took care of a problem. Let's move. We've got five minutes."

"We kidnapped one of the quarterbacks in the goddamned Super Bowl!"

"Shhh. Don't worry about it."

"Worry about it? Do you know how many people are going to be looking for Winde? And not just cops. Half the wise guys in the country will be on our butts."

Masco said, "Not if you keep your mouth shut."

"Keep my friggin' mouth shut? I ain't saying nothing to nobody."

Masco wheeled the cart to an elevator which brought them down into the bowels of the stadium. Less than two minutes later, they stopped the cart beside the back of a panel truck. It had the name *Mario's Fine Meats*

& Provisions stenciled across the side and the rear. Masco and Jimmy lifted Winde into the back of the truck, then tossed Mabel beside him. Jimmy jumped inside, while Masco walked calmly forward, sat behind the wheel and started the engine.

Inside the rear of the truck, Jimmy strapped a pair of plastic handcuffs around Winde's wrists, then around his ankles. He did the same with Mabel. Outside the truck, Masco began driving.

By the time Ben grew worried about Mabel and Winde, they were already on the road, gliding away from Sun Life Stadium as if they had never existed.

Chapter Thirty-Nine
V
____

Ben Johnson slipped into the hall off the Cantwell suite. He walked to the bathrooms, stuck his head inside the ladies room and hollered, "Mabel? Are you in there?"

Hearing nothing, Ben went into the men's room. "Mabel?" The room was empty, too.

Okay, thought Ben. Mabel was unpredictable. Maybe she'd convinced Winde to take her somewhere, maybe to other parties to meet some of the players, maybe Favre. He called Tony Trance, who was sitting inside a van filled with electronics, in the stadium's parking lot.

"Can you hear Mabel?" he asked.

Tony said, "Haven't heard a peep for five minutes or so. Just some rustling of fabric. Nothing at all for the past two minutes. She was heading to the bathroom."

"She's not there. Did she ask Winde to go somewhere?"

"No. They were just going to the head."

"Dang it."

"You think we have trouble?"

"I do."

"Hold on, I'll get McBride. He's inside the stadium."

A moment later, McBride came on the line.

"Ben?"

"Mike, I think Mabel Witherspoon has been harmed, maybe kidnapped."

"She's gone?"

"So's Winde."

"You've got to be frigging kidding me."

"Last we heard, Winde was escorting Mabel to the bathroom." Ben looked to his watch. "That was about seven minutes ago. Haven't heard anything since."

"Damn, damn, damn. Hold a sec."

Ben could hear McBride talking on the other end of the line. Then he heard a *click*. A minute or two later, McBride was back.

"I've got Chief Esposito and Agent Griffin on the line, Ben."

"Gentlemen," said Ben. "I'll get to the point. I was with Mabel Witherspoon in Cantwell's suite. Things were going well. Cantwell admitted to stealing money and dealing drugs. We got it recorded.

"Winde came for his meet and greet with Mabel. She asked to be escorted to the head—"

Esposito interrupted. "She used her time with Winde to take a leak?"

"She's got a weak bladder, and she wanted to wear leather pants...Anyway, they left the suite to go the loo, and we haven't heard from them since. It's been nearly ten minutes."

"Signs of struggle?" said Esposito.

"None."

"Any chance they went somewhere?"

"We'd hear them. The mic I've got on her is pretty sensitive. Any place you could use a cell phone, we'd hear her, to a range of a mile."

"What about Winde? He gone, too?"

"I'm afraid so."

"You lost one of the quarterbacks in the Super Bowl?" said Griffin.

Ben laughed at the irony. "I kinda did. Along with a very fine woman."

Esposito said, "The Pro Bowl is about to get underway, Ben. Seventy-two thousand in the stands."

"That's a hell of a dilemma, sir."

"We've got facial recognition software engaged," said Griffin. "I'll get their pictures on the grid. We'll start scanning. You have a photo of Witherspoon?"

"I do," said Ben. He put his PDA on speaker, opened his email and sent a picture of Mabel to Tony Trance. "I just emailed a JPEG to Tony. He'll forward it on to you."

A moment later, Griffin said, "Got it."

"We should lock things down," said Esposito.

"No," said Griffin. "If they're smart enough to take down a firebrand like Witherspoon and a man as strong as Winde, they're savvy enough to slip our net this quickly."

Esposito said, "We can search every vehicle leaving the stadium. Then circle in from there."

Griffin said, "This is damage control, chief. We keep this quiet. Keep this to yourself, Esposito."

"People are already worried. They've got to be. You know Winde's schedule."

"Put out a story. Say that he came down with something."

Esposito groaned. "If I were in charge—"

Griffin said, "You're not. I'll take full responsibility."

"Bet your ass, you will."

Chapter Forty
V

Mabel could sense little shreds of the world beginning to open up around her, as if she were awakening from a night of hard drinking. Consciousness came slowly. She could feel pain in her shoulders, radiating down to the hands bound behind her back. As her senses cleared, she noticed the floor, then the rocking from side to side. The floor was hard. It had an odd smell, like blood and cardboard, and something that reminded her of dry ice.

Mabel opened her eyes and focused. She was in the back of a truck. There was nothing inside it; it was just a hollow shell. Except for the body of Winde.

"Are you okay?" Mabel said.

Winde began to mumble. "Where…What the hell?"

"Are you okay?" Mabel said again.

"Where are we?"

"We've been kidnapped." Mabel remembered the microphone. "Ben? Ben, can you hear me? Ben, I'm in the back of a truck."

"What are you doing?" said Winde.

Mabel thought to tell Winde about the microphone, about what they'd been doing with Cantwell. But she decided against it. "Just being silly. I was hoping someone would hear us."

Half an hour later, the truck jerked to a squealing stop. Nobody checked on them. Hours passed. Still, nobody came. It began to get cold and damp and dark, like the inside of a tomb. Maybe it was their tomb.

Chapter Forty-One
V

Tony Trance looked across the conference room to the eclectic group he'd assembled to help track down Mabel and Winde. They were sitting in chairs, calmly waiting to see how they could help. Many would say that these people should have stuck to retirement, sailed off into the proverbial sunset with as little fuss as possible. Some might say that these people had long-since passed their primes. But Tony knew better. These were some of the toughest sons-of-bitches in Miami. You've got to be tough to get old, and these people had surely done their time.

"Gentlemen and ladies," Tony said. "We've got a problem."

Tony looked out to the expectant faces, their eyes laced with years of wisdom, some with cataracts. Three dozen of the finest operatives in SOSCADA, the Society of Senior Citizens Against Drug Abuse. These people, along with hundreds of others, spent their days doing the grunt work that the police and the FBI could no longer afford. These were the people that would sift through documents, hour after endless hour, until they had found some hidden gem, a deed registered to a dummy corporation that was registered to another shell, and so on. These were the people who would talk to their kids and their grandkids, learning what was really going on in the world. They didn't sit in front of their computer screens (although some of them did). They didn't peer at satellite images and hold meetings in tenth story conference rooms. They had their feet on the ground. They got things *done*.

Tony said, "As you know, Terry Winde has been kidnapped. He went missing with a woman named Mabel Witherspoon. Mabel was working with us to bust a ring of drug dealers. They were taken during yesterday's Pro Bowl, and haven't been heard from since. The FBI is working with NRO and the NSA. They've got satellite imagery of Sun Life Stadium and they're sifting through it as we speak. But there were hundreds of vehicles going in and out, and the grid has serious holes. There's some footage from the blimp and other media aircraft. But they're all focused on the field. The fact is, any car or truck that carried our people from the stadium is gone, and we probably won't find it.

"The FBI's got license plates and they're running them down. They've got some leads and they're running *them* down. But, so far…" Tony paused. "So far, they've got nothing."

Tony fiddled with a computer until an image flashed upon a screen behind him.

"This is Louis Masco. We think he's the one who engineered the kidnapping. Masco has been the fix-it man for an investment advisor by the name of Rial Cantwell. Masco is also involved with financing much of the southeast's drug trade.

"Cantwell has been embezzling from his clients. Together, he and Masco have accumulated billions in offshore accounts.

"Mabel Witherspoon threatened to expose the two men, unless they returned the stolen money to investors and stopped dealing drugs. Cantwell appeared to making preparations to do so. Masco worried that he and Cantwell would be executed by the cartels if they stopped dealing. He may be right.

"A week ago, Masco went rogue and vanished. We think he used this time to arrange the kidnapping of Witherspoon, to stop her from revealing his crimes. We think Winde is collateral damage. There is no ransom demand."

Tony took a sip of coffee. He looked to Ben Johnson, who was standing with him at the front of the room. Michael McBride stood beside Ben, acting as an unofficial representative of the law. Tony motioned toward the two men.

"Most of you know Ben Johnson and Chief McBride. Ben has intimate knowledge of Cantwell's operations. McBride is acting as liaison between the various law enforcement agencies involved in this case. I don't think that I need to stress the urgency here, but I will. These people must be found, and found soon."

Gumbo was seated closest to Tony. He was dressed in a pair of black slacks and a charcoal wool turtleneck sweater, similar to the one his informant had worn at the Essex hotel.

Gumbo said, "Masco's got to be holding them in a property that he, or Cantwell, owns. We need eyes inside every office building, warehouse, home, boat or truck they might possess. I'll task my people to find any word on the street, get my girls on it today."

Tony looked over to Murray Stein, the former mob-boss CPA, now SOSCADA'S Minister of Information. His job was to gather data. He had hundreds of retiree operatives pouring through records in dozens of states and countries. He had computer specialists who routinely hacked into the databases of known drug dealers and crooked foreign banks, gleaming information that could be discreetly forwarded to the authorities. He also had people still working in the various government agencies, people who weren't afraid to take a little risk to end the career of a criminal.

Murray said, "We'll see if we can run out more strings of property ownership, to find ones that Cantwell and Masco might own. It isn't easy, you know. A property could be owned by a company based in Grand Cayman. This company could be owned by a corporation in the Cook Islands, which is owned by a company in Luxembourg, which is owned by a trust in Panama, and so on. Some of the ownership strings go on forever."

Tony said, "We're looking for a place that nobody knows about. That means your work is vital. The FBI will get warrants to search all of the known Cantwell and Masco properties. If they can't find Winde and Mabel, we'll have to do better."

Murray said, "What if they're renting a place? Or borrowing one?"

"No stone goes unturned." Tony pointed toward McBride. "Chief McBride wants to say a few words."

McBride smoothed the edges of his tan silk suit, then adjusted his cufflinks so that they were square. He ran his fingers through his long, graying hair and cleared his throat.

"Most of you know that I worked in the Miami PD for thirty years. Ran the place for a decade. Some of you know that I have intimate knowledge about how effective *you* can be."

McBride tugged nervously at his cufflinks. He straightened his paisley tie and continued. "I did some stupid things while I was on the force, got in bed with a drug dealer named Cesar. Your organization helped take him down, along with me. I was lucky enough to get a presidential pardon, with the caveat that I would spend the rest of my career correcting my mistakes.

"I stand before you as a man who believes in what you do, who understands that regular people can affect the outcome of a nation. I understand that senior citizens have more to give to this country than most people realize, and I welcome your help.

"We have more than five hundred people tasked to this effort. Losing a quarterback right before the Super Bowl is not only a tragedy, but an embarrassment in the eyes of the world. Two lives are at stake. Hundreds of thousands of law enforcement officials will also be affected. If we don't find Mabel Witherspoon and Winde, we will become a laughingstock, the butt of jokes for years to come. Miami doesn't need that. Neither does the country.

"I have been authorized to work with you..." McBride paused. "...informally, but with full responsibility for your actions. I hereby deputize you, along with all members of SOSCADA, to help find Witherspoon and Winde, and bring their kidnappers to justice.

"I don't think I need to remind you, but I will. All of this remains confidential."

Chapter Forty-Two
V

"How are you feeling?" said Mabel.

It felt like they were in an underground cave—dark and as damp as midnight fog. *It must be night outside*, thought Mabel. The air inside the truck was growing colder, and Mabel was beginning to shiver.

"My bum shoulder hurts." Winde laughed. "Feels like after a game."

"Ice it in your mind."

"I'm too cold already." Winde paused. "Think that'll work?"

"Of course, it will."

"How are *you* doing, Mabel?"

Mabel's shoulders had grown numb. The plastic ties binding her wrists were cutting deeply into her skin. Her bad leg was beginning to throb and tremble. She had to pee so bad she could feel it in her eye sockets. "I'm feeling pretty good, considering."

"Where do you think we are?"

"In the back of a truck."

Winde chuckled. "Figured that out myself."

"We were kidnapped by a man named Louis Masco."

"Lou Masco? The guy that partners with Cantwell?"

"That's the one."

"Son-of-a-bitch. Never liked that man."

"You're a client, too?" said Mabel.

"Yeah."

"Then we're doubly screwed."

"Someone will save us."

After a pause, Mabel said, "We might have to save ourselves."

"You know something I don't?"

"Lots."

Winde grew silent. Mabel wondered what he was thinking. Probably fretting about his family, wondering if he'd get the chance to play in the big game and wondering if his throwing shoulder would be okay.

At that moment, the truck began to move. It backed up, with a high pitched *beep*, then started moving forward again. Soon, there were little flashes of light coming from the outside. Mabel could see that Winde had propped himself into a corner and was leaning awkwardly against the side of the truck, his arms behind him.

"What kind of a truck you think this is?" said Winde, making conversation.

"It's a meat truck," said Mabel. She'd had experience with packers and distributors during her farming days. She knew the smells. "Mostly beef."

"*Mostly* beef?"

"I smell a little lamb, too. No pork."

"Who are you, Mabel, other than someone who can tell the difference between beef and lamb and pork?"

"I was a dancer, Terry. Then a farmer's wife. Now, I'm a widow with a grandson. What about you, besides being a quarterback?"

"I'm a husband and a father. Got two little girls, pretty little things. I've got a mother in Georgia and a brother in Dallas."

The truck slowed to a halt. They heard the grinding of a motor, then a *thud*, as a heavy warehouse door hit the ground. The two front doors to the truck opened, then shut. They could hear footsteps shuffling outside. After a moment, the back of the truck slid up. Light flooded in, blinding Mabel and Winde for a long moment. Six men were standing outside the truck. They were arranged in a semi-circle, each holding an automatic weapon. A cavernous, empty warehouse spread out behind them.

Lou Masco stepped into view. "Greetings, Mabel."

"Hello, asshole."

Masco chuckled. "Hello to you, too, Terry. Sorry you had to get mixed up in this."

Winde looked over at Mabel. "This was about you? Not me?"

"Yeah. Masco and his partner were stealing from investors and I found out about it. Lou's been—"

Masco interrupted, "Yeah, yeah…I've been running with the wrong crowd. Buying and selling dope to teenagers. Well, lah-di-fucking-dah."

"He's a junkie," said Mabel. "And he can't stop."

"Shut up!" shouted Masco. "Shut the fuck up." Masco's eyes grew wide and unseeing, stabbing from side to side, as if he were watching an invisible fly. Glistening pimples of sweat had broken out along his forehead. A thin, oily stream was beginning to run down into his eyes. He kept wiping at it with the sleeve of his soaked white shirt, but it wouldn't stop.

"What are you going to do?" said Mabel. "Every lawman this side of the Mississippi will be looking for us."

"All I want…" Masco's breathing was heavy and harsh, as if his heart were stuttering. "…is for you to…back off."

"Are you okay, Lou?" said Mabel. "You look like you're about to freak, maybe pass out. I've got some Geritol in my purse. You want some?"

Masco leaned against the side of the truck. "I'd be far more worried about yourself, Mabel." He looked at Winde. "And you…What the hell were you doing with Witherspoon?" Masco looked at Mabel. "I thought he was Ben."

Winde said, "She won Cantwell's charity auction. For breast cancer."

Masco closed his eyes. "Oh, yeah. Forgot about that."

Mabel said, "How'd you know I'd go out to pee?"

Masco laughed. "You always have to pee."

"I could have used the bathroom inside the suite."

"There's always a line at this sort of thing. With your bladder, I knew you wouldn't wait."

Mabel looked to the floor. Her goddamned bladder. You begin getting old and things start to quit. The eyes, the ears, the knees and the hips. People don't talk much about the bladder. You never hear about it, except in those stupid TV commercials that show beautiful, pre-menopausal woman who should be doing makeup commercials, not ads about a problem they won't have for another twenty years. Yeah, the loss of bladder control is the real silent killer, the silent killer of freedom.

"I peed in my pants, Lou. Are you going to have the decency to help me with that?"

Masco chuckled. He walked around the end of the truck. He came back hefting a bulky contraption. It looked like a plastic toilet seat attached to a holding tank throne of PVC plastic. Masco handed the toilet to one of his men, who carried it into the truck. Masco went back around the truck. This time, he returned holding a fresh set of woman's clothing in a neat little pile. He also carried a white plastic grocery bag. He gave the clothes and bag to another one of his men, who brought them inside the truck. Mabel could see that the clothes were for her. The bag contained cylinders of Wet Ones hand and face wipes, along with a box of granola bars.

Masco smiled. "I knew you'd pee your pants, Mabel."

Mabel smirked. "If you're so smart, how come you can't cut ties with drug dealers?"

"Because you can't sever ties with that kind of animal, Mabel. They're inhuman. Once you've done business with them, they think they own you."

"Does that make you one, too? An animal?"

"Fuck you."

Mabel closed her eyes. There wasn't a rational bone in this man's body. Lou had lost touch with reality. Maybe it was the drugs. Maybe it was the drug dealers. Maybe it was the stress of having to give it all up. Whatever it was, he was a powder keg and she was a lit fuse, drawing closer and closer, ready to touch him off.

"Why don't you let us go, Lou? I'll have Ben destroy the evidence. We'll work with you to take down those dealers, take them out for good. We'll get you into witness protection—"

"Witness protection? Are you frigging nuts? I'd rather die."

"You're going to die."

Masco smiled. It was an eerie smile, a crazy, Jack Nicholson kind of smile. "You're right, Mabel. I probably am. And you're both going to die with me."

Mabel shrugged. "Well, if we're going to die, at least let us be comfortable. Is that too much to ask?"

Masco scrunched his lips. His head angled to one side and then to the other. "Okay," he said. He motioned with his head toward one of his men. "Secure their hands in front. New ties are inside."

The guard handed his weapon to Masco and jumped up into the truck. He reached for the box of ties on the floor and pulled out a fistful of new ones. He stuffed them into the back pocket of his jeans, then pulled a switchblade out of a holster on his belt. The knife opened with a deadly *click*. He cut the tie securing Winde's feet and then the one around his wrists.

With the quickness of a big jungle cat, Winde grabbed the guard's wrist. He squeezed until the knife fell to the floor. Then he spun the man by his shoulders, so that he was facing Masco. Winde draped an arm down across the guard's chest from behind and held him as a shield. He began to walk with him toward the edge of the truck bed. Masco calmly raised a rifle to his shoulder and shot the guard in the upper thigh.

"Owww!" shouted the guard. "Jesus, that hurts."

"Next shot's in the chest, Winde."

Winde let go of the guard, who hobbled out of the truck, whimpering.

"You want to be next?" Masco said.

Winde shook his head slowly. "Guess that was kind of stupid," he mumbled.

"Kind of," said Masco. He nodded toward one of the other men. "Let's try this again."

The second guard jumped into the truck. He slipped a new tie around Winde's wrists, this time in front.

"I'm going to leave your legs unrestrained," said Masco. "So that you can remain comfortable, as Mabel requested. The first move you make to fight or get away, someone puts a bullet in your knee. Got it?"

Winde nodded.

The second guard cut away the binding around Mabel's ankles. Then he replaced the tie behind her back with one in front.

Mabel said, "That's far more comfortable, Lou. Thank you."

"Don't abuse the privilege."

Masco began to pull the truck door down again. When the slider reached eye height, he tossed a couple of water bottles inside. "We'll bring you food in an hour or so." He laughed. "Until then, don't go any-where." He shut the door the rest of the way. A few moments later, they heard a tapping *clank* of a padlock, and then the metallic *swish*, as Masco released it from his grip.

"You think we'll die in here?" Winde said into the dark.

"No," said Mabel. "Better stay sharp. You've got a game to play. I sug-gest you start practicing."

"I'm a little tied up here."

"In your mind, you can be as free as a sparrow."

Chapter Forty-Three
V

Michael McBride stood at the front of the conference room, staring at the series of photos that were being shown upon the wall.

He said, "Cantwell and Masco own all of these places?"

The FBI's Griffin said, "They've got a shitload of real estate. They own some properties personally. Some is owned by their U.S. companies. Others are owned by offshore entities. Still more is held for investors. So far, we've found over ninety properties. No blanket warrants have been secured."

"We'll need a separate warrant to search each and every one?"

"In sixteen states and seven countries."

"They going to give us those?"

Griffin shrugged. "We've had some resistance. But in time, I suppose. We'll get them all."

"We have no time!" yelled McBride.

"Then that's a problem. We're already getting mucho political heat, saying this is a witch hunt."

"What about our evidence?"

"What evidence? What *legal* evidence do we have?"

"Have you been able to secure a warrant to ride Cantwell's computer?"

"We need probable cause."

"Isn't a kidnapping enough probable cause?"

"Apparently not. The judge is an asshole."

"Then find us another one."

"Doesn't work that way."

At that moment, the rest of this meeting's attendees began to filter into the conference room, including Jason Starr, the Special Agent assigned by the FBI to head the investigation.

Starr nudged McBride and Griffin away from the head of the table and positioned himself squarely in front. He picked up the handheld computer control and began sifting through the PowerPoint slides and photos. He didn't say a word until everyone else was seated.

Once the door to the conference room had been closed and locked, Starr said, "Time is of the essence, people. So, let's get this meeting underway." He turned to Jerry Giles, the Special Agent in Charge for the FBI's Miami field office. "Tell me what you've got. You change their minds about the warrants?"

Giles nervously cleared his throat. "No, sir. Not going to happen. We'll need to go jurisdiction by jurisdiction, property by property."

"Then, get out of here and get on it."

Giles picked up his papers and hurried out of the room.

Starr turned to Griffin, of the JTTF. "What do you have?"

"We've been able to search three warehouses, where suspected drug deals have taken place. We've taken fourteen people in for questioning. No one seems to know a thing. Except…Seems there's a saying going 'round that Winde and Witherspoon are 'dead meat'."

"What do you make of that?"

"Don't know, sir."

"What else?"

"We busted twenty-two kilos of marijuana."

"Not germane. What about Winde?"

"Nada."

"Get back to work."

Starr turned toward Esposito. "What about you, Chief?"

Esposito shrugged. "I've got officers beating the streets. We've remanded several dozen known informants and cohorts of Masco. Nothing solid. We heard the same saying. They're 'dead meat'."

"Gotta mean something. You have anything else worth knowing?"

"No, sir."

"Get back to work. Follow up on the dead meat thing."

Chapter Forty-Four
V
____

The interrogation room was small, perhaps eight feet by ten. It had a dented pressed board table and three metal chairs. The walls were bare, except for a large one-way mirror. The rest was just squares of acoustic tile.

Rial Cantwell sat in the room alone, his elbows propped upon the table, while he stared around at the walls.

"He looks calm," said Chief Esposito, as he watched Cantwell through the mirror.

"Yeah," said the man beside Esposito. The new man's name was Charles Akron, on loan from Quantico. Akron was short, with the smooth and rotund face of a chubby baby. He was forty years old, but looked thirty. His arms and legs were like pulpy white sausages. His fingers were short and squat. His only jewelry was a pinky ring, a high school class ring that was now too small to wear on its original target. Akron taught interrogation for the FBI, and there was no one better.

"How long you going to leave him there?" said the chief.

Akron peered at Cantwell, who was now drumming his fingers upon the table. Akron moved away from the window and reached for a round volume knob that was on the wall. He adjusted the knob until they could make out the beat of Cantwell's fingers.

"You hear that?" said Akron.

The chief looked puzzled. "What about it?"

"It's the Star Spangled Banner. He's drumming the frickin' Star Spangled Banner."

"Huh," said Esposito. "Never would have guessed."

"You can learn a lot from a man's fingers."

Esposito curled his lower lip and began to nod. What did Akron's fat sausage fingers say about him? That he ate too much? That he had a thyroid problem? Or, that he just didn't care? "Okay."

The two men stood watching Cantwell for another half hour. Most of the time Cantwell sat. Occasionally he would stand and walk around the room. A couple of times he stared at himself in the mirror, adjusting his hair.

Cantwell was peering at his teeth, when Akron said, "He's a vain mother."

Esposito said, "As far as I know, vanity is not a crime."

Akron looked sharply at Esposito. He frowned, then snorted, "You on his side?"

Esposito shook his head. "Nah. I'm on the side of the law."

"He's guilty as hell, and I'll prove it." Akron shrugged. "Okay, Espy. It's time. Go do your thing."

Esposito looked over at Akron, his eyes questioning. "Can I bring him something? Water? Food?"

"No."

When Esposito walked into the interrogation room, Cantwell was seated by the center of the cheap table, leaning back upon his chair, staring at the ceiling. Esposito took a chair directly across from him.

"Hello, Rial," said the chief.

"Hello, Álvaro."

"You've put us all in a very bad spot."

"Tell that to my lawyer."

"You want a lawyer?"

Cantwell smiled. "No. I've got nothing to hide."

Akron was staring through the window, reading Cantwell's face and measuring his voice. "Arrogant bastard," he mumbled. That was good. Cantwell was acting as he'd hoped he would. Arrogance got you screwed, every frickin' time.

Cantwell said, "Can I have some water or something?"

Esposito shook his head. "Later. First, I need to understand some things."

"Like what?"

"Like why two of your investors, one a Super Bowl quarterback, the other a dotty old lady, would get kidnapped at one of your parties."

Cantwell shrugged. "Beats me, Álvaro. Don't you guys have video or something? Surely you can see that I'm innocent of this."

"Isn't it true that Witherspoon was complaining about you?"

"Investors complain all the time, Chief. They're never happy…always want more."

"Isn't it true that she went to the police and complained about your partner?"

Cantwell leaned forward and pressed his elbows upon the table. He lowered his voice and said, "Do you realize how much of a target I am?"

"Right now you're the prime suspect in a kidnapping investigation."

Cantwell made *tssk, tssk, tssk* sounds with his tongue. "Do you seriously think that a man of my stature and visibility would try such a thing?"

"I sure as hell do."

Cantwell sat in silence for a long while. Esposito sat with him, looking at Cantwell, who simply stared back.

After several minutes, Cantwell said, "Have you been able to find Lou?"

Esposito shook his head.

"Think he's been kidnapped, too?"

Esposito laughed. "You are one cool shit, Cantwell."

"Innocence will do that to a man."

Esposito's eyes narrowed. "What if I were to tell you that we have financial records showing that you stole ten billion dollars from your clients? And that Masco has earned five from dealing drugs? That this sum is now worth thirty-three billion dollars, held in the following accounts…" Esposito pulled a paper out of his pocket and began reading a series of account numbers.

Cantwell's face suddenly lost its bravado, the color draining out of it as if a plug had been pulled. If they knew this, they could know other things, more dangerous things.

"How…how do you know this?"

"What do you think we are, dumb?" Esposito paused. "You want your attorney now? You going to shrink away behind some grease ball lawyer?"

Cantwell ran his fingers through his silky hair and straightened in his chair. "You don't scare me, Esposito."

"Well, you better be scared. Because we've got enough to send you away for the next forty years." Esposito peered at Cantwell and smiled. "Unless, you want to cut some kind of deal?"

Cantwell jumped up from the table and shouted, "I don't know where he is!"

"Who?"

"Masco! He must be behind this. I don't know where he is or what he's doing."

Esposito made his own *tssk, tssk, tssk* sounds. "Surely you must know where he'd be?"

"Not a goddamn clue."

"Do the words 'dead meat' mean anything to you?"

A flush came to Cantwell's face. Akron looked on with interest. Esposito was doing pretty well.

"That's a saying Lou uses. When someone becomes his target, he calls them 'dead meat'."

"Dead as in *dead*?"

"No! For God's sakes, Álvaro, we're not killers."

"That's not what I hear. What about Taylor? And Jameson? And Vermeer? What about them, Rial?"

Cantwell's breathing started to *huff* and *chug*, like a car caught between gears. He closed his eyes and tried to control himself. He took a long, deep gulp of air and held it in. He gripped his fists, then let them relax slowly. "I don't know what you mean."

"You want a lawyer now, Mr. Pretty Boy? Or do you want to cut a deal?"

"There is no deal. I don't know a goddamn thing."

"But Masco is your partner."

"I told you, he vanished. I don't know where he is."

Cantwell's breathing morphed into raspy gasps, as if he'd jumped onto a treadmill and was walking fast while trying to talk. "Can…I…have a drink of water now?"

The door clicked open and Akron poked his head into the room. "Chief? You've got some visitors outside."

Chief Esposito rose from his chair and said to Cantwell, "We're not done." Then he left the room.

Akron walked over and stood beside Esposito's seat at the table. He didn't sit down. Instead, he reached a hand across the table and said, "Hi. My name is Charles Akron. Call me Charlie."

Cantwell reached out and shook Akron's cool, dry pulpy hand.

Akron kept hold of Cantwell's fingers, while staring into his eyes. "I'm the guy who's supposed to beat the shit out of you for information."

Cantwell smiled crookedly. "If you must. But I can't help you."

"You sure you don't want a lawyer?"

"You going to beat me?"

Akron shook his head. "Nah. *I* think you're telling the truth." Akron looked around the table, as if suddenly noticing that it was empty. "You want something to drink? Water? Coffee? I'm starved. How 'bout a sandwich?"

Akron walked to the door. "Hey!" he yelled. "How 'bout some food here!"

A couple minutes later, an officer appeared. He was wheeling a serving cart, a special one that Akron had brought with him from Virginia. The cart had cans of Coke, Pepsi and Dr. Pepper. There were several bottles of Zephyrhills water, and a large coffee thermos, with a push down handle. There were also sandwiches wrapped in clear plastic.

"What kind of sandwich you want?" Akron fumbled through the sandwiches. "Me?" he said. "I'm a ham and cheese guy. You like ham and cheese? We've got two of them here."

"Sure," said Cantwell. "And a coffee…and a water, if you please."

Akron pumped some coffee into a Styrofoam cup and set it before Cantwell. He grabbed a couple of waters and two sandwiches, then placed them upon the table.

"Don't like to interrogate on an empty stomach," Akron said, smiling.

"Is that what this is, an interrogation?"

Akron shrugged. "They brought me down here to help find Witherspoon and Winde. That puts my nuts in a cracker. Do you realize the mess we're all in?"

Cantwell shook his head. "I'm sorry? I'm not following you."

"This Winde thing. A quarterback in the frigging Super Bowl? That's as bad as someone shooting the vice president, maybe worse. We've got the whole goddamned world watching us, a billion people set to tune their TV sets on the big game, and we've lost a quarterback. You see what I mean?"

"I know. It's a tragedy. But, I can't help you."

"I think you can. You just don't know it."

Akron took a large bite of his sandwich, as big a chunk as his mouth would hold. The bread stuck out from his lips as he chomped. He took a swig of water to help wash it down. After he'd swallowed the last of it, Akron leaned forward and farted loudly.

"There," he groaned. "I feel much better now." He settled back into his seat and said, "So, tell me what it is that you do."

Cantwell stared at Akron for a long moment, then said, "What I do?"

"Yeah. Tell me about your business."

"I manage money."

"Yeah, but how?" Akron leaned farther back in his chair. He took another large bite of his sandwich and motioned with it for Cantwell to speak. "Tell me," he said, through a mouthful of bread. "Tell me what you do."

"Well, we manage over a hundred billion in client funds…You know anything about the stock market, Charlie?"

"Yeah. Whenever I decide to invest, it goes down."

Cantwell smiled. "There are two important parts to the stock market, Charlie. There's the underlying financial condition of the economy, which ultimately breaks down to the specific companies. Then, there's the psychological part. I'm guessing that you decide to invest when your friends begin bragging about how much money they've made. Or, when *Money Magazine* starts touting how good the markets have been, how to get rich…"

"That's about right. I invest when stocks get hot."

"Now…" Cantwell sat forward in his chair, suddenly in his element. He forgot that he was being interrogated. He forgot about his missing partner. He forgot about Mabel Witherspoon and the Super Bowl. All he could think about were the financial markets, and how to spin them to his advantage. He was a shark and this was his ocean feeding ground.

"…Imagine a whole country of people feeling the way you do. Then imagine the brokers who take your orders for stocks, the mutual fund companies that accept the money you send, all of them forced to do your will, whether they think it's smart or not. Then, imagine this going on all around the globe. Everyone is reading the papers, watching the news, and watching the DOW or the S&P, as they go up and down like yos yos.

"The economy does not change in a day, unless Congress or the president do something myopic. But, our *perception* of the economy changes by the minute. I have dozens of people who analyze how this all interacts. If China threatens to restrict the money flow from banks, the markets react. If the president wants to regulate or tax the banks or energy, the markets react. If the Fed wants to raise or lower interest rates, the markets react. The thing is, the markets usually *overreact*. They can move ten percent in a week. That's where we can make some money."

"You make money off of stupid people?"

Cantwell laughed. "One way to say it. We have long, complicated algorithms that are programmed into trading models. These cause us to trade stocks without a human hand. All day long, these programs run, buying and selling all the time. As we sit here, my programs are hard at work. Buying or selling, sometimes both."

Akron took another bite of his sandwich. He walked over and poured himself a coffee. "Well, what do *you* do, Rial?"

"I help determine what gets written into the code. I also place big bets on major moves in the markets, both here and abroad."

Akron tongued at a piece of ham in his teeth. "So, should I be buying or selling?"

"Yes," said Cantwell. He laughed. "Right now, the markets are treading water, consolidating. No major moves. In times like these, we could shift money to stocks that we perceive to be undervalued. We might hedge in other areas of opportunity, sometimes buying, sometimes selling…gold, commodities, currencies…wherever things get out of whack."

"But how do you know? How can *I* know?"

Cantwell laughed again. "You will never know, Charlie. That's why you hire someone like me."

"Will you invest my money? For me?"

"How much do you have?"

"I don't know. Fifty thousand, maybe."

"Buy mutual funds."

"Aw, c'mon Rial. Won't you help me here?"

"I wish I could."

"What about Masco?" said Akron.

"What about him?"

"If you guys are so successful, why does he deal drugs?"

"Because he's addicted."

Bingo, thought Akron. This was his gift; with his odd looks and igno-rant demeanor, people never saw it coming, that stake to the center of the heart. It was coming, his kill shot. He could feel it, as easily as Cantwell could feel the markets.

"What do you mean, he's addicted?"

"In a way, we all become addicted. That's why we do it."

"You're addicted to stock trading?"

"I'm probably addicted to all kinds of trading."

"But Masco is addicted to drugs?"

Cantwell sighed. "Don't know how that happened."

Bingo.

Akron said, "Masco started testing product?"

Cantwell shrugged.

Akron continued, "Now he's in bed with Santiago and Diaz and Khan?"

Cantwell shrugged again. "I told him to stop. I *begged* him to stop."

"You think they have him?"

"Lou?" Cantwell shook his head. "No, they need him."

Akron took the last bite of his sandwich and said, between chews, "You're innocent of all this, aren't you?"

"I told you that."

"If Lou were to be hiding out, where do you think he'd go?"

"I don't know, one of the companies, I suppose."

"One of what companies?"

Cantwell's eyes grew suddenly wide. "You fucker," he said.

Akron smiled. "Yeah. I am."

"Is this when I call my lawyer?"

"No. You're free to go."

Chapter Forty-Five
V
___

"Do you think they'll ever let us out of this thing?" said Mabel. She looked over at Winde. He was sitting against the side of the truck with his eyes closed.

It was daytime. The warehouse around the truck was lighted by a series of windows high upon the walls. It wasn't bright inside, but there was enough light to filter into the truck. Mabel could just make out Winde's face. It had lost its spark. He was taking on the look of a quitter, not that of a winning quarterback.

Winde said, "What day do you think it is?"

"Wednesday, I think. Time for your workout."

Winde laughed. "You're worse than my coaches."

"You will throw three hundred passes today. And run three miles."

"Can't throw so many passes this late in the season, Mabel. My shoulder will fall off."

"Do it anyway. And I want you running fast. Sprints at the end."

"Yes, ma'am."

"If you're going to play in the Super Bowl, you'll need to be sharp."

Winde held up his bound wrists. "You expect me to throw like this?"

"The mind is a very powerful thing, Winde. The body can't tell the difference between reality and what's vividly imagined. You throw those passes in your mind, your body stays sharp."

Winde smiled weakly. "I'm still sore from yesterday's workout."

"Stop complaining and get to work."

Mabel looked over at Winde. She could see him drop back in his mind, read the defense and let loose with a throw. "I want every pass on the mark," she said.

"My receiver just dropped one."

"That's his problem. You do your job. Let him do his."

There was some shuffling outside the truck, then the door slid open. Light poured in, temporarily blinding them again.

"Can't you let us out of here?" said Mabel. "I need to stretch my legs."

A man tossed two paper bags onto the floor of the truck, then closed the door with a *thud*.

"McDonald's again," said Mabel. She looked over to where Winde was sitting with his eyes closed. She could tell that he was running through another play.

Mabel muttered, "I'm going to gain ten pounds." She leaned over and grabbed the two bags. She separated the meat from the buns, putting just meat into one of the bags and the buns in the other. She tossed the bag with meat, along with a small bag of French fries, toward Winde. "They know you're allergic to gluten and they still send this crap…Eat up," she said. "You've got to stay strong."

"Thank you, Mabel…How do you do it?"

"Do what?"

"Oh, I don't know…Age…Like your eyes. How do you deal with your eyes?"

"My eyes? They're just a minor stepping stone."

"You won't let anything stop you, will you?"

"Nope." Mabel leaned back against the truck and sighed. "It happened all at once, you know. One day, I'm an old broad slowly losing her eyesight and her hearing, nothing major, just enough to be a pain in the ass. I've got some macular degeneration in my retinas, like most of us seasoned folks. Turns black into gray, takes away the sharpness, but nothing we can't deal with.

"Then, *wham*. These plaque shards break off my blood vessels and lodge themselves into the arteries at the focal point of my retinas. Now, I can't focus, at least not on anything close. I can barely read without my 4x. Can't even make out those stupid little signs outside of bathroom doors. That's what got us into this mess, but that's a different story."

Mabel laughed. "Damnedest thing, though. Once I don't need to focus on the near stuff, I can see okay. Good enough to pass my driver's test, although I think the guy at the DMV was sweet on me. Gave me a little leeway when I started flashing my smile...I can still flirt, you know."

"They do that in Florida anyway, don't they?"

"Flirting?"

"Giving seniors leeway on the eyesight."

Mabel shrugged. "If they didn't, they'd have no one to ride the roads…All I know is that they still let me ride my Harley."

"You ride a Harley?"

"Of course, I do."

Winde laughed. "A bunch of the guys ride hogs. My wife won't let me."

Mabel smiled. "She just wants you safe, for the kids. Now, eat."

Winde reached into the bag and pulled out the meat. "I used to love Big Macs when I was a kid. Made me sick as hell, but I loved them…We didn't really understand my gluten allergies back then…just thought I had a weak stomach...Thanks for giving up your beef."

"You're going to pay for my diet when this is over…Maybe I'll go on that TV show, The Biggest Loser."

"You're a winner, Mabel."

"Yeah, yeah. I'm more of a filet-o-fish fan, anyway…" Mabel sighed. "Ah, I remember when a burger was fifteen cents. You could buy a burger, fries and a coke and get change back from a buck."

"If we get through this—"

"*When* we get through this," interrupted Mabel.

Winde laughed. "How come you're so strong? You've got more guts than half the guys in our locker room."

"And bigger boobs."

"Yeah. Except for the guys on roids."

"Getting old makes you tough, Terry. You see your friends die. You watch your body malfunction. You experience so much joy and so much disappointment…tragedy...Eventually, you realize that there are greater things in this world than you, that we're put here on this earth for a short time, to grow, to laugh and to die. You learn that no matter what you do, life goes on. That makes you strong. It gives you the strength to look Lou Masco in the eye and tell him to go screw himself. Because in the end, it just doesn't matter. The world keeps turning."

Winde said, "I'm not nervous anymore."

"Nervous about what?"

"The game. I keep thinking about my wife and my girls. I think about my mom and my brother. I think about my city, my state, all of the fans that I know are praying for my safe release. Somehow, the Super Bowl doesn't seem so important. It's just another game. It's what I do, not who I am. But the people…The people…They matter."

"You got it, kid. Now, eat and get back to practice."

Chapter Forty-Six
V
————————————

Ben

I was sitting on my balcony, staring out at the ocean with a notebook computer on my lap. It was a chilly, partly cloudy morning. I was wearing a pair of jean shorts and a Reebok wick golf shirt. I had a blue windbreaker draped over my shoulders and another one over my knees. It wasn't warm enough yet to go without jackets, but not cold enough to make me commit by strapping one on. Always the optimist, I am.

The throbbing in my leg was easing a bit. It had quieted down to a dull ache, a pain that three Advil every four hours was keeping at bay. I was just about to take my second dose of the day when I heard the front door to my office give a soft *creak.* I had spent half the night pulling off all my doors and wiping the oil off the hinges, so I would hear that telltale sound. I'd assembled two new video cameras, hidden in places no one but a serious pro would find. I'd wiped all the surfaces in the place, so that new fingerprints would stand out like a sore thumb. Now it was time. Someone was here for me, as expected.

I shut down the computer program I was writing, in hopes of finding Mabel's trail. No luck so far. To tell you the truth, I was getting big-time worried. Worried enough to make me look forward to what I knew was about to happen.

I accessed the Internet through my Wi-Fi and logged onto Halo. Halo's a war simulation game, mostly played by teenagers, but something a few of my old CIA buddies and I find stimulating. Makes us feel like *we're* still in the game.

I was searching to see if any of my usual gamer friends were online when I heard the distinctive *snap* of a bullet being chambered behind me. I kept playing with my computer, as if nothing was amiss, until I felt cold steel press against the base of my skull.

"Hello, Benjamin Johnson," said a voice behind me. Not Masco. Shit.

"Can I help you?" I closed my laptop and stared out at the ocean. There were just a few boats stirring, and only one hardy soul being pulled on a single water ski.

"Hands in the air. Then slowly stand and face me."

I placed my computer on the table beside my chair, raised my hands and turned to face the music. Masco's henchman was about six feet tall. He was emaciated, with the telltale look of a long history of drug abuse. His hair was fluffed out in some kind of hideous attempt to make him look *cool.* It just made him look petty. No amount of frilly haircut could soften the stark shadow of scar that ran from this man's temple, across his cheek and deep into his chin. His blue eyes flickered as I studied the scar, awkwardly revealing his sensitivity to it.

"Nice badge," I said.

"Gift from my fuckin' father," he said.

So much for compliments. "Are you here about Mabel?" I asked.

"I'm here to take your computers and recover your data, all of it."

"Sure." I said. I shrugged. "Anything to get Mabel back."

"That includes your online backup."

"Ahhh." I chuckled. "You caught me."

The man pointed with his gun. "Inside. Bring your notebook."

I picked up my computer. The man stepped aside and allowed me to pass, his gun trained on my chest. He was wearing vinyl gloves. No fingerprints today. Double shit. He said, "Take it downstairs and put it in the middle of the floor."

I did as I was asked. "What's your name?" I said.

"Pico."

He pronounced it peeko.

"Okay, Pico. What's next?"

"Your workroom."

Pico moved me with his gun toward my main computer station. I had four Dell desktops there, networked in a way that increased their speed a good tenfold. I walked over, sat in my *commander's* chair and flicked them all on.

Pico wasn't as computer illiterate as he looked. In fact, he was pretty good. He made me log onto my Carbonite account and copy it to a portable hard drive. Then he made me shred all I'd stored there. He made me open my hidden files, and all of my recent email correspondence.

He made me sift through my browser history. He searched my deleted files. Once he was convinced that we'd been through everything, Pico said, "Now, we do the same with your other computers." He frowned, then said, "Why do you have so many frigging machines?"

"I like them," I said. What I didn't say was that each computer held specific sensitive information, and that I never liked to put it all in one place. Except that they were all in my office. Stupid, careless me.

We spent the next couple hours turning on the dozen or so computers that I had spaced around the place. Pico wasn't interested in deleting any files from my machines; he was going to take them with him. He was interested in seeing where I'd been, what sites I had visited, what information I'd sent and where I'd sent it. He even made me go into my lame Facebook account to see what was written on my wall.

Good luck, I thought. Once data has left a computer and gone into cyberspace, there is no real way to know where it's gone, particularly if you know what you're doing.

We spent another hour unplugging computers and lugging them to the center floor of my office. Soon, we had quite a pile. The last computer that we looked at was my laptop. When we were done with that, Pico ripped out my Internet cable and phone lines, then confiscated my PDA.

"Now, your surveillance equipment," Pico said.

You screwed up there, buddy, I thought. How did he know I wasn't streaming surveillance to an online site or a security company? To give him credit, he'd checked for that in the beginning. But there was no way to know, to really know, without ripping into the walls. There were far too many ways to snoop these days, too many ways to hide things from others, particularly if you had some talent and experience.

Pico finally did make me pull out my cameras, except, of course, for the two hidden ones I'd just installed. He missed those. We retrieved the monster hard drives where my video data was archived, so there would be no record of what we'd just done. He missed the new drive I'd installed behind the wall. All-in-all, though, Pico did a pretty good job. I gave him a B-.

When everything had been lugged into the main area of my office, we had quite a pile of gear. Even I hadn't known how much there was. It just seems to accumulate over the years, I guess. Pico made me collect all of my cameras and scanners, as well as my plastic mask machine. That would be hard to replace, and I prayed he wouldn't take it.

"That everything?" Pico said.

I nodded. "Unless you want the rugs."

Pico smiled. "Funny." He spoke into a phone.

Soon, two men backed a truck into the reserved parking space outside my front door. They trudged in and began loading my gear onto the truck's flatbed. I began to whimper. There was a lot of good stuff going outside. Most of my equipment was state-of-the art, representing at least a quarter million of my hard-earned cash. There was also forty years of data stored on those disks. Some of those bytes were so sensitive they could take down governments. Of course, that was all encrypted, and only I had the keys.

When my life had been removed and loaded, Pico used his phone again. A minute later, an old Toyota Corolla pulled up beside the truck. A man stepped out of the passenger seat. I wouldn't have recognized him, except for the eyes, those jumpy ferine eyes.

"Hello, Ben," said Masco, as he sauntered inside.

"What's up, Lou?" I said. "I like the new beard. Makes you look like Grizzly Adams. Remember him? Almost didn't recognize you."

"Shut up." Lou began to walk around me, staring with a raw hatred that made me want to wet my pants. Finally, he said, "Took me a while to figure out who *you* were." He shook his head and laughed. "A financial planner…" He laughed again. "You had me going there for awhile."

"You here to cut a deal for Mabel?"

"Maybe."

Masco pulled a .22 caliber pistol out from the small of his back. I winced, because there was a silencer attached to its end. Silencers were bad news; they were for killing.

"Let's go outside," Masco said. "We should enjoy the day."

Masco pointed his pistol at my chest and motioned toward the stairs leading up to my balcony. I climbed as slowly as I could. It felt like a death march, like I was heading for a firing squad. I had no camera up top, so there'd be no record of my demise. I was about to become just another pile of bones in the sand.

Masco waited for me to take a seat, before pulling a chair about five feet away. Too far for me to make a move for his gun.

"How's Mabel?" I said.

"She's fine."

"And Winde?"

"Don't think he'll be playing ball anytime soon."

I groaned. As much as I didn't want to admit it, I'd had a big hand in ruining the Super Bowl. The frigging Super Bowl. This wasn't some tennis match at Mar-A-Lago, this was the biggest sporting event of the year. Thousands of players, coaches and owners and TV execs had put everything they had into this game, only to have it marred by the kidnapping of one of its stars.

Mabel had known what *she* was getting into. We'd discussed the risks, and she'd bulled her way onward, full force into the storm. But Winde? He was an innocent, and so were the billion viewers that deserved the best for this game.

"Tell me you haven't hurt him," I said.

Masco shook his head. "He's okay. Although, I'm not sure you've got what it will take to set him free."

"You've got everything," I said. "You've got my computers. You've got DVDs, tapes, flash drives and my hard drives. You've got access to my online backup. You've got it all."

"I'm not sure Mabel is…" Masco hesitated, searching for the right words. "…I'm not sure she's *teachable*…no, *redeemable*, at least in the short time we have before the Super Bowl. Maybe a few months in captivity will change her outlook." Masco shrugged. "Then again, maybe not…I think not." He paused. His eyes searched the sea, as if it had all the answers. "You'll never find her, you know."

"I know," I said.

"You went to the authorities."

"I went to McBride. He says you're too big to prosecute."

Masco angled his head, with a questioning look on his face.

I continued, "I also met with the FBI and the DEA."

Masco's face began to color. It started at the base of his neck, the redness rising gradually, until his whole face had the pink hue of a conch shell. "You fuck," he said.

"They won't *do* anything," I said. "They wouldn't even take my data. They say it would sap all their 'available resources' to go after you and Cantwell. They say you'd tie them up in the courts for a decade, and prevent them from putting away the scum they can convict. We *aren't* a threat to you. Let them go."

Masco smirked. He knew I was right. He probably had men on the inside, men who kept their fingers to the wind, men who kept him informed of all that went on within the various agencies.

Masco moved the table that was resting between us, until it was another five feet away from my chair. Then he reached into his pants pocket and withdrew a folded leather pouch. He unrolled the pouch onto the table. I could see its contents. There were plastic vials filled with white powder tucked into little pockets in the leather. There were several small spoons attached to the side, with elastic fabric that had been sewn into the flap.

Masco motioned toward the drugs. "Want some blow?"

I shook my head. Masco shrugged. He set his gun upon the table and picked up one of the vials. It had a stopper top, which he twisted out and laid upon the table. He picked up one of the spoons, dipped it into the vial, then brought it to his nose and snorted loudly. He repeated the ritualistic process with the other nostril.

Masco leaned back in his chair and sighed. I looked out to the water, wondering what was going to happen next. A killer, high on cocaine with a gun, a despot whose life was being threatened and spinning out of control, was not someone to mess with.

"I'm sorry," I said. "We screwed up."

Masco laughed. It was an inhuman, drug-induced rumble that started somewhere deep in his belly and made a kind of odd gurgling sound. The gurgle erupted into a cough, then a choking laugh. Was he sick? I wondered. Or, just too juiced up to care for himself?

"No, Ben. You fucked up." He coughed some more. "You really fucked up."

Masco grabbed his pistol and backed away from the table. He walked slowly around to the back of my chair. I stared out at the ocean. After a moment, I could feel the barrel of Masco's silencer tracing along the back of my head. He ran it down to my neck, then back up again. Then there was nothing, no sound, no metal against my skull. I waited.

I heard a *spit* behind my right ear. I felt a flick on my earlobe. Then I saw some blood and skin spatter along the floor of my balcony. I brought my hand up to the side of my head and felt around. Most of my right earlobe was gone.

"Thought I'd start with something small," Masco said.

I suddenly felt dizzy. My temples started to pound. Sweat began to break out across my body. My head felt like it was filled with wet cotton, and the world went fuzzy.

"Don't faint on me, Ben."

I looked back at Masco and he was smiling. No, he was laughing. Then his eyes narrowed into tiny angular slits and he growled, "Where else did you send the data, Ben?"

"Nowhere," I said. I looked into Masco's eyes. The world was spinning, but I sobered quickly, looking into those eyes. "I swear," I begged.

"I want the encryption codes."

"There aren't any."

Oh, shit, I thought. There was no way I could give those codes to Masco; I'd have to die first. I would die first. The data held in my computers was so sensitive, it would ruin lives. It would destroy the souls of good people who had made stupid mistakes, the kind of mistakes I had made. The data could alter the landscape of our Congress, maybe shift our entire government policy. It might even make Masco impregnable, give him the leverage to blackmail our government, and others around the world.

"I don't have codes," I lied. Masco pressed his gun against my other ear. I envisioned myself as Vincent Van Gogh…dead. I gave in with the most sincere reluctance I could muster. "Not most of them, at least. Those were kept by others, as a precaution against something like this."

"I don't believe you."

I closed my eyes. This was my worst nightmare come true. A crazy man on drugs with a gun and an agenda.

"You might as well shoot me again, Lou. I don't have them all. I've got a few. That's it."

Masco reached for his wallet. He pulled out two pieces of white lined paper and handed them to me. Then he tossed me a pen. "Write them down."

"Most are hidden in files," I said.

"Then give me the files."

I started scribbling, using the armrest on my chair. I filled up one of the sheets and turned it over. After I'd gotten halfway down the second page I stopped. I looked out over the ocean, staring briefly at a large yacht that was steaming southward. I scribbled a little more, then stopped again.

"That's it," I said. "That's all I've got."

Lou Masco walked around from the back of my chair, until he stood facing me. He lifted his pistol and shot me in the left thigh. I looked down and waited for the blood. It started slowly, as if my circulatory system had just been shaken awake. Blood began to come out of the hole in my leg like a small country spring, bubbling out and then dripping slowly down my calf and into my shoe.

"Jesus," I cried.

"Jesus won't help you now," Masco said. "The only thing that will help you is more codes."

"That's it," I said. "I swear, that's it. You can shoot me all you want, but there's nothing more."

Masco looked at me. I could see the flush of cocaine swimming in his eyes. They looked frantic, like a coyote in a fight for his life, snapping from side to side, looking *at* me, then *behind* me, *around* me, then *through* me. He seemed to hesitate. He lifted his pistol and pointed it at my forehead. He walked toward me, until the barrel of the silencer was about two feet away. Then against my skin.

"You sure you don't want to reconsider?"

I shook my head gently. "That's all there is, Lou. Really."

Masco let the gun drop to his side. He reached out his hand. I placed the paper with the codes and passwords inside it.

"Don't leave town," he said. "We'll be watching you. And if I find out you're lying..." He made a shooting gesture with his pistol. "...you know what will happen."

"What about Mabel?...What about Mabel!" I yelled. No answer.

Masco walked past me and down the stairs. He got into the old Toyota. I looked down from my balcony, watching him leave, before finding my spare cell phone and dialing 911.

Chapter Forty-Seven
V

Ben Johnson began the long drive into the old SOSCADA estate, his rented Nissan bouncing and creaking along the narrow road of white crushed shells. Now and then a palm frond slapped against the side of the car. The trees loomed above like city skyscrapers, closing in and drowning most of the light. Eventually, Ben emerged into bright sunlight. Before him stretched the expansive, Spanish style home, with Biscayne Bay gleaming behind it.

Ben parked his car in the circular drive. There was a curved line of vehicles already there, mostly government issue Fords. Ben hobbled with his crutches toward the grand patio, stretching out from the side of the mansion.

At least thirty people were clustering around the picnic tables. McBride was wearing a gray suit with a pink shirt and no tie. Chief Esposito was dressed in a tan suit, a white button down shirt and a yellow tie. His deputy chief, Cabrerra, sported a khaki uniform. So did Magnetti, the head of Special Investigations. Griffin and Trout had on blue pinstripes, as did a man Ben didn't recognize. Diane Magneson, from the Money Laundering Strike Force, looked crisp and regal in a navy blue pantsuit, white blouse and a red scarf. Reginald White, from the HIDTA wore a black blazer over gray slacks. The FBI's special investigator, Jason Starr, wore a simple, rumpled blue suit, a sweat-stained white shirt, black wing-tips and no tie. He looked like he hadn't slept in days.

Ben looked down to his khaki shorts, his boat shoes without socks and his stretched-out IZOD shirt. Guess he missed the memo about suits. Of course, he didn't want to put fabric over his wounds. His left thigh was bandaged and covered with a snug ACE elastic wrap. He left calf still looked like a railroad yard, with stitch tracks going everywhere. He felt better when he saw Tony Trance, standing beside the mansion, dressed much like he was, without the fresh wounds, of course.

"Okay," said McBride, as Ben joined them. "Let's get started."

"Sorry I'm late," said Ben. "But I got a call from Masco."

Everyone turned toward Ben. McBride said, "You get a trace?"

"The call came through a cell tower in Palm Beach. That's all I know."

"We've had no signal from his cell phone," said Esposito. "He's never turned it on."

"Probably used a burner," replied Ben. "He said he tried my passwords and encryption codes. Said I could live a few more days."

Starr said, "Anything about returning Winde and Mabel?"

"Wouldn't say."

"Tell him that if he returns them, we'll cut a deal. Tell him we'll help him get out from under the cartels."

"That's what I offered. He hung up."

"Shit."

Ben said, "It's been four days. Masco has all he'll get. Every day the chances are—"

"We all know the odds," interrupted McBride. "What else did he say?"

"That's it."

"Crap." McBride began to pace. "He's got your files and your computers. He's got your encryption codes."

"Some of them," interrupted Ben. "Not the critical ones, the ones dealing with the government. Or parts of this case." Ben hesitated. He looked over at the man he didn't know. "Who's this?"

The man walked toward Ben and held out his pulpy hand. "Name's Charlie Akron."

"Interrogator from Quantico," said McBride. "He met with Cantwell."

"Anything?"

Akron said, "Cantwell thinks Masco's hiding out in one of their companies, maybe one he doesn't know about."

"Any leads?"

"No."

Ben shrugged. "It's a very deep labyrinth." He looked over to Tony. "How're you guys making out?"

Tony said, "Murray and his team located eight more entities. Three buildings and five companies." Tony looked over at Griffin. "What about the FBI?"

Griffin smiled meekly. "Our people are not as…effective as yours."

Tony's lips edged into a small smile. "How many locations have you raided?"

"About half. We have to wait for warrants. That takes time."

"We don't have time."

"The government is a big machine."

Tony Trance looked from face to face. Tony's main objective was Mabel. He understood that everyone else was focused on Winde. Why wouldn't they be? Once the Super Bowl had passed, the FBI would move on. That gave them three days.

Tony said, "*We* could raid a few places, quietly, of course."

"That would poison our case against Cantwell," said Starr.

"I thought you guys had given up on Cantwell? Going to focus on the insignificant fish."

Starr smiled. "He kidnapped a football icon. That makes him fair game."

"I've still got my data," said Ben. "Terabytes. All stored safely, where even the FBI couldn't find it."

Everyone stared at Ben. They'd all assumed that when Masco had taken his gear, and wiped out his backup, that all of the evidence was gone.

"You do?" said Tony.

Ben smiled. "You don't think I'd store this stuff on Carbonite, do you?"

"We can't take it. Not yet," said Starr. "We're still getting permissions."

"Don't worry," said Ben. "It's not going anywhere."

Starr frowned and said, "What if they kill you?"

"Then it all goes public."

Starr groaned. "Don't die, okay?"

"I'll try not to."

Chapter Forty-Eight
V

Gumbo's white limousine screeched to the side of the curb. Four ladies emerged from inside, wearing short skirts, black fishnet hose and three inch heels. These weren't ordinary street workers. They were a little more 'seasoned,' at least forty years more seasoned, than the others that plied their wares on these streets.

"Happy hunting," yelled Gumbo, as his driver closed the rear door. A group of people began to crowd around the limo. Gumbo didn't disappoint them, as he stood up through a moon roof and began tossing hundred dollar bills into the outstretched hands.

Gumbo's 'ladies' waved, then began strutting down the street to their own personal corner. As they approached, four young hookers turned to face them. They put their hands upon their hips and waited, chewing gum with an exaggerated bite, like cows with their cud.

"Hey girls," said Sophie, known as "Rose" on the streets.

"We gotta move?" said one of the teenagers. She stood over six feet tall in her thin red heels. Her hair was blond and frizzed into a round cloud. She had on a pink tube top and purple hot pants that left nothing to the imagination. There was a round silver ring protruding from her navel, and a series of colorful tattoos along her right arm.

"Not today," said Sophie. "You hungry, honey? You and your friends? We're buyin' and payin' for your time."

Frizz girl looked to the others, who nodded. She looked back at Sophie. "It's a slow time. Sure."

Sophie pulled a thin phone from beneath the folds of her tight skirt and thumbed a quick text. Less than a minute later, Gumbo's limo came back around the corner.

"We'll go someplace nice," Sophie said, as Gumbo's chauffeur opened the door and ushered them inside. The limo was large, spacious enough to seat all eight, along with Gumbo, who sat inside, sipping a light gin and tonic.

"Thirsty?" Gumbo asked, as they settled into seats.

"Got a Diet Pepsi?" said frizz girl.

"Sure, if you tell me your name," said Gumbo.

"I'm Angel." She pointed at the other three ladies. "This is Veronica, Misty and Ginger."

Gumbo smiled. His teeth were so bright they were almost blinding, even in the low limo lights.

"Nice smile, Doc," said Angel.

"You know who I am?"

"Course. Everybody knows Doctor Love."

Gumbo opened a small refrigerator and pulled out a can of Diet Coke. "This okay?"

"Yeah."

Gumbo looked to the others. "Same?"

"Whatever," came the reply from all three.

The limo pulled into the entryway of the Four Points Sheraton, on Collins Ave.

"You'll be needing these," said Gumbo. He opened a narrow closet in the wall of the limo and produced eight white terrycloth robes. "Standard dress for vacationers. Throw these over your outfits." He then produced eight pairs of flip flops. "They frown on spikes."

The ladies wrapped the thick robes around their scanty clothes, donned the flip flops and were suddenly transformed into a group of grandmothers with their granddaughters on vacation.

Gumbo slipped Sophie a wad of cash, which she palmed into the pocket of her robe.

The restaurant was open and airy, with a yellowish-green wall on one side and open windows on the other. Palm trees in pots were sprouting everywhere.

Once they were seated, Angel said, "So, what's up, Rose?"

Sophie smiled. Her gaze was kind, looking with a motherly glow into Angel's wary eyes. "You've heard about Winde going missing?"

Angel laughed. "All my Johns can talk about."

"We're looking for him."

Angel began to looked puzzled, but her face straightened quickly. She'd heard about these old broads, about how they fought crime, that kind of shit. She said, "Don't know a thing about it."

Sophie reached into her robe's pocket and withdrew the stack of money. "You probably don't know anything, but we're looking everywhere, asking anyone who might have heard something, even if they don't know it's important." Sophie peeled off eight one hundred dollar bills and placed them upon the table.

Angel said, "Why you so interested?"

"One of our friends was also taken."

"One of…us?"

Sophie told a lie, a small white one, to help find Mabel. "Yes. One of us."

"That's cold."

"What're ya hearing?"

Angel grabbed the money off the table. She counted two hundred dollars for each of her friends, before stuffing the last two bills into her tube top.

"Mostly how frigged up the Super Bowl's going to be."

"What else? What about the kidnapping? You hear anybody use the phrase 'dead meat'?"

"I have," said Misty.

"Me, too," said Veronica. "And something about a truck. Heard that twice."

"From whom?"

Veronica shrugged. "I dunno. Some guys, I guess."

Sophie looked to the others. "You girls hear anything about a truck?"

"I did," said Veronica.

"You think they were killed in a truck?" said Angel.

"Don't know," said Sophie. "This is the first I've heard about a truck." She looked out the window. There were tables outside, with royal blue umbrellas shading guests from the sun.

A bubbly waitress came to their table. "Hi, my name is Sheila and I'll be your waitress. Are you ladies here on vacation?"

Sophie looked at the girls, quieting them with her eyes. She said, "We are. Us grandmothers thought we'd bring the granddaughters down here for some peace and quiet…to get away from all the men…You know how it is…You have a lovely hotel. How long've you been working here?"

"Six months."

"New to the area, Sheila?"

"Sort of."

"Plan to stay?" said Sophie, keeping tight control of the conversation.

"I hope to."

"I think you will. I've been coming here for forty years. From Michigan. Do you have our menus?"

Sheila handed them around.

"We'll need a few minutes, Sheila. I'll wave when we're ready to order. Thanks."

When Sheila was gone, Sophie looked back toward the young street workers. "You heard anything else?"

They hadn't. So they ate. When they were nearly done, Sophie said, "You know, we have a foundation that provides education for girls like you. Full tuition and a place to crash."

"Heard about that," said Angel. "You the ones got Paris off the streets?"

Sophie smiled. "We did. And others before her. You know Smokey Jones?"

"Big friggin' Amazon?" said Veronica. "Used to rule?"

"Yeah."

"Haven't seen her in years."

"She's in college and doin' real well. Going to be an art curator, for Jack Trance."

"Jack Trance, the super rich dude? Must be bangin' her, then."

Sophie laughed. "Doesn't work that way. There are no strings, girls. Just gotta stay off drugs and study hard." Sophie looked from face to face. "Interested?"

Veronica said, "Maybe."

"Good," said Sophie. "Why don't you come by the crib later and tell us your dreams."

"I said, 'maybe'."

"When you're ready, dear. Only when you're ready. And call me if you hear anything more about dead meat or trucks." Sophie pulled four business cards from a leather case held within her breasts, then handed one to each girl. "Here's the address and my number. You call me."

"I'll think about it," said Veronica. The others glanced at the cards, but remained silent.

Sophie paid cash for their lunch. Then they returned the young prostitutes to the corner where they'd found them. As the limo pulled away, Sophie looked out the window, to see Veronica staring after them.

Sophie winked at Gumbo. "We got ourselves another student."

"Which one?"

"Veronica. Let's give her two days, then come back."

"Deal." Gumbo looked expectantly at his other ladies. So far, the only one to talk was Sophie. That was normal; she always kind of took over. He asked, "Anything new on Mabel?"

Sophie said, "Something about a truck. Dead meat and a truck."

"Interesting. I'll pass that along to Tony."

Chapter Forty-Nine
V

It was coal mine black inside the truck, with not a single hint of light. They'd already been given their nightly ration of McDonald's. Fruit in the morning, Wendy's in the afternoon and McDonald's to finish. Different day, same old crap.

"How's it hangin', Terry?" said Mabel.

"Completed two hundred passes today. My arm's dead."

"Interceptions?"

"Not a one. Got sacked three times, though."

"All this sitting is slowing you down. I'm getting a spare tire big enough to ride on."

"Sorry," said Winde. "You got all the carbs in this deal."

"The big game's tomorrow. How d'you feel?"

"Awesome. I'm a finely tuned machine, ready to lead the charge."

"That's the spirit."

"It's your positive attitude, Mabel. You ever think of public speaking?"

"Makes me want to pee."

"You make *me* want to do great things."

"If you didn't, I'd kick your ass."

Winde laughed. "Don't I know it." He paused. "I love you, Mabel."

"Keep your hands to yourself."

Winde laughed again. "You'd like my wife and kids."

"I'm looking forward to meeting them. You would have liked Archie. He was a good, good man."

"You think the police will find us?"

"Probably not. But Ben Johnson and Tony Trance, they will."

"You talk of Ben like he's superman."

Mabel smiled in the dark. "Nah. He's just a man...If I hadn't met Archie first...he would have been the one."

"He could still be, Mabel. It's never too late for love."

In the darkness, Winde heard Mabel sniff. He didn't say anything more; he just waited. Finally, Mabel said, "Get some sleep, Terry. You've got a big day tomorrow."

Chapter Fifty
V

"It's over," said Ben. He was seated outside the Sanchez mansion on the patio, drinking coffee with Tony Trance. The day was already warm, with the daytime temperatures forecast in the seventies. By game time, it would be down into the low to mid sixties, with little wind. Perfect weather for football. Too bad the game was a farce.

"Don't give up yet, Ben," said Tony. "We've still got time."

"We've got nothing."

"We don't have nothing. We've got 'dead meat' and we've got a 'truck'."

Ben laughed. It was more of a high pitched whine than an actual laugh. "I feel useless. All these years of having information at my fingertips, ready to sing to the beck and call of my computer…All I get now is static…Nothing."

"Keep looking."

"There's nothing to see. I've been through Cantwell's files a hundred times. Not a shred that ties dead meat with trucks."

"They own warehouses, don't they?"

"The FBI says they've raided every one."

"Then think. Think outside the box."

"I've been trying, Tony. The only thing I can come up with is this: What if Masco owns a provisions company, maybe one that sells meats. What if one of his trucks was at the Pro Bowl, and that's what he used to get Mabel and Winde out of the stadium?"

Tony pulled his PDA out of a pocket, fingered a quick text message and said, "I'm calling Murray."

Ten minutes later, they could hear Murray's Porsche pull into the drive. Soon he came around the side. Rather than wearing one of his old baggy suits, Murray was dressed in one that actually fit him. It was made of light green silk. His shirt was a darker shade of lime and he had a new gold chain under his open collar.

"You been shopping with Gumbo?" said Tony.

Murray grinned. "You could tell?"

Tony shook his head, laughing. "You look like a pimp."

Murray smiled. "Gumbo says I'm stylin'." He grabbed a coffee mug and filled it from a thermos. He sniffed the brew and sighed deeply. "Starbucks Gold Coast." He set the mug down and said, "What's up?"

Tony said, "I think we missed something. We're betting Masco owns a provisions company, one that supplied the Pro Bowl. Maybe one that's supplying the Super Bowl today."

"We already pursued that angle. Went through all the aerial images. Nothing unusual. Can't find a thing."

"Damn."

"We'll get back on it, though. I'll have the FBI get us a list of every company that deals with Dolphin…Sun Life…Stadium. We'll try to backtrack ownership, but it won't be easy. They cover their tracks."

Ben said, "Maybe we should search every truck at the Super Bowl."

"On what grounds?" said Murray. "And what for? They've been kidnapped *from* the stadium. They're not going back."

"My gut says different, Murray," said Ben softly.

Murray stood, holding out his coffee cup. "I'm out of here, but I'm taking my Starbucks. We'll see if we can find anything for you."

Chapter Fifty-One
V

The door to the truck slid up rapidly. Lou Masco's twisted smile was surrounded by the sudden harsh light like a halo.

"It's Super Bowl Sunday, guys. Got to get you to the game!"

"You're letting us go?" said Winde.

Masco giggled like a five-year-old on a swing. The vision of what was to come. The thought of freedom from Mabel. The cocaine rushing through his system like a freight train. It all made him giddy. "No. But you're still going to have a big impact on the game, Terry." Masco motioned for his men to surround him, before saying, "You two need to get out of there. Step down, please."

"About time," said Mabel. "I was beginning to think we were going to die in here."

Masco's mouth opened, as if he were about to speak. He chuckled and shook his head.

Mabel and Winde shuffled toward the edge of the truck bed.

Masco looked warily at his men. "You ready?" he said. They all nodded. Masco retrieved a small step ladder from against the wall and set it up behind the truck. When it was in place he said, "Let's go."

Winde motioned for Mabel to leave the truck first. With her hands still bound before her, she sat unsteadily upon the back edge of the truck bed. Winde leaned over, struggling to help guide Mabel's feet onto the little step ladder. No one else moved.

"Aw, isn't that sweet," said Masco.

"Eat shit and die," said Mabel. She teetered on the ladder, but steadied herself by holding Winde's outstretched hands. She took the steps slowly, her legs wobbly after a week inside the truck.

"Can we get a shower?" she said.

"Won't make a difference."

Masco took two steps backward, as Winde slid his feet off the end of the truck and jumped to the ground. Masco squeezed the butt of his rifle, ready in case the quarterback tried to make another stupid move.

Winde looked toward Masco and said, "Let her have a shower, Lou."

"This isn't a friggin' football game, Terry. You've got no say here. So, keep your mouth shut."

"Can we go outside?" asked Mabel. "Maybe see the sun? Oh, what I'd give to see the sun."

"You can barely see the hands in front of your face, Witherspoon," said Masco.

"I see more than you think, asshole."

"Fuck you."

"You wish—"

"All right," interrupted Winde. "We all understand that you two hate each other."

"She ruined my life," said Masco.

Mabel snorted. "You ruined your own life. I just gave you a chance to save it."

Masco said, "You tried to kill me."

"Ha, ha, ha. I did nothing of the sort. I just asked you to return stolen money and stop dealing drugs. Is that so much to ask?"

Masco grabbed one of his guards' AK-47s and motioned toward the edge of the warehouse. "Over there."

"Where're we going, Lou?"

"I've got to fix your truck."

"You going to clean it? It smells like crap."

"So do you."

"So, let us take showers."

A smile seemed to slide across Masco's lips. His eyes narrowed and then widened. He grinned fully, showing his full set of coffee-stained teeth. "We've got a little shower here in the warehouse. You can take one there, together."

"Not on your life," shouted Mabel.

"Suit yourself."

Winde pleaded, "Please show some decency, Lou. Let Mabel shower."

"I just said she could shower. With her hands bound, she's going to need your help, just as you're going to need hers."

Mabel looked at Winde. "Well?"

Winde shrugged. "I take showers with people around all the time, Mabel. Doesn't make much difference to me, if you're game."

"You won't jump my bones?"

Masco laughed. "Fat chance, Mabel."

"I'm joking, dickface. I know he doesn't want a tired old lady." Mabel looked over at Winde and batted her eyes. "Do you?"

"Maybe if I weren't a happily married man, Mabel. But I am. And I'm faithful."

"Well, all right, then. Let's do get clean."

Masco motioned toward the far end of the warehouse. Winde and Mabel began walking, with Masco on their heels with a rifle. They came to a water-stained wooden door. "In there," said Masco. "There's only one way in and out. I'm going to have six men stationed here. So, don't try anything."

Mabel said, "What about clean clothes?"

"Clean clothes?"

"What are you, deaf?"

"We're not a laundry service, woman. There's a hand dryer. Wash your clothes and dry with that."

"That'll take time."

"You in a rush to get somewhere?"

"Well, duh. The Super Bowl?"

"You won't need dry clothes for the Super Bowl, Mabel. And I wouldn't be in a rush to get there, I assure you."

Mabel started to ask Masco what he meant, but he had already begun to walk away. He was done with her shit; she could tell. Anyway, she'd gotten what she wanted, a shower and a way to clean and dry their clothes. Compared to the last seven, this was turning out to be a good day. A very good day. Maybe their luck was turning. It was, but not as she'd hoped.

The bathroom had a white tile floor, with moldy grout the color of tarnished copper. The walls were made with simple plasterboard, painted white. The paint was peeling into circular rolls, and the drywall was crumbling into piles of pale yellow dust. There was a ripped, but workable shower curtain. It was white, with a pattern of faded green and yellow flowers. The shower stall was spacious and made of white fiberglass. Surprisingly well preserved. There was a metal railing against the back, with three brown towels and a single green washcloth. A large, mold-stained container of Head & Shoulders shampoo sat upon the washcloth. It was nearly full.

The main bathroom looked like it hadn't been used in a decade. There was a cracked porcelain sink with streaks of rust and lime that looked to be a quarter inch thick. Above it hung a blotchy mirror. It was as yellow as faded newsprint, with little black spots making it look like it had the measles. Beside the sink was a chrome toothbrush holder, with three toothbrushes laced with cobwebs and dead flies. A rolled up tube of Crest toothpaste was crammed into a soap dish. An old bar of Dial soap was sitting beneath it, looking like a dried out cucumber. As promised, there was an Excel hand dryer built into the wall. Mabel pushed its button and hot air began cloying the room like a sauna.

Winde walked to the sink. He looked at the toothbrushes longingly, as he turned the handle for the hot water. There was a long, low moan. Orange water began to sputter forth. After ten seconds or so, the water turned clear and began to steam. Winde grabbed the soap, whipped it into a froth and began to clean two of the toothbrushes. When he was done, he offered one to Mabel and said, "Ladies first."

Mabel took the brush as if it were sacramental bread, holding it reverently with both hands before her eyes.

Winde took the ancient toothpaste tube, squeezed a watery dab onto his finger and tasted it. "Huh," he said. "Tastes okay." He held it up and said, "Want some?"

Mabel grinned. "Boy, don't I."

Winde put a layer of toothpaste onto Mabel's brush, then squeezed some onto his own. They brushed their teeth together, groaning at the simple pleasure of having clean teeth. After brushing a second time, they addressed the shower.

Winde turned on the water. Mabel began to step inside, but Winde held her back. "Hold it, ma'am. Give it some time." Like the sink, the water flowed orange, long before turning clear. Winde retrieved a small trash bucket from the corner of the bathroom, returned to the shower stall and stood waiting.

Soon, a scorpion crawled out of the drain. Winde crushed it with the bottom of the bucket. "Normally, I'd take this outside and set it free," he said. "But we're a little handicapped here."

The first scorpion was followed by a second, then a third and a fourth.

Winde squished each one with the hard edge of the bucket. Once Winde was satisfied that all of the scorpions had escaped the drain, he turned off the water.

"All right, Mabel. You first. If you want me to scrub your back or something, let me know."

"Okay. But no feelies. You can't reach around me when you do."

"But what if lust overtakes me?" joked Winde.

"I'll kick you in the balls."

Mabel took the miniature microphone out of her blouse and set it upon the sink.

"What's that?" said Winde.

"Microphone."

"Do I want to know?"

Mabel shook her head. "I was working with the FBI. Doesn't matter now, Terry."

Mabel turned the water back on and stepped into the shower, wearing all of her clothes, except shoes. She just stood there, letting the water flow down around her. "Ahhh," she said. She bent down to touch her toes, mumbling, "I was so stiff, I thought I'd break."

After a long while, Mabel opened the curtain and handed the washcloth to Winde. "You're just the second man to see me this way," she said.

"In wet clothes?"

"You know what I mean…Vulnerable."

Winde reached up under Mabel's blouse and scrubbed her back, without reaching around for feelies. When he was done, Mabel closed the curtain back up and struggled to take off her pants. "Don't know why he couldn't have uncuffed us for this," she mumbled.

"It's a power thing."

After close to an hour, Mabel emerged from the shower. She had a towel around her waist, and her wet pants and underpants clutched in a tight fist. "I'm going to dry these while you shower, Terry. You toss me yours, and I'll dry them, too…before you step out with your naked self."

Winde remained in the shower for far longer than he was used to, negotiating the cuffs and the infected sores on his wrists, soaking in the simple pleasure of getting clean, and enjoying what may be his last free act on earth.

Mabel busied herself with the hand dryer. She dried both pairs of underwear and most of the crotch areas of their pants.

"Lucky I wear a thong," she muttered.

"What was that, Mabel?"

"Never mind."

Once Winde was dressed, he drew back the shower curtain and emerged. He made Mabel think of a drowned rat, his pants and shirt soaked, his beard scraggly after a week's worth of unkempt growth. Mabel was standing in front of the mirror, fully dressed, combing her hair with her fingers.

"You didn't see a hair brush anywhere, did you?" Mabel said.

"Sorry. You see a razor?"

"Sorry."

Nearly two hours after entering the bathroom, Mabel and Winde emerged. They didn't look much better, but they felt refreshed, almost renewed. Half a dozen of Masco's guards were outside the door, with automatic weapons in hand. One of them pressed the muzzle of his AK against Winde's shoulder and shoved him forward, back toward their rolling prison.

The guard laughed, saying, "We have a surprise for you."

When they reached the truck, they found Lou Masco waiting. There was a malicious grin on his face, his eyes wet and glinting red under the overhead lights.

He's had another good snort, thought Mabel. She was right. Masco was wired. A sheen of sweat stretched across his brow. His eyes shifted from side to side and his tongue kept darting out like a snake. His hands were trembling. Maybe it was the drugs. Maybe it was the excitement. Probably a little of both.

"Meet your new home," he said.

Masco stepped aside and allowed Winde and Mabel to see into the back of the truck. The far walls were now lined with explosives, maybe enough to level a stadium. There were stacks of rectangular, off-white blocks of C-4. There were sticks of dynamite coiled with red wires. All of it was held together with wire and duct tape. There was a tunnel down the center of the truck, ending with two metal chairs facing outward. The chairs were fastened to the back of the truck with wide canvas straps.

More straps were wrapped around the back of the chairs, ready to seal them in.

"You wanted to make a big bang at the Super Bowl?" Masco said to Winde. He cackled like a crow. "Well, now's your chance."

"Tell me you're not taking this to Sun Life Stadium," said Mabel.

"You'll be right below the fifty yard line."

"You're insane."

"It's your fault, Mabel."

Masco tossed his head toward the truck. His men began pushing Winde and Mabel with their rifles, up the ladder and into the back.

Winde looked at Mabel. There was a white flag of surrender in his eyes. "Sorry. Wish I could have done something more."

"There's nothing you *could* have done."

Winde shrugged. He allowed himself to be placed into the chair and strapped down. A few moments later, Mabel was put in beside him.

"I used to imagine that I'd die having wild sex," said Mabel.

"Maybe you will."

Mabel shook her head. "I'm an old goose, Terry."

Winde sighed deeply. He understood. "I wish I'd had the chance to tell my wife and kids how much I love them."

"Yeah. Archie died right beside me, and I never got…" Mabel closed her eyes. "Life is filled with should have dones. You know?"

Winde nodded. "I do, now."

"Don't give up," Mabel said. "The day's young. We're going to be at the stadium. They're going to find us and you're going to play in the game."

Winde closed his eyes and smiled, his lips tilting upward with a tiny, brief twitch.

Mabel suddenly yelled like a hard-driving football coach. "You will not give up, Winde! You don't think you did all that practicing for nothing, do you? Your team and your fans are counting on you. So, get your ass in shape!"

"My shoulder's so tight right now it could snap."

"Shoulder schmoulder. You'll do just fine."

Winde laughed. "You are a piece of work, Mabel."

"And you're a fine man, Terry Winde. And a pretty decent quarterback. You keep the faith."

Chapter Fifty-Two
V
____

Jack Trance maneuvered his black 1937 Bugatti Atalante through the darkly shaded drive leading to the Sanchez mansion. His wife, Lauren, sat beside him, looking very pregnant with the twins she would bear any day. Lauren placed a hand on Trance's knee, as he wound the Bugatti through the small bamboo forest.

"I like it here," she said.

"Like traveling to another world."

"And I love you."

Trance smiled. "You have very good taste."

The Bugatti emerged into piercing sunlight, nosing toward Biscayne Bay and the mansion before it. Trance parked along the circular drive of shells, opened the door for his wife and helped her out of the car.

"I feel like an elephant," Lauren said.

"You look beautiful."

"Yeah, yeah."

Trance and Lauren held hands as they walked around to the back patio of the mansion. They found Tony there, rocking in a chair with a baby sleeping on his shoulder.

"Hey, uncle Tony," said Trance.

"Shhh. I just got baby Jack to sleep."

"Oh, let me take him," said Lauren. She took the baby, pressed him gently onto her shoulder and began to sway from side to side.

Tony looked at Trance, and then at Lauren. "After the twins are born, you'll be begging for someone to relieve you, just so you can pee."

Lauren smiled and looked at her husband. Her eyes began to well with tears, as she thought of all it took to get Trance to this day. Twenty years of waiting. Nursing Trance back from near death, on far too many occasions. "Maybe," she said. "But I deserve it."

"Glad you came," said Tony.

Trance shrugged. "We're in Florida, until the babies are born, anyway. We were going to skip the Super Bowl, although my company always takes a suite at the game."

Trance's company, Hopewell Industries, owned sixty-six subsidiaries in the U.S., with many more overseas. It was the world's largest privately held company, netting Trance billions per year in profits. Trance had inherited the sprawling, mysterious empire, but had little to do with its day-to-day operations. Instead, Trance maintained a small legal practice in Cohasset, Massachusetts, trying to live life like any normal American.

The problem was, Trance wasn't normal. Trained as a Navy Seal, schooled in the traditions of Japanese martial arts, he was a Major General in the Marines. Inactive, but on call to the president. Sometimes he was forced to answer when his government came to call, with a crisis others couldn't handle. Trance was America's last resort, its weapon of choice when all else failed. Tony wouldn't have asked for his help, unless this were serious.

Trance said, "You said you had a problem?"

"One of Ben Johnson's friends was kidnapped, along with Winde."

"Ahhh," said Trance, smiling. "Should have known. If you'd asked me sooner, I would have come. We're just down the street."

"You're here now."

"What can I do?"

Tony looked at Lauren, as she rocked his son. *She's a natural*, he thought. Good for her. He looked out to the water. It was shimmering emerald green under the soft, sunny sky. The air smelled faintly of tidal brine and heavily of flowers.

"I consulted the *I Ching* and it said I should call you."

Trance closed his eyes. The *I Ching* would be the death of him yet. Sure, it had been used in China and Japan for thousands of years, as a way to converse with the Creator, the Universal One. Sure, it had helped him see into the depths of his own mind, to understand his true nature, his *Way*. But, whenever he, or his uncle, used the *I Ching*, things seemed to happen, monumental things that he would rather avoid.

Tony continued, "The *I Ching* said that things would happen today, things beyond my control, things that only *you* could manage."

"Aw, Tony..."

Trance glanced at his uncle. Tony Trance was in his seventies, but he didn't look a day over sixty. There were reasons for that, reasons that only a few could understand. Trance and Tony were part of a legacy stretching two thousand years into the past, a story that few would comprehend. So, when his uncle said he was needed, Trance understood. He may not like it, but he understood.

Trance said, "The last time you called, I was kidnapped, nearly killed, and hooked on cocaine and heroin."

Tony laughed. "I think you're safe this time, Jack. But others are in danger. Too many others."

Trance closed his eyes. "Don't tell me, the Super Bowl?"

Tony nodded. "The *I Ching* told me there was danger, and that you must be here."

Trance's lips curled into a resigned smile. He shook his head. *Not again.* "What's the plan?"

"Right now, we wait."

"Waiting works for me."

Trance took a seat at one of the picnic tables. It was early afternoon. The Super Bowl wasn't for another five hours. He'd wait. He'd wait all night, if that's what it took.

Trance closed his eyes and let himself fall into meditation. It took just a few seconds, before Trance found himself walking along the beach. Soon, he was joined by his dead father. His father was wearing a pair of cutoff jeans, a Red Sox T-shirt and a pair of old leather sandals. The two of them walked together for a long while, without speaking. Finally, Trance's father said, "It is good to see you, son."

"Hello, dad."

"You look rather well, for a man who should be dead."

Trance thought back to the trauma he'd recently endured, while helping to save the president and prevent a nuclear holocaust in Washington. "I'm feeling pretty good, considering," he said. "How are you?"

Trance's father tilted his head. "The great beyond is a calming place."

"And mom?"

"She misses her son, terribly."

"Tell her I love her."

Trance's father smiled. "She will like hearing that. She loves you, more than she ever knew."

At that moment, Tony shook Trance awake. "Jack…Jack…"

Trance opened his eyes. The sun had sunk far lower into the horizon. He had been in meditation for longer than he'd thought. He looked around. There were others at the picnic tables now. Gumbo and his ladies were there. Murray and Wendell Holmbs were there, as was Ben Johnson.

"Hi, everybody," said Trance.

Gumbo stepped forward and offered his hand. "Yo, Trance. What's shakin'?" He and Trance went into an elaborate handshake, ending with a jumping belly bump.

"Hey, Doc. How's the luv biz?"

"Sweet, like always. I just spread the happiness…"

Gumbo motioned toward Sophie and winked. "Our darling Rose has got us something. Thought you should hear it."

Sophie came forward. Beside her walked a tall, willowy woman with blatant tattoos and a round cloud of bleached blond hair.

"This is Angel," said Sophie. "She called me with information that might help us." Sophie stepped back, as if giving Angel the floor.

"My name's Angel," she said softly.

"Speak up, girl," said Gumbo.

Angel cleared her throat. "A couple days back, Rose bought us lunch and we discussed the kidnapping of that Super Bowl guy and one of us girls. We talked about 'dead meat,' and Rose asked us to tell her if we heard anythin'. So, I put the word on the street.

"I don't know if this means nothing, but last night, one of the Johns was talkin' about a 'Super Bowl barbecue'. There was going to be 'dead meat' at a 'Super Bowl barbecue'. He kept repeating it and repeating it, as if it was funny or somethin'. He was real drunk and tripped out, and I don't think he knew what he was sayin'."

"Who was this man?" said Ben. "You know him?"

"Wasn't my trick. But my friend said he had this shirt."

"A shirt? What do you mean, a shirt?"

"He wore this shirt. You know, a business shirt. A uniform shirt."

"What did it say?" asked Ben. "Did your friend see what it said?"

Angel nodded. "She did. She remembered, 'cause it was her brother's name, Mario. It said Mario's something or other…Meats."

Ben looked over at Murray. "Ring a bell?"

Murray Stein fumbled inside his attaché for a fat black notebook and placed it upon the table. "Mario's…Mario's…" Murray turned the pages frantically. "You don't know how many companies there are that service the stadium…" Murray stopped and jammed a finger against the notebook. "Aha! Mario's Fine Meats & Provisions. We've gone through five layers of ownership on that one. Got as far as…Walden Provisions, based in Brussels. Who owns that, we don't know."

"That's got to be it," said Ben. He pulled out his phone and dialed for Michael McBride. After a moment, he said, "Chief…It's Ben. We found something. Check out a company by the name of Mario's Fine Meats and Provisions. See if they were supplying the Pro Bowl."

Ben cupped his hand to his PDA and said, "McBride's with Starr, the guy from the FBI who's supposed to be running this show. They're at the stadium."

A moment later, Ben said, "Yeah? Uh-huh. They did? Are they there today?" Ben waited for another minute. "Really? Better get a warrant."

Ben hung up his phone and said, "Mario's has ten trucks at the stadium, right now. McBride's going to request a warrant so we can start searching them."

Tony looked at Trance. "This is where we need you, Jack. You get us into the stadium."

Trance laughed. "Is that what you wanted me for? Entrance to the game?"

Tony smiled slyly, almost meekly. "We've got this under control, Jack. But if we can't get inside, there's not much we can do, now. Is there?"

"I'm sure the FBI will let you in—"

"They don't want us, Jack. They say we're in the way."

"Well, maybe you are."

Tony picked up his phone, pushed the walkie button and called for the man who managed SOSCADA's vehicles. "Could you bring us four limos, please? To the house."

Ten minutes later, four limousines pulled out of the mansion's main garage and wound their way up to the house.

Trance said, "How many people are we bringing, Tony?"

"Oh, I don't know. Twenty. Twenty-five."

Trance groaned. "I can't get twenty-five people into the stadium, Tony. All my tickets have been distributed. We'd have a far better chance getting into the White House…"

"You know the commissioner of the NFL?"

"Yes, but—"

"You know the owner of Sun Life Stadium?"

"Yes, I know Stephen. But—"

"And your company is one of the Super Bowl's biggest TV sponsors?"

"Yes, but—"

"You can get us into the stadium, Jack."

Trance pulled out his Sectéra Edge PDA, while shaking his head. "You're going to owe me, Tony. Big time. Give me a true head count."

Tony counted out the people he'd assembled to go to the stadium and search the trucks. "Twenty-seven, including you and Lauren."

Trance dialed his phone. A moment later, he had Arthur R. Winthrop, III on the line. Art was the CEO of Hopewell Industries, a man with extraordinary influence, but someone who answered to Trance.

"Hi, Art. It's Jack."

"Where are you?"

"Miami."

"Coming to the game?"

"Thinking about it. I've got a problem."

"Jack, you've always got a problem."

Trance smiled. "I need to get twenty-five more guests into the stadium."

Trance was met by silence. Finally, Winthrop said, "Today?"

"The game's today, Art."

"You're joking, right?"

"No, Art. I'm not. It's essential that we all get inside. In about twenty minutes."

"You do know this is the Super Bowl?"

"That's the point."

Winthrop remained silent for several long moments, before saying, "How essential is this?"

"You want to be a hero?"

"I'm already a hero. Remember it at bonus time."

Trance chuckled. "I already pay you more than you're worth."

Winthrop laughed. "Call me when you're close…And, Jack?"

"Yes?"

"It will be good to see you and Lauren."

Trance smiled and hung up his phone. "Let's go," he said.

As the four limousines neared Sun Life Stadium, Trance called Winthrop, saying, "How're we doing?"

"Come to the center gate off Dan Marino Blvd. Passes are waiting for you there, along with someone who will guide you into the stadium."

"How'd you do it?"

"You don't want to know."

Trance groaned. "Thanks, I guess." He said, "Center gate," to his driver.

The limos were met by a white Ford sedan, with a flashing yellow light on its roof. They followed the car underground, beneath the stadium, into an area reserved for the owner of the Florida Marlins, the major lessee of the stadium.

As the limos came to a halt, the Marlin's owner himself was waiting to greet them.

"Hey, Jack," he said. "So nice of you to give me notice."

Trance stuck out his hand and said, "Twenty minutes not enough for you, Jeff?" As the men shook, Trance continued, "Will we be seeing you at Fenway this year?"

Trance and his wife owned the Boston Red Sox.

"Going to invite us over to the new house?"

"Be pleased to have you. Your whole family, if you'd like."

"Art said that you have a collection for me to see."

Ahhh, Trance thought. *The payoff.*

The Marlin's owner had made his fortune as an art dealer. Trance had the most extensive private art collections in the world, including newly found works by Da Vinci and Michelangelo. Most of Trance's collections were not publicly known. This had been Art's bargaining chip.

"Art told you about Da Vinci?"

"He also said something about Michelangelo."

Trance's lips spread into a tight, thin smile. "Yeah. Got a whole ceiling's worth."

Jeff looked over toward Lauren, smiled and waved. "The Loire Valley? In May?" he said.

Most of Trance's works by Da Vinci and Michelangelo were housed in a private chateau, on the banks of France's Loire Valley.

Lauren nodded. "We'll be happy to show you around."

"Marvelous." Jeff began walking away. "Gotta run," he said. "Bye, Jack. Bye, Lauren…Busy day."

"Was that the owner of the Florida Marlins?" said Ben.

"Yeah, and it cost me big time," said Trance. He looked around, his eyes searching with calculated experience. "What next?"

The area beneath Sun Life Stadium was close to bedlam. Trucks were coming in and out, carrying enough food and drink for almost eighty thousand people. Stadium workers were running in every direction. Some were driving carts laden with provisions. Others wheeled dollies loaded with every conceivable type of food and beverage.

"The authorities should be here soon," said Tony. As he spoke, Trance saw McBride, Esposito, Griffin and Starr converging upon them.

As McBride approached, his face broke into a wide grin. "Well, if it isn't Jack Trance, my reluctant savior." Trance had been the one to arrange McBride's presidential pardon. McBride opened his arms and gave Trance a meaty hug and a slap on the back. "Here for the game?"

Trance angled his head toward Ben and Tony. "Got caught up in this kidnapping thing."

McBride shook his head sharply. "We're more concerned with today's security, Jack...A thousand pair of boots on the ground, and that's nowhere near enough. We'll worry about the kidnapping tomorrow."

Ben said, "We think they're here, Mike."

"I heard. Mario's Meats."

"You get a warrant to search the trucks?"

"Didn't need one. They let us look inside them all, voluntarily."

"All of them?"

"Every one. There are a few still coming in. We'll check them out, too. So far, they're clean."

"That can't be," said Ben. "That just can't be."

McBride placed a hand upon Ben's shoulder. "I'm sorry, Ben. We're all sorry."

Trance said, "We'll need a list of every Mario's truck location. Including the one's scheduled to come in."

McBride handed Trance a map of the stadium spotted with red and green X's and said, "The reds are here. The greens are coming."

"We want permission to search them again," said Ben.

McBride shrugged. He looked at Starr. He shrugged, too.

McBride said, "Suit yourself." McBride's eyes narrowed as he surveyed the army of people gathered around the four limos. "How'd they get in here?"

Ben jutted his chin forward. "You think we don't have tickets?"

"I know you don't have tickets."

"Yeah, we do. Trance got them."

McBride looked at Trance, who shrugged. McBride began to back away, saying, "Look. We've got to get back to work. Security for this thing is a nightmare..."

As McBride left, Trance held up the map he'd received. He took a picture with his PDA, attached it to an email and sent it to Tony and Ben. "Tell me if you can read this," he said.

Ben fingered his PDA and opened the email. He zoomed in on the picture and said, "I see enough." He looked up at Tony. "Take ten people and cover the trucks near gates A, B & C. I'll take the others with me, to cover gates D, E & F. Trance, can you get gate G?"

Trance turned to his wife and said, "Honey, why don't you go up to the Hopewell suite? No need for you to be prowling around down here."

Lauren began to protest, but reconsidered. The others weren't carrying twins. Her legs were aching. She also needed food. "I'll do that," she said.

"I'll go with her," said Wendell Holmbs, ever the gentleman.

Trance shook hands with Wendell and nodded his thanks. He pecked his wife on the cheek and nudged her away. This could be dangerous, and he wanted Lauren as far away from trouble as possible.

As Ben and Gumbo reached their first Mario's truck, they found no one standing beside it. No driver. No sentry. The truck looked as harmless as a worm. A few workers were scrambling around, lugging cases of beer and boxes of frozen hamburgers and shrimp. Gumbo found a ladder on wheels and rolled it to the back of the truck. He locked the wheels with a stomp of his boot and climbed up the steps. He rolled the back panel of the truck upwards, yelling, "Anybody in there? Mabel?"

The back of the truck was filled with thirty pound cases of hot dogs. Gumbo stepped around the boxes and looked deeper into the truck.

"Hello?" he said. "Anybody there?" Gumbo walked all the way inside, shining a flashlight he'd brought from the Sanchez mansion. He banged the light's handle upon the side of the truck. "Hello?" Nothing.

"This one's empty," Gumbo said, as he climbed back down to the ground. He looked around, but Ben was gone. "Ben?" said Gumbo. "Ben?"

"Under here."

Gumbo looked around, but still couldn't see his friend. "Where are you, dude?"

Ben slid out from beneath the truck. There was a clover-shaped grease stain upon his forehead, and a thin coating of dust and dirt along his back.

"Just checking underneath," he said. "We're clear."

"Then it's onward, ho."

Chapter Fifty-Three
V
____

"How are you feeling, Mabel?" said Winde.

"Claustrophobic as hell."

The air around them was dark and lifeless, as desolate as a shuttered cabin in the wilderness, on a moonless night. They were surrounded by boxes of raw beef. The smell was almost overpowering. The cramped air, the blood and the bone and the flesh. Then, there were the explosives.

"I think I'm going to puke," said Mabel.

"Please don't," said Winde. "I'll throw up, too."

"Just kidding…Who do you think that was before? You think it was someone looking for us?"

"They ignored our screaming."

"They couldn't hear us, Terry. Probably too noisy out there in the stadium, and we're behind a ton of meat."

"What time d'you think it is?"

"Can't believe Lou stole our watches...Thinking about the game?"

Winde laughed. "Of coarse...You know, you start out as a kid. You play these games in your mind. The announcer in your head says, 'The Super Bowl comes down to this one final play. Fletcher goes out for a pass. Winde drops back. He lets it fly. Fletcher jumps for the ball. The defender sticks his hand in Fletcher's face. Fletcher fights through it like a madman...He catches the ball! He catches the ball! The crowd is going wild…Haaaa…Haaaa…' It sort of goes like that….Then you spend your whole life trying to get there. I've pounded my muscles in weight rooms every day since I was fourteen. I've spent thousands of hours studying film...just as many in the ice tub and on the trainer's table, nursing injuries.

"I've had six surgeries. Fought back from depression, problems with coaches, suffered the time away from home. All of it was to get here, the Super Bowl. And now? Now, I'm spending it in the back of a truck surrounded by dead cows."

"You've got me."

"That's true, Mabel. I've still got you—"

"Hello?" The noise was faint. There was a muffled tapping on the side of the truck. "Hello?"

"Oh, my God. Someone's out there," said Mabel. "Hello!" she yelled.

"Hello? Anybody there?" came the voice.

Winde began pounding his feet against the floor.

"Someone in there?"

Winde pounded some more. Mabel began stomping her feet, too. Then Winde started banging his head against the wall of the truck.

Mabel said, "Stop that, goofball. You'll get a concussion."

Winde stopped hitting his head, but yelled, "Hello!"

"Someone in there?"

"Hello! Hello!" *Pound, pound, pound* of the feet.

Then a voice seemed to be coming from below them, as if someone were crawling beneath the truck. "Hello?"

Winde stomped his feet, over and over, until his ankles felt like they would shatter.

Suddenly, the back of the truck slid open. They could tell, because tiny streams of light worked their way through the beef.

"Hello?" came a faint voice.

Winde yelled, "Here!" *Pound, pound, pound.* "In here!"

They could hear some shuffling. A bit more light began to show, and they kept yelling. There was more light. Then more.

"Someone there?"

"This is Mabel Witherspoon. Can you hear me?" screamed Mabel, more loudly than Winde thought a person could yell.

"Mabel? Is that you?" It was Ben. She could hear him now.

"Yes, you moron. It's me."

A bit more light. Some more shuffling. Then they saw one of the beef boxes move.

"Ben!" shouted Mabel.

"Quick," yelled Ben. "Help me move this meat."

"Be careful, Ben," said Mabel. "The truck is wired, with explosives."

A box broke free and sweet light streamed in. "What?" They still couldn't see him.

"Explosives, Ben. The truck is set to blow."

"Shit." They heard Ben say, "Slow down, guys. This thing's a rolling bomb…Clear back. I'll handle this."

"Hell, no," said someone near Ben. "You don't get all the fun."

"Suit yourself."

Within five minutes, Ben and Gumbo had removed enough of the boxes to create a thin center path to Mabel and Winde.

Ben said, "You guys okay?"

"Of course," said Mabel. "You think we're wimps?"

Ben began to cry.

Mabel said, "Don't start crying on me, Johnson. Find someone to drive this truck out of here. Mosca said there's enough explosive in this thing to level the stadium."

At that moment, Tony reached the back of the vehicle, followed closely by Trance and the others.

Ben held up his hands. "Careful, guys. The truck is wired. Looks like C-4, with a little dynamite thrown in for fun." He pulled at Mabel's straps, while Trance jumped inside and freed Winde from his bindings.

"We can't wait for the bomb squad," said Trance. "I'll run this out of here…get it somewhere it can blow and not kill thousands."

"The hell you will," said Ben. "*I'm* driving the truck out of here."

"Why you?" said Gumbo. "I was the one that found them."

Trance paused for a moment. He was an interloper here. These people had done all the work. They had given the sweat and taken the risks. They deserved this choice, even if it was to die.

"Sure you guys can *see* well enough to drive?" joked Trance. He was already on his PDA, searching for a place to bring the truck. "Okay," he said. "The parking lot will have tailgaters…Brentwood Park is just down the street. Bring it there."

"No," said Ben. "Too much risk. Find somewhere better."

Trance fingered his PDA. "The bomb unit is based in Doral. The Miami Gardens Landfill is on the way. 16300 NW 42nd Avenue. Know where that is?"

Ben nodded.

"We'll order a police escort, and have the bomb techs motor to the landfill. Get the truck there, then let the pros take over, Ben."

Ben was already jumping into the truck's cab.

"Be smart this time, Ben," said Trance. "Get out as soon as you can."

Ben stuck his head out from the open door. "Are you saying I'm reckless, Trance?"

Trance looked down to Ben's leg, raising his eyebrows, then nodding. "Yeah. I've seen you do some really dumb things, Ben."

"Well, not today."

Ben searched around the truck's cabin, but found no keys. "Figures," he mumbled. The truck was an older model, so Ben calmly reached under the dash and found the ignition wires. He pulled a jackknife from his pants, cut the two red wires, peeled the plastic sheath off both and twisted them together. He cut a brown wire, peeled back the sheath and touched it to the exposed red wires. The truck started with a low, grinding diesel chug.

Mabel hung by the open door. "You're my hero," she said.

"Aw, Mabel. I forgot my cape."

Gumbo jumped into the other side of the cab and shouted, "Let's roll, Ben."

Ben blew a kiss toward Mabel. He ground the truck into gear and they raced off through the belly of the stadium.

They all watched Ben and Gumbo speed away. When they were gone, Tony turned to Winde. "My name's Tony Trance. How d'you feel?"

"Great to be alive, sir."

"Up for the game?"

"It still on?"

Tony looked to his watch. "You've got a little over thirty minutes, provided you're able."

"Able? I've been coached up, big time. Haven't missed a pass all week." Winde looked over at Mabel. "You're going to take care of her?"

Trance stepped forward. "I've got the chief of surgery from Jackson Memorial waiting at my suite. She'll be in good hands." Trance looked at Winde's wrists. The cuts caused by the crude cuffs had become grossly infected and were oozing with yellow, greenish puss. "Get those wrists medicated and taped, Terry."

Winde grinned, "Just a flesh wound."

"This isn't Monty Python. I'm serious."

Winde walked over to Mabel. She opened up her arms and gave him a tight squeeze. "Glad you practiced?" she said.

"Thanks, Mabel. You put me in top form."

"Go win this game. For your family, your teammates, your city. And for all the little boys who dream."

Chapter Fifty-Four
V
____

"Ya think this thing's going to blow?" said Gumbo, as they raced west on the Palmetto Expressway, chugging toward the landfill.

Ben wiped a slick of moisture off his brow with the back of his hand. What the hell were they doing? They were in a rolling bomb. "We should have brought this to Brentwood Park. We'd be there by now."

"We can make it. They've got the roads cleared," said Gumbo. "It's just you and me, Ben. Just you and me and the grim reaper breathing down our scrawny little necks."

Both men looked out to the flashing police lights ahead and behind them. The roads were empty. If the truck blew now, they would be its only casualties.

"I'm thinking it's on a timer," said Ben.

"We should have checked."

"Impossible, with so little time. Anything could be a trigger, including a box of meat, or a loose string. We were lucky to get those guys out as it is."

"I'm glad *we* didn't die, Ben. At least not yet."

Ben pushed the truck as fast as he dared, fearful that even the jarring of the road could cause it to explode.

Ben joked, "I've been thinking…The bomb squad's facility is in Doral. Probably better equipped than a landfill. You want to take this thing all the way there? To Doral?"

"Got a death wish?"

Ben laughed. "Nah. But after driving on the back of Mabel's motor-cycle, nothing scares me. Besides, I think I'm beginning to like driving with a load of dynamite."

"Dynamite *and* C-4." Gumbo pulled open his shirt and puffed out his chest, his colorful American Eagle tattoo gleaming blood-red in the dying evening light. "It is a rush though, isn't it?"

"Still rather watch a beautiful lady walk by, particularly in a bikini."

Gumbo said, "I see too *much* skin, in my line of work." He lowered his voice. "So, you doin' it with Mabel?"

"Excuse me?"

"I said, 'are you screwing Mabel'?"

"That's none of your business, Gumbo."

"Haven't done it, hey?"

"It's not that I don't want to…But…well…"

"No need to explain it, dude. Women are like a rare, little-known species, one we men have yet to fully understand—"

At that moment, a loud-pitched whine began to come from the back of the truck.

"Uh-oh," said Gumbo. "You want to pull over?"

Ben shook his head. "No. We drive this thing to safety."

Chapter Fifty-Five
V
____

The volume of noise suddenly dropped across the Hopewell Industries Super Bowl suite, the air vibrating with a palpable sense of anticipation, as Jack Trance escorted Mabel Witherspoon inside. Mabel wasn't sure if the quiet was for Trance, who owned the conglomerate, or if word had gotten out about her. She soon realized that it was about Trance, which was fine by her. Guests began streaming by, greeting Trance with hugs or the shaking of hands. Several times, people said, "I heard about Washington…"

Mabel was about to ask Trance what they meant, when an elegant looking, brown-haired woman with a basketball belly came waddling up to her. "You must be Mabel."

"And you are?"

The woman offered her hand. "Lauren Haverford Trance."

"Ah, I know you! You're the new owner of the Red Sox. Archie, my late husband, he absolutely *loved* the Sox. We never missed a game; thank God for NESN."

Lauren's eyes shone with the jovial kinship that comes from a fellow lover of America's pastime. There was also a look of concern. "How are you feeling, Mabel? Are you okay? Can we get you anything?"

Mabel held up her battered wrists. "Maybe a doctor, for these…and a glass of scotch. On the rocks, if you've got it."

Lauren pointed toward a man who was approaching them, wielding a black doctor's satchel. "Have you met Sophie? This is her son…also Jack's personal physician, and here for you." Lauren smiled. "I'll get the scotch. You like single malt?"

Mabel's face crinkled into a smile. "What kind ya got?"

"Jack's got some Macallan '53 hidden behind the bar. That work for you?"

"That'll seriously work."

The doctor took hold of Mabel's wrists. He examined them closely, with a look of deep concentration stretching across his brow.

"You've got quite an infection here, Mrs. Witherspoon. Fortunately, it's not in the blood." The doctor strapped a head light onto his forehead and peered more closely at Mabel's wounds.

"I'm not taking any antibiotics until after I've had my scotch," Mabel said.

The doctor laughed. "Oh, I think you can handle both today." He reached into his bag and withdrew an orange prescription bottle. He unscrewed the cap, pulled out a yellow pill and handed it to her. "Can you swallow this, or do you need water?"

Mabel grabbed the pill and popped it into her mouth. "I'm old. I can swallow anything." She held out her wrists. "Clean these up and get 'em bandaged, fast. I've got a game to watch."

As the doctor finished bandaging Mabel's wrists, the Star Spangled Banner was beginning to play. Cheers grew in volume as the final strains of the song reverberated through the stadium. Then a roar erupted around them. Mabel looked to one of the TV monitors that were spaced throughout the suite. She could see the camera focusing onto #9, as he ran out onto the sidelines.

"I can't believe it," yelled one of the announcers. "Terry Winde has just run onto the field. I don't know where he came from, but this is a certainly a shocker." The announcer paused. "Hold it. It looks like Winde's wrists are taped. This is something new for him. Maybe some sort of injury…We're going to check with Steve Tasker on the sidelines and see if we can learn anything…."

"There's my boy," whispered Mabel.

Lauren, Trance and Tony converged upon Mabel. Lauren handed Mabel a glass filled with scotch and motioned toward a wide bank of windows at the far end of the suite. "Seats are over there, Mabel. We're going to open up the windows so we can enjoy the noise."

Mabel sat down, looking along the forty yard line. Winde was huddled with his players, jumping up and down, yelling something to fire them up. Then Winde thrust his fist in the air and they all sprinted onto the field, roaring.

"This is nothing short of extraordinary," said the CBS announcer. "We are hearing that Terry Winde has spent the past week in the back of a truck. He sent word through his wife, asking us to give thanks to a Coach Mabel Witherspoon…I think that's how you say it…for all her fine training tips. What do you make of that, Phil?"

"Not sure what that means, Jim," said the color announcer. "But this sure does change the complexion of this game." There was a pause, as the camera zoomed back on Winde. The color man continued, "As you know, Terry Winde set an NFL mark this year for passing accuracy, completing more than seventy percent of his passes. Under Winde's guidance, his team scored more than 500 points and averaged over 400 yards per game. This is an offense that explodes with him at the helm. Without him, I didn't think they had a snowball's chance to win. Now? This is anybody's game…"

Complete and total silence spread across the Hopewell suite, as Winde's wife slipped inside. She looked to a group of guests and said, "I'm looking for Jack Trance. And Mabel Witherspoon. Can you tell me where they might be?"

Winde's wife was guided to the back of the suite. The crowd outside was *roaring* through the open windows. Mabel was now standing, pumping her fists, yelling, "You go, Terry!"

"Mrs. Witherspoon?" said Winde's wife.

Mabel turned. "Yes?"

"My name is Daisy Winde."

Mabel's mouth opened and she let out a shriek. "Oh, my golly. It is so good to meet you!" Mabel gave Daisy a big, grandmotherly hug. "What are you doing here, dear?"

Daisy motioned toward an empty alcove of the suite, away from the crowd. When they were alone, Daisy reached into her purse. She located a jeweler's felt pouch, removed its contents and held it in her closed fist.

"I saw Terry, just for a minute, before he had to get ready for the game. He asked me to bring you this."

Daisy pressed something into Mabel's palm and closed her fingers around it. It was cool, something metallic.

"What is this?" said Mabel.

Daisy sighed, with a wistfulness that Mabel could feel in her bones. "That's Terry's lucky penny. His dad gave it to him when he was six. When he was in college, Terry put it on a gold chain. He wears it every game. He said he wanted you to have it." Daisy began to sniffle. She held back a sob and said, "He said he wouldn't be alive, except for you."

"I can't take this, Daisy," said Mabel. "And it was me that got him into this mess."

"He insists. He said you taught him more in one week than he's learned in a lifetime."

Mabel looked out to the field. They were preparing for the opening kickoff. Winde was standing on the sidelines, looking over in their direction, smiling. He gave a brief wave of the hand, then focused his attention on the game. Mabel turned to Daisy.

"What Terry learned was how important you and your children are, Daisy. Football is just a game. *You* are his life. He's a good man, and he loves you very much."

Daisy blinked back her tears and whispered, "I know."

"I can't take his penny, Daisy."

"He insists. He really does. He's stubborn, you know."

Mabel frowned. Then she smiled. "Okay," she said. "I understand stubborn." Mabel looked down to her emerald ring, the one Archie had given her after he'd first seen her on stage. She hadn't taken it off in half a century. She wet her finger and pried the ring off her right hand, mumbling, "Damned arthritis…" She held the ring out to Daisy.

"This is for you. My husband gave this to me, just after we met. It was love at first sight, you see. And it was the best kind of love, a love that endured everything God could throw our way. My Archie is gone now, but your love…your love is still young. Take this. Wear it if you like and remember—No matter what stands in your way, love will help conquer all."

There was a roar from the field. Mabel and Daisy turned, just in time to see Winde loft a pass high into the air. The pass must have traveled seventy yards, landing softly into the hands of a receiver running at full speed into the end zone.

"I don't believe it!" yelled the CBS announcer. "On the first play from scrimmage, Winde throws eighty yards for a score. I guess that answers the question of whether or not he's ready for this game…"

"He's ready all right," said Mabel. "The man understands his priorities." She pressed the ring into Daisy's palm and closed her fingers around it.

At that moment, there was a low *boom* in the distance. Then there was another one, this one much closer. Mabel looked out across the stadium. She could see a giant fireball erupting over its far edge. The flames looked to be about a half mile away, in the direction of Cantwell's offices. Mabel stared, stunned for a moment. Then she said, "That bastard."

"Excuse me?" said Daisy.

Mabel looked at Winde's wife. She took both her hands and squeezed them. "You need to go, sweetie. Go to where your husband can see you. He needs you now. His team needs you. And I've got some business to take care of."

Daisy squeezed back on Mabel's hands. "Thank you." She gave Mabel a brief hug, turned and headed back across the suite.

Mabel looked around to find Tony and Jack Trance, but they were already beside her. Mabel said, "The bastard did it."

Tony was on his phone, saying, "Are you there, Ben? Gumbo? You guys there?" He looked at Mabel. "Somebody picked up but didn't answer. All I hear is a lot of noise….Chaos, really."

Mabel closed her eyes. "Ben had to be stupid and take the truck."

Tony said, "Doesn't mean he's dead, Mabel. I'm sure he made it."

"He didn't have time, time to get the truck...to safety—"

Mabel felt herself swoon. She reached for her forehead, as her knees began to buckle. Tony caught her, gently and expertly, as if she were a dancer jumping lightly into his arms.

Mabel mumbled, "We need to find Cantwell."

Tony placed Mabel's feet upon the floor, holding her up like a marionette. "Are you okay?"

Mabel stiffened, then narrowed her eyes. "I'm fine. Let's go. The Cantwell suite." Mabel began to pull Tony across the room. Jack Trance followed, feeling as useless as a third leg.

Cantwell's suite wasn't far down the hall. Its doors were open. Music was thrumming out with a deep, heavy bass. A makeshift dance floor had been formed in the center of the suite, with bodies flailing. There was a raucous, uncontrolled party inside, far more boisterous than the one in Trance's suite.

"Cantwell!" shouted Mabel.

Nobody answered. A man bumped into Mabel, spilling beer down her blouse. The man wore a pair of rough work jeans with a silver rodeo buckle the size of a dinner plate. He had on alligator cowboy boots and a white embroidered shirt with a thin string tie. "I'm so sorry, ma'am," he mumbled, with a deep Louisiana accent. "It's been a long wait, and I sort of lost myself here."

"You a Winde fan?" Mabel asked.

"Yes, ma'am. He does great things for our city, and the team."

Mabel shook the man's hand. "Then you're okay by me."

Tony yelled, "Has anybody seen Cantwell?" Again, nobody answered.

Mabel spied little miss perfect, the receptionist with the blond hair, the blue eyes and the straight white teeth. She walked over and grabbed the woman by the shoulder. "Have you seen Rial?"

The receptionist was glassy-eyed and drunk. She hiccupped and slurred, "Haven't seen 'im all day. He was supposed to be here…but…haven't seen 'im all...day."

Tony Trance took a call on his phone. He nodded several times, then pointed out across the stadium. "The Cantwell Building is gone."

Mabel said, "He's destroying evidence. What about Ben?"

Tony drew took a long breath and shrugged. "The truck Ben was driving exploded. Can't reach anyone on his phone, now. Just rolls to voicemail. There's no news about him or Gumbo. They say it's a madhouse down there, but firemen and the bomb techs *are* on the scene. At the landfill."

"Ohhh," moaned Mabel. "This is all my fault."

Mabel shuffled slowly out of the Cantwell suite. She meandered down the hallway, with Tony and Trance trailing behind her, not knowing what to say. When Mabel had retraced half the distance back to Trance's suite, she sank to the hallway floor. She sat there, silent, staring forward as if seeing nothing at all.

Tony's phone rang again. He said, "Yeah. Uh-huh." He smiled and handed the phone to Mabel. "It's for you."

Mabel took the phone unsteadily. "Hello?" Mabel's voice was barely a whisper.

An unfamiliar voice said, "Ben Johnson says you owe him."

"Who's this?"

"My name is officer Cleveland. I'm at the Miami Gardens landfill. Mr. Johnson can't hear anything right now, and he's pretty shaken up. But he can talk…sort of...insisted I call you, to say he's okay."

Mabel dropped the phone and began to cry. "Damn you, Ben Johnson."

Tony picked up the phone. "Please tell Mr. Johnson that Mabel is glad he's okay."

"Sure. I'll write it down for him…Mr. Johnson also asked me to tell Ms. Witherspoon that he loves her."

Tony covered the phone and said, "Ben says he loves you."

Mabel grinned through the tears. "Tell him I love him, too."

Chapter Fifty-Six
V

Ben

By February, the days in south Florida begin to turn warm in a hurry. It's like winter's got just enough endurance to last through January. Then it gives out like a spawned salmon, to warmer days and cool, pleasant nights. The ladies break out their bikinis. Suntan oil flies off the shelves. Women stop looking like beached whales and start looking like bronze goddesses again. I just love this time of year.

I was hanging out on my balcony, staring at the smooth blue water, watching for any twenty or thirty-somethings that might be walking below me on the beach. I was beginning to hear again, and the ocean sounded as good as Sinatra.

I'd lost all my hearing when the Mario's truck exploded. Gumbo and I had just turned it off. The bomb squad was beginning to arrive at the landfill, but we hadn't bothered to wait. We'd gotten about fifty yards away from the truck when the whole thing exploded like a nuclear weapon.

The heat was immense. I could feel the air being sucked out of me, like I'd jumped into deep space. A flash of flame, burning like a firestorm, flew out from the truck. It melted my hair like candle wax. I breathed in some of the fire. Made me hoarse for days, but there was no permanent damage. Debris flew all around us. Chunks of meat came down like rain. A flaming hot dog landed on Gumbo's head and he ate the damned thing. We were lucky. All of us. A few seconds earlier or later, and…well, I don't want to think about that.

My leg was pretty much healed, now. My calf was still tender, but it was getting back to normal. Masco's twenty-two had nicked my femur, so it still hurt like a mother. But, by my second Corona, I'd forget about the pain. I'd start to remember my time at the CIA, pretending they were the good ol' days. I'd start to imagine that one of those bikini-clad beauties would look up at me and shout, "I love older men!" or, "I love a man with a shredded ear lobe!" I'd start thinking about fishing, how the water was beginning to warm, and how all the game fish would soon be rushing back into the bay.

I was still mustering up the energy to start putting my life back together. I had a pile of computers sitting in the middle of my office floor. I'd finished briefing the FBI about Masco and Cantwell, sharing nearly everything I had from my computers. Cantwell had gone missing, just like Masco. I had an idea where they were, at least where they were going to be. I wanted to talk to Mabel about it first, before I told anyone else.

I heard a loud rumble beneath my balcony and smiled. That would be our super hot biker chick. I reached into my cooler, popped the top on a fresh Corona, wedged a lime into the bottle and set it down on the table beside me.

After a minute or so, I heard a shuffling echo behind me. I didn't bother to turn. I just motioned with my beer toward the chair beside me. "Take a seat," I said.

Mabel sat down without saying a word. She was carrying a black canvas bag, which she slipped beneath the table. She took a long sip of beer and stared out at the water, just like me.

"How're you feeling, Ben?" she finally said.

"What?" I yelled. Then I laughed. "I'm good, Mabel. I'm real good. How about you?"

Mabel smiled. "Got my wire today. Nearly eight million dollars."

"Yeah," I said. "They let me send you your money, seeing how you helped break the case. The other investors will have to wait for the final accounting."

"You find it all? The money, I mean."

I nodded. "Yeah. It was just waiting there, like Cantwell wanted us to have it. I think he's trying to buy his freedom."

"You think they're alive?"

"I'm sure of it."

Mabel took another sip of her beer. "We made a deal with Cantwell, although I'd like to strangle the son-of-a-bitch. How much he keep?"

I shrugged. "About five billion, I recon. Fair. Left everything else right where it was."

"He could have taken more."

I inhaled deeply, my lungs rasping just a touch. *Ain't that the truth.* "There are going to be a lot of happy investors. Including your new boyfriend."

Mabel smiled. "Winde played quite a game."

"One of the best Super Bowl performances ever, they say." *Too bad I missed it.*

"I got a game ball."

"Did you, now?"

Mabel grinned. "It was after the game. I had heard that you were alive, but I was still pretty shaken up. They brought me down to the locker room. I think I walked in like a zombie. Winde was standing with a group of reporters, his hair all askew, naked to the waist, with a bottle of champagne in his hands.

"When I entered the locker room…I'll have to tell you about that later, because I saw some things you wouldn't believe…Did you know…Never mind…Anyway, Winde put his arm around me and called for quiet. Then he said something like, 'People will tell you that football is a game of preparation and training and skill. That's true. But there is nothing more important in football, as in life, than *heart*. We won this game today, but it was not because of our skill. It wasn't because we were the better team. We probably weren't. We won today because we had heart.'"

Mabel looked out over the ocean. Her eyes narrowed and she seemed to ponder something she saw out there. She shook her head slowly and continued. "Winde grabbed a football out of his locker. It smelled like dirt and grass and sweat, maybe some blood. He thrust the ball into my hands and said, 'Today's MVP game ball goes to my coach, Mabel Witherspoon. She taught me about life, and about heart.'

"Then he started spraying me with champagne."

Mabel reached into the bag under the table and pulled out a football. She tossed it into the air and said, "Catch."

I caught the ball and turned it over in my hands.

"The game ball should really go to you, Ben. You're the one that got things done."

I fingered the smooth, pebbled leather. Mabel was right. The ball did smell of dirt and grass and sweat, and maybe even a little blood. And champagne. It smelled good, like a full life.

"Thank you, Mabel."

"We haven't discussed your fee."

I couldn't get myself to look at her. My throat was choking up. Finally, I said, "A kiss would do the trick."

Mabel laughed softly. "You know I love you, Ben. But I'm like a goose; they mate for life. I'm still married to Archie. Always will be."

"I know," I said. "But I had to ask."

"Besides, you like women half your age."

I chuckled. I had to admit it; I did like watching them. "But they don't like me, Mabel."

"All good comes to those who wait, Ben Johnson."

Mabel pulled a piece of paper out of her bag and placed it upon the table. "That's your fee," she said.

I picked up the check and looked at it. The check was written out for one million dollars. I may not get the girl, but I did get paid.

"Guess it will have to do," I said.

Mabel took another sip of beer and sighed. "You'll get over me, Ben."

I nodded. I might, in time. But not all the way. Mabel would always own a big chunk of my heart. It made me sort of depressed.

EPILOGUE I

Ben

I took Mabel's check and used it to upgrade my place on Key West. Well, what I really did was to sell my old place, which was not on the water, and buy a new place, which *was* on the water. It wasn't overly large, but it did have a swath of sandy beach and a deep water dock where I could keep my Sundancer, to which I had given the name, *Mabel.*

I checked the car sites every day, to see if I could find a suitable replacement for my Jaguar. It wasn't easy. I was looking for one that wasn't filled with putty and didn't smoke like a coal factory.

I was looking through an *AutoTrader* one day when I saw an ad I wasn't sure could be true. There was a pristine, white 1964 XKE for sale near Daytona. I called the number and talked to a woman. She told me that the car had been owned by a neurosurgeon who had died at a very young age, of a heart attack. His widow had kept the thing in a garage for forty-five years, driving it occasionally on Sundays, to church. I am not making this up.

The woman had recently died. Her daughter was testing the market to see what the car was worth. I was bidding against some guy from Des Moines, who appeared to have more money than brains. So, I decided to go meet the seller face-to-face.

I pulled into the driveway in my rented Nissan. The driveway was made of smooth white concrete. The landscaping was neatly kept St. Augustine grass, with a little rose garden and a walkway of multi-colored flagstones leading to the front door. Very nice and neat. I could almost see the old widow walking around with a trowel in her hand, tending to every plant and blade of grass. The home backed up against the Intracoastal Waterway. It had a screened-in porch with a small oval pool, a perfect setting from which to watch the boats go by. The sky was blue. The water was a dark blue-green.

"Hello?" I yelled.

"Out back," I heard.

I walked around to the rear of the house, where I saw a woman. She was about sixty, with loopy graying hair and a trowel in *her* hand. Like mother like daughter, I thought.

"You the guy for the car?" she said.

"I am."

The woman tossed her trowel onto the ground and began walking toward the garage.

"I'm going to sell this place," she said, without turning around. "My husband and I live down in Lauderdale. I'm here to tidy things up and get rid of the junk. You wouldn't believe all the stuff people can accumulate in a lifetime…"

The woman opened the back door to the garage and stepped aside. "What d'ya think?"

It was an E-Type Roadster with the 4.2 liter engine, not the 3.8. There was not a single mark on the sweet little thing. I put a magnet to it and it stuck like glue. The car was perfect.

The woman pressed a button on the side wall and the garage door yawned. "Take her out for a spin," she said. Then she looked at me more closely. There was an odd look on her face, as if she'd just noticed that I had warts or something. Maybe it was the earlobe, which now looked like a red letter W. "Are you that Johnson guy? The one that saved the Super Bowl? We were at the game with our kids. You saved our lives."

"I didn't really *save* the Super Bowl, or your lives," I said.

"I saw you on TV. You were pretty funny, you and that Mabel chick."

"We had some fun." But that was over.

"Tell you what," the woman said. "You try the car. You like it, it's yours."

That's how I got my new ride.

It was about ten in the morning when I pulled off NW 183rd Street into the parking lot of Jiggles. I felt myself looking around, to make sure that I hadn't been spotted outside the place. It was one thing to furtively watch women in their bikinis. It was something far different to do it in the open, or to pay for it.

There was just one other car in the lot. It was a Mercedes E550, a Mars red convertible with the top down. Elmer Bagwell was doing okay, I thought. Now, he was about to sell the place, maybe move to some island somewhere. Probably be bored as hell, like I was about to be.

I leaned against the side of my car, wearing my usual pair of khaki shorts, a red striped polo shirt and sandals without socks. I had brought sunglasses this time, and they were propped up on the top of my head. I was facing into the sun, working on my tan, when a powder blue, 1957 Chevy pulled into the lot beside me. A woman stepped out of the car. She was long and sleek; made me think of a cheetah. She had silky auburn hair. Her skin was smooth and untroubled. Her eyes were blue. Her smile was white. My knees were jelly.

"You must be Ben," she said, as she stepped out of the vintage car. She offered her hand.

"And you are?"

"Katherine Colter. People call me Kate." She looked at my car and began to walk around it with admiring eyes. "I'm an accountant. A CPA, actually. I do Bagwell's books."

"Oh," I said. She looked to be about thirty-five, and she looked nothing like a CPA. She looked more like the wife of some baseball player. You know the type. All beautiful and bubbly and as hot as fire.

"This your car?" she said.

"Yeah."

"Everything real?"

"Driven only to church on Sundays." She laughed. I looked over at the Chevy. "How 'bout yours? Everything real?"

"You mean me, or the car?"

I smiled. "The car."

Kate smiled back. "Not a speck of bondo anywhere. Took me ten years to refurb the darn thing. Did it all on my own." She held up her hands and I could see the dark, grease-stained calluses of a back-yard mechanic.

I didn't know what to say. I snuck a quick glance at Kate's legs and tried to imagine her in a bikini. It didn't take much, and I felt little Johnson start to stir. It took a lot to wake up that old soldier, but Kate did it without moving a muscle.

Kate said, "I saw you on Leno. You looked pretty good on TV. Your ear looks rather sexy." She paused. "I'm a career woman."

I tilted my head. "I'm a career man."

"It's not that I don't like men." Kate looked at me with those solemn coral eyes. I got the odd feeling that she was trusting me without question, like she might her therapist. "I do."

I looked at Kate and wondered where she was going with this. We had just met and she was telling me her life story. Maybe it was the magic of Leno. I'd received a ton of email, a bunch of requests for work, plus five marriage proposals after the show. Now I was getting the intimate details of a woman's psyche.

"You're just married to the job," I said.

"Exactly. That and my hobbies—cars, computers and game fish."

She sounded like the Yin to my Yang. "I like computers. I like fish," I said. I was sounding like a goof.

"I've got an '88 Mako 261 center console," Kate said.

"I've got a SeaRay Sundancer."

"What size?"

"Forty-eight footer."

Kate smiled. "I love a man with a big boat."

I laughed. I wanted to give her a wisecrack about my other big thing, but settled on, "I helped Mabel bag a grander."

"Did you, now? Will you take me out sometime?"

"You serious?"

"Very."

We stood in silence, looking at each other's cars. I peeked again at her legs, to her tight black skirt, then to her white blouse with the camisole underneath and no bra. I don't know why I was acting this way. I hadn't been with a woman in years. I hadn't been with a woman her age in thirty years. Probably longer. I shrugged. No law against imagination.

Mabel broke the awkward, heat-filled silence with her hog. She roared into the parking lot, sidled her Harley up beside me, shut off the engine and looked at us both.

Mabel said, "Hello, Ben, Kate. You two meet?"

"Yeah," I said. "Just did."

Mabel's lips rounded into a little smile. I'd seen that smile before, and I wasn't sure I liked it. Her eyes fixed on me, saying something I couldn't decipher.

After a moment of awkward silence, I nodded approvingly. Mabel looked pretty good. "Got yourself looking shapely again there, dear."

Mabel smoothed out her leather pants. "That's just my Depends, riding up my crotch."

I laughed. "Really. You look great."

"I made Winde pay for a personal trainer and a membership at Curves." Mabel grew impatient with the small talk. She looked over at Jiggles. "Let's go," she said, tossing her head. "Let's get this done…I've called an employee meeting for noon. Buddy and my attorney should be joining us in about an hour."

The door was unlocked, so we walked into the club. Elmer Bagwell was sitting alone at the bar, sipping a club soda with lime. He greeted Mabel with a hug, me with a handshake and Kate with a friendly nod. He motioned over to a round table that was piled high with papers. "Your people satisfied?" he said to Mabel.

Mabel said, "Yep."

"You sure you want to do this?"

"No doubts."

"Let me show you around then."

Bagwell took us on an hour-long tour of the place, explaining everything about it, including a short bio on each employee.

The lawyers came. Money and paper exchanged hands. By eleven thirty, Mabel was the new owner of Jiggles. By noon, the place was filled with her employees.

We all gathered near the stage. Mabel stood upon it and said, "Jiggles has new owners."

There were groans from a few of the employees. Most of the dancers remained silent, staring with their fresh, fearful young eyes. New ownership meant changes, and changes weren't always good.

Mabel said, "My name is Mabel Witherspoon. Some of you know me. The rest of you will." Mabel looked around the room. There were about thirty dancers, and another twenty or thirty others who did all the jobs required to run the place. "I used to be a dancer in Vegas, back when it was one of the only places to find such work. I want you all to know that I understand that this is not a strip club. It never will be."

There was a quick spark of cheers and a lot of clapping. The roar reminded me of the Super Bowl I'd missed.

Mabel motioned over toward Archie, III. Buddy was a slim, youthful twenty-three. He was wearing a pair of Levis and a blue button down shirt, with no tie. He sported a pair of black, Elvis Costello eyeglasses. They made him look like a nerd, but cool at the same time. A cool nerd. The girls were going to love him.

"This is my grandson, Buddy. He will be handling the day-to-day management of this place. His word is law. Don't come running to me behind his back." Mabel paused, then chuckled. "Unless it's about something illegal or immoral."

"Grammmm," moaned Buddy.

Mabel smiled. He was a good kid. I already knew that.

Mabel continued. "There *are* going to be some changes, though. First, we will be putting in a retirement plan, a 401(k). For every dollar you put into the plan, we will match it. At the end of the year, if we've made money, will make a profit sharing contribution.

"If Bagwell's books are correct..." Mabel snuck a glance at Kate, who nodded. "...We should be putting up to five grand into each of your accounts next year."

Another cheer went up from the employees. Mabel held up her hand. "I have made arrangements with the Hopewell Foundation for education financing. The foundation will pay tuition for any of you who want to further your careers."

"You're going to pay for education?" said one of the dancers. "Even to blow this soda stand?"

"To any accredited school. To study anything you want. We will also be bringing in some of the region's best dance teachers and choreographers, to help you develop your craft."

Mabel clapped her hands sharply, like a farmer might, to get the attention of her animals at feeding time. "Here's the deal. We don't drink on the job and we don't do drugs. Do either and you lose all privileges. If you need counseling, we'll pay for it."

Mabel stared out at her new family. She would mother these girls, as if they were her own. Some would stay and dance. Others would go on to school, become professors, scientists, choreographers or housewives. Still others would drop out. Mabel would give these girls a chance at a good life, like the one she'd been given by Archie. What they did with the opportunity, well, that was up to them.

It was nearly five o'clock when I waved goodbye to Mabel and Buddy.

They were working now, attending to all the little details of small business ownership. They were oblivious to a small-time detective who was now just in the way.

I dropped heavily into the seat of my Jaguar. I leaned back and closed my eyes. What now? I wondered. When this was finally over, what would I do? I could go back to sitting on my porch, drinking beer and watching the sun sink into the sea. I could go out and catch some more fish. I felt a little stir of excitement, but that was all.

I had to admit it. This thing with Mabel had left me drained. I was physically and emotionally beat. I'd let myself fall in love, for the first time, really. And I'd been left behind like an abandoned dog at the pound. Mabel wanted no part of me, at least not how I'd hoped.

There was a shuffling beside me and I opened my eyes. Kate was opening the door to her car. I waved and she waved back. Kate began to get inside her Chevy; then she stopped. She stood for a moment, half in her car and half out. Then she stepped outside and slammed her door shut. She leaned over the passenger door of my car and said, "Look, I've never done this before. But, I was wondering…do you want to go get some dinner?"

I looked around to make sure she was talking to me. Here she was, this beautiful, talented thirty-something asking me…old, retired me…to dinner.

"Are you coming on to me?" I said.

"Don't flatter yourself. I'm just hungry."

"I know a great place on Key West."

Kate opened the door to my car and jumped inside. "Drive," she said. "Before I change my mind."

"You sure you want to do this?"

"Drive."

And that's how I got my groove back.

EPILOGUE II

Jack Trance's two hundred fifty-foot yacht, the *Lauren*, glided serenely into the small private cove near Maiquetia, Venezuela. The sky was cloudless. The sea was green. The air smelled of sea salt and cooking spices, with the occasional whiff of diesel exhaust.

As Nikko, the ship's captain, dropped anchor, a pair of twenty-foot Boston Whalers raced out from the shore. The boats pulled alongside the *Lauren* and waited for the ship's occupants to emerge from inside. A few moments later, Jack and Lauren Trance stepped onto the aft deck. Trance waved at the people below. Lauren cradled a sleeping baby on each shoulder.

"Just another minute or two," yelled Trance, in Spanish. He tossed two flexible ladders overboard, one into each of the boats.

Mabel Witherspoon walked up beside Trance. Behind her came Ben Johnson, holding hands with Kate Colter. Half a dozen men soon joined them on deck, wearing battle fatigues.

Mabel and Ben climbed down into one of the boats. Kate edged over to stand beside Lauren. She took one of the twins and cuddled it against her breast.

Trance kissed his wife and climbed down into the second boat. Using nylon ropes, his men began to lower gear into the Whaler—four large duffel bags and two six-foot-long fiberglass crates. When Trance had secured the gear, his men slithered down the ladder like chimpanzees. Trance waved up at the boat and yelled, "Back soon."

"Be safe!" yelled Lauren. She hated when he did this.

The two Whalers sped to the shore. They tethered to a wooden wharf, where Trance was greeted by a man wearing a gray business suit, black wing-tips and a white Panama hat.

Trance said, "Hello, Enrico. We all set?"

Enrico bowed stiffly, formally. "Two cars are waiting, sir. With a military escort, as requested by our president."

Trance nodded. He grabbed one of the canvas bags, hefted it over his shoulder and began walking to a warehouse at the end of the dock. Inside the warehouse, there were two black, armor-plated Humvees. A man stood at attention beside each one. Both wore military uniforms. Trance saluted and the men saluted back.

"At ease, men," said Trance.

"You sure we need all this?" said Mabel.

Trance smiled grimly. "Better safe than sorry. It's one thing to challenge Cantwell at his office in Miami. It's a far different thing to do it on foreign soil. He'll have guards, I assure you."

"But, what if we're stopped and searched? With all these weapons? You've got rocket propelled grenades in those crates!"

Trance laughed. "We do?" He motioned toward the two military men. "These are officers from the FAN, the Fuerza Armada Nacional of Venezuela. I had the U.S. president make a call to Chavez. We have permission to be here."

"I thought he hated America?"

"This isn't politics, Mabel. This is about criminals. If Chavez helps us with ours, we help him with his."

Mabel blinked. "Oh." She glanced over at Ben and mumbled, "Nice to be legal, for once."

Ben laughed and patted Mabel on the back.

"Let's roll," said Trance.

They jumped into the Humvees and began the short drive to Caracas. They stopped outside a modern office building, made with smooth brown marble and smoky glass. Trance, Mabel and Ben emerged from one of the vehicles, while the two uniformed military officers walked out of the other. Trance's men remained behind, taking discreet positions across the street.

They entered through a revolving door into the twenty-story building. The officers showed their credentials to the building's armed guards, who surrendered a bright red key. When the elevator door opened, Trance inserted the red key into a red slot above the bank of buttons. He pushed for the top floor and said, "To the penthouse we go."

The elevator opened into a narrow, but elegant reception area. There were six modern chrome chairs, with black leather strapping, lined against the wall, to the right of the elevator. Freshly cut flowers were sitting in three waist-high Chinese porcelain vases spaced about the floor. The flowers couldn't mask the telltale scent of a medical facility.

There was a middle-aged woman sitting behind a mahogany desk, typing into a computer. She looked up, as if startled. "You don't have an appointment," she said, in English.

One of the Venezuelan officers held up an ID and replied, in Spanish, "Tell Dr. Campos that the FAN is here to see him."

The area stretching behind the receptionist looked like a miniature hospital. There were two empty gurneys resting in the hallway, along with three futuristic-looking, designer wheelchairs. The walls were barren of artwork. The floors were brightly polished and smelled strongly of disinfectant.

Dr. Campos came scurrying out of an office, sputtering loudly. "You have no right—"

"Shut up," interrupted Trance, in fluent Spanish, "You are not in trouble, unless you make it. We know that you provide plastic surgery services for…" Trance hesitated. "…for criminals who don't want to be recognized."

Campos began to protest, but Trance raised a hand.

"Don't argue with me, or we will shut you down."

Campos looked at Trance and began to blink, saying nothing.

Trance continued. "You have two surgeries scheduled for this afternoon, for Rial Cantwell and Louis Masco."

"We have no such patients—"

Ben Johnson handed Campos a computer printout. The document detailed the transfer of one million dollars, made three months prior, from an account controlled by Rial Cantwell.

"The names they are using are John and Robert Canedy. Here is their receipt for payment, as well as their reservations for the next two weeks—here and at your hotel."

Campos took the printout, but didn't bother to read it.

"I run a legitimate practice here—"

Trance interrupted, "These men are fugitives from United States justice, Doctor Campos. We have no issue with you, as of now. We are here to speak to them. Let us do our job and you will remain unharmed."

The bravado dripped out of Campos like hot sweat. His shoulders finally slumped and he shrugged. "What do I do?"

"We are going to wait in your reception area. When they come…" Trance looked to his watch. "…in sixty-five minutes, we are going to have a little talk with them. Then, you do what you were paid to do. You operate, then you help them recuperate."

"That is all?"

"That is all."

Campos shrugged. "Okay."

Trance, Ben and the two Venezuelan guards took seats in the reception area. Mabel seated herself at the receptionist's desk.

An hour later, the elevator door swung open. Mabel kept her head down until Cantwell and Masco, along with their two bodyguards, had stepped inside.

After the door closed, Mabel raised her head and smiled. "Hello, Rial. Hello, Lou."

"Guards!" yelled Cantwell. But Trance and the two FAN officers had already disarmed the men that Cantwell had thought would protect him.

Ben waved. "Hello, Rial!"

"You," Cantwell muttered. "How did you find us?"

"Because you're stupid," said Ben.

Cantwell's eyes darted from Mabel to Ben to Trance. "You here to kill us?"

"On the contrary," said Mabel. "We had a deal. You give the money back to investors and stop dealing drugs, you walk away."

"But what about—"

"The fact that you tried to kill me?"

"It wasn't personal—"

Mabel yelled, "You bet your ass it was personal! So, you shut up and you listen." Mabel closed her eyes and counted to ten. After a few moments, she continued. "This is where the killing, the cheating and the dealing stops. We're going to let you go free, because we had an arrangement, however lenient it might be. We're going to let you get your faces changed. We're even going to forget we had this meeting.

"But if you ever steal money or deal drugs again…If you ever set foot on American soil…If you ever do anything to hurt me, my friends or my family, you are going to wish you were never born. We will always be able to find you and we will make you pay. In spades. You got that?" Mabel looked at Cantwell and then at Masco.

"Yes," both men said.

"No matter what you do or where you go, we will be watching. You got that?"

"Yes, ma'am," said Cantwell.

Mabel stared at Masco, until he said, "Yes, ma'am."

"Nobody screws with Mabel Witherspoon. Nobody."

"Amen," said Ben. "Amen."

The End

From The Author:

I hope that you have enjoyed the fourth installment in the Jack Trance series of books. This story is also the sequel to *The Varicose Vigilantes,* available from Shaksper Books. If you liked this book, you may also enjoy *The Varicose Vigilantes, The Alchemist Conspiracy* and *The Presidential Pretender.*

You can order these titles through your favorite bookstore, or online at major retailers. Please visit my website, www.jaylumbert.com. Please feel free to contact me directly. You can link to me through my website. My direct email is jay@lumbert.com. Because of security and spam filters, it would be helpful if you add a book title to the Subject heading of your email.

I enjoy hearing from readers. Don't be a stranger. Let me know what you think.

Life is what you make it… Enjoy!

**Please note that Jay Lumbert's books are available
through local bookstores everywhere.
They can be purchased at all major online bookstores, such as
www.BarnesAndNoble.com (BN.com), www.Amazon.com and
www.Borders.com. eBooks are also available.**

You can send an email to Jay Lumbert through his websites,
www.jaylumbert.com and www.lumbert.co.m
If you have difficulty going through his website, Jay's direct email address
is
jay@lumbert.com.

Because of security and spam filters, it would be helpful if you added the
title to one of his books to the Subject heading of your email.